· IT'S A GIRL THING ·

Dear Little Black Dress Reader,

Thanks for picking up this Little Black Dress book, one of the great new titles from our series of fun, page-turning romance novels. Lucky you — you're about to have a fantastic romantic read that we know you won't be able to put down!

Why don't you make your Little Black Dress experience even better by logging on to

www.littleblackdressbooks.com

where you can:

* Enter our **monthly competitions** to win **gorgeous** prizes

* Get **hot-off-the-press** news about our latest titles

* Read **exclusive** preview chapters both from our **favourite** authors and from brilliant new writing talent

* Buy **up-and-coming** books online

* Sign up for an essential slice of romance via our **fortnightly email** newsletter

We love nothing more than to curl up and indulge in an addictive romance, and so we're delighted to welcome you to the Little Black Dress club!

With love from,

The *little black dress* team

Five interesting things about Julie Cohen:

1. In high school in the USA, my best friend and I used to spend our chemistry lessons writing novels about us having sex with rock stars.

2. Despite this lack of scholarly application, I graduated summa cum laude from Brown University. While I was there I wrote a daily comic strip about an Elvis impersonator and his pet squid.

3. I came to live in England because of the Beatles, and because I fell in love with a guitar-playing Englishman.

4. I have a postgraduate research degree in fairies in children's literature, which has very few practical applications.

5. The Englishman and I have recently had our first child, who will be English as well, I suppose.

By Julie Cohen

Featured Attraction
Being a Bad Girl
Delicious
Spirit Willing, Flesh Weak
Married in a Rush
Driving Him Wild
All Work and No Play . . .
One Night Stand
Honey Trap
Girl From Mars

Girl From Mars

Julie Cohen

little
black
dress

First published in 2009 by
LITTLE BLACK DRESS
An imprint of HEADLINE PUBLISHING GROUP

A LITTLE BLACK DRESS paperback

1

Cataloguing in Publication Data is available from the British Library

ISBN 978 0 7553 4139 9

Typeset in Transit511BT by Avon DataSet Ltd,
Bidford-on-Avon, Warwickshire

Printed and bound in Great Britain by
Clays Ltd, St Ives plc

HEADLINE PUBLISHING GROUP
An Hachette UK Company
338 Euston Road
London NW1 3BH

www.littleblackdressbooks.com
www.headline.co.uk
www.hachette.co.uk

For Theresa Isabelle Langlais, my Grams

Acknowledgements

Many, many thanks to writer Paul Larson and *2000AD* editor Matt Smith for generously sharing their experience of the comics world, including the omnipresent Stormtroopers. Your jobs are so cool. All errors, omissions and deliberate distortions of reality are my own. Thanks also go to Roger Sanderson, Scott McCloud and Batman.

Thank you to Brigid Coady, Kathy Love, Anna Louise Lucia, Ruth Ng and my mother Jennifer Cohen for helping to scare away the crows. And thanks, as always, to Wonder Woman and Super Girl: my agent Teresa Chris and my editor Catherine Cobain.

What's Not to Like?

I t all started when Stevo fell in love.

We were in the middle of an *X-Files* marathon weekend. It was about four o'clock on Sunday morning and we'd got halfway through season three. We'd paused the DVD player so that Digger could put some waffles in the toaster and Jim and I could chip away at our long-standing argument about which episodes were better. Jim liked the 'monster-of-the-week' stand-alone episodes; I preferred the continuing story about the government/extraterrestrial conspiracy.

'It's the show's *whole point*, it's what ties the *whole world* together,' I said, sitting forward in my comfy flowered chair so that my feet touched the ground, and waving my hands in emphasis. 'You need a central mythology, something to believe in, otherwise there's no continuity. Without the conspiracy the show wouldn't have lasted two seasons. Look at *Girl from Mars*—'

'Don't bring your work into this, Fil. A comic book is different from a TV show.' Jim tossed his long hair behind his shoulder and had that suppressed grin that meant he knew he was winding me up. 'Only losers and nerds read comic books.'

'Losers and nerds!' I exploded, loving every minute of it. I looked to Stevo for his customary support in this argument. He was sitting on one end of the couch, staring at the paused TV and biting one of his fingernails.

Digger came into the room and plunked a plateful of waffles on to the already crowded coffee table. He squeezed honey from a plastic bear on to two of them, put them together to make a waffle sandwich, and settled himself on the couch. Digger always sat in the middle, and his weight made the ancient cushions tilt up a little bit at either end. I'd drawn a caricature of this – big bearded Digger in the middle of the bowed couch, with slim Jim and slight Stevo perched on either side, dangling in the air. It hung, framed, behind the couch.

I plucked a waffle from the pile and took a joyful bite from the corner of it. 'Look, all I'm saying is that people like continuity and consistency, even in fiction. Look at you and me, for example – we've been having this same argument since we were in school.'

'Popular, were you?' asked Digger, reaching for the honey bear again.

'There are more important things than popularity,' Jim told him. 'Particularly being right. Look, Fil, even you have to admit that it's a hell of a lot more exciting to see, say, a human-eating Flukeman bred in nuclear waste than to catch yet another half-glimpse of some dead aliens.'

'I've got something to tell you guys,' said Stevo suddenly. Something about his voice made me put down my waffle.

I'd had a funny feeling about Stevo all night. He'd been off, withdrawn, even quieter than usual.

I looked at him. He was biting his lip and his compact body was perched stiffly on the couch, as if he were preparing himself for some sort of blow.

'What?' Jim asked. 'Don't tell me you're going to take my side instead of Fil's in this for once.'

A long pause followed. If it were a comic, it would be drawn as four still panels – no words, just close-ups of our faces. Jim framed in long brown hair, smiling and in his element. Digger the opposite physical type, chosen for contrast, with sharp eyes and waffle crumbs in his beard. Stevo, the focus of the scene, his high cheekbones casting dramatic shadows, his black eyes narrowed in an advance wince. And me, the character who reflected the dawning understanding of the reader, my eyes widening, my brows shooting up, my hair electric blue and the knowledge clear on my face.

Nothing was going to be the same ever again.

'I can't stay for series four,' Stevo said.

Digger frowned.

'Wimping out, are ya?' Jim, the only one who hadn't started to twig, reached for the remote.

'I'm sorry,' said Stevo. 'It's just that I need to get home because I've got . . . er, to meet someone later.'

'Work?' I asked.

'Uh, no.'

'Plumber?' asked Jim.

'No.'

'Your mum coming over from Hong Kong?' Digger asked, and I knew him well enough to hear through his nonchalance.

'No, it's not my mum. It's, er, for lunch. A date.'

It had been quiet before. It was twenty past four in the morning, after all. But now it was Quiet, capital Q, the kind evoked in art by vast landscapes, huge skies muffled with clouds, everything dark and unmoving.

'You what?' said Jim.

'I've got a lunch date. We'll probably go for a walk afterwards. Fly some kites, if it's not raining.'

More Quiet.

'You have a date?' I asked.

'Yes.'

Stevo looked as if he wanted to flee or, barring that, to dive under the couch and hide there with the lost crisps and forlorn fuzz balls. Shy Stevo. I felt a wave of affection for him, strong enough to make me suppress my dismay.

'Stevo, you sly dog, we never even suspected,' I said, and I smiled. A big, crazy, I-am-so-so-ecstatic caricature of a smile, which normally wouldn't fool anyone, let alone Stevo, but I saw him seize on it.

'It's – we met on the plane back from San Francisco when I went to see my brother and we've sort of been seeing each other since, and I wanted to introduce you guys but, you know, I didn't want to jump the gun. It's early days.' His relief was palpable. I wondered how long he'd been keeping this a secret.

'Does this mean that you have also been having sex?' Digger asked.

I'd never seen Stevo blush so hard. 'Might have been.'

Digger punched Stevo on the shoulder. 'Nice one, Stephen.'

Jim was staring at Stevo as if he were Flukeman. I dug an HB pencil out from behind my chair cushion and threw it at him. It left a faint black mark on his forehead and when I had his attention I gave him a pointed look through my manic smile.

'Oh,' he said. I watched him rearrange his features

into a more socially acceptable configuration. 'So, er, well, what's her name?'

I caught my breath.

'Um . . . Brian.'

Jim went back to staring.

'He's great,' Stevo said. 'Such an amazing guy. He used to do voiceovers for cereal ads but now he's a – um – a mortgage broker. You'll – I'm sure you'll like him.'

'That's cool,' I said, despite the heaviness settling in my chest.

'You went to San Francisco two months ago,' said Digger. He exchanged glances with me. I spent more time with Stevo than any of the rest of us; we both drew for Union Publishing Corporation comics, though on different titles. And yet he'd never once mentioned Brian.

It must be serious.

'Anyway,' Stevo said, 'I won't be able to make our gaming session on Thursday night. It's Brian's dad's birthday. I'm really sorry.'

'Right,' said Jim. 'Right. Well, okay.'

Stevo stood. 'Okay, well, I should go home now and get some sleep. Thanks for being so happy for me, guys.'

'Are you kidding?' I said. 'We're thrilled for you, Stevo. You wanna rub some of that luck off on the rest of us?'

He laughed his usual hesitant chuckle. 'Later, dudes. See you Wednesday for the pub quiz.'

We waited until we'd heard the front door close before we said anything else.

'Shit,' said Digger.

'You can say that again,' Jim said. 'What's all this Brian crap?'

'You didn't know Stevo was gay?' I asked.

'I never really thought about it.'

'Men,' I said. 'You're so unobservant.'

'Hey, you never knew he preferred *Babylon 5* to *Deep Space Nine*,' Jim pointed out.

'At least I noticed him sitting up straighter every time Jean-Luc Picard came in shot,' I countered.

'I thought he was girding his loins in case you did your Borg impression.'

'Jim! Fil!' Digger broke in. 'You seem to have missed the big point here. Stevo. Has got. A *boyfriend*.'

That shut us up.

'And he's having sex with him,' Digger added.

One of the side effects of being an artist is that you have far too visual an imagination. I quickly looked at the pattern on my chair.

Stevo's sexuality didn't bother me. I'd always known he was gay, though I'd considered him more of a theoretical than a practising homosexual. Sort of like how Digger, Jim and I were theoretical heterosexuals. If we were to have sex, it would be with a member of the opposite sex, but in real life, the topic was moot as we never got the opportunity anyway.

In any case, these guys were my friends. I loved them, but I didn't want to picture their sex lives, whomever they might be with, theoretical or otherwise.

'Well, that's it,' Digger said at last. 'We've lost him.'

'Come on, Digger,' I said. 'He's only got a boyfriend; it's not like he's dropped off the side of the earth.'

Digger shook his head. 'No, this is only the beginning. I've seen it before. First he drops out of an *X-Files* marathon and the occasional Thursday night. Then weekends are out, because weekends are when couples do all their couply things together. He meets Brian's friends, he meets Brian's family, maybe they go to Hong Kong for a week or two to meet Stevo's family. Gradually we see less and less of him. Then they move in together, and wham!' Digger clapped his huge hands together. 'We get a card at Christmas if we're lucky.'

'You're overreacting. He said we'd like each other.'

'Ah, and that's where you're wrong, Fil,' said Jim. 'You've just disproven your "women are more observant than men" theory because what Stevo actually said was that we would like Brian. Nothing about Brian liking us.'

'Of course Brian would like us,' I said, though my heart was sinking as I said it.

I looked around the living room of the house Jim and I shared, the scene of most of our quartet's gatherings over the years. The ratty tartan couch, bowed with Digger's weight; the coffee table littered with plates, mugs, empty beer tins and *Star Wars* action figures; my 'girl's chair', so called because it was upholstered in something that had once been flowery chintz and all the boys refused to sit in it; the elaborate, empty shrine on the mantelpiece, decorated with candles and sparkly bits, with the naked plinth labelled FIL'S FIRST PEREGRINE, waiting in hope that one day I might win a Peregrine award for best comics artist; one entire wall taken up by shelves of *Star Trek* and other science fiction DVDs; two pairs of Digger's spare boots; and an iguana called The Baz.

'What's not to like?'

Magic Paper and Fake Coffee

Whenever I walked into the offices of the Union Publishing Corporation on Vauxhall Bridge Road I could never believe I was really there.

It wasn't that the offices were anything special. The squat 1930s brick building had been gutted and renovated in the seventies, which meant suspended ceilings, draughty aluminium windows and a tendency to put carpeting on the walls. Reception was a few burnt-orange chairs and a bored woman behind the desk; most of the work space was open-plan with grey partitions separating desks cluttered with paper and dirty coffee cups. On the ground and first floors, it could be any office space in any part of London, or indeed the world, producing a variety of consumer magazines, mainly for the male market, mainly about cars.

The third floor was different. It looked exactly the same – grey partitions, cluttered desks, stacks of paper. But on the third floor, the paper was magic.

The perfect fusion of pictures and words, line and colour, technology and imagination, art and narrative, time and space: comics. And among those comics, the most amazing comic ever to be invented anywhere in the universe.

The Union Publishing Corporation was the birthplace of *Girl from Mars* and every time I pushed through the creaky revolving door I offered up thanks to the god of comic books.

It was Monday, three weeks after Stevo had abandoned us for his lunch date, and while I was offering up thanks, Stevo was grumbling. I'd met him outside Victoria station at 10.15 a.m., which was the compromise time we'd come up with years ago. I always wanted to be early for the monthly editorial meetings for all of UPC's comics titles, so I had extra time to absorb the atmosphere, maybe browse through a few *Girl from Mars* back issues. Stevo, left to his own devices, would have been fashionably late or even more fashionably absent. He hated editorial meetings and only showed up because the chief comics editor and editor of *Girl from Mars*, Anthony Alwards, insisted and because I nagged him.

We fell into step together as if nothing had changed. 'I don't see why I have to be here,' he said for the thousandth time. 'UPC has got to be the only comics publisher in the world that makes its artists do stuff like this.'

'Blame Dennis McKay and his revolutionary vision,' I said, though Stevo knew full well that I would stand for no criticism of the creator of *Girl from Mars*.

'I don't care who's to blame, I really could've done with some extra time in bed this morning.'

He dug his employee badge out of the pocket of his ironed indigo jeans and showed it to the receptionist. I tucked mine carefully back inside my jumper.

'Stop bitching,' I said. 'It was *X-Files* again this weekend and I haven't slept since Friday. I tried to nap during season six but Jim kept prodding me with his foot.'

Stevo didn't say anything and I realised he probably didn't want to stay in bed to sleep. I felt my cheeks flush as I punched the lift button for the third floor.

This was my chance to ask Stevo about Brian, maybe even arrange a day when Brian could come and meet Jim, Digger and me, and therefore put Digger's fears at rest. But Stevo was staring at the lift doors, and something about him radiated 'keep off' vibes.

None of us had mentioned Stevo's boyfriend, not in the pub, through the gaming, or during *The X-Files*. But I'd thought about him, out in the fresh air, flying kites and laughing with a man whose features I couldn't make out, while Digger, Jim and I were left behind in a stuffy room watching stories we'd seen before.

The lift arrived and I examined Stevo surreptitiously in the smoky mirror. What did a person who was having lots of sex look like?

He was the same. His job at UPC was drawing for *Combat* comics, and you'd never guess from his exterior that he was a genius at drawing mega-violent battles. He was short, slight, tidy, with combed black hair and round glasses. No love bites, no rumpled clothes or bed hair. I knew that most of his air of privacy and self-containment was shyness, a quiet barrier meant to keep others out of his space. I didn't have a problem with that, as I had barriers enough of my own, but I'd never felt as if it had excluded me before.

I was the one who'd brought Stevo into our little social circle in the first place, when we'd both started working at UPC three years ago. We were the newbies at the company and ended up sitting together at the monthly meeting. He'd doodled a picture of a dwarf cutting off a giant's head with a battleaxe and rolled his eyes when Anthony introduced him to the assembled throng, as if to say, *What is this, a tea party?*

He came around to our house initially to talk about work, but stayed to hang out. He'd been shy at first, but eventually he'd blended in. He taught Jim mahjong; he impressed Digger because, for a small guy, he could put away vast amounts of curry; and he was an awesome artist, with an encyclopaedic knowledge of war films and pop music.

But right at this moment I felt as if I'd never known him at all.

When the lift stopped we were the last two to get off. I cleared my throat, wondering how to broach the subject.

'So, how's Br—' I began, and then the door to the conference room down the corridor slammed open.

'Brown! Ng! Get your ratty arses in here so I can start the goddamn meeting!'

If Anthony Alwards's speech were put into a speech balloon, it would consist mostly of the symbols @$%*!.

'All right, Chief,' I said, hastening into the room. I wasn't sure how he'd got the nickname; I suspected he'd cultivated it himself. When I'd told Digger and Jim about this, Digger was very impressed at the concept and spent several days suggesting alternative nicknames for himself, including 'André' and 'Stud Man'.

Stevo and I squeezed on to the last free corners of a table. Aside from me and two women from sales who were wearing near-identical skirt suits and sitting together on a single chair, everyone else in the room was male. After shooting Stevo and me a look of daggers, Anthony began.

'Right, so now that you lot have bothered to show up, we'll start with *Lacey* . . .'

I immediately zoned out. The structure of UPC, based on founder Dennis McKay's democratic and artistic ideals, meant that although artists and writers were technically freelancers, the more regular contributors were treated as staff. In theory, at these monthly meetings, we were able to offer input about editorial direction and to participate in decisions about sales and marketing.

In practice, it meant that I had to sit around listening to guff about UPC's other comics titles.

This didn't bother me, because it was my chance to gaze happily at the walls. Here, framed, hung original *Girl from Mars* issues dating all the way back to the comic's creation in 1951. Near the door was the splash page for Issue 1, showing Girl from Mars's spaceship crash-landing on Earth, drawn by creator Dennis McKay. Pages from every decade since, including issues I'd read under my duvet at night as a teenager, circled the room. And then, glory of glories, three hundred and sixty degrees round the room, was my own front splash for Issue 662, *Sirius Business*.

A dream come true.

'Are you with us, Brown?'

'Um. Yes, Chief.'

'About shitting time. Now sales on *Girl* this quarter have been down seven point six per cent, and reader feedback says . . .'

Sales. I studied one of Wayne Jayson's covers from 1984. I liked his angles and his starkness. Maybe I'd try a bit of a tribute with my next project, a nice little extra for long-term fans. I squirmed in my seat, picturing the geometry.

'– And we're very excited about it. Sound good to you, Brown?'

'Um.' I sat up straighter and tried to figure out from Anthony's face what he was very excited about. Unfortunately he looked about as excited as a brick in the rain.

'Sure,' I said. Damn. I didn't need to pay attention to sales figures, but I came to these meetings to find out what was going to happen to *Girl from Mars*, and I'd just missed it.

He nodded grimly. 'Obviously we'll discuss this in more detail once we're under way. That's enough for today, get the hell out of my fucking face, you lot.'

I listened hard as we filed out of the room, trying to overhear someone discussing what Anthony had said about *Girl from Mars*. Mostly people were talking about lunch and their weekends.

Sixty seconds! My attention couldn't have lapsed for longer than that. How much information could Anthony have conveyed in a minute? I jiggled on my feet until the lift door opened and then I pulled Stevo out of the building, fast.

'What was he talking about?' I demanded as soon as we were on the pavement of Vauxhall Bridge Road, pulling up our collars against the April rain.

'Who?'

'Anthony! He said he was excited about something. What was it?'

'Hmm,' said Stevo. He began walking towards Victoria.

'Anthony never gets excited about anything. It must have been something big. What was it?'

'Hmm,' he said again. 'I don't recall. Must not have been listening.'

I shoved my hands in the pockets of my jeans and exhaled sharply in irritation.

'You could at least pay attention, Stevo, it's your job.'

'Doesn't seem like you were paying attention.'

'I was! But then I was thinking.'

'I come to these things because I have to, Fil. Not to act as a tape recorder for you.'

'I was only not listening for like ten seconds!'

He shrugged. 'Sorry.'

But he wasn't. He was all detached again.

I rubbed my eyes, which felt full of grit.

'Let's have a coffee,' I suggested, to change the subject, though I didn't really have to say it because Stevo and I always had coffee after editorial meetings to immerse ourselves in happy conversation about what Jim and Digger would call 'art-wank': our favourite artists, or exhibitions we wanted to see, or technical ideas we wanted to try.

We never talked about our private lives, or our feelings. He'd never once told me the basic fact that he was gay, for example; I'd inferred it from other things. We didn't have that sort of a friendship.

But we were close. We'd spent so much time together for the past three years, and besides, none of the four of us spent time talking about our feelings. We didn't need to. We understood each other perfectly.

I pulled open the door of O Solo Mio Café, anticipating the blast of coffee aroma. But Stevo had stopped on the pavement.

'Er,' he said, 'sorry, not this week, Fil; I've got to be getting on.'

'Brian?' I asked.

'Yeah.'

'Again?'

Stevo looked sheepish. 'Call you later, all right?'

So it was that I entered O Solo Mio Café solo, for the first time ever.

'Americano with an extra shot, black,' I said to the woman behind the counter before sitting at one of the tables along the side wall, under the posters of sausages.

It would be okay. Stevo was a good guy. He wouldn't drop us in favour of romance, no matter what Digger thought.

I shook off my wet jacket and pulled out my pocket sketchbook and a pencil. If I wasn't going to get to talk with Stevo, at least I could spend the time observing people and capturing some gestures and expressions. Maybe Girl from Mars would visit an Italian café sometime soon. I liked capturing bits of machinery to integrate into the frequent drawings I had to do of space station interiors. The espresso machine had a few nicely chunky metallic bits, and I liked the design of its dial.

'Americano, extra shot, black,' someone said, and I accepted my coffee with a thanks and barely a glance. I reached for it straight away, took a blistering and much-needed sip, and then spluttered.

I brought the offending cup up to the counter. 'Excuse me,' I said, 'but I think this is decaf.'

To her credit, the barista didn't ask me how I knew. 'Oh, I'm sorry,' she said, and took the coffee back. I stood at the counter to wait for my new cup, tracing the outlines of the espresso machine with my eyes.

'Hi,' said a voice at my side, and I turned, thinking someone was speaking to me. But it was a businessman in a shirt and tie, and he was addressing the barista. 'Are you sure this is decaf?'

He was holding a cup, and from my position next to him I could see it was an Americano, black. I took it from his hands and tasted the coffee. It zinged in my mouth.

'This one is mine,' I said. 'Heavy on the caffeine, zero everything else. I think they gave me your decaf.' I said the word, as always, with a half-restrained shudder.

'I'll make them again for you,' the barista said, and got to it.

I didn't understand the point of decaf. It was like sugar-free cake, or a flat fizzy drink. Or a bald cat. It removed the whole essence of the thing. You might as well drink hot water and stop pretending.

The man was staring at me. His eyes were dark blue, more or less exactly the same colour as my hair.

'Do you usually drink other people's coffee?' he asked me. He had an American accent.

Oh, God. I realised I'd just forgotten both social norms and germs in one fell swoop.

'Uh, sorry,' I mumbled, looking at the floor.

'What's so bad about decaf, anyway?'

I swallowed. 'It's—'

Fortunately, my rightful coffee appeared at that point. I snatched it, knocking half a dozen packets of sugar to the floor along with my spoon, which fell with a clatter. I bent, scooped them all up and retreated to my table.

I could feel the man looking at me. I bowed my head and made rapid sketches of the espresso machine.

This was what Digger had been going on about. My friends and I were too odd for normal human consumption. In public, we were bound to humiliate ourselves in some way. No wonder Stevo was hiding his boyfriend from us. A science-fiction-obsessed long-haired computer programmer, a six-and-a-half-foot tall role-playing-game addict who made most of his income by selling stuff on eBay, and a serial hair-dyeing female comic book artist who hung out with males so much she wasn't even sure she still possessed both X chromosomes. We all lived in a deeply unfashionable part of South London and none of us had jobs that required us to wear business clothes, or even to leave the house except on rare occasions.

I gulped my very hot coffee and made furious pencil lines. Drawing calmed me. It made sense of things. The dial connected to the gleaming body of the machine, snug and purposeful. The stiff tentacles of the milk steamers had their own logical place. By the time I'd finished half my coffee, my brain was singing with stimulant and my fingers wanted something else to draw.

I drew the lady by the door, who fitted into her black coat as if she'd sewn herself into mummy wrappings, her hair flattened at the back. The angular woman who needed only the tiniest fit of exaggeration to become a four-legged insect. The two sleek Italian men gesturing as they talked over their espressos. The businessman sitting in the corner who had taken my coffee, who had black hair with a Superman stray lock on his forehead, black eyebrows and long black eyelashes. His dark blue eyes were looking straight at me.

My pencil fumbled. I looked away quickly.

Of course I'd started to draw him. I turned over the page and drew my coffee cup. Then my coffee cup with my hand round it. Then the Italians' hands, fingers forming a vocabulary of their own.

Hands are nearly as important as faces in expressing emotion. You have to think carefully about their size, their shape, their placement and gesture. Big hands can be powerful, gentle, threatening, clumsy, protective. Small hands can be helpless or clever. A villain with blunt hands poses a different sort of threat from a villain with spidery fingers. A hero needs capable hands.

Like those hands, there. Wrists that were strong, but not thick enough to hide the beauty of bone and sinew. A hint of veins in the back, orderly procession of knuckles, long fingers, broad thumbs that signified masculinity. My pencil shaped them joyfully until I felt the pressure of eyes on me and realised that I was drawing the guy in the corner again and he was still watching me.

Damn. I snapped my sketchbook shut, shoved it back in my pocket, and concentrated on drinking my coffee. With my eyes closed.

'I'm not sick or anything.'

An American accent, and it was right next to me again. I opened my eyes and he was standing beside my table.

'Uh,' I said, 'what?'

'I thought you might be worried that after drinking from my cup you might have caught something. So I thought I'd reassure you that I'm not sick.'

'Um. Well. Thank you.'

He stood there as if he were expecting me to say something else. But what could I say? *Sorry for staring at you, it's just that you're handsome and I can't help drawing you, you know, just as an exercise?*

So I was quiet. He cleared his throat a bit.

'I'm Dan.' He held out his hand to me. He had a broad palm, but not square or clumsy. A deep-grooved lifeline, and a broken love line. I looked at it.

'Like I said, I'm not contagious,' he said. 'Not at the moment, anyway.'

'Oh.' I shook his hand, which was what he'd meant for me to do all along. I noticed how small and scrubby my hand looked, how untidy the nails, how smudged with pencil.

'What's your name?' he prompted.

'Philomena.' I wondered if I should ask him to sit down, though I couldn't imagine anything more embarrassing.

'That's an unusual name.'

I nodded. My parents were both university lecturers in literature. I was lucky I wasn't named Eustacia Vye.

'Do you live around here?' he asked.

'No, I work nearby.'

He nodded. I nodded back. Was it my turn to say something?

'Well, I've got to—' I began at the same time that he said, 'Do you mind if I sit down?'

'—be going,' I finished.

'Oh. All right. Nice meeting you, Philomena.'

'Um. Yeah.'

I pushed aside the rest of my coffee and stood up, even though I didn't have to be going, even though I could really use that coffee, because Daniel's smile made me all hot and twitchy, like a feverish hamster.

I should've drunk the decaf, because then he'd never have talked to me. He could have ignored me like every other attractive man in the world usually did, which was really for the best because I was such a fool when I felt this way.

'See you around,' he said as I left.

I hope not, I thought.

It's Not Rocket Science

'Fifty-seven weeks,' Jim said, staring glumly into his half-empty pint of bitter.

'I know,' said Digger.

From two tables away, we could hear the celebrations of the team of accountants who had trampled all over our pub quiz winning streak.

'I should've known that question about the Pet Shop Boys,' I said.

'Stevo would've known,' said Digger, polishing off his Beamish.

Jim pounded his fist on the table. 'I'm not a bad loser, but *fifty-seven weeks*.'

'I know,' said Digger.

The accountants set up a rousing chorus of Queen's 'We Are the Champions'.

'They want to gloat a little bit more; I don't think the whole pub is getting the message,' I said.

'Why isn't Stevo here?' Jim demanded for the sixth time at least. 'What did he tell you?'

'I could only get his answerphone,' I told him,

again for the sixth time at least.

'It's like I said, when romance rears its ugly head—'

'Romance my arse,' Jim said to Digger. 'He didn't come to the quiz because he's too busy shagging.'

'Maybe he forgot,' I said.

'You don't just forget something you've been doing every Wednesday night for fifty-seven weeks.'

'I know.'

'You guys must be gutted,' said the woman collecting glasses as she stopped by our table. She was tall, with masses of red hair piled on top of her head. 'That's a hell of a winning streak to break.'

'Don't,' we all moaned, and all put our heads down on the table in despair.

'Who was that?' Jim asked when we'd raised our heads and she was gone.

'Dunno,' said Digger. 'She must be new.'

'She knew we'd won every quiz for over a year, she can't be that new,' I said.

'She's probably heard of our fame.' Jim banged his hand on the table top. 'Dammit, I hope Stevo screws himself to death.'

'You don't mean that,' I said.

'Fil, there are a lot worse things I could wish him, believe me. At least he's getting some.' Jim downed the rest of his pint in one. 'Right, there's only one thing for it. We must get steaming drunk.' He got up and went to the bar.

I swirled my lager around in its glass. 'The thing is, there isn't much to choose from between sex and a pub quiz, is there?'

'Certainly isn't,' Digger said right away, and then he looked at me more closely. 'Are you saying you'd rather have the pub quiz?'

I shrugged. 'At least the quiz comes with beer.'

'Fil, have you ever actually had sex?'

'I –' I glanced over at Jim, who was well out of earshot and seemed likely to be at the bar for some time. 'Yeah, of course I have.'

'When?'

'I had this thing with a guy in art college.' *Thing* wasn't quite accurate; *massive puppy-dog crush* was more the correct term. But Digger didn't have to know everything that had happened between me and Pierre.

'And this thing involved sex?'

'Yeah.' I shrugged again. 'It's overrated, as far as I'm concerned.'

'Sounds like you weren't doing it correctly.'

'We were doing it correctly! It's not rocket science.' And Pierre had had more than enough practice, even if I hadn't. 'I can think of several things that I'd rather be doing with my precious time.'

'Does Jim know about this?'

'What, that I like pub quizzes better than sex? I don't think he's ever asked.'

'No, about the thing in art school.'

I shook my head. 'Don't tell him, okay?'

'Why not?'

'Um. Well, it all ended up being a bit of a mess, so I didn't really feel like going into it when it happened. And if we bring it up now it would seem like I was concealing it or something, which I wasn't, but it was ages ago, okay?'

Digger seemed to accept this, though it wasn't the truth.

'Anyway, wouldn't you choose a pub quiz over sex any day?' I asked Digger.

His eyes went dreamy. 'I'm enjoying imagining a

situation where I would have to make that particular choice.'

'Drink,' ordered Jim, putting a glass in front of each of us.

'What is it?'

'Quadruple gin and tonics. Down the hatch.' He swigged from his.

I took a sip, shuddered, and then held my nose and drank. When I'd got to the bottom of the glass, all the colours in the room seemed a little bit brighter.

'I'll get the next ones,' I said and went to the bar. When I got back the conversation was still on sex.

'What else would they be doing?' Jim was asking. 'That's the whole point of a relationship, isn't it?'

'Some people might say it had something to do with mutual affection and support.' Digger accepted his gin and polished half of it off without any noticeable effort. I always thought I deserved more credit than I got for matching Digger drink for drink, considering he weighed at least two and a half times as much as I did.

'What do people in love do with all their time anyway?' I asked, sliding into my seat. 'Sex only lasts so long.'

'According to rumour, they spend a lot of time going around like this.' Digger rolled his eyes to the ceiling, fluttered his lashes, and plastered on a huge dopey smile.

Laughter pushed me off my chair. As I hit the floor, I realised I was actually quite dizzy.

'How do people know what to do?' Jim asked. 'Is there a guide to getting into a relationship that everyone's read except for us?'

While I was on the floor staring at the squashed chewing gum on the bottom of the table, I had a sudden blindingly great idea.

'Hey,' I gasped, hauling myself to my feet, 'here's what we have to do. Let's go and pick up people.'

'You mean, carry them somewhere?'

I pictured Jim and Digger lifting random strangers and slinging them over their shoulders, and laughed again.

'No, I mean let's go to a club and flirt and dance and stuff. Like normal people do.'

Digger and Jim stared at me.

'Come on. Everybody else does it. Let's not sit here like a bunch of chickenshits. How hard can it be?'

Jim spoke first. 'Fuck it. Yeah. Okay. Let's go.'

Digger shook his head slowly. He downed the rest of his drink, and then he picked up my untouched second gin and downed that, too.

'Better make it fast before the booze buzz wears off,' he said and pushed himself to his feet.

I giggled and followed my friends to the door of the Swan Inn, ignoring the fresh chorus of Queen that came from the accountants. I regarded Digger's and Jim's backs affectionately. They were great guys. I was a great girl. Despite the pub quiz humiliation, despite my total embarrassment two days before with that American in the café, we were intelligent, interesting, personable individuals.

All kinds of people went to nightclubs to get off with each other. It was only reasonable to suppose that we had as fair a chance of succeeding at our goals as anyone else.

What could possibly go wrong?

Nuclear Holocaust

The Manhattan Project was set between an employment agency and a shop selling leather sofas. Until tonight, it had formed no part of my life other than causing me to wonder why in the world anyone would name a nightclub after nuclear arms development.

Now, when I stepped through its open doors, paid the twelve-pound cover charge, and walked down a black-painted corridor to the strange new world of a normal Wednesday night in clubland, I saw that the name referred to the vaguely New York-style themed decorations. A cut-out Statue of Liberty loomed over the DJ desk and the bar was backed with a silhouette of the city at night. The loud, unfamiliar music consisted of a driving beat and a woman moaning.

'I expected some explosions,' Jim said beside me.

'I think there are nuclear-holocaust-level fashion disasters here, at least.' I nodded towards a gang of girls on the dance floor. They all wore shorts, tights, and skimpy tops that barely contained rolls of spray-tanned flesh.

'Then again, the three of us are sporting the latest style in black and baggy,' said Digger, which was true.

Someone laughed and a group of four men and three women swept past us, every one of them young, well groomed and well built. The women had bust lines which I could only achieve with a Wonderbra and two rolls of toilet paper. As we watched, they went on to the dance floor and began effortlessly dancing.

'Do you think they're an alien life form?' Jim asked.

'I think we probably need to drink more.' Digger began wading his way through the other punters to the bar. As he was so big, he created enough of a wake for Jim and me to follow behind him easily.

In the light of the club, the gin and tonics glowed radioactive blue. The three of us found a railing to lean on and took sips for courage, watching the crowd.

'I wonder what the average IQ in this room is,' said Jim.

'Stop being a snob,' I said. 'And we're not here for conversation, anyway. We're here for action. So who's it going to be?'

'What?'

'Pick one. Who in this room do you most want to have sex with?'

'Um.' Jim put both hands round his glowing glass. '*Who* in this room do I most want to have sex with?'

'Whom. I meant whom. There's no need to correct my grammar. Look, there are dozens and dozens of women here. Choose one, walk up to her, start talking.'

'Um,' he said again, and his eyes began darting from side to side as if someone had pulled a gun on him.

Bullying him into getting laid didn't seem to be working, so I changed tack to supportive and encouraging.

'The world's your oyster, Jim. You're good looking, smart and funny. You've got a well-paid job and half of your own house. You're the best guy I know and any woman would be lucky to have you.'

He focused on me. 'Do you really think that?'

'Of course I do. Now you've got to believe it too. That way when you walk up to a sexy woman and start talking to her, she'll sense your inner confidence and fall at your feet. You are a fierce warrior of love.'

Jim didn't say anything. He took a long drink of his gin. The positive affirmations had made him perk up a little, but perking up was no good without some action.

'So who's it going to be?' I prompted.

'Actually,' he began, but he wasn't looking around at the crowd. I sensed he was going to start a conversation about something else, in order to put off talking to a stranger, so I scanned the room rapidly.

'Look at that one, over there,' I said, pointing at a blonde who was standing, like us, leaning on a railing and watching other people dance. She had bobbed hair and was wearing a black dress with some sequins on it, and she seemed to be on her own. 'She looks all right. Go and talk to her.'

'You want me to go and talk to that blonde girl?'

Stuff the support and encouragement, it was time for bullying again.

'Get your skinny arse over there before I have to kick it,' I said, and pushed him in her direction.

Jim looked from me, to the girl, back to me again. He squared his shoulders, turned away, and headed for the girl.

'Wow,' said Digger.

Jim leaned beside the girl and spoke to her. From this

distance, and with the loud music, I couldn't hear what he was saying.

'Don't choke,' I whispered. From my limited experience, I knew the next few moments were crucial. People judged you within seconds of seeing you and if you messed it up, they were finished with you for ever.

The girl smiled at him.

'Go on, my son!' I cheered.

Jim said something else and the girl laughed, but she wasn't laughing at him, because he laughed along with her and she said something back.

'He's actually doing it,' Digger said, shaking his head. 'You know what that means, don't you?'

'Yeah, if she wants to dance we're going to get to rip his back off all week.'

'No, it means that now you and I have to pick someone and go and talk to them.'

'Huh.' Digger didn't say anything for a minute. 'Couldn't you and I just pretend we're strangers and have a conversation with each other?'

The suggestion was actually quite tempting. It was one thing to force your best friend to interact with someone, and quite another to risk humiliation yourself. It wasn't as if The Manhattan Project was full of people who were celebrities or fantastically good looking or rich or cool; most of them looked more or less normal. It was just that 'normal' was out of my league. Only two days ago I'd been practically struck dumb in O Solo Mio with the American, and I hadn't even been trying to pick him up. Imagine the disaster if I'd actually attempted to flirt with him.

I closed my eyes for courage and felt the room sway slightly, which was hardly surprising given that my veins were flowing with pure gin. Without the distractions of flashing lights and lame Americana it seemed as if I could hear Jim's voice – not what he was saying, but the timbre of it, sounding, as usual, sarcastic and comfortable – as if I were listening to him from upstairs in my studio while he was hanging out with Digger in front of the TV.

When I opened my eyes he was still talking to the blonde and from his grin and her giggles he was evidently telling her a joke.

How bad could it be?

'No,' I said. 'Jim did it, now we can't let the side down.'

Digger accepted this glumly. 'What are we going to do?'

'We need to split up, because nobody will talk to us if they think we're together.'

'I don't think I have anything in common with most of the people here.'

'You can always find something in common if you try hard enough,' I lied. 'Listen, you go to the left and I'll go to the right. If we haven't met anybody to talk to, we'll bump into each other halfway around the room.'

'And then?'

'And "then" won't happen because we'll both have found somebody sexy and wonderful before we get there. Let's go.'

I did an about-face and began marching round the room anti-clockwise, swigging from my gin as I went. My direct path would have brought me close to Jim and the blonde, but I swerved widely round them. As curious as I was, I didn't want to cramp Jim's style.

The dance floor was sunken slightly from the level of the rest of the club, so that as you walked round it you mostly saw people's shoulders and the tops of their heads. The extra height made me feel like a spectator, as if I were in a theatre and the dancers were providing me with a show.

Except it wasn't quite like that, because the spectatorship went both ways. How much easier would it be if I were the camera, if I occupied the place in a picture of the observer's eye, and wasn't involved in the action.

But action was what I was here for. I fortified myself with another slug of gin and scoped out the men around me. In an ideal world, I'd find someone who was good looking enough for me to be attracted to but not so good looking that he wouldn't even glance twice at me. He should be taller than me, which wasn't difficult because I was only five foot two and therefore a shortarse, as Jim and Digger were constantly reminding me (Stevo, at five foot five, had stayed out of these arguments). He'd have some sense of humour. Maybe he'd be a comics fan.

I spotted a Spiderman T-shirt and instantly rejected its wearer because he looked about thirteen. I added another item to the list: he had to be over the age of consent.

Right, then. I wasn't being very demanding. I needed an adult male, of normal height and more or less normal weight, who wasn't repulsive. The room was full of them. In fact, there were two of them, drinking pints, right in front of me. The one with the big shoulders had an Arsenal football shirt on and the slimmer one had ginger hair but he was actually quite cute in a freckly Jimmy Olsen sort of way.

I took a deep breath, walked right up to them, smiled and said, 'Hello.'

'I don't know, mate. If you ask me, he acted a complete

muppet in the last match. He couldn't find the goal if it was shoved up his nose. I can't believe we wasted fifteen mil on this guy.'

'Hello,' I tried again, a bit louder.

'You've got to give him a chance, mate,' Ginger Olsen said. 'It's early days yet.'

'Hello?'

'Excuse me, did you see his shot at goal yesterday? Was he trying to hit the moon? No, mate, I'm telling you, he's bloody useless. We should've saved the cash.'

I sucked in a lungful. 'Hello!' I yelled.

Shoulders and Ginger stopped mid-argument, their beers poised on the way to their mouths.

'Uh, hello,' I said. They stared at me.

What did I do now?

'Uh, you're talking about football, huh?'

'Yes,' said Shoulders.

'Oh.' I racked my brain for anything I might have heard about football at some point or other. A sudden inspiration struck me: according to rumour, men loved it when women acted all clueless around them, so they could get alpha and superior.

I swallowed. Girl from Mars would never do it. Girl from Mars would blast these two with her laser ray just for looking at her funny and being a bit too ginger and/or shouldery.

But these were desperate times.

'Uh, the offside rule,' I said. 'Will you explain it to me?' I performed the manoeuvre known, I believed, as batting my eyelashes. With the strobe lighting, it made the room flash on and off very quickly.

When I stopped confusing myself with my eyelids, Shoulders and Ginger were still staring at me. Shoulders took a drink of his pint. The music thundered and cursed around us.

Neither one made a move to explain the offside rule.

'Forget it,' I mumbled, and moved off.

Ka-Zam! That was the sound of Philomena Desdemona Brown horribly shot down in flames while attempting to flirt.

And I knew the damn offside rule already.

I stashed myself behind a slender pillar and looked around for Digger. He was nowhere to be seen. This could be because of the other people and the dodgy lighting, or it could be because he'd already got off with a seductive little vixen and was flagging down a taxi to get home, quick. My money was on the dodgy lighting, but the vixen was a possibility. Digger wasn't much of a talker with strangers, but in a place like this, who was looking for conversation? He wasn't bad looking, if you didn't mind beards. A lot of women liked brick walls of men.

Which would mean I was the only failure.

Why the hell was I here and where was Digger? I hated clubs. I hated dancing in public (unless it was to David Bowie whilst smashed out of my head). I hated most of the male population except for my beloved best friends and safe, non-sexy guys who liked comics as much as I did and didn't treat me like a girl.

But the point of this whole exercise was to be treated exactly like a girl by someone I couldn't possibly have anything in common with.

I went to the bar and ordered a glass of water, which was probably the only wise thing I'd done all night. Then I girded my loins (whatever that means) and began my anti-clockwise trek round the club once more.

It was my bad idea, and I had to see it through. The

problem was how. It was like mocking up a page that wasn't working, and trying to figure out what to change so that the layout and the art and the narrative would fall together.

Talking, as I'd learned, wasn't a good idea; as soon as I opened my mouth the bloke would know that I didn't have a clue how people spoke in clubland. I obviously couldn't use my sexy body to attract the men like flies to a spider's web. For one thing: what sexy body? I had the hips of a sixteen-year-old boy and the breasts of a thirteen-year-old girl, and ever since Jim and borrowed my Venus ladyshave to remove a stubbornly sticky piece of vegetation from The Baz's tank, I hadn't bothered shaving my legs.

For all I knew, ink-stained jeans and a plain black T-shirt were the height of this week's *Vogue* fashion, but as none of the other females in the club were wearing them, they probably weren't. Plus my hair was . . . well, it was blue. There was no getting around that.

I had two options for success. One was that I caught someone's eye by mistake and we just, for whatever reason, clicked.

The other, infinitely more likely, scenario was that somewhere in this crowd there was a guy who was so drunk and desperate to get laid that he didn't give a shit whom it was with.

My strategy to attract both of these options was to boldly and promiscuously cast my eye around in the hope of catching a clicker or a desperado. After several minutes it became obvious that far from attracting anyone, this strategy resulted in men backing quickly away from me. In one case, so quickly that he dropped his pint.

I was staring quite hard at a group of six men, hoping

one of them would look in my direction, when I bumped into someone else.

'Watch it, mate,' he growled.

'Sorry,' I said, and then, of course, I immediately went into my catching-eye routine, which didn't quite work because the guy was pretty much on top of me. I saw him give me the once-over.

'Ah sorry, love, I thought you were a bloke.'

This wasn't exactly a pick-up line but he was the only man who had spoken to me all night. Never mind that he was bow-legged, lantern-jawed, had a hairdo like a bog brush and smelled like a brewery gone wrong. He was taller than me (barely), he was an adult, and he was male.

'Do you want to dance?' I asked.

He gave me the once-over again. 'I like my girls with more tits on 'em.'

There wasn't much of an answer to this, so I just waited.

He considered, then shrugged. 'Might as well.'

We went on to the dance floor together and he immediately started jerking and twitching. I swayed back and forth a bit and took the opportunity to appraise my conquest. He wore a striped shirt that was too small for him in the neck and too long for him in the sleeves and he had a missing top incisor. His right hand was spasming in the air so I couldn't see it clearly but his left hand had small mats of hair between the second and third knuckles of each finger.

I wondered if, now that we were dancing together, the incomprehensible rules of the mating game meant that we had to get off with each other. Against my will I imagined it as a series of panels: us in a cab, his hand on my thigh; a close-up of his mouth with missing tooth as he went to kiss me; the speech bubble issuing from his figure in the darkened room: *Are those really all the tits you've got?* And then, in perspective from below, lots of shadows but not enough to conceal his hairy shoulders as he loomed shortly above me on the bed –

I shuddered, apparently in time to the music because my partner said, 'Nice moves,' and then made a grab for my chest.

Something barrelled across the dance floor, something in black with hair flowing behind it, and sent my partner sprawling.

'Jim?'

Jim scowled at my pick-up, who was scrambling to his feet. 'Watch yourself,' he said.

The guy took a swing at him and Jim stepped back. Then, to my utter amazement, he lifted his own fists.

'You want to try something?' he growled.

My dancing partner sized Jim up. Jim was skinny, but tall, and spitting mad. The guy turned round and beat it.

Jim grabbed my arm. 'Let's get away from this dickhead.'

'Where did you come from?' I asked as we hurried through the throngs of dancers and off the dance floor on the other side.

'Just bumped into you, I guess,' he said. 'Where's Digger?'

'I think he got off with someone because I haven't seen him. Where's your blonde?'

'Uh, she had to go.'

'Good job dodging that punch.'

'I've got the reflexes of a jungle cat. Do you really think that Digger found some—'

Both Jim and I saw him at the same time. He was at

the bar, a second bar which was smaller than the main one. Instead of a Manhattan skyline behind it, this one had a giant neon American flag. It was so bright that we could only see the silhouettes of the people standing near it, but Digger was unmistakable and larger than anyone else there.

He was talking to the girl next to him, and maybe it was because Digger's voice was so deep that it carried, or maybe the neon behind him made it particularly easy to lip read him, but either way I could tell what he was saying. 'Excuse me, would you like a drink?'

I didn't have to hear what the girl said. When she turned to look at Digger her face caught a ray of red and blue light and I saw her expression perfectly as it shifted from surprise, to shock, to contemptuous laughter.

If Jim had been fast in dodging that punch, he had nothing on me running to Digger.

I got there so fast, in fact, that I was able to see the hurt on his face before he hid it away.

Do I Have to Say That Thing in Klingon?

'Hey, Jim and I want to get the hell out of here,' I said.

'You saw her laugh.'

Guilt twisted in my stomach. For insisting my friends come here and for making them do something they didn't want to do. For my protective instincts that had led me to Digger too soon to pretend I hadn't seen anything.

'She was a cow,' I said.

'She was a dog,' Jim added, having appeared at my side.

'She was a flibbertigibbet,' I said, hoping the word would give Digger an excuse to smile. He didn't.

'Whisky,' he said to the barman, and when it came he downed it in one and grimaced.

'We have Glenlivet at ours,' Jim said, and as one we headed for the exit. I caught a glimpse of the blonde Jim had been talking to, standing on her own over by the DJ desk, and started to tell Jim she hadn't left after all, but then I had the horrible thought that she might have told him she was leaving as an excuse to get away from him.

And it was all my fault. We rode the taxi home in silence and nobody spoke until we were in our habitual seats in our living room with tumblers of Scotch in front of us. When I took a sip, the whisky mixed with the gin inside me and made me feel bad.

'It was only an experiment,' I said. 'You know, just to see if we could do it.'

'Sort of like making an atom bomb?' Jim said, and that shut me up.

Digger drank steadily and refilled his glass. His face was expressionless, but I watched him miserably. Giant, hairy Digger had the tenderest heart of anyone I'd ever met. For example, once when I'd been round his flat I uncovered a bank statement by mistake. He had a monthly direct debit donation to Childline which was nearly as much as his monthly rent. I never asked him about it, but I did notice afterwards that he was always in the kitchen making a cup of tea whenever one of the harrowing NSPCC adverts came on the telly.

Hurting him was unbearable, and I couldn't apologise to him because that would make him lose even more face. So I opened my foolish mouth again to explain. 'It's just that Stevo is one of us, and he found someone, so it doesn't seem so unlikely that we might—'

'Do we *want* anybody else?' Jim interrupted.

The anger in his voice made me cringe a bit. Obviously he'd been more hurt by the blonde's rejection than he'd let on. 'Well – no, of course we don't.'

'We're happy with our friends, right?'

'Yes, of course we are.'

And I was happy. It was obviously the booze talking in my head that gave me a sudden glimpse of an alternative reality of myself in another house, or in a restaurant, sitting across from a man whose face I couldn't quite imagine. We held hands across the table and laughed and I knew that I could tell him anything, anything at all, even the feelings I kept buried and secret, even the doubts. Even the hopes.

I blinked and the vision disappeared.

Jim took a fierce slug of his whisky. 'Who needs sex anyway?'

For the first time since we'd left the club, Digger looked at Jim, and then at me. He put his whisky on the coffee table and ponderously rose to his feet.

'We need to do something,' he said.

Maybe it was all the booze sloshing around inside me, but his pronouncement seemed full of dreadful portent. He stood up and took down three of the four candles surrounding my empty Peregrine shrine. Then he went into the kitchen and we heard him clattering around.

Jim and I exchanged a glance, and he shrugged.

'Which knife is your sharpest, and where are the matches?' Digger called from the kitchen, and we both bolted in there after him. He was contemplating the knife block.

'Why?' I asked.

'I want to go on a killing spree and then burn the neighbourhood down, stupid.' Digger poked in the cutlery drawer. 'Ah, there are the matches. So which knife, bread or butcher's?'

'I just sharpened the bread knife,' I said, relatively reassured by his sarcasm that he wasn't planning harm to himself. Digger drew the bread knife from the block and swished it through the air a couple of times. Satisfied, he opened the back door into the garden.

'Coming?' he asked. 'Jim, will you bring the Glenlivet?'

I followed Digger outside. The fresh spring air made me blink and realise quite how drunk I was, which was very drunk. Nevertheless, when Jim appeared with the Scotch and handed me the bottle, I took a swig of it to steady myself. Jim was none too firm on his feet, either.

Digger, though, was meticulous as he pressed the ends of the three candles into the earth so that they were standing up by themselves. He patted down the dirt around them and then lit their wicks. The moon was almost full, a waning gibbous, so it wasn't dark and the candles added a golden flicker to the steady silver light.

'What are we doing?' I asked.

'We're making sure we never have another disaster like tonight.' Digger took the Scotch from Jim and gulped it down.

'How? Are we going to summon a demon or something to make the club explode?' As well as I could with my head spinning, I considered the idea. 'Actually, that's pretty appropriate.'

'No. We're going to take a vow.'

'What kind of vow?'

'It's like Jim said. We're friends and we don't need anyone else. Let's promise to keep it that way for ever.'

'You silly,' I said, waving my hand in a drunken fashion. 'We don't need to promise to be friends, we're already friends.'

'No, I mean we promise not to need anyone else.'

I was still trying to catch up with this reasoning when

Jim said, 'You mean we'll stick together, just the three of us. No relationships.'

I scratched my head. 'You mean you guys won't try to get girlfriends?'

'And you won't try to get a boyfriend,' said Jim. 'Just you and me. And Digger.'

'Imagine if one of us three pulled a Stevo,' Digger said. 'And then another one did. The person who was left would be alone.'

'That wouldn't hap—'

'You said it wouldn't happen with Stevo,' Digger interrupted. Which was true.

Imagine Digger alone. Jim alone. Or me.

Waking up every morning, not knowing what to do. All those hours stretching out. I could lose myself for days on end with my drawing, but I always knew I had someone to come back to: Jim and Digger and, until recently, Stevo downstairs waiting for me.

'And anyway,' Jim said, 'if we take a vow we won't have to put ourselves through anything like tonight. No worries about –' He glanced at Digger and then at me and stopped.

No worries about being laughed at. About being lied to. About settling for someone just because he hadn't rejected you yet.

Surely anything was better than doing all that again.

'Okay,' I said. 'What do we have to do?' I looked at the knife. 'We're not becoming blood siblings or anything, are we?' Blood made me woozy, which Stevo was always saying was ironic seeing as I liked splashing my comics panels with it.

'Hell no,' said Digger. 'I might be swearing eternal fealty to you idiots, but I'm not cutting myself for you.'

'Digger, that's so sweet.'

'Shut up, I'm concentrating.' He thought for a moment, a task I didn't envy him. 'Okay, here goes.' He pointed the knife straight at the moon so that the beams gleamed off the blade and made it look a little like a lightsaber. He fixed his gaze on the infinite stars above.

'I, Douglas Michael John Mann, promise to forsake all romantic relationships and to stay true to my friends, James and Philomena. By the stars and the moon, by the earth and the fire, by the fellowship of three, I do swear it.'

'Now say "bItu Hpa' bIHeghjaja",' Jim ordered. The phrase sounded like someone growling whilst choking on a ham sandwich.

Digger unfixed his gaze from the infinite stars and raised his eyebrows at Jim.

'Hey, if you get to make up the ritual, at least I should be able to put some parts of it in Klingon,' Jim said.

Digger considered this, and then shrugged. 'It fits, I guess.' He re-adopted his solemn and dramatic pose and growled and choked, 'bItu Hpa' bIHeghjaja!'

Then he swung the knife downwards and with one mighty swipe, decapitated one of the three candles. The still-lit wick landed on the grass and Digger stamped out the flame with his massive foot.

'There. It is done, and done well.' He passed the knife to Jim. I resisted the urge to ask him why he was suddenly speaking like someone out of *The Lord of the Rings*.

Jim planted his feet wide on the ground and pointed the knife at the moon. With his long hair flowing around his face he did look a bit like one of the elves. 'By the stars and the moon, by the earth and the fire, by the fellowship of three, I, James Thomas Lousder, do solemnly swear to forsake all romantic relationships and stay true to my friends, Philomena and Digger. *bItu Hpa' bIHeghjaja!*' He roared the last phrase, and then visited fearful Klingon vengeance on his candle. The burning end flew through the air and snuffed itself out on my leg.

'You could have immolated me,' I said to Jim as he handed me the knife.

'Stop whining and take the vow,' he said.

I pointed the knife to the heavens. I tried to summon the requisite solemnity for pronouncing a vow which, after all, could conceivably change the course of my entire life. Instead, I felt very drunk and incredibly silly.

'I, Philomena Desdemona Brown, do swear by the stars and the moon and the earth and everything that I will forsake all romantic relationships – although, frankly, I'm unlikely to have any in the first place. But if I do, I'll forsake them. And stick with my friends Digger and Jim.' I lowered the knife. 'Do I have to say that thing in Klingon?'

'Yes,' said Jim.

'Uh. Bitu Hpa—'

'bIHeghjaja,' Jim prompted, spitting a bit in the process.

'Bijaja.'

'Your Klingon is absolutely appalling.'

'You know, weirdly enough, that doesn't bother me. What does it mean, anyway?'

'Death before shame.'

'Oh,' I said. Suddenly the gravitas which had eluded me when saying the actual vow hit me with a vengeance. I'd just sworn to a lifetime of chastity, and the alternative, apparently, was death.

What if I *wanted* to get married one day? And have kids and do all that stuff?

I looked around at my friends. They were looking back at me. Marriage and love and children seemed so very remote, something that other people did, something other people could earn in some way by being normal, by living up to expectations.

'Cut the candle,' Digger prompted me.

'Right.' I raised the knife again and swung it down in a great arc towards the candle. Drunk as I was, it was hardly surprising that the knife struck the candle a glancing blow, uprooted it from the ground, and sent it hurtling six feet through the air to land on a pile of leaves, immediately setting them alight.

'Shit.' I grabbed the Glenlivet from Jim and ran to the fire.

'Don't pour the—' Digger yelled before I realised it was extremely stupid to throw alcohol on a fire. I tossed aside the bottle and began stamping on the fire instead.

'Ouch! Ow!' I yelled as the heat burned through the thin rubber soles of my Converses. It occurred to me that I was in danger of my jeans catching fire, but the flames were spreading so I kept on stamping. 'You guys think you could help out here – ouch!'

Jim appeared at my side and threw something over the fire and my feet. It was a beach towel that had been hanging on the clothes line since last September and was nice and damp. I jumped out of the way as he and Digger took care of the edges of the fire with their boots.

'You hit that candle like a girl.' Jim snuffed out the last of the flames.

I checked the bottom of my trainers: a little singed,

but they would live another day. 'In case you hadn't noticed, I *am* a girl.'

'Hmph.' Jim retrieved the Glenlivet from where I'd tossed it, wiped off the mouth of the bottle, and took a swig. 'Let's go indoors.'

I was the last inside, and, before I went in, I took a last look over my shoulder at the beach towel covering the doused remains of my potentially very serious mistake.

If I believed in omens, that wouldn't be a very good one.

There's a Distinct Difference Between Sucking and Biting

With all the vows of infinite friendship and everything, you would think that the three of us had known each other all our lives, but we hadn't. Jim and I became friends when we were both thirteen, which meant I'd been friends with him for nearly fifty per cent of my life. But I'd only met Digger five years before the night we stood in the garden decapitating candles. I was still at art school and Jim was at university on the other side of London.

That particular day had started off brilliantly. I was in my single hall-of-residence bed with Pierre, naked and warm with his lovemaking. He was sipping from a chipped mug of instant coffee and smoking a cigarette while I lay beside him gazing up at his beautifully Gallic features. My hands ache when I'm attracted to somebody. It's weird, I know. My hands were aching like crazy now.

Frenchmen knew the art of making love, I thought happily. They appreciated sex as if it were a fine wine. I sighed and pictured a troop of beautifully Gallic children frolicking through sun-drenched vineyards, and Pierre and me walking behind them, hand in hand. In my daydream I had instantly been transformed into the sort of person who wore floaty white dresses.

'Oh darling,' I said in my imagination, 'I am so lucky you walked into the student union all those years ago without your money and had to ask me, a total stranger, to buy you a plate of chips and a pint.'

'No, my darling,' he replied in my dream, 'it is I who am lucky, to have found such a desirable woman as you.'

Pierre flicked ash on to the floor by the side of my bed. 'Got any lectures this afternoon?' he asked, and I jumped a bit, because his French accent was actually much less pronounced than in my dream.

'Nothing I can't bunk off, why?'

A slow and sexy smile crossed his face. 'I have an idea for something we can do.'

'What's that?' I asked, my toes curling in pleasure. He was going to suggest something wildly romantic, like a picnic in the rain. Not that Pierre had ever suggested anything wildly romantic before, in the three months that we had been seeing each other. His usual *modus operandi* was to turn up at my hall of residence every now and then at about midnight, fag hanging out of his mouth, bottle of red wine in hand, his clothes splashed with clay and the light of lust in his eyes.

But last night, for the first time, he had stayed. He'd fallen asleep in my arms and woken me in the morning with kisses along my neck.

My first real boyfriend. It flashed across my brain that maybe I should introduce him to my parents, and the prospect filled me with pleasure. A French sculptor, with a reputation for brilliance among the students and staff: they couldn't fault that.

They might even be proud of me. The thought was both thrilling and alarming.

Pierre ran his hand up my thigh. 'There's someone I want you to meet,' he said.

Oh, my goodness. We were even thinking the same thing. 'You want me to go to Paris with you?'

He opened his mouth to reply and my phone rang. 'Just a second,' I told him. There was no way I wanted this memorable moment of my life soundtracked by a ringing phone. I rolled the short distance to the edge of the bed and reached for my mobile phone.

It was Jim. 'What?' I asked him.

'What time are we meeting up at Covent Garden?'

Oh, damn. I'd forgotten that I was supposed to meet Jim and go to Forbidden Planet with him, usually a prospect that filled me with the incomparable joy of shiny new comic books in plastic sleeves. But not today.

'Um, I'm not sure.' I glanced at Pierre, who was smoking his fag with a dreamy expression on his face, doubtlessly picturing the happy moment when he introduced me to his fabulously sophisticated, talented and accepting family. 'I think I have a lecture, actually.'

'Fil, *Nemesis* is out on DVD today.'

'Jim, that movie bites and Jean-Luc's clone doesn't even look like him.'

'It's out today and I need it.'

'It'll still be out tomorrow. Or next week.'

'It won't be the same and you know it. You said you would, what's up with you?'

Pierre finished his cigarette and put it out in the dregs

of his coffee. He shifted, as if he were about to get up, and I put my leg over his to keep him there. Instead, he reached over and picked up his packet of fags, grunting at the awkward position.

'Is there somebody there?' Jim asked. 'I can hear somebody.'

'No. It must be the radio.'

'You're acting weird.'

No, Jim, I wanted to say, *as a matter of fact, I'm not acting weird at all. I'm acting like a normal woman who has a boyfriend for the first time in her life.*

'Listen, I've got a really important lecture. But I'll ring you if I can skip out of it, okay?'

'My battery's about to go.'

I sighed with exasperation. 'You work with technology all day long, can't you remember to charge your mobile phone without my reminding you? You do have to do some things for yourself, you know.'

'Is it your time of the month or something?'

I ran my fingers through my bedhead hair, which happened to be platinum-blond at that time. Pierre was looking bored, and I sounded like a nag. He'd hear me nagging and decide blondes weren't that much fun after all.

'Okay, so just go to Covent Garden for three, and if I can make it, I'll be there, otherwise go on to Forbidden Planet without me, all right? You can manage to buy a DVD on your own, can't you?'

'Do me a favour and go take a Nurofen.' Jim hung up.

I tossed the phone to the floor. 'So what was your great idea?' I asked Pierre, hoping he wouldn't ask what my conversation had been about. Somehow I didn't think that moody continental sculptors kept track of when the latest *Star Trek* films were out on DVD, nor would they be impressed by my having friends who did.

He smiled. 'I want you to meet my friend Marie.'

My hopes sank. So it wasn't a family introduction after all. But then again, he wanted me to meet his friend. That was a good sign, right?

'Sure, that sounds great.'

'I think we could really have some fun together, you know what I mean?' He nuzzled my ear, and I could smell cigarettes and coffee.

Not the romantic afternoon I'd planned, but maybe I could salvage something. 'How about a picnic in the rain?'

'I think we should go to Marie's place. It is more private.'

'Oh. All right.'

Pierre slid out of my bed and scooped his trousers up off the floor. His naked penis pointed upwards towards his chest. His erections astonished me. I could hardly believe that such an impressive physiological change had been inspired by my body. And this was the second time this morning. Maybe I was some sort of a sex goddess.

'Are you sure you don't want to come back to bed?' I asked.

'No.' He tucked his manhood into his trousers in a matter-of-fact way and zipped it up out of sight. 'Let's go now; we can get decent coffee.'

'Oh. Okay.' I held the sheet up to my chest and found my T-shirt where it had been balled up at the end of the bed. Once that was on, it was long enough so that I could pull on my underwear without it being too awkward. It wasn't that Pierre hadn't seen me naked before; just never in the light of morning, which was different to night-time.

I didn't want to put him off. By the time I'd put on my jeans and trainers and run my fingers through my hair, Pierre had lit another fag and was standing, slouched and attractively bored, by the door.

I tugged at my hair in the mirror. 'Do I look all right to meet – Marie?'

'Yes. Let's go.'

He strode down the long, breeze-block corridor of the hall of residence and I tripped beside him happily. How brilliant was this? We were off on an adventure, some-where other than the student union and my room. Did this mean we'd officially passed the point in our relationship where we did nothing but shag each other senseless and could now venture out into the big wide world as A Couple?

At the café on the corner, Pierre bought us each a paper cup of double espresso. I watched him drink his. His full lips, his darkly stubbled chin. Perhaps I could hint that he should wash his hair before he met my parents. Then again, clay dust was sexy. The caffeine added to the feeling I always got when I was with Pierre; that breathless, I-can't-quite-believe-it knife edge of nerves, where everything was sharper.

Outside the café, he raised his strong hand to hail a cab and once inside, he pulled me over to sit on his lap. 'I think you and Marie will like each other, eh?' he murmured in my ear, his hand on my thigh.

'I'm sure we will,' I lied. I wasn't really good at making girl friends; I found myself tongue-tied, even with the art college set, who exuded creativity and sensuality and seemed fond of bracelets and sandalwood. But perhaps it would be easier with Pierre there to introduce us.

'I will like that very much.'

And what wouldn't I do to please him, my Gallic sculptor who was making my life a fairy tale? I smiled and settled into his lap.

One day I might even confess to him that I'd been a virgin when we first met. Imagine how touched he'd be, how emotional. Of course he would never have suspected it previously. I'd been doing everything I could think of to cover it up.

The cab pulled up in front of a warehouse. 'I spent all my money on the coffee, eh?' Pierre said, and I took the hint and dug into my pocket for cash to pay the driver. Then I followed my gorgeous, brilliant French boyfriend to the door of the warehouse. He pressed a button and spoke a few words in French through an intercom, then hauled open the big sliding door, which was crawling with graffiti. Our footsteps echoed in the green-painted stairwell.

At the top of the stairs was a dented wooden door. Pierre pushed it open without knocking, and I followed. The space beyond was vast, with rough wooden floors, unfinished brick walls and floor-to-ceiling windows looking out over South London. One of those artsy lofts I'd heard about, but never actually been in. For a moment I thought the room was full of people – strange, still, pale people – but then I realised they were sculptures. Standing in every position, hands up, bent over, twisted round, leaning backwards. All nude.

'Wow,' I said.

Pierre wasn't listening. He was walking towards the only furniture in the room, a king-sized mattress lying on the floor in the centre. A woman stood in front of it. She had straight black hair and wore a tight black knit dress and no shoes.

'*Salut*,' Pierre said and kissed her on the mouth.

I frowned. I wasn't all that sure about what French people did to greet their friends, but I thought it was cheek kisses, not mouth kisses. Still, I was prepared to have an open mind; after all, that's what having a boyfriend, especially a foreign one, was all about, wasn't it? Learning new things?

I shifted a little bit and my elbow brushed one of the statues. It appeared to be made out of plaster, and it was a woman. A naked woman, of course, with straight hair. I looked from the sculpture's face to the woman's, and saw they were the same.

Okay. So Marie, whoever she was, liked to make naked statues of herself. It was art, fair enough. Maybe if I had a body like hers, I'd do it too. My gaze fell on the statue's full breasts, and then I looked away quickly: maybe not.

The real-life woman was approaching me. 'Welcome,' she said to me, smiling with the mouth that had just kissed my man. She took my hand in hers. It was very warm.

'Thanks,' I said. 'Uh, nice place.'

'Isn't it?' She had an accent, though not quite French. 'Please, make yourself comfortable. It is very good to meet you at last.' She led me by the hand through the statues towards the mattress, where Pierre was still standing. We passed by several more sculptures of her, which presented various parts of her anatomy.

'At last?'

'Yes, Pierre has told me all about you.'

'Oh! Well, that's good.' If he was telling his friends about me, he must think it was serious. For a split second I thought about Jim, and what I wasn't telling him, but then Marie put her arm round my waist and pulled me closer to her, so we were standing hip-to-hip.

She was really very friendly. Pierre smiled and nodded. 'Ah yes, you are very suited together, proper opposites,' he said. He sat down on the mattress, and patted the space beside him.

I joined him. It was the only place in the loft to sit down, after all. I took his hand in mine, just in case, for whatever reason, Marie didn't quite understand the nature of my relationship with Pierre. She smiled again and I expected her to offer us some coffee, though I certainly didn't need any because my nerves were jangling all over the place. Instead, she sat down too, on my other side.

From this angle the statues looked very tall and I had a perfect view of their buttocks and crotches. They were very detailed. 'Are those, um, sculptures or are they body casts?' I asked.

'Both. Do you like them?'

'Yes, they're –' I searched for a description from my art-school vocabulary but was a bit too distracted, squished between two people here on this mattress. 'Nice.'

'I am glad.' Marie tossed her hair behind her shoulder and licked her lush red lips.

I wondered exactly what Pierre meant about us being opposites. Marie was tall, I was short; she was brunette, I was (currently) blond; she was voluptuous, I was skinny; she was exotic, I was English. He seemed to approve of this, but was it a comparison where I came up lacking? I shuffled over a little bit more towards Pierre, but he shook his head and lay down on the mattress, his hands behind his head, as if he were watching some kind of a show.

Marie put her hand on the side of my face. She had

calluses on her fingertips, and she ran them over my jaw, my cheek, my forehead as if she were testing me for a sculpture. 'Lovely,' she said, in a detached way, and then with her other hand she reached for my T-shirt and began to pull it up over my head.

'Um.' I scooted backwards and held down the hem of my shirt. 'I'm not sure I'm into posing just at the moment, you know, without any clothes on or whatever.'

Marie raised a shaped eyebrow.

'Don't worry,' said Pierre from where he lay on the bed, 'you can pose afterwards, if you like.'

'After what?'

In answer, Marie, with leisurely movements, unzipped her dress at the front and pushed it off her shoulders. She was nude underneath, the living model for all the art around us. The smile still on her lips, she took my hand from my T-shirt and put it on the slope of her left breast. Then she leaned forward, her mouth aimed directly at mine.

I jumped backwards on the mattress, snatching my hand back. 'Um, I'm sorry, I don't think that's –' Oh God, I didn't even have any experience turning down a man, what was I supposed to say to a lesbian? 'I mean – I'm with *Pierre*,' I said, looking to Pierre, who hadn't moved. Why wasn't he protesting?

'Don't worry, Pierre will join us.' Marie smiled, and I could see she was amused. 'He enjoys watching first.'

'He –' I scrambled off the bed. 'You mean he –' The truth clunked into my brain like a stone. 'You mean that's why we're here, you want us to all—'

Pierre's smile was the echo of Marie's. 'I said I think you'll like Marie, yes?'

'You – but –' I backed away, my brain refusing to make

words. My backside hit something solid and I whirled round to look at it. It was another sculpture, this one male, its penis jutting upwards at a horribly familiar angle.

I gazed from the sculpture to Pierre. The same face.

'You – are you – hold on, are you and Marie – have you been sleeping together?'

He didn't have to answer; it was obvious from the lack of shock on both of their faces. As opposed to mine, which was flaming.

'You've been cheating on me with Marie?' This time they both raised their eyebrows at the same time. 'You've been cheating on Marie with *me*? And now you want to have a threesome?'

He held out his hand to me. So did she.

My vision of white floaty dresses and Gallic children traipsing across sun-drenched vineyards shrivelled like a punctured balloon.

'Oh my God.'

Pierre sat up. 'You don't want to?'

'No!'

'I thought you were an adventurous girl. I thought you were different.'

'I thought you were my boyfriend.'

He took his cigarettes from his pocket. 'I see now that you are conventional.' He lit a cigarette between his lips and handed it to Marie who lay down beside him, nude. The bitter smoke formed a cloud between them and me.

'I –'

I choked. Anger, despair and shock wrenched round in my belly, all trying to rise up and say something, something that would make me less inadequate, make Pierre mine again, erase the past half-hour and get back to thoughts of picnics in the rain.

'Can't we just go to France?' I asked him, but he was already kissing Marie's neck. She blew smoke rings towards the ceiling and casually slipped her hand inside his trousers.

I fled past the stiff, naked statues, each one wearing a knowing smile.

A bit over three hours later I emerged from the lift into Covent Garden tube station and the sound of falling rain. I spotted Jim right away; he was huddled in his black coat under an overhanging bit from the shop across the way. His hair was plastered to his head and I knew the end of his ponytail would be dripping a steady stream of rainwater down his back. He looked shorter than usual, but then at second glance I realised that was because he was standing next to a giant.

As usual on a rainy day, there were several people sheltering in front of the shop. The guy next to Jim was at least six and a half feet tall, broad in a massive denim jacket whose shoulders were soaked with rain. He had a bushy brown beard and curly brown hair, both of which looked as if they hadn't been cut in quite some time.

He looks like a bear escaped from the zoo, I thought. I would mentally apologise for that thought later, but at the time I wasn't in a charitable mood. After leaving Pierre and Marie, I'd gone back to my hall of residence and spent a frantic hour sweeping up ash and opening windows and energetically trying to clear the smell of Pierre's fag smoke out of the room, and then just as energetically slamming the windows shut because the smell was the only thing I had left of him. Finally I'd gone for a walk and then gravitated towards meeting Jim, because I couldn't think of anything else to do. I pulled up the hood of my jacket and scurried over to the shop.

'You decided to turn up, then,' he said, as we set off in the direction of Shaftesbury Avenue. Coincidentally, the giant pushed off at the same time we did and strode along beside us, continuing to make Jim look shorter than usual.

'The lecture sucked.' I felt my cheeks heat with guilt and remembered humiliation.

'So does *Nemesis*, according to you.'

'No, if you'd been paying attention correctly to our conversation you'd have remembered that I said that *Nemesis* bites. There's a distinct difference between sucking and biting. Though with your table manners I wouldn't expect you to know it.'

We'd turned off the pedestrianised bit on to the crowded pavements of Long Acre, and I couldn't help noticing that Giant Bear Man was still walking beside us – not an easy job, given his size and the size of the pavement. Jim didn't seem to notice.

'I'm surprised you can remember my table manners,' he said.

'What's that supposed to mean?'

'Nothing.'

'I've been busy.'

'Of course you have. They work art students down to the ground, so I hear.'

We crossed a street and Bear Man got tangled up with a tide of people crossing the other way; I could see his head towering over them all. Within a minute or two he'd caught up with us again.

'I tried to call you,' I lied, 'but your phone was off. It probably ran out of charge again.'

The look Jim gave me cut straight through the rain to leave a slash of guilt on my heart.

'You don't have a radio in your room, either,' he said.

'Oops, pardon me,' said a man who knocked his arm against Bear Man beside us. Bear Man nodded and stepped round him, keeping pace with me and Jim.

'Jim,' I said, lowering my voice, 'this is a little weird, but I think that big bearded guy is following us.'

'Oh him?' Jim glanced over at him. 'That's Digger, he lives down the hall from me. I told him I was probably going to end up going to Forbidden Planet alone because you couldn't be bothered to come, so he came along with me.'

I stopped. Jim and Bear Man stopped too.

'You know him?'

'Yeah,' said Jim. Bear Man nodded.

I spread my hands. 'And you didn't think it was a good idea to introduce us?'

Jim shrugged. 'You didn't seem all that interested.'

'Of course I'm interested in your friends. And it's manners, Jim, you introduce people.'

Unless, of course, one of the people was a brilliant sexy French sculptor. You kept that one quiet and lied to your friend about it.

I swallowed.

Now was not the time to bring that up, though. What was the point? *Listen, now that we mention it, I've been seeing this guy without telling you but it doesn't really matter now because he dumped me today when I wouldn't have sex with him and his girlfriend at the same time.* Yeah. That was going to go down a treat, especially seeing as this huge Digger man was listening to every word.

'Fil, this is Digger,' Jim said. 'Digger, Fil.'

'Nice to meet you, Digger.'

Digger nodded.

We began walking again, both of us as silent as Digger. I wasn't really sure what you were supposed to say to a giant man who appeared to be mute. Did you ask polite questions, or would that just be embarrassing for everyone? Jim wasn't helping any, either.

It was easier to take up sniping again. 'Sheesh Jim, you'd think you'd been brought up in a barn or something. You got any other friends stashed away that I don't know about?'

'No,' Jim said, sounding petulant, and I felt sorry I'd said that because I knew better than anyone that making friends had never been easy for Jim.

Fortunately at that moment we reached Forbidden Planet and Jim made a beeline for the *Nemesis* DVDs, while Digger lumbered off silently to another end of the shop. I sloped off to my own personal heaven, the comics section.

Little slices of adventure, all sandwiched in slippery plastic sleeves. Comics weren't quite guilt-free – nobody who grew up in my household could ever pick up a comic without hearing a sharpened voice saying, 'But they're *trash*, darling.' But that guilt, at least, was one that I had dealt with long ago. Not like the new feeling of somehow having betrayed your best friend just by trying to be happy.

I let my fingers and eyes feast, and tried to lose myself for a little while. I started with the art comics and indies because there was some good stuff in there. But my real love were the superheroes and the sci-fi comics. The bulging muscles and the tights, the bright colours and the action and the complex multiverses. All the Marvel and

DC stuff, *2000AD* and, of course, *Girl from Mars*. I already had this month's issue but I picked it up off the shelf anyway and flicked through it, with the feeling of visiting an old friend.

The thing was, why hadn't I mentioned Pierre to Jim in the first place?

We didn't talk about sex or boyfriends or girlfriends or anything like that. I mean, sure, I'd got off with one or two blokes at parties and stuff since I'd got to art school, in an amateurish sort of way, and quite often I formed crushes on the kind of handsome, talented, terrifying men that were too good to notice me, that is (I'd believed) until Pierre. Most likely Jim had got off with girls, too. That was the sort of thing you did, right? He sort of liked those fey Goth girls with long hair, Arwen types; he stared at them whenever he visited me at my art school. Maybe he'd been seeing one himself, without telling me.

It all seemed too embarrassing to talk about. Which was probably a good thing, because nothing could ever be as embarrassing as what had happened with me and Pierre.

Pierre. While I'd been glorying in the idea that finally I had a normal boyfriend who cared about me, he'd been using me as a booty call when Marie had a headache or was busy sculpting her own genitals or whatever. The truth sank in with sickening inevitability and even the thousands of supertechnicolored superheroes surrounding me didn't make me feel any better.

In my head, I went through every conversation I could remember. Had he known that I thought we were having a relationship? Was he aware of my pitiful little hopes? I remembered my last words to him, and cringed.

I might as well have thrown myself at his feet screaming, 'Please, please, please love me, I am so pathetic!'

I sighed in sadness and utter humiliation.

God, I did want to talk to Jim about it.

He knew sadness and humiliation. He knew what it was like to look around and realise that everyone else was playing a game, and they all knew the rules, and you'd been left out and didn't know anything. He'd be able to sympathise and understand.

But of course I couldn't talk to him about it because I'd left him out of the game I'd been playing.

This wasn't helping. I put the comics back on the shelf and wandered around the shop. Digger, I noticed, had bought the latest Terry Pratchett hardback and was standing by the exit, reading it, seemingly oblivious of everyone around him. If he couldn't talk, he could at least read.

I didn't see Jim anywhere. I threaded through the aisles of action figures and models and wished I could scroll back in time to the moment where I could have told Jim about Pierre. It would've taken thirty seconds or less. What had I been afraid of, anyway? That Jim would be upset that I thought I'd found someone I liked? I knew him better than to think he'd be so selfish.

Jim rounded the corner of an aisle in front of me. He had an armful of DVDs and books. 'Look, Fil, this one's been signed by Michael Dorn!'

His cheeks were flushed, and his grey eyes were all sparkly with excitement. They shone like silver at times like this and made his face look lean and handsome.

I felt a rush of affection for him at the same time that I realised the real reason I hadn't told Pierre about his existence.

It was because I hadn't thought Pierre would think

Jim was interesting and cool enough, and if he didn't think Jim was interesting and cool enough, he wouldn't think I was, either.

'That's great, Jim,' I said, but I guess it fell flat of what he expected because he looked at me and frowned.

'Where are all your comics?'

'I decided not to get any.'

He frowned more deeply. 'What is up with you today, Fil?'

I bit my lip and tried to think how to tell him about how he was the most important person in my life and he knew me the best and I was so grateful for it that I could never repay him. How I loved him like the brother I'd never had. And yet how, at the same time, though I didn't want to be, I was ashamed of him because I was ashamed of myself. And I was even more ashamed of myself because I felt that way.

I couldn't do it.

'Nothing,' I said. 'Here, let me help you carry that stuff to the till.'

'You are definitely riding the crimson highway. Crazy women.'

The four guys in the aisle beside us all looked at me, and I blushed.

'Will you shut up about that?' I snapped. 'Give me your stuff.' I grabbed for it, and he turned away.

'I can do it myself.'

I tagged along behind him and watched him pay for his things. Then I went with him to the exit, where Digger tucked his book beneath his arm and fell into step beside us without, of course, a word.

I could sympathise with him. I couldn't think of a damn thing to say.

Jim's face was like thunder and he stomped along the wet street with his carrier bags of booty in his hands. He'd been looking forward to this day for ages, and I'd ruined it for him. I couldn't blame him for making himself a new friend, even a big, bearded silent one. I'd turned my back on him.

I love you, I wanted to tell him, but we never said stuff like that. *I'm sorry*, I wanted to say, but I couldn't explain what I was sorry for. I walked along with him, beside him but not with him, miserable.

The rain rained and the sky lay on the city like a wet wool blanket. For London, it was eerily quiet but maybe that was because I was so desperate to hear something. Because the pavement was so narrow, Digger was walking slightly ahead of us and his shape was a vast lumbering shadow. I thought about going back to my hall of residence, alone, and lying on my bed hating myself for trying to detect a whiff of cigarette smoke.

Digger suddenly stopped in front of us. Jim bumped into him, and I bumped into Jim. Digger turned round.

'Sweet holy cats,' he said, 'will you two stop sulking and find a pub?'

Jim and I stared at him.

'"Sweet holy cats?"' Jim said, and Digger's big mouth quirked up on one side, and I began to giggle.

'I thought you didn't talk,' I said.

'I only talk when I have something worth saying. Unlike some other people. There's a pub across the road, first round's on you, Fil, for nearly standing us up.'

We went inside the pub; it was orange with light and nearly steaming with wet warmth, and I caught the flash from Jim's smile. I dug in my pockets for my money, glad I hadn't bought any comic books.

Some magic spell of Digger and holy cats meant everything was normal again. Of course I couldn't say anything to Jim; I'd been silly to think I could. I'd just have to show him how I felt about him instead. I went up to the bar.

It's Strange Being a Stranger

Five years after the day after Jim, Digger and I took
our no-romance vow, I awoke with the worst head
I'd had in a very long time. Noticing blearily that I'd
fallen asleep wearing all my clothes and that my trainers
had smeared soot all over my duvet, I hauled myself out
of bed, downed a pint of water that I seemed to
remember having put on my bedside table two days
before, and dragged my feet all the way to the bathroom.

A shower failed to help. Fresh clothes didn't help
either. As I walked past Jim's bedroom on my way downstairs I heard him snoring like a chainsaw. Or maybe like
a Klingon.

Digger was asleep on the sofa, his feet sticking over
the end as they always did. He slept as quietly as a kitten.
I went to the kitchen and made myself some coffee and
toast, which I consumed while slumped on the sink. They
made me feel, if that were possible, worse.

There was only one cure for this feeling, aside from
the last slug of Glenlivet still in the bottle. I grabbed my
bag and UPC badge. Outside the sun shone painfully, but

fortunately it didn't take long to get to the cool cavern of the tube station and once I was on the Northern line I closed my eyes and attempted to drift off. One good thing about being a creature of habit: I could change at Stockwell for the Victoria line even when half asleep.

I suspected I was one of the few people in the world who went to work when she had a hangover because she knew it would make her feel better. The closer I got to the UPC building, the more the world began to fall into place, and by the time I'd shown my badge to reception and punched the lift button for the archives floor, my head had stopped pounding quite so relentlessly. The archives smelled of dust and paper and ink, and I went straight to the *Girl from Mars* section.

Here, collected in one place, was every single issue of *Girl from Mars* dating all the way back to the first one in 1951. The comic's creator, Dennis McKay, had had enough foresight to see that he'd made something special with *Girl from Mars* and he'd kept several copies of each issue – even the September 1954 issue that had to be hastily reprinted when a distributor had noticed that the accidental placement of a bullet on the cover made it appear that Girl from Mars had a very large nipple erection.

The archives made it possible to check continuity with stories dating over fifty years ago. Past artists hadn't always done this; in fact, for a few issues back in the nineties, Girl from Mars's skin colour had inexplicably changed from green to turquoise and then back again. But in general one of the things that readers liked about *Girl from Mars* was that even with different writers and different artists and different types of storylines and con-texts, the main character stayed, essentially, consistent.

This wasn't to say she stayed exactly the same. She'd been born in the aftermath of World War II, in a country wanting excitement and escape, created by a man who wanted a heroine who would reflect the strength of the women he'd seen helping the war effort. She'd first appeared wearing a sort of Martian uniform, complete with knee-length skirt and pillbox hat. Her fashion sense had changed quite a bit over the years, as had her spaceship and her vocabulary and her sidekicks. Although the profession of 'space alien' wasn't subject to a glass ceiling, she benefited from feminism in that males didn't tend to talk down to her any more (though even in the fifties, she usually responded to such patronising and chauvinistic behaviour with a few well-placed kicks).

But these were external things. Girl from Mars developed, she learned from her mistakes and the tragedies of others, but her essential Girl-from-Mars-ness remained the same through all of it.

To illustrate how extraordinary that was, I can use the parallel example of Batman. The Caped Crusader was created in 1939 and has, over the years, been portrayed as a logical detective, a masked and violent vigilante, a law-abiding police helper, a darkly suffering and fallible human, a right-wing militant, and an ultra-camp dude in tights.

Not Girl from Mars. She was always kind, always brave, always ready to use her accurate fists to promote justice and attitude adjustment. She was touched by tragedy, and above all, she was always alone. Even among friends, she was the alien. She didn't even have a real name. And yet she made that loneliness, that alien-ness, so inspiring, so much the foundation for everything good that she did, that you couldn't help but wish you were from Mars like her.

Of course, every artist and writer added something that was essentially his or her own, too. What I liked about my contribution was that as the first female artist in the comic's history, I got to show Girl from Mars from the point of view of what a woman wanted to be – rather than from the point of view of what a man fantasised about. Less heavy on the tits and big girly eyes, more acute on the action and street smarts. The smarts had always been there along with the tits, of course, but I played up the former rather than the latter.

I located some Wayne Jayson issues from the eighties, carefully removed them from the shelves, and brought them over to a table so that I could study them. Jayson had brought some darkness to Girl from Mars, but again, that had been there from the beginning. I opened issue 402, *Mars Memories*, which was Jayson's rendering of Girl from Mars's back-story. The beautiful Martian landscape and architecture became even more haunting because you knew, as you read, that Girl from Mars was never going to see them again.

By the time I'd finished reading, my mind was zinging with ideas. I dug in my bag and got out my sketchbook and a pencil.

What seemed like minutes later, I looked at my watch and saw to my surprise that it was nearly two o'clock in the afternoon, which meant I'd been here four hours at least. With that realisation, my throat told me I was parched and my stomach told me I was ravenous. I filed away the Jayson comics, packed up my work and went off in search of sustenance.

A coffee and a mozzarella and tomato panini got rid of the last vestiges of my hangover and I sat happily at my normal table in O Solo Mio with a second coffee and an almond pastry, reading a gossip magazine that someone had left behind on the table and wondering why on earth anybody would be interested in the doings of pop stars and movie actresses. It was one more in the ever-growing list of things I didn't understand about most normal people.

'Philomena?'

American Dan was standing by my table with a mug, doubtlessly containing decaf. He was wearing a white shirt and a tie, as before, and he had a briefcase.

'Dan, remember? We met on Monday. We switched coffees.'

'Yeah, I remember. Uh, how are you?'

'Great. Would it be okay if I joined you?'

I looked around briefly. There were plenty of empty tables. 'Sure, yeah, that would be okay. I mean it's the best table, right?'

'Is it?' He sat across from me and set his mug down.

'Yeah, well, you were sitting here last time.' As soon as I said it I realised it made me sound like I was stalking him or something.

'I guess I was. You're not drawing today?'

I held up my pencil-smeared hands. 'I've been drawing all day, I thought I'd take a break.'

'What kind of an artist are you?'

'Oh. Um, an illustrator for magazines.' It was the standard answer I gave to people who I didn't think would understand my real job. I was immensely proud to be a comic book artist, but I'd discovered that people who didn't read comics usually responded with casual contempt when I told the truth. Either they assumed that it was easy to do and mentioned how they'd drawn Danger Mouse a lot when they were a kid, or they dropped a comment that made it clear that they thought comics were trash for children and they'd never picked one up in their lives. Since my response to both of these attitudes was to launch into a twenty-minute lecture, with citations, about the value of comics as a narrative and art form, I found it was easier for all involved if I just lied in the first place. And it wasn't a lie anyway, really; *Girl from Mars* was a magazine of sorts and I did freelance as an illustrator sometimes.

'That's interesting,' Dan said. 'Will I have seen your work anywhere?'

'No. I mean, it's doubtful. You're not English, are you?'

'I'm from Philadelphia. I'm over on business,' he said, 'but I'm hoping to stay for a while. It all depends on how well this new project goes, I guess.'

'Oh.'

'It also depends on my dad,' he continued. 'He's English and I'm hoping to reconnect with him while I'm here. I haven't spent much time with him since my parents split up when I was a kid and he went back to London.'

'Oh.' Why couldn't I come up with anything else to say?

He shrugged, as if I'd asked him a question. 'I'm not sure how much reconnecting is happening, though. I don't really know him enough to tell. He works a lot. English people are so reserved, aren't they?'

'I don't think we generally go up to strangers in cafés and tell them about our family dilemmas, no.' There! A whole sentence!

'Whereas in Philadelphia you have to wear earphones in Starbucks if you don't want to hear the life histories of all your fellow customers.'

'Earphones! I knew I'd forgotten something this morning.'

His smile faded. 'Look, if I'm bothering you, just say so.'

'No, no, it's okay.' I blushed furiously into my coffee.

He drank his through a long pause, during which I tried not to squirm. 'My father says it's one of the things he likes least about Americans,' he said finally, 'how they spill their guts at the least provocation. Given his choice, he'd only ever talk about the weather and soccer.'

'Football,' I corrected, and then cringed in case he took offence. 'It's probably safer to stick with those topics,' I rushed ahead, to forestall any more silence. 'My parents, for example, are devastatingly articulate in their disapproval about my life choices.'

He laughed. Actually laughed! I nearly toppled off my chair.

'Blue hair bother them?'

'Blue hair is the least of it, believe me.'

He went quiet again and I wondered if it was up to me to keep the conversation going now.

'What's this new project you're over here for?' I asked.

'Oh. It's – well, it's a different direction for me. Something I've never done before. I should know whether it's going to work out in a couple of weeks.'

I nodded.

'The thing is, the project I've been asked to work with has been stuck in a rut for years. The whole company has. The minute you walk into the building you can tell that nobody's going to change anything without a grappling hook and a few tonnes of dynamite.'

'And you're the dynamite.' I pictured a Dickensian version of an office, with rows of balding clerks in dusty jackets clicking their abacuses and scratching their ink pens, and Dan sneaking around behind them hiding sticks of TNT under their chairs.

'I hope so. I get the feeling that without some new blood to drag them kicking and screaming into the twenty-first century, they're going to fade away.'

'So the rusty English brought in a sparkling new American to get them all fired up again.'

'Something like that,' he said, 'though I have one or two other particular qualifications for this job. Besides being American.'

I could see that he did. He had an easy confidence, a belief that he deserved to be liked. It would be far too weird to ask him how and where one could find such a belief, as if it were a nice hat I admired.

'Well, good luck with it,' I said, knowing it sounded lame. 'Being dynamite and everything.'

'Thanks.' It went quiet again, but it didn't seem so bad this time, maybe because we had some words behind us already.

'It's strange being a stranger someplace,' Dan said, after a minute. 'Living in Philly all my life, I know the city backwards. You always run into someone you know there. But then here, it's weird, I keep on seeing people and thinking I recognise them and then realising I don't know them at all because I was thinking of someone back home. It's a little isolating. I guess that's why I'm talking to strangers in cafés.'

'Oh, have you been talking to lots of strangers in cafés?'

'No. Just the one.'

His smile was so warm, so genuine, so aimed directly at me, that I almost forgot how to breathe.

'Listen,' he said, 'I know this is out of the blue and you don't know me from Adam, but maybe you could show me around London a bit, if you have some free time? Not the tourist stuff, the real things that real Londoners do?'

I stared at him. This had suddenly careened on to an entirely new level.

'I think it could be fun, don't you?' he said. 'You've been working all morning. Can you take some time off?'

'I'm not—' I stopped, because I had no idea how to end that sentence. *I'm not free? I'm not sure why you want to spend time with me? I'm not the type of person who suddenly makes friends with people like you?*

'Come on,' he said, smiling, 'take pity on a foreigner. I'm here in London all alone, hardly know a single soul. If you leave me by myself this afternoon I'm liable to do something stupid like buy a great big Union Jack and use it to tickle one of those guards who aren't allowed to laugh.'

'I think they can deport you for that,' I said, feeling relief because I knew why he was asking me now: he didn't know anybody else and he was bored. Being someone's last resort was a situation I could understand.

'See? You'd be saving me. Come on, what do you say?'

'Well,' I said slowly, 'I don't have any plans for this afternoon, and I have been wanting to see the crack.'

He'd been about to take a sip of his coffee but he burst into laughter and had to put down his cup. 'The what?'

I stood up. 'You'll understand when you see it.'

The Crack

U sually I went to Tate Modern with Stevo. We'd take the tube sometimes on a Monday after an editorial meeting, when there was a new exhibit, and especially each time a new installation was opened in the turbine hall. It was always just the two of us, because neither Digger nor Jim was particularly interested in art and they were actively not interested in modern art. We'd read magazines on the way and once we got there, we'd each wander off to see the bits that interested us most and meet up for more coffee later.

The journey felt different with Dan. For one thing, we spent the whole time in conversation, though thankfully he did most of the talking. He told me about the first time he'd used the Underground and mistakenly taken the District line all the way to Barking when he'd meant to take the Circle to the Barbican; he asked questions about the station names; he acted every inch the cheerful tourist.

'Why are you smiling?' he asked me as we swiped our cards at the Blackfriars turnstiles.

'Oh, those people looking at us in the carriage, because we were talking,' I said. 'You said hi to them.'

He thought back. 'So?'

'People don't look at each other on the Underground,' I told him. 'There's a science to it. You need to do everything you can to avoid eye contact, especially when it's busy.'

'Everyone seemed so bored.'

We climbed the steps to the street level and watery sunshine. 'That's the idea,' I said. 'You have to seem bored so nobody will look at you.'

'Why? What horrible thing would happen if people looked at each other?'

'They might end up talking to each other.'

He clapped his hand to his forehead in mock despair. 'A fate worse than death.'

'You just don't do it.'

'But why?'

We went down another set of steps, to the walk along the Thames, and I thought about it. I knew why I didn't talk to strangers; I was unlikely to have anything in common with most people and I'd just as soon avoid the weird looks. But I wasn't sure why normal people didn't.

'I think – in London, anyway – it's the fear of getting stuck talking to some nut case. It's easier to keep quiet.'

'But who knows, the person sitting next to you might end up being a fascinating genius. Or a long-lost relative. Or the love of your life.' He grinned, the breeze tousling his hair. 'Or someone who's taking you to see a crack.'

'*The* crack,' I corrected him.

'Sorry.' He gazed at the Thames and I tried to see it through his eyes, as if it were new and strange instead of a river I'd seen thousands and thousands of times. It was brownish grey and sluggish like a huge snake. In fact, a few months before, in *Girl from Mars* number 682, *The Thames Terror*, I'd drawn a huge snake coiling around and crushing the slim girth of the Millennium Bridge which lay ahead of us now.

We climbed a third set of steps up to the bridge itself, and Dan looked around at everything: St Paul's dome framed by modern buildings and gazing down across the river like an elegant uncle; the silver thread of the bridge stretching towards the looming brown edifice of the former power station on the south bank; the views of London either side of us glittering and pointing towards the sky, grey and black and brown and white.

I usually saw London through a distorted film, part my own imagination, part familiarity. Following Dan's gaze, I saw the fat finger of the Gherkin, the gorgeous cliché of Tower Bridge, the squat thatched ring of the Globe and the swoop of the London Eye. I heard the faintly metallic sound of our footsteps, wisps of conversation from strangers, and I smelled traffic and water and cigarette smoke.

It was beautiful.

We didn't speak until we were on the South Bank. 'For a terrifying moment I thought you were going to show me a crack in the bridge,' Dan said.

'No, it's in here.' I gestured at Tate Modern. 'It's best to go in the side entrance.' Suddenly I felt that rush of excitement you get before you're going to see something you've been wanting to see for ages, and I had to stick my hand in my pocket because I had an impulse to grab Dan's hand and pull him along with me.

We walked together to the side entrance and went through the glass doors into the great hall. Dan looked up into the giant space where the turbines had stood when this had been a power station. Black beams and bricks and empty space formed an industrial cathedral that drew the eye up and up towards a grim and looming heaven.

But I looked down at the cement floor.

There it was: a hairline, between my feet. I scuffed my trainer next to it to get Dan's attention and he looked down too.

The crack zigzagged across the vast grey slab floor. It grew from a tiny line and gaped open, splitting into a jagged chasm. We stood and followed it with our eyes.

'It's art?'

I nodded. '*Shibboleth* by Doris Salcedo. There's an installation in the turbine hall every year. This one has been here since October.'

We walked along the crack. I noticed that the other visitors were doing the same thing. It was as if the fissure had a strange power to draw people to it and determine the path they took across this huge field of concrete. It removed our choices and forced us to follow the disruption.

Had this powerful thing really been here for months and I hadn't seen it? Usually Stevo and I went to a new installation within the first few days. In fact, he usually insisted. But this time . . .

I stopped, my gaze glued to the crack. Had Stevo been here with Brian instead, and was that why he hadn't taken me? Had the break between us been there for so long?

What other cracks were there in my life, great gaping canyons maybe, that I hadn't noticed?

'*Shibboleth*,' said Dan. 'Interesting title.'

Suddenly I was filled with dread that he was going to start talking about the artwork. Trying to explain it, to pin it down with words and make it an intellectual thing. It was something my parents would do and something I hated because somehow it made everything so much smaller and so much less mine.

I started walking again, hoping Dan would get the message. He kept pace with me.

'You know what it reminds me of?'

I winced. He was going to spoil it. 'What?'

'When Wile E. Coyote follows the Road Runner to the edge of a cliff and the rock cracks underneath him. It looks like this just before it falls.'

I looked at him. He was trying to appear serious but a crease in one cheek gave him away.

'I'm relieved you're not an art snob,' I said.

'Believe me, I wouldn't dare.' We had reached the end of the crack, and both of us turned to visually trace the path up to its beginning.

'The crack is making you sad, though,' he said.

This time the crease in his cheek had gone, and he looked truly serious. Our eyes met and my hands ached.

'Philomena,' he said, 'I wasn't expecting to ask you this, but I wonder if you'd like to have dinner with me? Not tonight, but sometime soon? Maybe tomorrow?'

We were standing on either side of the crack, which by this point was several inches wide.

'Sick of eating alone, huh?' I asked, but my voice wavered a bit and I could tell I hadn't done a good job at sounding cool.

'No, it's because I'd really like to have dinner with you.'

This was more than my hands aching. This was a rush of excitement and desire so strong that I felt a little dizzy, a little sick to my stomach. I asked, 'You mean like a date?'

'I mean exactly like a date.'

My body, my treacherous body, made like it was going to jump joyously over the crack and join Dan on the other side. His side, where you said hello to everyone and asked people out for dates and then went on them. A side that was an entirely new world and was separated from my world by only a few inches of empty space.

I swallowed.

And then again there was the other side. My side.

'I'm sorry, Dan, I really need to use the loo. Too much coffee. I'll be right back.'

'Philo—' he began, but I pretended not to hear him. I turned away and hurried through the glass doors on the side of the turbine hall, to the black-clad lavatories.

I shut myself into a cubicle and dialled Jim's number on my phone. He answered after two rings.

'Morning,' he said cheerfully. 'Where are you? Making a tour of newsagents?'

'No, I'm—'

'Me and Digger went down to the newsagent as soon as we got up and I'm glad we did because you are officially a genius. I love the killer sea urchins! We made sure all the copies were at the front of the stand.'

It was the first Thursday of the month; the day that *Girl from Mars* hit the shelves, this particular issue being my *The Neptune Nightmare*. I must have felt really rough this morning to have forgotten. And then, of course, I'd been distracted, though I hadn't realised I'd been *that* distracted.

'Thanks for remembering,' I said. 'And putting them in front.'

'Hey, you deserve it. I've read it twice already. How are you feeling? We found the best hangover cure ever.

You get some mouthwash and some lemonade, and you put it in a glass with –'

He sounded so happy, so familiar, so overwhelmingly Jim, it was as if I were sitting on my flowery chair back at home, safe and secure, never having heard of Dan or a date.

'– and then you pour the whole thing down the sink. Makes you feel instantly better. Where are you, anyway?'

'Oh, I'm at work,' I said automatically, and then I felt a wrench of sickening memory of lying next to Pierre and lying to Jim. 'I mean, I went to work, and now I'm at Tate Modern.' *With a man*, I tried to say, and couldn't, and felt worse.

'Ugh, modern art,' Jim shuddered.

'Listen,' I said lightly, 'do you remember that thing we did last night out in the garden, right before we all passed out? When we were really drunk?'

Jim laughed, and I bit my lip. It had all been a joke. None of us had meant it. Which meant I could go on the date with Dan, but I'd be all open and honest about it with Jim and Digger, not like Stevo had been. Not like I'd been before with Pierre. The date wouldn't change anything.

Or would it?

'Too right,' Jim said. 'That was the best idea we've had in ages.'

'You mean . . . did we really mean it? Not to get in a relationship and stuff?'

'bItu Hpa' bIHeghjaja!' he yelled and even through the phone it echoed off the toilet walls.

'Death before shame, Fil. Damn right we meant it. I'm never going through that nightclub shit again.'

'Oh. Yeah. Right, of course.'

I leaned my head against the black wall. If the vow

was real, I didn't have to worry. A date was out of the question.

'Listen, I'm making us Jim's Special Curry tonight to celebrate your total *Girl from Mars* triumph. Okay? Digger and I have been slicing onions for the past half an hour for the bhajis, he's got tears in his beard.'

'Fantastic,' I said. 'Looking forward to it already. I've just got to do – one thing.'

'All right, see you soon.'

I stood in the toilet cubicle, my phone off, with Jim's voice still in my ears. *Ceci n'est pas un urinoir*, someone had scratched on to the toilet door. A little modern art joke. I didn't laugh.

What was I going to say? I didn't turn down dates very often. In fact, never, because I'd never been asked out on a proper one before. Did I lie and say I was already seeing someone? Or lie and tell Dan I wasn't interested in him?

I certainly couldn't tell the truth: *I'm sorry, I can't date you because I made a vow last night not to date anyone, partly in Klingon, and then nearly set my garden on fire.* It was a bit too much like carrying around a large sign saying WARNING! SOCIALLY INCOMPETENT FREAK!

Like he didn't think that already, from my reaction when he asked me out. Even I knew that running to the toilet wasn't perfect etiquette.

I sidled out of the Ladies' room, hoping Dan hadn't come over to wait on the benches outside. I needed the little bit of panic time before I spoke to him, to rehearse, so I wouldn't blurt out the real truth, the thing that was even truer than the vow: that I couldn't date him because I was too scared to and I was pretty sure I would fail.

He wasn't there, but I spotted him right away through

the glass walls that separated the mundane corridor of shop and coat check and toilets and escalators from the grand turbine hall. He was still standing on his side of the crack. At the sight of him my traitorous hands ached because they wanted to touch him.

He was looking up at the ceiling. He had his hands in his pockets and an expression of good-natured wonder on his face. A stranger in the city enjoying its new and unusual pleasures. Including me.

I nearly smacked myself on the forehead with my aching hands. Here I was, angsting all over the place because a man had asked me out, thinking it was something special and unusual and tempting, and really it was for one simple reason: Dan was a tourist. He didn't know anybody else his own age. He'd asked me to dinner for exactly the same reason as he'd asked me to show him London. He was bored and it was something to do.

If I marched over there and told him I couldn't go out with him, he would shrug and smile and say, 'Sure, all right,' and he wouldn't give it a single further thought.

I, on the other hand, would think about it a lot. I would think about sitting across a restaurant table with him, maybe in candlelight. I would think about spending an evening basking in his attention. I would think about talking easily and memorising his features to draw later and maybe even about reaching across the table to push that Superman curl back from his forehead.

I would think about that so much that I would be tempted to be disloyal to my friends, and to throw myself into a situation that would only end in pain for me.

He was still looking up at the ceiling. I ducked behind the escalators and, as quickly as I could, hurried through the shop and out of the museum.

I Hate Lunch

If this were a story or a television show or a film, now
would be about the time when I would be wondering
why the hell the heroine turned down a hot date with a
hot guy, because of a stupid vow taken while drunk.
Stories are about going on hot dates, or at least refusing
to go on them in an interesting manner, preferably whilst
forcibly subduing an eighty-tentacled beast from outer
space. Stories aren't about running away while someone's
attention is on the ceiling.

But there are other types of stories besides romances
and adventures and even comic books, or at least there
should be. Stories about good friendships are quieter and
usually less dramatic; they rely on humdrum events and
repetition for their power. But they were the most
important stories in my real life.

It's not too much to say that my life pretty much
began the day I met Jim. And even now, thirteen years
later, though we didn't have a gushy or demonstrative
friendship and, in fact, spent a lot of our time having
sibling-like arguments, there were things Jim did for

me that nobody else in the world had ever done.

For example, the moment when I was standing in the toilet at Tate Modern and he told me he'd been down to the newsagent to make sure my comic was in a prominent place. Or when I got home later that day, my heart still hammering even though I'd had a seat for the whole tube journey, and the house smelled gloriously of curry and he'd scanned, enlarged, and printed out my drawings of the killer sea urchins in *The Neptune Nightmare*. He'd Blu-Tacked them all over the house in unexpected places – sleeping on the couch cushion, climbing up my toothbrush, peeping out of the tea canister, lurking underneath the toilet seat.

No one had ever been proud of me until Jim came along. Since I'd been drawing *Girl from Mars* I sometimes got fan mail, and I heard via online fan forums and at conventions that my art was pretty popular. But other people saw me through my work, whereas Jim saw my work through me. He knew me better than anyone, all my weaknesses and most of my failures, and he still made a big deal out of everything that I achieved.

I'd met him by accident. I was thirteen years old and I was having an awful morning, even compared with the general awfulness that was part and parcel of being thirteen years old. For one thing, two days before I'd been given back a maths exam with a big red 'F' written at the top. I was supposed to get one of my parents to sign it, but instead it had stayed crushed at the bottom of my school bag for forty-eight hours, while its presence burned a hole in my brain. Mrs Wilson was going to ask for it again today, and I could only say so many times that my parents were off lecturing at a conference.

I was, I will admit it, a wimp. My parents weren't going to beat me or anything for failing an exam. They wouldn't even yell, as they believed in collaborative parenting strategies. Instead, when I showed the mark to my mother, she would examine the paper minutely, as if analysing it for hidden metaphors, and then she would look at me and sigh. Then she would call my father, and he would do the same thing, including the sigh. Then one or other of them, whoever's turn it was, would say sadly, 'We're very disappointed with this performance, Philomena. You're such a bright girl. Why don't you apply some of your considerable intellect to your school work?' And I would try to explain about not being interested in maths, and finding it difficult, and that I thought they were seriously misguided in their estimation of my intellect because, as far as I could see, I was a hell of a lot less bright than just about everybody else in my class.

And they would shake their heads and look disappointed. My father, the more methodical of the two, would point out the doodles in the margin of the paper and suggest that if I'd spent more time on algebra than on illuminating the manuscript, I would perhaps understand maths better. My mother, the more ambitious, would mention that one didn't get very far in life these days without a proper education. And there, somewhere in the room, standing like a phantom between them and me, was the image of the daughter they really wanted: pretty, focused, sharp, witty, someone who applied herself in school and who looked set for a brilliant career in literature or, failing that, astrophysics.

Sometimes, when my eyes went unfocused during these lectures, which I suspected even bored my parents,

I could swear I saw that perfect daughter actually standing there. She was wearing a dress.

My dread of this conversation was, at the moment, stronger than the dread of any punishment Mrs Wilson could levy for failing to bring the test back signed. But the thought of facing Mrs Wilson was enough to get my guts churning as I got off the bus for school.

I spotted Alicia and Belinda and Claudia right away and, shouldering my backpack which felt as if my maths exam had transformed into a ton of bricks, I headed towards them. I could listen to their chatter about magazines or boys or whatever for ten minutes until the morning bell went and not have to think.

'You should invite Diana,' Claudia was saying, 'she's got an older sister who can get us—'

'Hey,' I said to them, my usual morning greeting, and though I knew better than to expect effusions of joy at my presence I was surprised when suddenly they all shut up.

'What?' I said.

'Nothing,' said Belinda, who was my neighbour and the reason I hung out with the three of them in the first place. I saw her roll her eyes at Claudia.

'What?' I said again, my mind performing calculations much more quickly than I'd ever done algebra. Invitations and older sisters who could get something. 'Are you talking about a party?'

'No,' said Belinda quickly. 'We were talking about *EastEnders*.'

'Oh,' I said, trying to sound wise in the ways of soap operas. I wasn't. My family's television was practically from the nineteenth century and watching it was more of a chore than a pleasure. This was handy for my parents since they thought of television as a 'useful resource for understanding contemporary culture' rather than as a form of entertainment.

Alicia and Claudia immediately launched into a discussion about people I'd never heard of. I nodded at what I hoped were appropriate places and tried to figure out how these girls felt so comfortable being girly. All three of them had hitched up their uniform skirts so the hems flirted with their thighs. Alicia and Claudia, who had naturally curly hair, had straightened theirs; Belinda, who had naturally straight hair, had curled hers. All three of them were curvy and coltish, having blossomed at some point when I hadn't been paying attention into that magical sexual creature, the teenage girl.

Whereas my skirt stuck resolutely to my knees, even when I tried to roll the waistband; my hair refused to do anything but be stuffed into various permutations of bunches; and I was commonly mistaken in the school hallways for an eleven-year-old first year.

As we entered the school building together, Alicia said, 'Oh, I *love* talking about *EastEnders*, don't *you*?' I saw a look and a smirk flash between her and Belinda and Claudia, and I knew I'd been had. They'd been talking about Diana George all along. Suddenly I remembered a rumour that Diana's sister was willing, for a small fee, to buy alcohol for teenage parties.

There really was a party going on, and I evidently wasn't invited.

I walked to our form room with them anyway, because being alone in school was utterly unthinkable.

A.B.C., as I thought of them, chattered all through registration. They were a self-contained unit, natural as the alphabet progression. They passed notes back and forth during the morning lessons, and I pretended not to notice. I drew a caricature of Mrs Wilson with steam coming out of her ears and nose and from beneath her omnipresent flowered skirt. I drew a picture of a hundred smiling girls all having a good time, and myself standing alone.

'My mother had a migraine last night,' I found myself telling Mrs Wilson when I was held behind at the end of period four. 'She'll sign the paper tomorrow.'

I was, and always have been, a rubbish liar. 'Do you really think that avoiding the issue is going to make it any easier, dear?' Mrs Wilson asked.

'I'm not avoiding the issue, miss, my mother had a migraine.'

Mrs Wilson shook her head. 'See you have it for me tomorrow. Or I'll have to give you school detention.'

By the time I was finished with my excuses A.B.C. had gone to lunch, with nary a backwards glance. I stuffed my books into my bag, muttering a curse as my pencil case toppled out of the side pocket and sent writing and drawing implements all over the floor. Mrs Wilson clucked her tongue at me. I gathered everything up and shoved it all into my bag every which way.

I continued cursing under my breath all the way down the corridor to the cafeteria. I hated maths, I hated being condescended to and, most of all, I hated myself because I was hurrying to sit with three girls I had nothing in common with and whom I didn't even like, because I was too scared to be on my own.

At the entrance of the cafeteria I paused to look for A.B.C. Lunchtime was an eternal scramble. The school, trying for a more pleasant and grown-up atmosphere, had done away with the long refectory-style tables and instead had arranged individual tables around the room, four or six seats to each table, as if it were some sort of a restaurant. Each of the tables filled up quickly with cliques. In practical terms, this meant that if you were someone like me, you had to plan your lunchtime carefully if you wanted to end up sitting next to someone you could call your friend, instead of perching on the edge of someone else's group or sharing a table with a bunch of people you didn't know at all.

I was craning my neck, hoping that A.B.C. had saved me a seat and doubting that they had, when I overheard the conversation.

'Shove off, Lousder, we're sitting here.'

The voice belonged to an older boy, one who I'd noticed on the periphery of my vision before just because he was tall and particularly unpleasant looking. He was standing with two of his other unpleasant-looking friends and talking to a pale, skinny boy, who sat alone at an empty table for four with a packed lunch.

'It looks like there's enough room for all of us,' the skinny boy said.

'No, there isn't, because we don't want to sit with you, Lousder. Loser.'

The skinny boy didn't get up. He tilted his head. 'I'm sorry,' he said, 'I didn't understand you.'

'Lousder. Loser. Same thing.'

He shook his head. 'No, I didn't get that either. I'm afraid I don't speak "Idiot".'

The bigger boy bent down so that his face was level with the smaller one. He spoke slowly. 'Your name is Lousder because you're a loser. So move it.'

The skinny kid paused for a long moment, seeming to think, and I was amazed at his courage. Finally he shook his head again, almost sadly. 'It's no good, I just don't seem to be understanding you. Hold on, though, I think I have an Idiot–English dictionary in my bag.' He bent and unzipped his rucksack. I saw anger gathering on the bigger boy's face.

I quickly pulled out the chair next to the skinny boy and sat down.

'Hey,' I said, 'thanks for saving me a seat, sorry I'm late.'

The skinny boy looked at me in some surprise. Before I could think about the monumental stupidity of what I was doing, I smiled up at the bigger boys. 'Oh sorry, were you all going to sit here? I don't think there's room now.'

I saw them calculating silently the difference in effort in bullying two people out of seats instead of one. I held my breath.

It seemed for ever before their leader shrugged and they moved off. I let out my breath and turned to the skinny guy.

'Thanks,' he said.

'No problem. I loved your line about the Idiot–English dictionary.'

'I think it was lost on them. I'm James Lousder.' He pronounced his last name carefully, emphasising the 'ow' sound of the first vowel and the 'd'.

'Philomena Brown.'

James nodded. 'You're that girl who's good at art.'

I was surprised at this; I'd never noticed James before and expected him to be equally ignorant of me. 'Uh, yeah, I guess so.'

He took a bite out of his white bread sandwich. I noticed that one of the shoulders of his school jumper was covered with ginger fluff as if, out of school hours, he were accustomed to carrying a tom-cat on his shoulder, like a pirate's parrot. He smelled a bit of cat, too.

'Where are your friends?' he asked.

'I don't know.' I looked around again and this time I saw them: they'd pulled up an extra chair to a table for four, and were joined by Diana George, she of the older sister, and by Emma Cleary. Alicia happened to look up at the same time I spotted them; as soon as her gaze met mine she looked away, and then bent her head to talk quietly to the other girls. Emma and Claudia glanced over their shoulders in my direction, then away. I saw them laughing.

'I sort of felt like sitting somewhere different anyway,' I said.

James nodded. He ate his sandwich. I didn't have a packed lunch; I'd planned to buy something, but in order to do that, I would have had to walk by A.B.C. with the added delights of D and E. And I wasn't feeling very hungry anyway. Instead, I got my jumbled pencils and pens out of my bag where I'd shoved them and began putting them into order, back into my pencil case.

We didn't say much, but I was sort of enjoying the silence. Usually at lunchtime I had to listen to a lot of talk, and you had to really listen to it, because at any point someone could ask you a question and you had to keep on your feet so you could make up some sort of answer, even if you hadn't had a clue what A.B.C. were talking about in the first place. Because if you didn't answer correctly – say, for example, you didn't know the difference between mascara and concealer – they would look at you as if you were some sort of freak.

I had become fairly good at saying 'Yeah!' enthusiastically to cover up my ignorance or my lack of interest.

But it wasn't exactly relaxing. I preferred sorting pencils, next to someone who didn't feel the need to gossip.

I heard a snort beside me. I glanced up; James had picked up one of my coloured pencils and was examining it. 'Why do they call this one "green-blue"?' he asked.

'Because it's a cross between green and blue,' I said.

'Why don't they call it "blue-green"?'

'It's more green than blue. If it were more blue than green, they'd call it "blue-green".'

He turned it over in his fingers. 'It looks more blue than green to me.'

'No, it doesn't. It's way more green.'

'No, if it were more green, it would be darker. But it's not. So it's bluer.'

'Darkness has nothing to do with it,' I said. His blatant disregard for common colour knowledge was exasperating, but at the same time I was conscious of a sense of relief. This was the first time today when I'd been able to behave in the way that felt natural.

'Anybody can see that pencil is more green than blue,' I said. 'Look, hold it against your blue jumper.' He did. 'See? It's green.'

James shook his head in disagreement.

'What the hell are you, colour blind or something?' I asked.

He took the pencil away from his jumper and squinted at it. 'I am, as a matter of fact. Do you think that's relevant?'

I laughed, loudly enough so that people on other tables looked over at us.

'I hate lunch,' James said, when I had finished.

'So do I.'

For a moment, we looked at each other, and we had

one of those rare moments of empathy, where we, two strangers, understood each other completely.

'Anyway, I've got to go; my mum's picking me up for a doctor's appointment,' he said. He tossed the crust of his sandwich into his paper bag and stood up. 'I'll see you later, Philomena.'

'Yeah. See you later, James.'

'Jim,' he said, and he smiled at me. He picked up his rucksack, and turned and walked out of the cafeteria. I noticed that although his bag was so big, he walked with his shoulders back and his spine perfectly straight.

'It's not that I haven't tried to understand it because I have, it's just so boring I can't keep my mind on it, that's all. But I think this means I should move down a set in maths. I think that would be a good idea, don't you?'

My mother's eyes scanned my exam paper. She seemed to be taking her time about it, even more than usual.

'I mean, if I moved down, then they'd probably go more slowly and I could catch up. Plus it's a smaller class size, which has got to be a good thing, hasn't it?'

My mother pushed her glasses up her nose and transferred her attention from the paper to me. She didn't have quite the weight of disappointment that I'd expected. Instead, she looked concerned. I waited for her to open the door to her study and call for my father.

But she didn't. 'Aren't all your friends with you in the top set?' she asked me. 'Wouldn't you miss them?'

This was a new one. I'd asked to move down sets before, and the normal declaration was that I needed to be challenged.

'I thought this was about maths,' I said.

My mother sat down among the notes for her latest book, another feminist reinterpretation of Victorian literature. She was a pretty woman, in a buttoned-down, frizzy-haired way. She mostly wore brown clothes in a range of different textures and shades. Today she had on a tan woollen skirt, a chocolate-brown silk blouse and a coffee-coloured corduroy jacket. She claimed always wearing brown meant she never had to think about matching anything; when I was a little girl I'd loved climbing in her lap and touching all the different soft materials.

That had been some time ago.

'Your father and I have been researching pedagogical theories for learning in adolescents, and most concur that peers are far more influential than teachers for children your age. It seems to me that you should be surrounded by children as bright as you are. That way you would learn more.'

I thought about mentioning that my peers were more interested in boys and parties and gossip magazines than algebra, and that the most useful thing I'd learned in school today was that bullies preferred to pick on lone targets.

'Could you just sign the paper, Mum, please?'

She held it in her hand, unsigned, and made no movement for a pen. 'You haven't brought any friends here for some time.'

So that they could get crushed by stacks of books and paper, laugh at our television, and be forced to sample my father's bizarre cooking? 'I've been busy.'

'What about that girl who lived down the street? The Waterhouse girl?'

'Belinda's been busy, too.' Planning a party she wasn't inviting me to.

'Oh? You two seemed to get on well. She seemed a lovely girl.'

Belinda's parents didn't have a single book in their living room. Their shelves held artfully arranged bric-a-brac. I had never mentioned this fact to my parents, which probably accounted for my mother's positive opinion of Belinda.

'Like I said, we've both been busy.'

My mother sighed. It wasn't the sigh I'd been expecting. It sounded sad.

'You spend so much time alone, Philomena,' she said. 'Aren't you lonely?'

She looked at me searchingly, the way she normally looked at my schoolwork, and I felt the usual urge to explain, to excuse, to justify. This time about myself.

A failing mark in maths was much easier to explain.

The doorbell went. 'I'll get it,' I said quickly, and practically bolted out of the room.

When I opened the door, James was standing on the doorstep. He'd traded his cat-hair-covered school jumper for an equally hairy jacket, and he was holding his enormous school satchel, which should have been big enough to bend him to one side.

'Hi,' he said, and I saw that he was blushing like mad. 'Sorry for disturbing you, I sort of thought—'

'Who is it, Philomena?' My mother appeared at the doorway of her study.

'It's James. I mean, Jim. Come in, Jim.' I grabbed Jim's jacket sleeve and pulled him into the house. He came along willingly, looking surprised and more than a little pleased.

'Jim's my friend,' I told my mother triumphantly. 'We're going upstairs to my room.'

I was still hanging on to his jacket sleeve; I hauled him past my mother. I wasn't sure whose eyes were wider.

We went upstairs and down the corridor to my bedroom, where I closed the door firmly after us. Jim looked around at my walls, covered with drawings and paintings and a bookshelf full of children's classics.

'Wow,' he said.

I sat on my bed, among a jumble of mildly dirty clothes. 'Thanks,' I said, 'you just saved me.'

'What from?'

'Um. I failed a maths test and had to get my mum to sign it.'

'Oh.' He looked around again. He took quite a while looking at each of my drawings. I squirmed, seeing them from an outsider's point of view, all the misrenderings and mistakes suddenly apparent. And speaking of mistakes, why had I hauled this boy, whom I didn't know, up here to my room?

At last he'd worked his way around the room. 'You're not bad, you know,' he said, coming to stand by my single bed.

'Thanks.'

He stood there in silence for a few minutes. He still smelled of cat, and from the state of his trousers I thought that a feline had been using them as well as his jacket for a bed, but I didn't mind. It was a comfortable smell.

'Do you like *Star Trek*?' he said eventually.

'Our television doesn't work for toffee,' I admitted. 'I've given up watching it because it gives me a headache.'

He nodded, seeming to accept this as a reasonable problem to have.

'Why—' I began, and then stopped because the

question seemed rude. But I wanted to know, so I went on. 'Why did you come over to my house?'

'Oh,' he said, and he blushed again. 'I just thought you might like to look at these, if you had some time to waste.'

He put his big bag on the bed beside me, unzipped the top, and held it open. It appeared to be full of magazines.

'Comics,' he said, sounding apologetic. 'I've got *2000AD*, and *Girl from Mars*, and quite a few *X-Men*.'

I reached in and pulled out a comic book at random. On the cover, a woman with green skin, wearing a white minidress, was clinging on to the outside of a rocket that was hurtling through space.

'You're allowed to read these?' I asked. I'd seen them in shops and in the dentist's waiting room, but I'd never owned one.

'My mum buys me all the new ones.'

I looked over the comic again. The glossy paper was so flimsy, and yet the picture on the cover was dynamic, full of action and power and certainty.

This Martian girl didn't look as if she had to hate lunch.

I sat back on the bed, my back leaning against the wall, and pushed the laundry to the floor so that Jim had a space to sit down. 'Do you have a bunch of these ones about the girl?'

'Yeah, I've got a ton.' He climbed on to the bed and rummaged through his bag, selecting issues and handing them to me so I could arrange them by month. When we had an entire year's worth collected, he took a copy of *2000AD* for himself and settled with his back against the wall, too.

Side by side, we began to read.

The TIME Temptation

Jim and I had bought our seventies semi-detached house in South London together a year after we'd finished university. It seemed like a sensible thing to do: separately, we couldn't have afforded a house the size we wanted, but when we pooled our resources, we could.

The loft had been converted into a large room with skylights installed in the sloping walls. This became my studio. I put in my drawing board, a radio, a little refrigerator and a kettle, my Mac and scanner, and a ratty old couch I had left over from my student days. I plastered the walls with the work of artists I admired and I put an umbrella plant up there, which promptly died.

Jim took two of the three bedrooms for himself, one for sleeping and one for working. I took the other. I'd tried to convince him that he should have the third bedroom as well, if only to house his science fiction collection, because it seemed fair that if I had a whole floor to myself he should have a whole floor too, but he insisted I had to have a separate bedroom from my studio. 'At least if you're sleeping on the same floor as me I'll have a chance of seeing you every now and then,' he'd said.

When I had an issue of *Girl from Mars* to do, I would go up to my attic room with a packet of tea and a jar of Horlicks, six pints of milk, two bottles of red wine, six bars of Green & Black's organic dark chocolate, a loaf of bread and some Marmite, and I would emerge only when either I'd run out of some element of my supplies or I'd finished a major bit of work – for example, when I'd done with the layout and rough sketches and needed a brief dose of reality before I firmed up the pencils and started on the inks. I slept in naps on the ratty couch.

Even when I came downstairs, I couldn't claim to be actually there. I went through the motions of talking, or watching TV or going to the pub for the quiz or whatever the others happened to be doing, but my mind was still upstairs, on my drawing board, thinking through that line or this scene or whether a splash panel worked, wondering how the narrative would fit the images and whether I needed to make things bigger or smaller or more spaced out, whether I'd lost the vitality of the line when I'd inked it, how I could balance out light and shadow and colour. I interacted with the outside world through a screen of *Girl from Mars*, not really seeing anything except for the pages in the eye of my imagination and memory, and usually Jim and Digger had to remind me much later of what I'd said and done. Stevo didn't bother; he knew what it was like and knew that nothing could ever be as important to me at these times as trying to live up to my vision.

When I was finished with a job, it took some time for me to readjust to daily life. I felt equal measures of elation and depression when I sent off my picture files to UPC. Though this was my normal reaction, I was perpetually surprised at how strong the emotions were.

Digger would bring me a string bag of oranges and make me eat them. 'I'm not letting you get scurvy,' he'd say. Then he'd drag out my wellies or my trainers, depending on the weather, and force me to walk around in the fresh air. For a big guy, he could move fast when he wanted to.

I would begin the walk absolutely certain that I had failed. I tackled every comic with enormous ideas, with tremendous ambition. This time, on this one, I was going to capture the universe. And yet with every bit I drew, the ideas and ambition got smaller, as if the lines were hemming in my vision somehow, making it finite and small and flawed.

The fresh air and the movement blew things back into proportion. For the first part, I'd be silent. Digger would stride beside me, as always waiting for the right time to speak.

After an hour, I would be talking about what I'd done wrong. After an hour and a half, I'd be talking about what I'd done right. By the time the afternoon and the walk was over, I might even be talking about something unrelated to *Girl from Mars*.

Because I worked so intensely, I tended to get things done far before their deadline, so I had periods when I didn't have to do any work at all. This was when I could enjoy Jim's DVD marathons, or properly join in Digger's endless *Dungeons and Dragons* campaign. I was in one of those periods now, and had been for a couple of weeks while I waited for the next script for *Girl from Mars* to turn up.

I cleaned the house, including my studio which was the worst of any of it; I moved all my stuff that had migrated upstairs back down to my bedroom. I overhauled the garden and went for long walks and read some library books and re-dyed my hair. I attempted to play with The Baz, thinking he needed some fun in his life, but he merely stared contemptuously at me and my ball in the way that only a lizard can do.

I tried not to think of the dinner date I could have had with Dan.

Finally, it became impossible not to notice that the latest script was over two weeks late coming to me. Especially as I was checking my email inbox about every five minutes to see if it had come. I took my courage in both hands and rang Anthony, but his assistant said he was in a meeting all day. I hated to ring up any of the writers because it wasn't my job to hound them for editorial, and besides, *Girl from Mars* had several scriptwriters and freelancers and I wasn't sure which one was due to deliver my script.

I rang Stevo, though I didn't expect him to answer. First I tried his mobile, but just got the recorded voice asking me to leave a message. Then I had the bright idea of ringing him on his landline, where he wouldn't be able to see the number of the person calling. I sat at the kitchen table, doodling in the margins of Jim's sudoku with his ballpoint, thinking of what message I should leave on Stevo's answerphone, since he hadn't replied to any of the other ones.

He answered on the second ring. 'Yeah?'

So he had been avoiding me. A great wash of sadness swept through me.

'Hi, it's me,' I said, and then added, 'Fil.'

'Oh, hi, Fil.' He didn't sound ecstatic.

'I tried ringing you on your mobile just now.'

'Oh, uh, yeah, it's broken. How are you doing, anyway?'

'I'm fine, how about you?'

'Fine.'

His voice was familiar, but two weeks without seeing each other had made us into strangers. I sighed.

'We could have done with you at the quiz,' I said. 'We came in second last week and the week before we totally bombed.' In more ways than one.

'Look, I'm sorry about that. I've been busy, with work and with, you know, other things.'

'How's it going with Brian?' I tried to keep my voice cheerful, but I don't think I succeeded.

'Great, actually.'

I waited for him to elaborate. He didn't.

'Uh, right. Well, Stevo, the reason I'm calling is that I have a question about *Girl from Mars*.'

'What's that?'

'My next script hasn't turned up and I was wondering if you've heard anything about why?'

'Why would I know?'

'I don't know, I thought you might have heard office gossip or something.'

'No. Though it could have something to do with that new initiative Anthony was talking about in the meeting.'

'What new initiative?'

'The one you weren't listening to.'

'Oh, crap.' This meant now I couldn't ring Anthony to ask, in case he discovered I'd missed everything he'd been talking about. 'What was it about, do you know?'

'No, I wasn't listening either, remember? I never listen.'

'We should probably bring in a tape recorder or something.'

'Anthony would sack us on the spot. Industrial espionage.'

'Comicsgate.'

He barked a laugh, and for a moment it felt as if the past few weeks hadn't ever happened.

'Listen, Fil,' he said slowly, 'do you want to come over for dinner next week? To meet Brian?'

'I would love it!' I bounced up and down in my chair, suddenly feeling light. 'Oh my God, Stevo, you have no idea how much we've missed you. Jim and Digger are going to be so pleased. What day should we come?'

'Oh.' He paused. 'I, uh, sort of meant just you.'

I let this sink in.

'I think it's good to ease Brian in gently, you know? He might be overwhelmed by the whole gang experience.'

'We're not a gang, Stevo, we're your friends.'

'Yeah, but you have to admit that you're a little – well, full on.'

It was the *you're* that did it. As if Stevo was officially telling us that he was no longer part of *we*, that Jim and Digger and I were no longer required.

But that hurt too much, so I focused on the last couple of words. 'What do you mean, "full on"?'

'Oh, you know, like the whole private jokes thing, and all the arguing between you and Jim.'

'We don't argue.'

I could almost see his eyebrows raising behind his round glasses.

'We agree to disagree, that's what friends do. Anyway, you didn't think we were too full on when you came to London from Hong Kong and didn't have any friends and we welcomed you with open arms.'

'That's not exactly how I remember it,' he said.

I felt the crack getting wider.

'Of course that's how it happened. We both started at

UPC, I took you home, and you fitted right in with us. And now three years later you get a love life and suddenly disappear.'

'I haven't disappeared. I'm still here.'

'No, you're not. You haven't answered my calls in weeks. And you haven't done anything with us.'

'You know where I live, if it's that important to you.'

'I can't just turn up at your house, Stevo!'

'Why not?'

Because you might not want me there. 'We hang out here, we always have.'

He sighed. 'So do you want to come for dinner, or what?'

'You mean just me, myself? I can't leave Jim and Digger behind like that.'

'You don't need to share every single thing, Fil.'

'So what would I tell them I was doing?'

'Whatever you want to. Don't tell them if you think it will bother them.'

Stevo and I had done plenty of things together without Jim and Digger before, but nothing secretive. Nothing Jim and Digger would want to be included in, or that we couldn't tell them about.

'These are my friends we're talking about. Our friends. I can't go and do something behind their backs without telling them about it. Not something to do with you,' I added quickly.

'Fine. Suit yourself, then.'

'So what are you saying?' I asked, my heart in my throat. 'You don't want to be friends with us any more?'

'Oh, Fil, stop being so melodramatic. Things can't always be the same, over and over again. That's all.'

'Why not? We were happy, weren't we?'

'Doing the same thing, every day, week after week? The quiz, the gaming, the TV, the same people and nobody else?'

'Well, we weren't *unhappy*, anyway, not till you left.'

'Fil, I want more out of my life than to be not unhappy.'

Which meant that yes, he didn't want to be friends with us any more.

'Oh,' I said.

'Listen, I've got to go. I'll see you at the next editorial meeting, okay?'

'Okay.' I put the phone down and sat in the empty kitchen.

So Digger had been right.

Jim was working upstairs; I thought about going up and telling him about the conversation, but then I thought better of it. It would hurt him, especially the part about Stevo wanting to introduce Brian only to me. It was one thing to suspect that you'd lost a friend; it was another to know it.

I felt as if I'd been slapped in the face and punched in the stomach at the same time. I wandered into the living room, but that was worse because I saw the end of the couch where Stevo used to sit with Jim and Digger, underneath the caricature I'd drawn of the three of them.

Dammit! Why'd I bring him home with me in the first place? It had seemed like a good idea at the time. Jim had brought in Digger; it was fair that I brought in a friend of my own. When I'd met him, he'd known nobody and I'd thought I'd recognised something in him, something that needed other people in a way I understood.

But maybe I hadn't understood a single thing.

This was the trouble with change. You introduced too

many variables, left yourself too open to being hurt. It was just so much safer to stay the same.

I stomped upstairs to my studio, which was my space for me and *Girl from Mars*. I was about to slam the door but then thought Jim might emerge from his office and ask what was wrong, and I needed some time to think about how I was going to tell him.

I wandered around the room for a little while, picking up pencils and sketches, putting them back down in a different place and then getting annoyed with myself for messing up the newly clean space. Finally I put the kettle on and sat down at my computer to check my email for the sixtieth time that day.

There it was, on the top of my inbox: GFM SCRIPT 679. 'Thank God for that,' I muttered. I needed work, something to absorb me, stop me from feeling this awful empty tension. I clicked on the attachment, GFM679, opened it in Word, and sent it to the printer straight away. I preferred to read a hard copy, so I could make notes and little sketches in the margins. I always read as slowly as I could, going back over pages, savouring the words, taking time to close my eyes and imagine what I would draw.

The printer spat out a fat stack of A4, words for me to transform into pictures. The stuff of magic.

Girl from Mars and The TIME Temptation, Episode One: Temptation, said the cover page, but I flipped that aside quickly, eager to get into the story. I settled down into the couch, my sock-clad feet nestling underneath the knitted throw on the end, feeling that, for the next three-quarters of an hour, all my troubles were behind me. I began to read.

Thirty minutes later, I was on the tube to Victoria with the script in my hand.

Even Space Aliens Need a Little Tenderness

'What the hell is this?'

I'd had plenty of time to think up a reasoned, polite, professional opening line. For one thing, the Northern line had been delayed between Balham and Clapham South. For another, when I'd arrived at UPC, Anthony's assistant Martina had informed me, again, that Anthony was in meetings all day. I had always wondered what publishing professionals could possibly find to talk about in all-day meetings, and half assumed that 'in a meeting' was a euphemism for 'in the pub'. But when, despite Martina's dire warnings that he wouldn't like it, I went to the conference room and put my ear to the door, I did indeed hear Anthony's voice going on about something to do with marketing strategies.

So I pulled up a chair and sat down outside the meeting-room door until twenty past six. This also gave me lots of time to think up how I could phrase my thoughts and concerns in the way most calculated to preserve my much-loved job.

Unfortunately, when I saw Anthony emerge from the meeting room, his tie loosened, his jacket off, his shirt sleeves rolled up, my only impulse was to wave the script for *Girl from Mars* number 679 in his face and yell, 'What the hell is this?'

'Fuck me, Brown, what's wrong with you?' he asked mildly.

'This is what's wrong with me.' I waggled the script. 'How am I supposed to work with this?'

Instead of telling me to bugger off and go home and start drawing, Anthony squinted at me and nodded. 'Right, come into my office,' he said.

I followed him down the corridor and through the glass door of his office. Every other door in the UPC building was made of wood. I think Anthony had specially requested a glass one so that he could survey his domain from the comfort of his chair. His chair did look very comfortable: it was large and leather and cushy. Anthony sank down into it with a grunt of satisfaction and tented his fingers together in a way that was supposed to make him seem wise.

'What do you think is the matter with the bloody script?' he said.

I didn't sit down; I was too mad. 'Everything!'

'Calm down, Brown. Surely it can't have every single thing wrong with it?'

'Not far off. Have you read this thing?'

'Yes, as a matter of fact, I have.'

'And you okayed it?'

'Yes, as a matter of fact, I did.'

'Are you insane?'

Anthony narrowed his eyes, but his hands remained steepled. 'Why don't you tell me point by point, or is that too technical for you arty types?'

'Right. Point one. Listen to this.' I flipped to page three and read theatrically. '"PAGE TWO, PANEL ONE: Girl from Mars standing in half-lit alleyway. Camera angle slightly from above; she is standing in the left-hand third of the page and the light is coming from a streetlamp out of sight to the left. The edge of a rusty fire escape creates a line bisecting the panel diagonally from left to right. Blue and black shadows run along from her feet and up the red brick wall beside her. Three trash cans line the wall to her right and the shadow ripples over them. A copy of yesterday's *Times* blows loose along the ground."' I finished and raised my eyebrows, waiting for justified outrage.

'Well, that sounds fine,' Anthony said. 'I can picture it in my head exactly.'

'That's exactly the problem! It outlines every single thing in this panel, including its composition, point of view, and colour.'

'That should make your job nice and easy. Why are you bitching?'

'Chief, you know full well why I'm bitching. I'm the artist. *I'm* the one who decides composition and point of view and size and how much shadow there will be and where and how the fire escape cuts up the page. And every panel is described like this! The script is twice as long as it normally is.'

'So that's your problem with it. It takes away your goddamn artistic licence.'

'It takes away my art! With prescriptive scenes like this, I'm nothing more than – than a photocopier for the writer's imagination.'

'Right. Right. So your ego has been bruised. Is that all?'

'No, it's not!'

'What's point two, then?'

I took a deep breath. Anthony didn't seem to be taking my concerns as seriously as they should be taken. On the other hand, he hadn't kicked me out yet.

'Point two,' I said. 'The whole script is about Girl from Mars trying to get home.'

'And?'

'Girl from Mars can't get home. There's her addiction to water, and the gravity difference, and that whole negative energy thing that means that if she re-enters the Martian atmosphere she'll—'

'So?'

'So it's a pointless storyline.'

'More pointless than saving a bunch of council homes from being incinerated by a fleet of bulletproof robots when the bloody government's going to go and knock them down next week anyway?'

This was a reference to *Girl from Mars and the March of Progress*, a Thatcher-era storyline that was a particular favourite with fans.

'Every regular reader will know this is ground that's been covered before.'

'Brown, we've been running for over fifty years. There's very little ground we haven't covered before.'

'There's one ground we've never touched, which brings me to point three.' I took a deep breath and paused, the better to get across the enormity of what I was about to say.

'Chief, this script is a *romance*.'

Anthony regarded me over his fingers. His face did not register shock, surprise or disgust.

'You say that as if it's a bad thing, Brown.'

'It – Chief – I –' Clearly I wasn't getting through. I turned to page six and stabbed at a paragraph with my finger. 'Look here, when Girl goes to see the scientist Jackson Silver – there's a two-page description of what he looks like, including the dimple on his chin; he's basically Cary Grant, as far as I can tell. And then' – I turned pages furiously – 'on page nine they accidentally brush shoulders and end up looking deep into each other's eyes! And then' – more page flipping – 'look at this! It's banter! And here, while they're supposed to be sneaking through the network of underground caves, Girl from Mars actually grabs his hand and keeps holding it!'

'Take a couple of deep breaths, Brown, you're hyperventilating.'

'And this is the start of a six-part series, it says at the beginning! What will she do next? Kiss him? Go steady? Get *married*?'

'Even space aliens need a little tenderness.'

'You are not taking this seriously!' I flung down the script in frustration. 'Girl from Mars doesn't fall in love! Men can fall in love with her, that's fine, she's gorgeous and everything and who could help it, but she doesn't love them back. She can't. She wouldn't let herself. She's independent, she's strong, she's alone. She doesn't turn into some soppy love-sick bimbo the minute a Cary Grant lookalike comes strolling into the scene.'

Anthony sighed. He stood up and poured a coffee from the flask on the side of his desk and to my surprise, he offered it to me. Never having been offered a coffee before by Anthony, I took it even though, for once, I had no desire for it. Indignation was an even better stimulant than caffeine.

'Sit down,' he told me. I did. The chairs on the non-Anthony side of the desk were considerably less cushy. He sat down again and regarded me levelly without doing the steepled fingers thing.

'I take it you were too busy being outraged to actually read the title page of the script,' he said.

'*The TIME Temptation*,' I said. 'I read it. Random capitalisation and all.'

'Did you read the author's name?'

'It's obviously someone new. Paul or Mike or Kioshi would never—'

He selected the title page from the stack of script and passed it to me.

Girl from Mars and The TIME Temptation, Episode One: Temptation. By D. McKay.

I stared at the name. 'It's not – Dennis McKay died in 1992.'

'You're right, it's not Dennis McKay.'

'Who is it? His son or something?'

'His grandson. Who also happens to be a very successful screenwriter and director. Have you seen *Blue-Eyed Daughter*? Or *Mixing Desk*? Or *Ninety-Eight Point Six*?'

'No.' But I'd heard of them. Romantic comedy box-office smashes, every one.

Written, apparently, by the grandson of the man who'd created *Girl from Mars*.

'Why is he writing for us?' I asked.

'Brown, you were in the last editorial meeting. You know what *Girl from Mars*'s sales have been like this quarter.'

'Uh. Yeah. I guess.' Should I smile, because they were good? Or look worried, because they were bad? Anthony always looked grim, so it was impossible to take a cue from him.

'So you can see that a serious rethink is required.'

Oh. So sales had been bad, then.

'Chief, *Girl from Mars* has been around for over half a century. It's weathered out bad quarters. It can do it again.'

'It's not only this quarter, Brown, as you know.'

I didn't have the first idea, but that wasn't going to stop me from arguing. 'But—'

'We need new ideas. That's the bottom line. Now we have a successful Hollywood screenwriter, who just happens to be the grandson of the comic's creator. We can get this covered in the national media and pull in new young readers as well as the nostalgia market. We'll get people who don't normally read comics. And McKay's films have that winning formula at the box office. And then, of course, there's the ready-made Hollywood connection for future film deals.'

'The *Girl from Mars* film sucks.' It had been made quickly in the late seventies trying to cash in on the *Superman* craze, and had the most wooden acting and lamest alien creatures I'd ever seen.

'You haven't yet seen the twenty-first century version with full CGI and a massive budget.'

God, wouldn't Jim love that. I shook my head, bringing myself back to my grievances. 'That may be, Chief, but the fact remains that this script flies in the face of over fifty years of *Girl from Mars*.'

'And the fact also remains that *Girl from Mars* will be lucky to last another two years if we don't change our direction to appeal to the market.'

'We're going to lose our core readership with this script.'

'There aren't many to lose. Besides, Brown, that's where you come in.'

'No.' I stood up and put my full coffee cup on Anthony's desk, not caring if I left a ring. 'I don't come in anywhere. I'm not going to participate in the ruination of my favourite character of all time.'

'Fine,' said Anthony. 'We'll get another artist.'

'Fine,' I said, though that wasn't fine at all. In fact, it was the opposite of fine. Drawing *Girl from Mars* had been my dream ever since I was thirteen. The idea of turning down an assignment went against everything I loved.

Oh well, I thought, trying not to scream. This whole McKay debacle was bound to blow over quickly. They'd do his series, it wouldn't be popular, and then we'd be back to the right kind of stories again, and I could get back to drawing.

'Though if you care about that core readership,' continued Anthony, 'I'd think twice about resigning.'

Resigning? Who'd said anything about resigning?

'What?' I choked.

'The plan was to team you up with McKay from the beginning. You're our most popular artist with the fans. In fact, not to give you a big head, you're the most popular artist we've had for a decade or so. Research indicates that the core readership will stick with you, even if they're presented with a new storyline. Of course,' he said, sighing, 'we can try someone else, maybe Bushey or even pull Ng off *Combat*, but there's a risk we'll end up alienating the very readers who have stuck with us all this time.'

I sat down again.

'So what you're saying is that I need to work with this

guy, or *Girl from Mars* is going to change beyond all recognition.'

'No, what I'm saying is that you're part of the dynamic new team finally moving *Girl from Mars* into the fucking twenty-first century. Now are you going to stop whining?'

Since I couldn't answer 'No', I kept quiet.

'How about this,' Anthony said, with the air of doing me a great favour. 'Why don't I set up a meeting between you and McKay. You can air your concerns.'

'I'll air them all right,' I muttered.

'Not too bloody freely, because we don't want to scare the bugger off. UPC is one hundred per cent committed to this new direction, Brown.'

'And what per cent are you committed to my being an artist for you?'

'We have some opportunities in *Lacey* comics, if you like. Or the agony aunt picture poser.'

I didn't think he really meant it. I didn't dare to call his bluff.

'I'll meet him,' I said.

The Essentially Deconstructive Nature of Sequential Narrative Art

'Unbe-bloody-lievable,' Jim said, shaking his head. 'I hope you told them where to shove it.'

'Yeah,' I said. 'Well, actually, no. I can't. If I don't do this comic, I'll lose my job.'

'Damn.'

'Hiya.' The Swan's redheaded barmaid came to stand opposite the bar where Jim and I perched on stools. 'What are you guys up to?'

'Pre-parent drink,' I told her. Long ago Jim and I had discovered that parental visits went much better when we had a pint's worth of alcohol in our system, and made it a habit to go to our local before we hopped on the bus to Wimbledon.

'I get you.' She nodded. 'Are you two brother and sister?'

'No,' Jim said.

'It's not far off,' I said. 'But we have different parents.' Sometimes I wished we didn't. Jim's mother drove him crazy, but despite her faults and the surfeit of cats she was a kind and gentle woman who made no secret of the fact that Jim was her entire universe. That sort of parent was a lot of responsibility; Jim visited his mother lots more than I visited my parents. But there were compensations.

'So what are you going to do?' Jim asked me.

'I'll meet with this McKay bloke and try to make him see sense, I guess.'

'You should challenge him to a duel.'

'Yeah, I'm sure that would help.' I swirled the last bit of lager around the bottom of my glass. 'Anyway, what was that phone call that had you stamping around when I got home?'

'Oh, Compugist are hounding me to take that desk job again.'

'How much more money is it?'

He told me. I whistled.

'So you're going to take it?'

'No,' he said, draining his bitter and putting the glass down with a thump. 'What would it be like if I went into the office every day? You'd get lonely, wouldn't you?'

'Don't turn down the job because of me. Most of the time I'm in my own world drawing. I wouldn't miss you.'

'I'm not an office person,' he said, sounding irritated. 'There are too many people around all the time.'

'You might like some of them.'

He gave me a look as if I were insane.

'Have you ever worked in an office, Fil?'

'No.'

'People who work in offices are droids. And I'm not talking cute wisecracking droids like C3PO and R2-D2, I'm talking Daleks. Mindless, conscienceless, Earth-destroying monsters who follow orders blindly and have no respect for human life.'

The barmaid laughed, and Jim and I both looked at her in surprise. 'You're not far wrong there,' she said. 'Do you want another drink?'

'Better not,' I said regretfully, 'I'm already half an hour late.'

We stood up and the barmaid waved to us as we left. 'She seems nice,' I said.

'Who?'

'The barmaid. I wonder if she knows anything about pop music,' I mused as we reached the bus stop and lounged against it. 'Or war films. We could use some help now Stevo's gone.'

'What is it with you and this making new friends idea? I thought we agreed we didn't need all of that crap.'

Actually, we'd agreed not to get girlfriends and boyfriends, not any friends at all, but I didn't point out the distinction because Jim seemed touchy enough, suddenly. For all his many wonderful qualities, he had a way of getting annoyed by my saying what I thought were the most innocuous things. Especially lately. I put it down to some sort of male PMT.

Though in this case, he was probably right. No new friends equalled no new heartache.

The bus drew up and we got on it.

'Anyway,' he said, 'let's not talk about work any more, parental visits are gruelling enough. I spy with my little eye something beginning with D.'

I looked out the window. This, too, was a well-established routine. 'Dog.'

'No.'

'Daewoo.'

'No.'

'Damn ugly building.'

'Got it.'

'I Spy' didn't take much thought, so I had some brain space to think about why else Jim might be annoyed with me. All I'd said was that I didn't mind if he took the job, that I'd be fine in the house on my own. I thought I was being supportive.

Our mouths were being kept too busy by the game for me to ask him, though, and then we were in Wimbledon. Jim walked with me to my parents' front door to drop me off. 'The Mitre afterwards?' I said, standing on the doorstep, opening the front door. The Mitre was the pub next to the bus stop at this end.

'The Mitre,' he agreed. 'Text me when you're on your way.'

I waved at him and then took a deep breath before stepping into the house. I had to get through the next two hours and dinner, and I'd be in a pub with Jim relaxing.

My mother poked her head out of her study as soon as I came in, her reading glasses halfway down her nose, her brown cardigan unbuttoned. 'You're late,' she said, 'your father's got dinner on the table already. Who was that outside?'

'Jim.' I kissed her on the cheek and we went together to the dining room.

'He didn't come in to say hello?'

'No, his mum probably has dinner on the table too.' I didn't mention the barrage of questions that my parents usually hurled upon every visitor I was so foolish to bring into their house. Not that there had been many visitors. The few times I'd brought Digger around he'd sat at the dining-room table, taller than everyone else, his face bright red as he tried to deal with the embarrassment of talking so much with people he didn't know. As soon as he'd stumbled through one answer about his younger brother and sister, he was hit with more questions about his job, his flat, his television-watching habits and his opinion of Trollope. Jim had been the target of my parents' attention many times over the years, and I couldn't blame him for slipping away.

'Oh, is Jim here?' My father came into the dining room, spectacles flashing, with a covered casserole in his hands. The casserole smelled of fish, but you could never quite tell with my father. 'You look nice, Philomena,' he added, as he always did, though I had learned that his fashion sense, like his taste in food, was questionable at best. He was wearing too-short tracksuit bottoms and a T-shirt, although he had never exercised in his life. He just liked to be comfortable when he was writing up his research.

'No, Jim had to go.'

'Odd boy,' said my mother, sitting down at her place and dishing out vegetables.

'He's not odd.' I passed my plate to my father to put some casserole on. It was pink, with red flecks. Fortunately, I was used to not being able to identify what I ate in this house.

'I don't see why he hasn't asked you to marry him yet.'

'Mum! We don't have that sort of relationship.'

'How long have you been living together now?'

'Nearly five years, but—'

'You'd think that after five years of living together you'd think about getting married.'

'We don't –' I paused, pouring us all glasses of wine, and waving the bottle in a way meant to signify not having sex. 'We're just friends, and always have been. Platonic friends.'

'"Friendship is certainly the finest balm for the pangs of disappointed love,"' my mother said. '*Northanger Abbey*.'

I gritted my teeth.

'Is he gay?' my father asked, his mouth full. 'Is he with that Douglas, and that's why the two of you aren't together?'

'Dad!'

'He needn't be afraid of us just because he's gay. You know I've been doing some research on Richard Stanswick, and after that there's very little that can shock me. Amazing what they used to get up to. There's a theory that his entire Dusky Princes sonnet cycle is a coded description of one particular homosexual orgy.'

'He's not gay. Digger's not gay either. We're all just friends.'

'It would be nice to see you happily settled down, though,' my mother said.

I reflected on how strange it was that as a teenager, I'd been embarrassed about how weird I believed my home life was, with books on every available surface and genius parents who thought about literature more than they thought about mowing the lawn or getting the car serviced. And now that I was an adult, my parents seemed to have reverted into the most conservative roles possible, pestering me to get settled down. Especially my supposedly feminist mother.

'Forget it,' I said. 'I'm going to be an old maid for the rest of my life. I'll live with Digger and Jim until we're all old and senile and then I'll outlive them because women live longer than men and when I finally die I'll be eaten by The Baz.' Did iguanas live that long? I didn't care; I was only saying it to annoy my parents.

'Sarcasm doesn't suit you, Philomena,' said my father, helping himself to more casserole.

'It's not sarcastic, I mean it. We've taken a vow and everything.'

My mother munched peas and regarded me sadly. 'Having a child is one of the most profound joys in the universe. I hate to think of you missing out on it.'

It's a profound joy until your child grows up and becomes a trash-drawing freak, I corrected her mentally, but there was no sense in saying it. She'd only act hurt and pretend she hadn't been thinking it in the first place.

'Almost as profound as the joy of discovering a forgotten sonnet, I bet. How's your research going?'

This sent them both happily chattering away, about their work, about concordances, about university politics and iambs and poststructuralist theory and a little argument about the semiotics of gardening. I pretended to listen, letting the words wash over me as I had during a million meals before. I thought about what I'd said about Jim and Digger and me growing old together and dying.

My father was right; I'd been sarcastic. I didn't really believe that in fifty years Jim and Digger and I would all be wandering around our semi with Zimmer frames.

But that was the logical extension of our vow. The three of us would get old and wrinkly together. Our parents would die off, we'd retire from our jobs, and we'd spend our dotage arguing about *The X-Files*, with nobody else in our lives.

The thought made me feel as if I were trapped and suffocating inside too-close walls. Which was stupid, because I loved Jim and Digger, and there wasn't anyone else I'd want to grow old with. And as for the profound joy of having children . . . well, I had Girl from Mars. She was my creation, my legacy to the world.

If D. McKay didn't mess her up completely.

'. . . the argument seems to be almost proto-feminist, almost to anticipate Cixous's theories of *écriture féminine*. In 1842! You can imagine.'

'Yeah,' I said, nodding.

'It's all very exciting,' said my father.

'It sounds it.'

I must not have sounded enthusiastic enough because both my parents put down their forks and exchanged a glance. In unison, they stood and began collecting the plates. I got up to help them.

'No, Philomena, you stay here and relax and finish your wine,' my father told me, and they both disappeared into the kitchen.

While my father's cooking was questionable at best, his wine was always excellent. This one was white, which also made me suspect that the casserole had been piscine in nature. I sat in my chair, sipping, and gazed at the familiar dark green walls, hung with photographs. The photos were material proof of the profound joy of having a child: row upon row of my baby pictures, and then carefully framed school photographs of me, gap-toothed in my school uniform. Lazily I watched my progress, from gummy chubby lump to skinny pre-teen tomboy, smiling as I remembered the big upset I'd caused when, aged fourteen and on a dare from Jim, I'd dyed my hair turquoise the evening before School Picture Day. Turquoise was a good colour; maybe I should try that again. I searched for the picture. It was hung far down in a corner near the sideboard, half-hidden by a crystal decanter. And then . . .

And then that was it, actually. There were no later photographs of me.

My parents had obviously become lazy about getting photos framed. Either that, or my teenage years were about the time their profound joy had started to wear thin.

Mum and Dad returned from the kitchen, bearing bowls of crumble and custard. Well, custard, anyway; the brown thing could have been crumble, could have been pie, could have been flapjack. It seemed to have apple in it. And what I hoped was a currant.

'So,' my father said carefully, 'how is your job going, Philomena?'

They never asked me about my job, preferring to avoid the distasteful subject; they had obviously been conferring in the kitchen after my blatant lack of interest in their intellectual discussion, and wanted to bring the conversation back to something in which I could participate.

And those were the two topics they could come up with: my lack of a love life and my job, which they hated. Apparently the only common ground we had were the places where I failed to live up to scratch.

'Great,' I told them, shovelling up pudding. 'Girl from Mars is selling like crazy. I really think the title is going from strength to strength. Only yesterday my editor told me that I was the most popular artist they'd had in a decade.'

'That's fantastic,' my mother said. 'You should be able to use that popularity, too, to get you other illustration commissions, don't you think?'

'I don't want other illustration commissions,' I said, my attention fixed on my bowl where I was chasing down another currant. 'I'm very happy working on *Girl from Mars*.'

'Of course you are,' my father said quickly. Too quickly. 'Fine art was never going to hold your attention, was it?'

I nearly flung my spoon across the room. They said they were happy for me, why couldn't they actually *be* happy? Why did they need to mention *other commissions, fine art*?

'In fact, all sorts of exciting things are happening; my next piece is working with a Hollywood screenwriter and director who's written some big box office hits.'

'Oh, well, that's nice,' my mother said blandly.

I quit eating my pudding and drained my wine glass. What the hell was I doing, talking about D. McKay's shitty script as if it were the best thing in my universe instead of the worst? Was I trying to impress my parents with his Hollywood credentials? Aside from the fact that I was lying my arse off, my parents were the least likely people in the world to be impressed by anything resembling pop culture, including box office smash films.

Was I really that desperate for approval from them?

'I think Johanna Edwards said she was doing a book about the essentially deconstructive nature of sequential narrative art – that's what you do, isn't it, Philomena?'

'Comics,' I said. 'I draw comics. Comic books. About a space alien. They've got ray guns and big monsters in them. There's nothing intellectual about it, Mum, Dad. I'm sorry to disappoint you, but there it is. Do you need some help with the washing-up?'

A Fearsome Amazon
Warrior Queen

Why was I so many different people?

With my parents I was alternately a little girl wanting approval and a teenager wanting to rebel. With Jim and Digger I was funny, confident, one of the guys. With strangers I was ill at ease, tongue-tied, abrupt. While drawing I was powerful, absorbed, only present as eyes and hands and ideas.

Surely there was one person, one Philomena Desdemona Brown, that I could put my finger on and say, once and for all, *that's me*?

Maybe this was why I had spent the morning of my Anthony-scheduled meeting with D. McKay rifling through my wardrobe. Should I try to dress up and look professional to confront McKay? Or should I dress like an eccentric artist, everything as paint-splattered as possible?

In the end, of course, I went for black. Comic book artists know that if you want to create drama and menace, you go for shadow. We also know that big blocks of black are really marvellous for taking up space that you don't have to fill with drawing. Black gives your work a presence, and it lets the reader use their own emotion and imagination.

In my case, it also made my blue hair really stand out.

Sometimes I wish I could just grow a bushy beard like Digger, I mused, stuffing all the clothes back into the wardrobe wherever they would fit. Being so big and hairy made him invisible, in a way. People only noticed the obvious outside bits of him, and he never had to think about what he wore because his bigness and hairiness said it all. I supposed that was part of my dyeing my hair different colours, too, though it was also because my real colour was a boring and ugly mousy brown.

The clothes conundrum had made me late and Jim was already working by the time I got downstairs, but he'd left me a 'good luck' Post-it on the fridge. I thought about having breakfast, but my stomach was too jumpy. Being hungry could give me an extra edge, too. I stuffed the Post-it in my pocket and headed for the Underground, buying myself a large coffee on the way.

Nobody talked on the train. I noticed it more these days because of what Dan had said. Some people read the free papers; some stared at the advertisements or at the floor. Some played with their mobile phones, though they couldn't possibly be getting reception. All of the reading and the staring and the playing was, I realised, a signal, sort of like Digger's beard and my hair, meant to tell others that they were occupied in their own worlds, that they weren't to be looked at or talked to or bothered.

Of course this meant that they didn't look at other people, so I was free to watch them. The woman next to me was wearing a baseball cap and staring at her sudoku, pen in hand. She'd only filled in three clues. She was breathing in sort of a funny way, with a hitch every now and then, and I saw that she had tears in her eyes. Not enough to spill over, but enough for her mascara to start to smear.

What was it? Was she in the middle of a vast personal tragedy? Had her boyfriend chucked her, had her cat got run over, was her mother terminally ill? Was she really bad at numbers, or allergic to the Underground?

Her breath hitched.

What horrible thing would happen if people looked at each other? I heard Dan ask in my head, and I said to the woman, 'What's wr—'

The train stopped at Clapham Common. The woman put away her pen, stood up, and left. As she was stepping off the train I realised that she was the barmaid from the Swan. I hadn't recognised her with her hair up beneath a hat.

I wondered about her all the way to Victoria, what was wrong, and whether she'd got up because I'd started speaking to her. And whether if I'd been crying and someone had started speaking to me, I'd have got up too.

The UPC building looked the same as always, boring and marvellous, and I took a few deep breaths outside it in order to strengthen my resolve. I was going to go in there like a five-foot-two blue-haired hurricane. I tried to forget that in my eyes, D. McKay's grandfather had been practically a god. The man was ruining my comic and he had to go.

I wondered what he looked like. He was probably some young stripling, wearing a tailor-made suit and puffed up with a sense of his own importance after three box-office smashes that were most likely flukes. Or a chubby, self-satisfied brat trying to be cool in a T-shirt and jeans. Or a big, purple, warty troll with three eyes and teeth dripping in drool.

Whatever he looked like, I was well and truly going to kick some McKay arse.

Exactly how I was going to do this, I did not know. I figured I'd make it up as I went along. Like the black clothing, I was adaptable.

I dug the script out of my bag, ready to wave it in McKay's face if necessary, and showed my badge at reception. In the lift mirror I stared at my pale face and rehearsed my reasons to be here today. Normally I was far from confrontational, and yet this was the second time in two days that I was preparing to wave a script in someone's face.

Whoever Philomena Brown really was, deep down underneath everything, today she was a fearsome Amazon warrior queen, ready to do anything to defend her territory.

Anthony had told me the meeting was in the same conference room I'd eavesdropped outside a few days before. I marched down the hallway to the bland beech door, my mind set on business. It was probably my imagination, but I fancied I heard and felt the entire office settle into a hush. Like the quiet that descends over two gunslingers who are about to test their quick-draw skills in a conflict that will leave one of them dead.

Right. The best defence was offence, I'd been drilled in that concept by Jim through hundreds of hours of Nintendo. I heaved in a deep breath, clutched the script in my left hand, and while I opened the conference-room door I tried not to think about how silly I would look if

D. McKay was late and I was attacking an empty room.

I stepped in, brandishing the script. 'What the hell—'

And then I stopped.

Sitting at the conference table, with a stack of A4 and a notebook in front of him, flicking through a copy of *Girl from Mars and the Neptune Nightmare*, exactly where the purple troll was supposed to be, was Dan.

Dream Team

'Philomena?' he said, in some surprise.

My mouth had dropped open. I got control of it with difficulty. '*You're* his grandson?'

'What are you – oh.' He glanced down at the comic in his hands, and then back to me, and I saw him making the connection. 'You're Fil Brown.'

'Philomena Desdemona Brown. Fil for short. And you're Daniel McKay.'

'Yes.'

We stared at each other, me in the doorway, him still in his chair. My guts were all cringing with embarrassment and my heart was beating very fast.

Stupid body. Calm, I needed calm and a sabre-like wit. This man, American Dan, Daniel McKay, whoever he was, was the enemy.

'I thought Fil Brown was a man,' he said, as if it were an accusation. He stood up and stared at me.

'Join the queue,' I said. 'Why didn't you tell me you were Dennis McKay's grandson?'

'Why did you lie to me about being an illustrator?' he shot back.

'I didn't lie,' I retorted. 'I am an illustrator. And at least I didn't pretend I was a businessman here in the country on some new project.'

'I am on a new project, and I never said I was a businessman.'

I clenched my free fist. 'You said *Girl from Mars* needed a grappling hook and some dynamite!'

'It does. It's hopelessly old fashioned. It's exactly the same as it was when I was a kid, and it was outdated then.'

'That's the point; it's got continuity.'

'It's got stuck in a rut, more like.'

I realised I was still holding the script as if I were about to wave it, but I hadn't got around to that part yet. I did now.

'And this story is supposed to be the big saviour? The dynamite?'

'Yes.'

'And you're the answer to all the world's problems?'

He wasn't the Dan I'd met before. His dark blue eyes glinted with anger.

'I seem to recall you wished me good luck when we talked about it in the café,' he said.

'I didn't know you were talking about *Girl from Mars*.'

'Right, so you're not against change in principle, just about this change in particular?'

'I'm against this script. It's totally wrong.'

'So that's why you had Anthony arrange this meeting with me.'

'You mean you didn't know?' Indignation bubbled through my veins. 'Have you ever actually read any *Girl from Mars*, besides that one you're holding right now? Because if you have, your script doesn't show it.'

'I didn't know why you wanted to meet with me. It crossed my mind when you walked into the room that it might have been to apologise, but I can see I was wrong.'

'Apologise for what? Having integrity? Consistency?'

'For leaving me standing next to a giant crack.'

Agh. I'd hoped he wouldn't mention that.

'We have more important things to talk about,' I said.

'It seemed pretty important to me when I was standing waiting for you in Tate Modern for forty-five minutes.'

We were the only people in a big room but the air felt close. I shifted my feet, trying to figure out how I could justify running out on him.

'I had to be somewhere else.'

'I figured that out. It took me a little while, but I got it, loud and clear.' He sat down in his chair and crossed his arms over his chest. 'So since standing me up isn't important, let's talk about what is. The *comic book*.'

I flushed with fury at his sarcasm. 'Comic books are important!'

He shrugged. To him, this was obviously nothing more than another job, another achievement to tick off. Making blockbuster films – tick. Being good looking and confident – tick. Ruining a fifty-year legacy – tick.

'What's your problem with my script?' he asked.

'If you cared at all about your grandfather's creation, you wouldn't be able to sit there and ask me what's wrong. You'd know.'

'Well, let's assume I don't know, so spell it out for me. What don't you like? The title? The characters? The caves? What?'

I sat down across from him and put the script carefully between us, as if it were a shield.

'Jackson Silver, for a start,' I said. 'It would take more than a rent-a-hunk like that to make Girl from Mars's knees weak.'

'He's also an astrophysicist who knows the key to getting her home.'

'I don't care what he is or what he knows, Girl from Mars only goes weak at the knees when she's slammed into by a fifteen-ton truck. And here she's actually flirting, for the first time in nearly sixty years.'

'The comic needs something new. That's why I was asked to do it.'

Grandson or not, famous or not, how dare he waltz in and say what the comic needed?

'"New" doesn't mean "a hopeless collection of clichés",' I burst out. 'You've made *Girl from Mars* into one of your romantic comedy movies.'

'Have you seen one of my movies, Fil?' His hands were on the table. Spread out, pressed hard on the surface.

'No. But—'

'So you're judging them by genre. That ever happen to you about being a comic book artist?'

'*Girl from Mars* is not a romance! She doesn't go all ga-ga over a man!'

He stood, suddenly, his chair scraping back behind him, his voice loud. 'Are you saying that Girl from Mars has the guts to tell somebody who asks her out that she's not interested, to his face?'

I stared up at him, wide-eyed and breathless. 'I—'

The conference-room door swung open. 'Brown and McKay, my creative dream team,' boomed Anthony, striding into the room.

Relief swept through me at being saved from having to try to justify what I'd done. Of course, if I'd known what Anthony was about to propose, I would have run out screaming. But I didn't.

'You're having a productive discussion, I hope?' he said in a jovial tone, the effect of which was similar to a party balloon at a funeral.

'Very,' said Dan.

'You were surprised Brown was a woman, I bet.'

'It's been one surprise after another,' I said.

'And you're ironing out all your little difficulties, I trust.'

Neither one of us said anything to that. We were both frowning.

'It's been a long time since we've had spirits running high around here and, I for one, think it's about time. Too much number-crunching. We forget that this business is all about passion.'

'That's funny,' I muttered, 'it seems like only yesterday you were saying that it's all about roping in shiny new famous people with built-in media coverage.'

'We can't ignore the bottom line, of course,' Anthony carried on, ignoring me, 'but the fact remains that quality speaks for itself. That's why I'm so excited to have the two of you on board for this project.'

He wasn't fooling me. Anthony wasn't a sweet-talker, he never got excited, and he had something brewing in that big brick-like brain. He hadn't even sworn since entering the room. All in all it was highly fishy and my relief had fizzled away.

Arguing with Dan was clearly going to get me nowhere so I tried one last time with Anthony. 'Chief, nobody has more passion about *Girl from Mars* than I do. That's why I wish you would just listen to—'

He held up his hands to stop me. 'No, Brown, I'm not the creative one here. I've already discussed it with McKay, and he's got complete carte blanche for this story arc.'

'Carte—' I looked from one to the other. This had all gone on behind my back. Anthony had essentially handed the reins over to Dan, so he could drive the comic over a cliff.

'I want the two of you working closely together on this project. That's why I've got some great news for you.'

'What?' we both said together, both, I noticed, not without suspicion in our voices.

'I've had the boys clear a room for you on the fourth floor, behind the archives. We're moving in a drawing board and a computer – two, if you need them. It was the way your grandfather used to work, McKay, everything in-house.'

'You want us to work in the same room?' I gasped.

'It's a great idea, isn't it?' As always, Anthony's voice was deadpan. 'That way any of your little niggling issues can be worked out straight away. And it means that you can spark off each other's creative process.'

And that you can keep an eye on me in case I decide to make more trouble, I thought.

'I usually like my own space,' Daniel began. Thank God, he wasn't up for this stupid idea either. I started nodding. 'But if you think that a shared office would genuinely help the creative process go more smoothly here, I'm willing to go along, Anthony.'

Anthony. What a two-faced suck-up. 'I don't think this is a good idea,' I said. 'I'm a nightmare when I'm working, just ask my housemate. I work irregular hours and I make a mess everywhere, and I like really loud music. And lots and lots of caffeine. You wouldn't like it,' I told Dan.

'I think if you expect compromises from other people you're going to have to be willing to make some yourself, Brown,' said Anthony. 'If you absolutely have to work from home, we're always looking for talent for *Lacey*.'

Damn. I bit my fingers.

'That's settled, then.' Anthony clapped his hands together. 'The room will be all ready for you tomorrow, and I'll get you security cards that will give you access outside of office hours. I know you creative types like to work round the clock. I'm announcing the news on our website tomorrow and we're sending out press releases. With a big hitter like McKay on our side I'm expecting a lot of attention.'

'Whatever's good for *Girl from Mars*,' said Dan, and I glowered at him. He raised one eyebrow in the infuriating manner of the victor. And I'd thought he was a nice guy.

Bastard.

'Right,' I mumbled, and headed for the door. Anthony touched me on the shoulder as I passed him.

'Don't fuck this up, Brown,' he said under his breath.

'Don't worry,' I replied, because right at that moment I couldn't see how I could make the situation any worse.

The Comics Sweatshop

Of course, I did make it worse, because that night in my dreams Daniel McKay was standing in front of me in the fourth-floor UPC archives department. His tie was unknotted and the top button of his shirt was open, so I could see the base of his throat, and his arms were folded on his chest and his deep blue eyes were full of anger.

'Your sea urchins are judging me based on genre!' he thundered.

'You are incredibly sexy when you're angry,' I heard myself say. I glanced down at myself; I was wearing a lime-green Martian uniform, which was unzipped partway down the front. I had somehow acquired a magnificent pair of breasts.

'That's a romantic cliché.'

I looked back at Dan, who had suddenly grown blood-red horns on his forehead. 'You're an arrogant creep and I hate you!'

'I will destroy your precious comic! Bwa-ha-ha-ha!'

'Cliché!' I yelled.

'I'll show you cliché,' he said, and he pulled me into his arms, bent me backwards, and kissed me.

Ka-Zam! shouted a thousand voices in my head.

And I sat bolt upright in bed, panting, with my hand pressed to my mouth where I could still feel Daniel's lips on mine.

Sunlight peeped through my blackout curtains and I could hear, faintly, Jim's music from down the hall where he was working. I lay back into the warmth of my pillows, closed my eyes, and indulged guiltily in the memory of warm lips, strong hands, and an electric current powerful enough to vaporise a small town.

It had been the best kiss of my entire life, it hadn't been real, and it was with the enemy.

My mobile phone rang, pulling me out of my sexy wallow. It was in the pocket of my black jeans, which were thrown over a chair. I checked the clock beside the bed: it wasn't even half past nine in the morning; way too early for anybody who knew me to expect me to answer. I buried my head under the pillow until it stopped ringing, and then I crawled out of bed and went down the hallway to the bathroom.

The mirror showed me that my hair was stuck straight up on one side of my head and that the magnificent breasts had existed only in my dream. Still, I hesitated before stepping into the shower, because I didn't want the water to wash away the imaginary feeling of being in Dan's arms.

'You are pathetic,' I told myself finally, and got in. As I soaped up I reminded myself of the plan I'd formulated the night before. I was clearly expected to be in my and Dan's joint office today, to sort out the script problems. But trying to argue with Dan was a waste of breath, and

Anthony hadn't said when I was expected. I'd spend the day farting around, and turn up at UPC around eight or nine tonight and use my new all-hours entrance key. With any luck, Dan would have finished his work and gone home by then, and I could avoid seeing him altogether.

And then . . . well, I'd do something. I'd have to follow Dan's script. But maybe I could arrange things so that my protest was subtle, but clear. For example, I could draw Jackson Silver, the love interest, slightly deformed. I smiled as I rinsed my hair, picturing Jackson's chin so big that he'd never get close enough to give Girl from Mars a snog.

Speaking of snogging. I twisted the tap to cold and blasted my dream out of my head.

I dripped icy water all the way back to my room. I was pulling on a pair of tracksuit bottoms when my phone rang again. This time I took it out and checked it. It registered six missed calls, and the number on the screen was Anthony's.

Yikes.

'What is it, Chief?'

'Don't you answer your shitting phone, Brown?'

'I was in the shower.'

'Get your arse down here now. We're having a press conference at half ten to announce your partnership with McKay. Star Bar.'

'What?' I checked the clock: five to ten. 'Why didn't you tell me this yesterday?'

'If I'd let you think about it all night you wouldn't have come. Get your skates on.' He hung up.

I swore in a manner becoming the Chief, discarded my trackies for a pair of paint-spattered jeans and a vintage seventies *Girl from Mars* T-shirt, and ran as fast as I could for the tube.

By the time I'd reached the Star Bar, which was a newish, trendyish wine bar not far from UPC, my watch said twenty to eleven. I opened the heavy glass door and saw that the place was full of people, presumably journalists. They chatted to each other, holding coffee cups gilded with stars and eating from several large platters holding bagels and cream cheese and pastries and other assorted things I was too frazzled to identify.

I fought through people to the front of the room, where Anthony and Dan both stood, wearing suits. Anthony muttered, 'About time' and Dan, chatting with one of the photographers, didn't seem to register my arrival at all.

Except he did, because when Anthony cleared his throat and the chatter faded, Dan looked straight into my face for a split second. I scowled.

'What the hell is this?' I asked.

'Brunch,' said Anthony.

'*Brunch?*'

'Apparently you have to feed journalists just to get them to cover a goddamn story. Good turnout, though, eh?'

'Whose idea was this?'

Dan's conversation paused long enough for him and Anthony to exchange a look and I had my answer. I should have known it as soon as I walked in; I doubted Anthony had even heard of the concept of 'brunch' before last week. This smacked of Hollywood.

I grimaced, and turned to find out where I could get a cup of coffee, at least, but before I could do anything Anthony cleared his throat and banged on a nearby table for attention.

'Right, you lot, thanks for coming. I'll make this short and sweet, and then after we pass on the news you can have your one-on-ones.'

One-on-ones? What the hell were those? I glanced at Dan, but he was smiling winningly at the journalists.

'As you may know,' Anthony continued, 'UPC's lead title, *Girl from Mars*, is nearly sixty years old. It's been one of Britain's most popular comics since it was created in 1951 by artist and writer Dennis McKay. These days the girl is looking pretty good for her age, thanks to talented artists such as Fil Brown, here.'

The attention of the entire room focused on me and I took a step back and nearly tripped on the chair behind me. Someone steadied me with a hand on my arm: Dan. His hand was gone before I properly registered it, and he never took his eyes off Anthony. But I had plenty of time to grit my teeth and reflect that he had some cheek, after yesterday.

'The big news is that UPC have commissioned a story arc for *Girl from Mars* from Daniel McKay, writer and director of *Mixing Desk* and *Ninety-Eight Point Six*, who also happens to be Dennis McKay's grandson. UPC is incredibly excited –'

Blah, blah, blah. I zoned out and looked at the stars painted on the ceiling instead of the reporters and photographers as Anthony went through a huge spiel about how famous Dan was, how brilliant this new direction would be, and threw in all sorts of comments about close collaboration that, as far as I could tell, were a warning to me.

Since when did UPC give press conferences? Since never, as far as I was aware; if there was an innovation, they usually sent out releases and posted a notice on their website, and usually it was to the comics media, which wasn't big. But with the amount of people here, Anthony had to have attracted the mainstream media, too. I risked a glance at the journalistic horde. Many of them were female, and some of them were well dressed. Definitely not comics media.

It was obviously the draw of Superstar McKay. Who was now taking the spotlight and saying, in his enthusiastic, deceptively pleasant American voice, how pleased he was to be here in England, how happy he was to follow in his grandfather's footsteps, and how he was enjoying the challenge of writing in a new medium. Nothing about grappling hooks or dynamite, I noticed, though it did get me thinking about his motivation. With all this fuss and the special office for us and everything, UPC must have dropped a load of money on to McKay, but he probably didn't need it after his hit films. So why was he doing it? Sheer arrogance? Ego?

'I've read *Girl from Mars* since I was a little boy,' he was saying now. 'My grandfather would send copies to America in the mail, months' worth at a time for my birthdays and at Christmas. I'd look forward to them all year and then read them in a single weekend. Then I'd reread them slowly, making them last until the next bunch came. You can imagine the effect Girl from Mars's tight costumes had in forming the libido of a young boy.' There were chuckles, sycophantic, no doubt, from the collected throngs. 'When UPC sent me some recent issues and asked me to contribute some scripts, I was immediately blown away by the quality of Fil Brown's artwork. As a director I'm obsessed with the visual. I specifically requested to be partnered with her, so this is a dream come true.'

I was clenching my fists so hard that my palms hurt where my short nails were digging in, and my teeth were squeaking as I ground them. Where had he learned to lie so convincingly? Was this something they taught you in Hollywood?

'Anyway, I'd like to thank Anthony and UPC for this opportunity, and to thank my grandfather, Dennis McKay, for creating the most exciting female in comics. And I'd like to thank Fil, too, for her talent and commitment to *Girl from Mars*.'

He turned to me slightly, and once again I felt the focus of the room on me. They were, I realised, waiting for me to say something. Dan was smiling, hypocrite that he was; Anthony was glaring, sending me 'don't fuck up' vibes.

My palms and neck broke out in a sweat. I hated, hated, *hated* speaking in front of people. I had avoided it since compulsory drama lessons in year nine at school.

I swallowed hard, and then cleared my throat noisily. I didn't look at the audience, because I knew what they were thinking. A woman? Comic book artist? What kind of weirdo is she?

'I love *Girl from Mars* and I will do my best to make sure she continues in the tradition of Dennis McKay and all of her other wonderful writers and artists,' I managed, and then stepped back, hoping that message would be clear enough for the fans so that I didn't get crucified when the series came out. Comic fans were pretty vicious when you crossed them; I knew because I was one myself.

Though I wasn't doing a great job being vicious today.

There were some questions for Dan, predictably, about the mega-stars who had been in his films and what his next film project would be, but he responded in a good-natured and charming way that didn't answer anything, and which I was familiar with from our conversation when he had failed to mention who he was or why he was really in England. Then the photographers took some pictures which I couldn't quite muster a smile for and it was all over except for the spots in front of our eyes.

'Okay, now we've got some time for one-on-ones,' Anthony announced, and he shooed me into a chair. He and Dan each sat at tables and the journalists instantly clustered round Dan's table. There was even a bit of a tussle until Dan said a few words and they formed a more or less orderly queue, waiting for their turn to ask individual questions.

None of them even glanced in my direction. I waited exactly two minutes and then stood and left the Star Bar.

I went to O Solo Mio, ordered a double espresso which I downed on the spot, and then bought a double Americano to take away. I muttered to myself all the way to UPC. I was waiting by the lift, tapping my foot, when Anthony appeared by my elbow.

'Going to your office, Brown?'

'Might as well.'

'I'll show you what we've done.' The lift doors opened and we got in. 'I'm depending on you, you know,' he said to me.

'Right.' Why argue when there was no point in doing so? He had me effectively trapped.

'And so is McKay. He was telling the truth about specially requesting you.'

Yeah, when he thought I was a man and expected me to be star-struck and easily pushed around. 'That was nice of him.'

'Nice has nothing to do with it, as I'm sure you well know. Here we are.' The lift stopped and Anthony ushered me down the hallway and through a door.

Right away I could see that the word 'office' had been a euphemism. The true term would be something closer to 'underground lair'. The UPC building wasn't exactly airy and the archives weren't known for being bright and cheerful, but this room had evidently been rejected as being too grimy and dark even to house books. The one window was obscured by broken Venetian blinds and a stack of cardboard boxes and there were water stains on the ceiling and the carpet tiles on the floor. Into this temple of gloom had been shoved an aluminium desk with one ancient desktop computer, and a scarred wooden drawing board. The room was small enough so that the desk and the drawing board rubbed shoulders.

'Of course you'll want to put your own homely touches in it,' Anthony said. The two of us standing near the doorway filled nearly all the available space.

'Yeah, I can probably fit a sofa bed and a potted palm in that corner. Maybe a paddling pool.'

'This is the first time since 1979 that a creative team have had their own office at UPC,' said Anthony. 'I'm going to have a job explaining your preferential treatment to everyone else.'

'Hmm, I don't envy you.'

'Well, happy working. We're counting on you, Brown.' Anthony disappeared and I was left alone in the room.

'How am I supposed to work in here?' I sighed to the stale air. I was used to my attic eyrie, where I could shout, pace, sleep, dream, dance, talk to myself, create. I was used to my friends being nearby, my cabinet of supplies, my music and my memories. But this place, this was a—

'I see you found the comics sweatshop.' Dan's voice came from behind me.

He had a coffee-maker and a bag of coffee under his arm. He set it on top of one of the cardboard boxes and I noticed the coffee was decaf.

'All done with your fans?' I asked lightly and crossed the room to check on the supplies stacked next to the drawing board. I was pleased to find a supply of Bristol boards and India ink, though I never used mechanical pencils. I clanged them into the metal bin, aware of Dan standing in the room, watching me, breathing the same air.

'You gave me a hard time yesterday,' he said. 'I don't think I deserve it.'

I found another mechanical pencil. *Clang.* 'Apparently Anthony and the national media would agree.'

'You're acting as if you're the only one who cares about *Girl from Mars*. What I said before was true. I grew up with the title. Some of my clearest memories of my grandfather were of him telling me stories from his comics.'

'Weren't you lucky.' It came out sarcastic, but I actually meant it. Imagine sharing something like that with your family, instead of hiding it under your duvet.

'And I've read all of your work from the past two years,' he said. 'Anthony sent it to me. I meant what I said, I did want to work with you because I think your art's amazing. But the comic needs a change.'

I stopped sorting through the art supplies and faced him. He looked remarkably like he had in my dream, without the horns, of course, so I couldn't say anything right away. He took it as a cue to continue.

'I'll admit that I wouldn't have said that about a

grappling hook and dynamite if I'd known who you were.'

'But that's what you think.'

'Listen, if you love *Girl from Mars* as much as you say you do, surely you've got to realise that the title can survive a few new ideas, and that it might even be improved.'

'Change is one thing. It's a totally different thing to come in from out of nowhere and trample all over everything with no idea what you're playing at. You don't know *Girl from Mars* at all.'

'I told you, I—'

'Being related to Dennis McKay and reading a few issues is nothing, Dan. This comic has been going for twice as long as you've been alive. You can't just come in and shake it up because you think it might be fun. You need to eat, breathe, and sleep *Girl from Mars* for months before you start working on a comic. Do you know anything about Wayne Jayson, for example?'

Dan thought. 'Wasn't he a sidekick?'

'No, he was an artist – *the* artist – of the late eighties and early nineties. The sidekicks were, in order of longest- to shortest-lasting: Rufus, then Antoinette, F-8 the Android, Berger, Kingsley the Talking Ant and Dicky.'

'Dicky?'

'He was a silicon-based life form from the Ffrytl system whose real name consisted of all consonants. He only lasted three issues in 1967.'

'I – see.' He seemed amused, which made me angrier.

'It's not just artists and sidekicks, Dan. Do you know the specs of Girl from Mars's spaceship? Do you know how many times she's tried to go back to Mars and failed, and why? Do you know why she can't form emotional connections with Earthlings?'

'Because she's afraid of losing them for ever, like she lost her home world.'

So he'd thought about that, at least.

'But it's more than just fear. There's this whole history behind her, and you don't know it. Not like you should, if you're going to mess with it.'

He pulled out the chair to the desk and sat on it. 'Sort of like how you don't know my films but you felt like you could criticise them anyway?'

'I didn't criticise them,' I said, though I thought I probably had. 'I just said they were romances, and *Girl from Mars* isn't.'

'You implied more than that.'

'Listen, Dan, I think you'd be insulted too if I decided to step into your studio and direct a film without bothering to learn anything about how to do it. Your script isn't even a comics script, for God's sake.'

He frowned. 'What do you mean?'

'The panel descriptions, for a start. They're too detailed, except when they're not detailed enough. And they don't match up with the dialogue.'

'I don't understand.'

I sighed, picked up my bag from the floor where I'd dropped it, and rummaged around for the script I'd stuffed in there yesterday. 'Look,' I said, spreading the battered pages out on the drawing board. Dan got out of his chair to stand beside me. He had a lemony smell, which I realised I'd included in my dream, although I hadn't consciously noticed it.

Ignore it, I told myself. Since he seemed to be willing to pay attention, I decided to start with the easy stuff, so maybe we could get that sorted out once and for all. 'When you write a film script I'm guessing you have two people standing in front of a camera and they can say whatever they want, whenever they want, and move around the room and stuff. But comics are static, so there are some major differences. For example, here in the panel description you have Girl from Mars and Jackson standing at a table looking at some plans, with Girl on the left. But then in the dialogue, you have Jackson speaking first.'

'And?'

'A single panel of comics reads from left to right. People will start with the top left-hand speech balloon. So generally it's easier if you have the left-hand character speaking first.'

'You mean, every time?'

'There are ways of getting round it, but it's easiest if you stick to that rule for the majority of panels. In this panel, you just need to switch the characters' places.'

'But what if Girl is moved to the right but then she speaks first in the next panel? Oh wait, I see – then it's a close-up, or you switch point of view.'

'Or you get them to move, or something else. Whatever works for the story. Here's another thing.' I shuffled pages. 'Here you say that the hidden door creaks open slowly, and Girl creeps into the cave and then draws her ray gun. All in one panel.'

'So?'

'Well, in a film you could show all that with a few seconds of footage, but in comics we only have still pictures. For example, I can't show that the door is hidden and have it opening at the same time, because as soon as it opens, it's not hidden any more. I'd have to do it like this.'

I grabbed a sheet of paper from the stack, a HB pencil

from my jeans pocket, and drew a blank cave wall. Then, beside it, I drew the same cave wall with the crack outline of a door in it. Then a third drawing with the door halfway open, and Girl from Mars coming through it, her hand on her ray gun. I wrote 'CREAK!' coming out of the bottom of the door.

'Just that part of the sequence takes three panels. You could skip the first action and just have this one' – I covered the first two drawings with my hand, so we could only see Girl coming through the open door – 'but that means the reader doesn't know it's a hidden door. You could skip this middle one, but then the reader doesn't know the door's opening slowly. If you're writing a comics script, you have to make these decisions.'

'Right.'

'And how it's placed on the page depends on how important it is. For example, if this is a big part of the suspense, I can use all three of these panels, blow them up, and put them in the centre of the page with the other action happening around them. But if they're minor, I can use just the last panel and put it wherever it happens to come. You don't need to give me all of that, I can make the composition decisions myself, but I will need to know if I need to emphasise something in particular because it's going to be a major plot point later. Like does the reader need to know it's a secret door because episode five will hang on that fact?'

Dan was nodding. I realised we'd been talking for several minutes without arguing.

'Okay,' he said. 'I get it. Essentially I need to give you more detail.'

'Well, no.'

He frowned. 'What?'

'You're writing like a director. But you're not. You don't have the camera; I do.' I tapped my forehead. 'I'm in charge of the visuals.'

'Ah.' His mouth twisted up on one side. 'This is what it's all about. You think I was too bossy with the camera angles and composition, and your artist ego's been hurt. So you're objecting to the entire script because of it.'

'No, I'm objecting to the entire script because it's wrong and you don't know your subject or your medium. But if you're going to work with me, you can't insult me by trying to do my job for me.' He opened his mouth, but I overrode him. 'If you want a particular feel, if you want things smooth or jagged or dark or whatever, that's cool, I can do that. Or if you want a particular panel to be emphasised, or to bleed over the page, or you need a colour theme throughout, all of that's fine. If you've got a splash that needs to be just so because it's a tribute to something, or because you're going to refer to it again, go ahead. But you're writing like you're doing a film, like you're talking about time instead of space. It's not going to work for comics. The reader sees everything at once, the whole page or two pages, and then focuses down on the individual panels, and then sees it all at once again. I need to be the one making the decisions about the entire page, and if you've got a strong diagonal line here on panel one' – I pointed to a script page – 'that leads the reader's eye in the wrong direction, I end up fighting against that.'

I was looking at the page, picturing how I'd do the composition differently, and so I didn't notice that Dan hadn't answered. When I glanced at him, he was leaning with his hands on the drawing board, staring at me.

'What?' I said.

'You really know what you're talking about.'

'Of course I do. It's my job.'

'It's more than that, isn't it? It's how you think about the world. It's who you are.'

It was like that moment when we'd been standing at the crack and I'd been nearly suffocated with loss, thinking about Stevo, and Dan had said what I was feeling out loud. Without even asking, just from looking at me and being near me. As if he could reach inside and take something out and then show it back to me.

It made me want to shiver, and back out of the room.

'Thank you so much for your insight, O Great and Powerful Hollywood Director.'

He frowned and stood up straight, away from me.

I shuffled the script back into order. 'Are you going to change the script, or what?'

'I'll think about the stuff you mentioned,' he said to the air above my head. 'About who speaks first and how to show action. And the visuals.'

'And the whole romance thing.'

Dan walked to his desk and turned on the ancient desktop computer. It started up with a whine and the buzz of a hundred flies.

'Fil, you might be in charge of the visuals. But I'm in charge of the story. And if there's one thing I do know, it's how to tell a story.'

'But—'

'I've got some work to do. Are you going to work, or do you want to make the coffee?'

Make the coffee like a good little girl. I glanced at the bag of decaf and grimaced. 'I'm going home. I'll be back tomorrow with some decent supplies. Will there be something here I can draw?'

'You bet.' He wiggled the mouse and then banged it on the table. Seemingly satisfied, he shrugged off his jacket to reveal his white shirt. He squinted at the screen and began to type.

My Perfect Man

As I expected, the *Girl from Mars* internet fan loops were going crazy with the news about Daniel McKay. I'd been hoping for a general outcry which I could show to Anthony, but actually the response was pretty mixed. For every fan who said we didn't need Hollywood commercialism, there was another who said that a higher profile for the comic could only be a good thing. And then, of course, as is usual in online discussion groups, everything descended into petty bickering, private jokes, and one-upmanship. I scrolled through over a hundred messages and didn't really find anything useful. But before I set off for UPC I logged in as Desdemona, the pseudonym I used when I didn't want to be known as an insider, and posted a question: *Yeah, but how would you guys feel if McKay somehow changed the essence of the character? Even if he pulled in loads of sales?*

Then I left it, threw my iPod into my duffel bag on top of everything else, and dragged it all downstairs.

'You want some help with that?' Jim asked through a mouthful of toast. He was sitting at the kitchen table, leaning his head on one hand and flipping through a book about film history. We'd only achieved third place at the pub quiz the night before, and he was evidently feeling the worse for wear and also in need of extending his knowledge base.

I shifted my big duffel bag back on my shoulder, leaned my portfolio full of drawing boards against the table, and pinched a slice of toast from his plate. 'That's all right, I can handle it, and you look like you've got your work cut out for you there.'

'Third place. It's a travesty.'

'Ugh, so is the amount of Marmite you put on your toast.' I dropped the slice back on his plate, with a semicircular bite taken out of it.

'Make your own toast, then.'

'We would have been second if you'd let the barmaid slip us that answer.'

'I am an honourable man and I resent your suggestion that I should cheat, even in so slight a form.'

'I think she just wanted to help.' I'd spent a good portion of the evening wondering if I should ask her if she was all right. In the end I'd decided it would only embarrass her if she knew I'd seen her crying on the Underground, and besides, she seemed to be fine. My dilemma did make me miss a picture-round question about Norman Lamont, though.

'Oh, how the mighty have fallen,' Jim said, and stuffed the toast I'd bitten into his mouth. 'All that for your new office?'

'My home away from home. I can't wait until this is all over.'

'Like I said – a duel. Guns at dawn will sort that McKay out. What's he like, anyway?'

'He's an arsehole, and he's not changing the romance.' I picked up my portfolio.

'Sure you don't want me to help? I don't need to start work till noon.'

'No, I'm fine; you do your studying. Later.'

I clumped up the road to the tube station, manoeuvred my bag and portfolio on to the train, and collapsed gratefully into a seat. It was actually very heavy. I should have got Jim to help me. But I hated to be a helpless female and besides, I—

I didn't want Jim to meet Dan.

If they met, Jim would see that Dan was attractive. He might even see that I was attracted to him, though I didn't want to be, and that was embarrassing. And then he might ask about it, and I'd have to go into the whole Dan asking me out on a date malarkey. Even though I'd kept our vow and not gone on the date, it complicated things and Jim would keep on asking me if I was managing not to date Dan, and he'd tell Digger, and then I'd have both of them on my back about it; it was going to be difficult enough sharing an office with Dan without having my friends taking the piss.

It was better to keep everything separate.

With that all figured out, I hauled my stuff off the train at Victoria and up the Vauxhall Bridge Road. I had some difficulty getting everything through the revolving door, and then I had to pause and dig my ID card out of my pocket to show to the receptionist. By the time I'd reached the fourth floor, my arms were aching.

I could smell the coffee as soon as I stepped out of the lift, and it made my mouth water and my body sing with the promise of caffeine. My Pavlovian response was fruitless, though, because the coffee was bound to be decaf.

I paused in the doorway. Dan was sitting at his desk. He'd pushed the buzzing desktop computer to one side and had a laptop open in front of him; he was chewing on a pencil and staring at the screen. He'd abandoned his business suit and was wearing jeans and a sweatshirt, and his hair looked as if he'd spent quite a bit of time running his hands through it.

Dan registered my presence, looked up, and jumped out of his chair. 'Morning,' he said and took my duffel bag off my shoulder without asking permission. He took my portfolio, too, before I could protest and brought them both over to the drawing board and what, I assumed, was now officially designated my half of the room. 'What have you got in here, bricks?' he asked.

'Boulders. I can carry my own stuff.' He didn't give me it back so I followed him to my end of the room. There was a neat stack of paper on my drawing board; I read the front page.

'You've rewritten the script already?'

'Yup. Spent most of the night doing it. Look underneath.'

Underneath was a DVD of *Ninety-Eight Point Six*. 'Emotional and uplifting' said the review on the front, next to a photo of an actor and actress laughing.

'In case you want to learn more about the genre,' Dan told me.

I don't, I was about to say, then thought better of it, not wanting to start another war. I shrugged and put the DVD on a corner of my drawing board, where it wouldn't get in the way.

'Want some coffee?'

'Only if it's this.' I pulled out a bag of dark roasted Ecuadorian.

'That's right. My coffee is an affront to taste.' He went back to his desk and sat down. I noticed he was wearing battered trainers. The whole casual look suited him. Pity he was the enemy.

First things first. I set up my own coffee-maker on the cardboard box next to Dan's. Then I began unpacking my bag. Boxes of art supplies, a stack of drawing boards and paper, a squashy cushion for my chair. Sketches, an action figure of Girl from Mars, a plastic cactus, my digital camera, chocolate bars, Horlicks, two Simpsons mugs, a box of tissues, iPod and earphones, a crocheted blanket made by Jim's mum, a stack of architectural magazines. I had retrieved a blob of Blu-Tack and was climbing on to the drawing board to stick some sketches up on the wall when I realised Dan was watching me.

'Like to settle in, do you?' He sounded amused.

'I'm very particular about my work environment.'

'It looks like you're marking your territory.'

'Don't you?'

He shrugged. 'I can work anywhere. All I need is a laptop or a pen and paper.' He nodded at the DVD on the side of the drawing board. 'I wrote the second half of that screenplay riding a bus around Philly because I couldn't stand to be in our apartment.'

Our? Despite myself, I wanted to ask him. Instead, I climbed back down, stowed the rest of the Blu-Tack on the side of the board, and picked up the script. As I settled on to my now-cushioned chair to read, I heard him begin to type again.

He stopped, though, as soon as I turned the last page, so I could tell he'd been keeping track of my reading. 'Is it a comics script now?' he asked.

I neatened the pages and turned them over so that the

title page was on top again. 'It's better,' I said grudgingly, and then relaxed and conceded, 'Much better. I can draw this one.'

'Good.'

His smile was so wide and he was so pleased with himself that I had to add, 'You've kept Jackson in there, though. Girl from Mars is still flirting with him.'

'I told you, you know about comics but I know about stories. Trust me, Fil.'

I grunted. I wouldn't admit it, but I could do more than draw this script. I could make it come alive. The gloominess at the beginning, the nearly film noir splash, to match the caves later on; I could use a bit of my Jayson tribute. The bright sterile contrast of Jackson's lab. The hints of a writhing underground monster, that might, it struck me in this reading, have something to do with Girl's own psyche. The romance thing still sucked, but I could maybe do enough so that the issue wasn't a total disaster.

I pulled a sheet of paper off my stash and began sketching rapidly. The caves were alternatively vast and claustrophobic . . . lots of shadow and dramatic lighting from the torches . . . and Girl and Jackson's silhouettes making jagged lines up the walls . . . I thumbed through the script to find exactly how tall Dan had described Jackson as being, because I was sure he'd specified down to the last quarter inch, but I couldn't find it. It had been on page six, on his first appearance. Now it was gone. And not just the height, but all of it, including the dimple in the chin.

'You cut your description of Jackson,' I said, and Dan had clearly gone back to his own little world of work because he looked up, blinked, and shook his head to clear it. I recognised the action as one I did sometimes, too.

'Oh. Yeah, I took it out. I thought it would be better, more authentic, if you created what he looked like. I can describe what I think is a handsome man, but he's going to be more appealing if you give us your version of a handsome man. It's a visual, and you're in charge of the visuals, right?'

I thought of my plan to give Jackson an enormous chin. 'Right. Um – thanks.'

'No problem. Your coffee's been ready for ages.'

'Oh, yeah.' I got up and poured myself a mug. I had a nose at Dan's desk as I did. He had his laptop, a notebook and a pen, and his mug of coffee. That was it. He was making notes in his notebook, in bold incomprehensible handwriting.

'Is that episode two you're working on?'

'Uh huh.' He kept writing. I tried to read it, but upside down and from a distance, it was no use.

'They're not kissing or anything, are they?' I asked.

'You'll find out everything when you read it.'

I went back to my drawing board and got some fresh paper for the preliminary sketches of Jackson Silver. I held my pencil poised over the page as I tried to figure out where to begin.

A handsome man of my own imagination. Someone who would suit Girl from Mars. He'd be athletic, but not too brawny. As a scientist, he'd look intelligent but he wouldn't need the clichés of glasses or a lab coat. His hair would be dark, and his eyes, in close-up, would—

I stared at the sketch I'd produced. It was Dan.

No, no. I grabbed a rubber and erased half the face. I'd make his jaw wider, his mouth sterner, and get rid of that Superman lock of hair. There.

It still looked like Dan, with a lantern jaw and a stern mouth.

I crumpled up the paper, then tore it in two for safe measure, and threw both the wads into the bin. A fresh sheet of paper, a new approach. Think Cary Grant. Think Brad Pitt. Think Matt Damon. Think – oh God, I wished I spent more time looking at gossip magazines.

Okay, I could do this. I watched enough movies and telly with Jim. I needed a man with the build of Apollo from *Battlestar Galactica*, except maybe taller. The intelligence and drive of Fox Mulder from *The X-Files*. The gravitas of Jean-Luc Picard from *Star Trek*, but the swagger of Han Solo from *Star Wars*. The mouth of Daniel Craig's James Bond; the hair of Luke Skywalker. No, that was silly, nobody had Luke Skywalker hair any more. The hair of . . . oh dear God.

I'd drawn someone with the swagger of Luke Skywalker, the gravitas of James Bond and the hair of Jean-Luc Picard.

More paper in the bin. 'What kind of a stupid name is Jackson Silver, anyway?' I grumbled.

Dan looked up from his notebook. 'What's that you're complaining about, Philomena Desdemona Brown?'

'At least my name has the virtue of referring to a real person.' I drew a line, rejected it, started again with a foot. A bare foot. I'd never seen Dan's foot, so I couldn't possibly make it like his. It was a very male foot, well formed and strong, with the second toe slightly longer than the big toe. A small dusting of dark hair. And of course that was what Dan's foot looked like, who the hell was I kidding?

'Agh!'

'Do you need a little help with—'

'No!' I crumpled up the foot sketch and threw it away before Dan could see his own foot on the page.

'Then if you don't mind, Fil, I'm trying to do some work here.'

He began typing. I stared at the empty page, where I was supposed to create a man for my heroine to fall in love with. My perfect man.

How on earth was I going to do this?

Ghosts

'What are you going to do, Fil? Fil!'

I blinked and focused my eyes. Digger was leaning towards me, his palm full of dice. As I was sitting on the floor and he was on the couch, he loomed even more than usual.

'What?' I asked.

'You've got a huge bad-ass demon coming towards you with a flaming sword in his hand, what are you going to do?'

'Oh. I, uh. Where did he come from?'

'Hell,' Jim told me. 'You've conjured him up by mistake. Remember? I'll take a swipe with my broadsword, though I don't expect it will make any difference, knowing our sadistic Dungeon Master.'

Digger tossed him a twenty-sided die, and looked at me expectantly. I checked my character notes to see what kind of spells I could use against a bad-ass demon, but all I seemed to have were various things to make me invisible.

I dropped my head into my hands. 'I'm sorry, Digger, I'm too brain-dead for gaming tonight.'

'Been battling Hollywood script demons at work all day, eh?' Digger put down the dice and stroked his beard sympathetically.

'Something like that.' Actually, the script wasn't the problem. I'd been using office hours to work on the splash and the first five pages, before Girl from Mars met Jackson Silver, and all of that was going fine. Objectively, it wasn't even so bad sharing an office with Dan, because he got on with his writing and left me alone. The problem was all the extra hours I was putting in at home, trying to draw the hero. I'd quickly decided that I couldn't risk doing the sketches at UPC, because what if Dan saw that I kept on drawing him by mistake? So I came home from a full day of work and then put in five or six more hours upstairs in the studio, except when Jim and Digger dragged me out for the quiz or for gaming.

And then there was the commute. And then, of course, my dreams. Because spending hours in the company of someone I didn't want to be attracted to was a task of repression so great that apparently all my desire had to burst out of its bonds during the night as I slept.

And whoo-boy, was it bursting its bonds. I was having sexy dreams of all descriptions, every one of them featuring Daniel McKay. He'd even appeared in one of my standard walking-down-the-street-and-suddenly-realising-I'm-in-my-underwear dreams, by striding on to the street in his own underwear and, strangely, offering me ice cream.

'I haven't been sleeping much,' I said to Digger and Jim. 'And I've been drinking too much coffee.'

Walking to the coffee machine meant passing close to his desk and I breathed in his scent, saw the way his hair curled on the back of his neck, and watched his long fingers flying over the keyboard. I tried not to do it. But I'd always had a weakness for coffee.

'All right, we can save the demon till later,' Digger said, and put his dice back into their tiny leather pouch. For a big guy, he had surprisingly nimble fingers. Whenever we needed a fuse changed or the curtains repaired or something like that, Digger always volunteered. Jim was good at abstract concepts, I was good at two-dimensional visuals, and Digger was good at manipulating things. It was sort of nice, how we all fitted together into a whole.

'What about my broadsword attack?' Jim asked.

'You missed.'

'I rolled a nineteen!'

'I know. You missed.'

'Damn! That's one evil demon. Hold on, Fil, I just remembered I've got something for you.' Jim disappeared upstairs.

'Jim says you've been talking in your sleep,' Digger said, once it was clear that Jim was out of earshot.

'Really? Does he – did he say what I said?'

'Muttering and stuff, I guess. He hears it through the walls.'

For a moment I considered telling Digger why I was talking in my sleep. He might find it funny, and he was discreet enough not to mention it to Jim if I asked him not to. For example, he never gave away what Jim and I were giving each other for our birthdays, even though I usually begged him to tell me what Jim had bought me for weeks beforehand. One time he'd hidden a life-sized Chewbacca cut-out in his flat for two and a half months, after I'd dragged it home from a ComicsCon for Jim. Apparently he had to shove it under the bed every time Jim came around, and once, when Jim had turned up unexpectedly, he'd thrown a sheet over Chewie and pretended it was an ironing board.

But I balked. Talking about my attraction to Dan out loud would somehow make it real, and if it got any more real, it would make my life even more hell. It was just safer to keep it to myself.

'It must be the caffeine,' I said, folding my character notes in halves and then quarters.

Digger rearranged his dice pouches, pencils and rule books. 'He worries about you.'

'Well, he doesn't need to.'

'He's not used to you being gone all day, working in an office.'

'Tell me about it, neither am I.'

'We also thought maybe – you know, Stevo. You probably miss him most.'

Digger and Jim had been talking about me. The idea touched me, but it also made me worry a little about what they'd said. 'Well, you know, as long as I keep busy I'm okay. Want a coffee?'

'In a minute.' Digger yawned.

'You quit that game without too much of a fight,' I said. Digger's *Dungeons and Dragons* stamina was legendary, transcending the need for sleep, fresh air and even, in certain cases, food. One time he'd poured a glass of iced water down Jim's back because Jim had dozed off during the third day of a campaign to reclaim the lost Amulet of Malarakhad.

'Ah, well, I'm tired too. I've been busy. Spent today cleaning cages at the CPL.'

'CPL?'

'Cat Protection League. They've got a whole room full

of strays waiting to be adopted. I go down there a couple of times a month when I need a change. I saw Jim's mum there today, getting another kitten.'

'Don't tell Jim.'

'I know.'

I sighed. 'I know she has too many cats, and she worries about Jim a lot, but there are worse parents out there, you know?'

Digger looked at me with a bit of a frown. 'Do you think—' he began, but then Jim came back down the stairs with his typical tread, hitting every second step harder. Digger and I immediately acted casual.

Jim handed me a sheaf of paper, printouts from his computer. 'I did an internet search on Demon McKay,' he said. 'Know your enemy, that's what I always say.'

Panic leapt in me. Had he seen photos? Had I been calling out Dan's name in my sleep?

'Thanks,' I said, but Jim didn't say anything else, just went to tidy up his character sheets, so I risked the conclusion that he didn't yet know the truth. I flicked through the paper. There were several articles, without, I noticed with relief, any photographs.

'So,' Jim said to Digger, 'you want to explain to me how we're supposed to defeat this demon if it's immune to a good old sharp bit of metal?'

'That's for me to know and you to find out,' Digger replied with the infinite smugness of the Dungeon Master.

I knew they could comfortably discuss this for the next hour at least, so I curled up in my girly chair and turned to the top article, which was dated last summer:

CURING SADNESS WITH ROMANCE:
DANIEL MCKAY

Daniel McKay, writer and director of box-office hits Mixing Desk *and* Ninety-Eight Point Six, *talks with E!ntertainment.com about the tragic inspiration for his romantic films.*

If you'd asked Daniel McKay as a kid what he wanted to be when he grew up, he wouldn't have chosen the career he has now. 'I wanted to be a fireman,' says the writer/director, a sparkle of humour in his blue eyes. 'Either that or a war journalist.'

But for McKay, fate had different ideas, and the biggest one was named Elizabeth Soucy.

'Elizabeth and I were childhood sweethearts,' McKay recounts. 'Our families were close and we'd always planned to marry, from the time we were about five. When we grew up a little, we decided to wait until we'd both finished college.'

Then fate intervened.

Elizabeth contracted cancer, a rare and fast-growing form. Although doctors attempted aggressive treatment, nothing seemed to work. McKay, aware that they might not have long together, cut short his education and the couple married.

I lowered the papers and stared at the chintz of my chair. Dan was *married*? I pictured his hands, which I'd drawn the first time I'd met him. He didn't wear a wedding ring.

'But you have to be able to kill it,' Jim was insisting. 'Demons are immortal, aren't they?'

'Nothing's immortal, there's always a way to defeat these things, you're just being deliberately obtuse.'

'Ah, well, it depends what you mean by "deliberately" –'

Married to his childhood sweetheart: the phrase conjured up picket fences, apple-cheeked innocence, a sunny summer wedding with a white dress and confetti. I could picture it easily, with Dan in a dark suit, smiling. It made my heart ache a little.

'It wasn't an easy time, after the wedding,' McKay says. 'Elizabeth was very ill, but she was fighting hard. I spent a lot of time at the hospital with her. I'd been fiddling around with writing screenplays for a friend of mine who was starting up his own production company, and I began writing *Ninety-Eight Point Six* while I was in the hospital, mostly for something to do to keep my brain occupied. I was about halfway through it when Lizzy died.'

Ah. Thus the lack of a wedding ring. I gnawed on my thumb.

Here was a different world, a different perspective. Poor, tragic, newlywed Elizabeth. Her grieving family around her hospital bed.

And Daniel McKay had married a woman who was about to die. I tried to put this together with him cheerful in the Underground, angry in the office, confident in the press conference.

It didn't fit, not easily. But I didn't know any other – what was the word? widowers? – to compare Dan with. Jim's mum was a widow, with her cats and her plastic coverings on the floor to save the carpet when you walked in. She'd always acted, since I'd known her, as if there was something missing in her life, something she needed Jim to fill. Dan didn't act like that.

But maybe I just didn't understand human nature enough.

I watched Jim and Digger talking, both totally absorbed in their conversation about the game. They acted consistently. I could predict what they would do in any situation, how Jim used his hands to express himself, how Digger absent-mindedly stroked his beard. They always acted the same way. Maybe other people were just more confusing.

I went back to the article.

McKay's screenplay languished while he picked up the pieces of his life, but eventually, when he had begun doing some directing for his friend's independent film company Pegasus, he took up the script again, finished it, and pitched it as Pegasus's new project.

It's not difficult to see where McKay got the idea: *Ninety-Eight Point Six* is the story of a beautiful young woman, Emily (played by a then little-known Isabelle Axenby), on the cusp of success and happiness, who contracts a quick-growing disease, and decides to do the hundred things she's always wanted to do in the short time before she dies. The love interest (played by Edward Harringdon) is a physician who is racing against time to find a cure for Emily's disease.

'It's the first film I did, and it's close to my heart. We had hardly any budget, but we did the best we could on our resources and I couldn't believe it when it won an indie film award and ended up with nationwide distribution.'

His next film, *Mixing Desk*, was produced under the aegis of a mainstream studio, with a Hollywood-sized budget, but it also owes something to his tragic past. The story of a rock DJ who is haunted by the ghost of his classical music-loving wife, it's funny despite its sad premise, and McKay admits it's because 'At that time I felt that Lizzy was watching over me a lot. I used to talk to her, like Micky does in the film.'

What did she say to you?

'Most of the time she told me to pull my finger out and get to work!' McKay laughs. 'And to stop listening to such rubbish music.'

So what's next for Daniel McKay, after two big box-office hits?

'Well, I've decided war journalism isn't for me. My next film, *Blue-Eyed Daughter*, is out in September.'

And what about that fireman job? Rescuing people from burning buildings?

'I haven't ruled that out yet.'

I turned over the page. Jim had printed out a *Time Out* film review for Daniel's latest film, *Blue-Eyed Daughter*. My brain still reeling from the magazine article, I skimmed though it. It wasn't a good review; two sentences caught my eye:

McKay goes over familiar ground in his third film: a man rescues a woman from tragedy, against the odds. It's a potent fantasy, but it falls flat in this tame comedy, which tanked in its native USA.

Rescue fantasies. Dan's films were all about saving his wife.

I put down the papers.

'You're just drunk on power; admit it, you love being Dungeon Master because it means you get to make up the rules.'

'And what's wrong with that?' Digger asked mildly. 'That's the point of making up your own world. Don't tell me you don't like science fiction for the same reasons.'

'Yeah, but *invincible demons*, Digger –'

I stood up and reached for my coat, which was tossed over the back of my chair. My friends looked at me.

'What are you doing?' Jim asked.

'I've got to do some work at UPC.'

'It's a quarter to one in the morning.'

'I've got to check out something.'

'I'll come with you.' He stood up.

'No, no, I'll be fine, I'll take a cab.' I waved at him and Digger, swung out the door before they could follow me, and jogged to the corner of the street. Fortunately, there was a free cab nearby, and doubly fortunately, I found a twenty-pound note crumpled in my jacket pocket.

It was only when I was well on my way that I realised I had no idea why I was going to UPC. Dan wouldn't be there. Nobody would be there. Not even the shadow of his wife.

But I seemed to remember, that afternoon before I'd left, that there had been a printout on his desk, and the more I thought about it, the more I convinced myself that it was the draft of the script for his second episode of *The TIME Temptation*. If it were there, it would tell me if Dan was writing his same rescue fantasies all over again, with Girl from Mars in the place of his wife.

It made sense. Girl was doomed – not to death, because she was immune to most Earth diseases and because her metabolism effectively made her age about a hundred times more slowly than humans, but because she was a hopeless exile, isolated from her family and friends and home. That was why, in Dan's script, she was turning to Jackson Silver. He was going to rescue her.

The cab dropped me off outside UPC and I swiped my new ID card at the entrance. While it was extremely cool to be able to get out-of-hours entry to the centre of the comics universe, I wasn't really in the mood to appreciate it. I headed straight for the fourth floor. Everything was much darker and quieter than usual.

I hit a switch when I came out of the lift, which turned on a single fluorescent tube. It flickered as I went to our office and opened the door. With the dim light from the hallway, I negotiated the room and found my desktop lamp. Blaring lights, somehow, seemed inappropriate at this time, for this task.

As soon as I got the lamp on I saw that Dan's laptop was gone. The desk was completely empty, except for the desktop computer he'd shoved to one side. I hovered over it for a moment as if I could summon the script by will, and then I took the plunge and opened the top desk drawer.

Inside there was a tin box of strong mints, and Dan's notebook.

From what I'd seen, he wrote out his scripts in longhand before he typed them, or at least took extensive notes. I looked around the empty room, then sat in his chair and opened the book.

I couldn't read it at first. The visual impact was too great. He wrote with thick black pens, I'd seen him doing it. Bold black strokes on white paper, mostly capital letters but some, more fluid, sentences in script. He pressed down hard enough to dent the paper.

Holding his handwriting, I held the reality of Daniel McKay that I hadn't quite grasped before. This was a person with a past, with a whole life, with people he loved and sorrows and joys that I had no idea about.

In the close circle of light, it felt as if I were touching him.

It took me a little while before I could turn the page, and then I realised I was looking at a draft version of the script I'd already seen. I flipped forward, the written-on pages crackling, until I reached a page where Dan had printed EPISODE 2: DEEPER across the top:

PAGE ONE
SPLASH
They're deep in the caves. Dark, gloomy shadows, against which Jackson's torch and GfM's skin glow. The space around them is vast, with distant stalactites above. There are rats here, but they aren't what's really frightening. Hmmm, how much more will Fil let me get away with describing?

I smiled when I saw my name. It was all lines and angles in his handwriting. That was probably how he saw me: prickly, difficult, harsh.

A faint noise came from behind me, out in the corridor. It could have been the lift door opening; it could have been a rat. No, hold on, there weren't rats in the UPC building, were there? I was imagining Dan's cave.

A footstep.

I dropped the notebook back in Dan's desk and shut

the door with my knee on my way to my drawing board and my wooden box of art supplies. I grabbed an X-Acto knife and pulled off its plastic sheath.

The footsteps, stealthy and unhurried, approached the door. I saw a flickering shadow cast on the linoleum floor of the corridor. It was tall, and broad-shouldered, and—

Dan poked his head round the office door. 'Morning,' he said cheerily. 'What's with the little knife?'

'I didn't know who you were,' I explained. I put down the X-Acto.

'You were going to attack me with that? Very Girl from Mars.'

'Well, it's dark.'

He turned on the overhead light, and I blinked with its brightness. 'Not any more. What are you doing here, anyway?'

'I, uh . . . needed this.' I picked up a sketchbook at random from my stack. 'What about you?'

'I couldn't sleep.' He pulled out his chair and sat in it. I hoped he wouldn't notice it was warm from my backside.

'Why not?'

'Ghosts.' He laughed. 'Ghosts and the long procession of every mistake I've ever made.'

He had sadness etched into the corners of his eyes and his mouth. As soon as I saw it I knew the sadness had always been there, but it had taken his handwriting and the article about his wife to make me see it.

'Anyway,' he continued, 'I thought I'd catch up on my reading, since you told me I had so much to do. I figured maybe there were some *Girl from Mars* comics here to help me expand my knowledge base.' He glanced around the room. 'You got any lying around?'

'A few. But if you want to read, I've got something to show you. Come here.'

He got up and obediently followed me down the flickering, shadowy corridor to the archives. 'Do you know what's in here?' I asked, pointing at the door.

'No.'

'Really? Nobody's shown you?'

'No. What is it?'

'This is going to knock your socks off.' I couldn't help a smile and a little skip of anticipation as I opened the door, turned on the light, and led Dan through the stacks of cases to the corner where more than half a century of *Girl from Mars* lived.

'Every issue,' I said, my voice hushed, looking over the neatly numbered boxes. 'Right from the beginning, up to last month.'

'You're kidding,' Dan said, and his voice was nearly impressed enough even for me. 'Even the first one? The ones my grandfather drew?'

'Your grandfather was the one who collected them, at least at the beginning.'

He stood, and though he was tall he was dwarfed by the stacks of comics. I pushed over a stepladder for him and he reached right up to the top, to the box containing Issue 1 in its plastic bag. He removed it with gentle hands.

'Where can I read it?' he asked me.

'There's a table. You can't take them out of this room.'

He brought the box over to the table, and took all the issues out and spread them over the table. 'Wow,' he said. He touched the covers through their plastic: first Girl from Mars in her fifties uniform, then her spaceship, then the soaring title lettering. I stood behind him, but he seemed oblivious of everything except the comics.

He'd said ghosts. Maybe one of them was of his grandfather. In this shuttered room, stacked with shadows and history, they were face to face.

I couldn't help it. The line of his shoulders and neck, the expression on his face, even the way his hair fell forward – they were all of a piece with his handwriting, with the sudden perception I'd had of him as a real person, someone with so many private thoughts and moments. I reached out and I put my hand on his shoulder.

'*Girl from Mars* is the best escape I know,' I said quietly.

He looked away from the comics to meet my eyes, and I knew this was the first time I'd read his feelings, although he'd read mine before.

'I've got a good collection myself,' I told him, 'especially from the eighties onwards. I'll bring some of it in for you tomorrow, if you like. That way you can take them home and read them.'

He raised an eyebrow. 'Are you sure you want them in the hands of an infidel?'

'Sure. Though I'll have to sue you for every penny you've got if you put a coffee ring on them.'

Dan nodded. 'Thanks,' he said, and then he was looking at Issue 1 again and all the joking in his face was replaced by a sort of pensive wonder.

And I wasn't wanted here. This was between Daniel McKay and his ghosts. I slipped quietly out of the archives, down in the lift and out on to the Vauxhall Bridge Road, where I flagged down a cab.

The lights were still on at my house, and as soon as I

let myself in, Jim jumped up from the couch, turning off the TV. 'What's up?' he said. 'Where have you been? You didn't take your phone with you.'

'I was at UPC, like I told you,' I said, a bit taken aback at his concern. 'Where's Digger?'

'He was tired, I told him to go home. Why did you have to go in to UPC? Were you meeting someone?'

'I needed to see Da—' Even as I stopped myself, I knew that although I really hadn't thought there was any chance of bumping into him there at such a late hour, checking the script, or even snooping in his notebook, wasn't what I really wanted. I'd read about Daniel McKay's tragic past, and I wanted to see him to find out if it was true. And it was.

'– Some drawings,' I amended. I hung up my coat on the banister.

'Where are they?'

'Where are what?'

'The drawings you needed.'

'Oh.' I put my empty hands in the pockets of my jeans. 'I meant, I needed to look at some drawings before I went to sleep. Let my subconscious brain work on them. You know.'

Jim glared at me. 'You shouldn't be whizzing around London at this hour by yourself.'

'Since when are you Mr Protective? You've never worried about me whizzing around London before.'

'I'm usually with you. It's only since you—' He stopped himself. He was still holding the television remote; he put it down and tucked his hair behind his ear. 'Anyway, what did you think of those articles I printed out? Because I think I've figured out what's going on here with McKay.'

'Have you?' I'd been about to go upstairs to bed, but I halted with my foot on the step.

'Isn't it obvious? McKay has worn out his welcome in Hollywood because he keeps on telling the same kind of stories, and now he's coming to tell exactly the same story with *Girl from Mars*. He doesn't care if it's right for the comic, all he cares about is writing his happy romances so he can pretend his wife never died.'

'I think you're probably right,' I said.

Jim frowned. 'Aren't you angry about this? I'd be furious.'

'I'm really tired, actually. I'll see you in the morning, Jim.'

I climbed a few steps and something made me look back down. Jim stood near the bottom, all by himself.

I turned around. 'Think I'll watch TV for a little while to relax my brain. What's on?'

'Not much. Want to watch a film?'

We went into the living room together and I started looking through the pile of DVDs near the telly, which was where we kept the ones we hadn't seen yet. About a quarter of the way from the top I saw it: *Ninety-Eight Point Six*.

'How about this one?' I asked, pulling it out.

Jim raised his eyebrows. 'I noticed that there. Isn't it one of McKay's?'

I swallowed. This would be the time to tell Jim what I'd learned about Dan tonight, that undertone of loneliness and sadness that I hadn't seen before under his smile. How I still didn't like what he was doing to *Girl from Mars*, but how I couldn't dislike *him* any more.

But I didn't know how to start, or how to explain it without also explaining how I'd met Dan before I knew who he was, and if I did that, it would look as if I were hiding something.

'Like you said, know your enemy.' I put it into the player and sat down in my chair. Jim took his place on the couch.

We sat, side by side. I remembered doing this with him a million times, in this room, in other rooms, on chairs and on the floor, on my single bed at uni, and on my single bed at my parents' house. Watching or playing or reading, with no need for conversation.

This was fine. We didn't need to talk; we were friends. It was enough to be sitting here. And I had a lot to think about.

Because the movie was exactly what the article had said it was. It was a love story between a man and a woman who was doomed, but it was funny and it was warm and I could hear Dan's voice in the lines.

The credits rolled and I kept looking straight ahead so that Jim wouldn't see the tears in my eyes.

He snorted.

'It's not that bad, actually,' I said, blinking hard.

'Not enough explosions for my taste,' he said, and then his voice quietened a bit. 'Did you like all that stuff, Fil?'

'What do you mean, the movie?'

'I mean the lovey stuff. All the kissing and holding hands and happy ever after things.'

I shrugged. 'Dunno,' I said, but the insistent longing in my chest told me I was lying. 'Yeah, I guess. I mean, yeah, it would be nice, to have this great romance or whatever.'

'I don't think it's really like that.'

My eyes were finally clear enough for me to glance at him, but now he was watching the last credits and all I could see was his silhouette. The light from the telly made him look different, or made me see him differently; it made me notice his straight nose, well-made mouth, high cheekbones. See how handsome he was.

'What do you mean?' I asked.

'It's not showy and flashy and all charm and wit. That's the problem with these films. They make love seem all sweet and perfect, but I think it's more like this, like living together and just getting on with it. Don't you think?'

Dan's film had given me the exact opposite impression: that love was something deep, rare and precious, special and different, and worth doing anything to keep. Was that just another fantasy? As comforting and dangerous as Digger's *Dungeons and Dragons* world?

But maybe Jim was right. Maybe they both were right. Maybe love was rare and precious *and* just like this. For a split second I imagined leaning over and kissing Jim on the lips, as Emily had kissed Gabe in the film.

I could picture it, watching it from a distance as if Jim and I were phantoms on a television screen. I could almost imagine how it would feel.

I had no idea what would happen afterwards.

'They don't make movies about just getting on with it, I guess.' I stood up. 'I'm going to bed, it's late.'

Jim rubbed his face with his hand. 'Yeah. Yeah, me too.'

We went upstairs together and said goodnight. He turned left at the top, I turned right, and as I took off my trainers and jeans I heard him running water in the bathroom.

In the morning, I woke up late, and the first thing I did was to reach for my sketchbook and a pencil. I sat up in bed and drew Jackson Silver, with no hesitation or problems.

Jackson wasn't real. He was tall and blond and had a bit of a dimple in his chin and he didn't look like Daniel McKay at all, because Daniel McKay wasn't a cartoon character. Not any more.

And this complicated everything.

Them's Fightin' Words, Cowboy

With Jackson Silver drawn, my last block was removed. Rainy April slipped into warm May nearly without my noticing, immersed as I was in *Girl from Mars*. I drew in the comics sweatshop, I drew at home, I doodled on the Underground, and the times I couldn't draw, like when I ate or slept or showered, were like pauses between breaths. There was something about the caves that got to me. Maybe it was the hint in Dan's notebook that there were very frightening things in there, and my inkling that they might represent something important to Girl from Mars, possibly the hopes and desires she'd been keeping underground for so long.

Dan spent a lot of time in the archives, so that distraction was gone, and of course Jim and Digger were used to how I worked by now and they wouldn't be offended when I seemed not to hear anything they said to me. On Sunday I took an hour off, because it was a sunny day and Jim and Digger wanted to take The Baz for a walk in the park. As The Baz's normal response to sunshine was to sit absolutely still to absorb as much of it as possible, we didn't get very far, but Jim had a great time tugging on the lead and trying to bribe the iguana to move with carrots and nice fresh bits of foliage pinched from the flower beds, while Digger ate an ice cream and I an ice lolly while watching sitting cross-legged from the grass.

But my mind wasn't on the sunshine and the park and the lizard and my friends; it was with Girl from Mars and Jackson Silver. I tossed the stick of my ice lolly into a nearby bin and said, 'I'm going to UPC just to get a few things down.'

Jim looked up from The Baz, his hair blowing across his face in the breeze. 'Already?'

'I won't be long. I've got an idea I don't want to lose.' I headed for the Underground.

UPC was empty on a Sunday, of course. I brewed some coffee, turned my mobile off, and got to work. The caves had chasms in their floors, and every niche was cloaked in darkness. So many unnamed things lurked just beyond sight. Some of the panels were from their point of view, seen through cracks, through shadow.

The next thing I knew an alarm was going off beside my ear. I sat upright, my hand clapped to my head, and my aching neck and back told me I'd fallen asleep over my drawing board. The alarm was coming from a chunky watch lying next to where my head had rested. I picked it up; there was a takeaway cup from O Solo Mio next to it, and a Post-it note saying, in Dan's all-caps handwriting: HEY, SLEEPYHEAD, ED. MEETING 10.30 A.M.

I checked the watch. Twenty past ten. On Sunday night? No, I amended, seeing the light filtering through the grimy windows, on Monday morning. I must have worked through the night and dozed off.

The coffee was still warm, though not hot. An Americano, black, with two shots. I slipped Dan's watch in my pocket and made my way down to the conference room.

'Nice of you to visit us, Brown,' Anthony said with his usual charm, from his place by the door. I nodded at him and slipped into the room. There were still two empty seats, right at the front, and I figured hey, with the sweatshop and the press release and everything, all of UPC probably thought I was a total suck-up anyway, so I might as well take the seat and act like one. Dan was in the middle, chatting with Bradley who did my lettering and someone who I thought was an assistant editor on *Lacey*. He looked at me briefly and smiled.

Oh, God, my hair was probably sticking straight up on the side that had been pressed to the drawing board and my cheek was probably covered with ink. I tugged at my hair and rubbed at my cheek, and then remembered to mouth 'thank you' for the coffee, but by that time he was talking to Bradley again.

Anthony came in and clapped his hands for attention. 'Right, now that all of you bug— oh, hello, Ng, decided to join us I see; you're even later than your sidekick Brown for once.'

Stevo ducked into the room muttering, 'Sorry.'

'Seat at the front, bloody nice to see your sunshiny face. Now first order of the day is to introduce our new writer on *Girl from Mars*, Daniel McKay, though you'd have to be living on Mars not to have heard of him.'

Stevo slipped into the seat beside mine as everyone else's attention was on Dan. I didn't know where to look, or what to say to Stevo even if he did want to talk to me, so I stared at the floor and concentrated hard on what

Anthony was saying. I don't think I had ever learned so much about Lacey sales figures, or what the next cover of *Combat* was going to be.

And for the first time I actually paid attention to the sales information about *Girl from Mars*. I didn't have to pretend to be fascinated, because I immediately boggled at Anthony in shock.

It was that bad? Really?

'So you can see it's about buggering time we got some interest in our so-called lead title,' Anthony continued, 'and if any of you have any complaints that McKay and Brown have been given their own office, you can sodding well come to me and I'll start cracking the whip over your sorry arses, as well. There's a lot of pressure on these two and I don't think anybody in their right mind would be envious.'

He paused bulldoggishly, waiting for anybody to raise their voice in complaint. You could have heard a pin drop.

'Fine. Speaking of which, there's ComicsCon in six weeks and you're going to be there, McKay and Brown, to push this title like a dealer selling heroin. I'm rushing through the production so that the first instalment is out the week after the Con. I've booked you for a panel discussion. I want every comics fan in this country to be slavering into their little clip-on tie to get hold of Episode One.'

'No problem,' said Dan easily.

'Yes, Chief,' I said.

'Good. Now get out of my face, you lot, and get to work.'

Stevo stood up, and I stood up too, and because everyone around us was moving and shuffling and trying to get to the door, we found ourselves stuck together. He was only an inch or two taller than me and everything about him was the same, his neat hair and his smooth-shaven face, except that he was wearing cologne and he didn't smile.

'Sorry,' I said, not quite sure why.

'Guess you found out what the new initiative was, huh?' he said.

'Yeah.'

We stood there for a moment, not able to move. I searched for something to say. 'Uh, how's Brian?'

'He's fine,' he said, sighing slightly. Someone brushed past us and we both had to lean backwards into our chairs.

I looked down at my now-cold coffee, remembering how normally Stevo and I would be on our way to O Solo Mio together. Before he'd decided to dump me and my friends.

'There's no use asking you how Jim and Digger are, I suppose,' he said.

'What's that supposed to mean?'

'I can see you're working.' He pointed to my ink-stained hands. 'You probably haven't seen them in days.'

'That's not true. I saw them today. I mean, yesterday.'

'That's good.' He had that same tone of irony that he'd had when he'd said Brian was fine. Like he meant something completely different, like he was trying to make a comment about me and my life, after he'd decided not to be part of it any more.

'I hate these meetings,' he said.

'Better run on home to your boyfriend, then,' I said, and saw a sudden path clear to the door. I hurried through it.

I paused to dump my coffee down the sink in the

Ladies', watching it swirl down the drain like so many afternoons with Stevo. Then I went straight to the sweatshop and tidied up the drawings that had been displaced by my sleeping head. There were lots of them. In fact, I only had one page to go. Even with the delay while I'd wrestled with Jackson Silver, it had to be one of the quickest comics I'd ever drawn. I looked over the work I'd done last night, wishing I could show it to Stevo. Digger and Jim were always supportive and enthusiastic about my art, but Stevo had been the one who really knew what I was trying to do, who understood how hard I'd had to work. Now, I had nobody like that.

Within a few minutes, Dan came in. He made the room seem fuller, more important.

'Glad you woke up in time,' he said cheerily, swinging into his seat.

'Oh. Yeah, thanks for the alarm.' I dug his watch out of my pocket and handed it back to him. As I did so, I realised I'd forgotten to check my hair or my face in the mirror when I'd been in the loo.

'I can see why everyone calls those meetings the Circle of Hell,' he said, strapping the watch back on his wrist. It suited him; it was big and masculine. If I put it on my wrist it would fall right back off again, over my hand.

'With Anthony as Satan,' I said.

'Mmm.' He got out his notebook from the desk drawer, and started up his laptop. 'With a flaming whip and everything. Nice of him to mention all the pressure we're under.'

'I didn't know the sales figures were that horrible,' I said, and felt sad. It seemed only a few weeks ago that I'd thought everything in the world was hunky-dory, and my biggest worry was whether I could stay awake for a whole weekend of watching *The X-Files*.

'Well, that's why we're here. Speaking of which, I've never been to a comics convention. What are they like?'

'Different.' It would certainly be different for Dan, who was used to Hollywood and glam film festivals. Next to those, ComicsCon would seem pretty pathetic. 'You'll probably hate it.'

'I'll have to judge for myself.'

'Don't expect luxury. Anthony likes to save as much money as humanly possible.'

Dan glanced around the office. Although it was now decorated, in a fashion, with my sketches and my junk, there was no disguising that it was a gloomy hole.

'Now that's a shock,' he said.

Then he looked at me, and his expression was a bit weird.

I knew it. There must be ink all over my face and I probably looked like the tattooed lady.

'Listen, Fil, are you all right?'

'Uh, fine.' I scrubbed at my face again.

'It was just that I couldn't help noticing you and that guy sitting next to you. There seemed to be some tension there. Tell me to get lost if it's none of my business, but—'

'Oh. Stevo. Yeah, you could say that.'

'Is he an ex?'

'An – oh, you mean an ex-boyfriend?' The appropriate response to this, of course, would be to fling myself on the ground laughing hysterically at the idea of my having exes hanging around everywhere. But I didn't quite feel like it. Instead, strangely, I felt like talking to Dan about it. 'No, he's more of an – an ex-friend.'

'That's difficult if you work together.'

'It's not like that. We didn't have a big argument or anything, it just sort of happened.'

Dan nodded. 'I know what you mean. Things happen, your life changes and you grow apart. It's happened to me, too.'

When his wife died. He would've had friends who couldn't handle his grief, who didn't know what to say. Or married friends who only knew him and Elizabeth as a couple. I couldn't really ask about that, though, because he'd never told me about Elizabeth, and I didn't want him to know that I'd been checking up on him behind his back.

'I hate it,' I told him. 'It's not supposed to happen. We used to be so comfortable together, and now – whoompf. It's gone. It's as if we were never friends, except worse, because I still remember everything.'

'Yeah, it hurts. On the other hand, something like that shows you who your real friends are.'

'That's true,' I said, but I was hearing Stevo's voice: *There's no use asking you how Jim and Digger are, I suppose.*

I picked up my mobile from where I'd flung it on the floor after turning it off. There were four missed calls when I switched it back on.

'Shit, Jim,' I said. He'd called yesterday afternoon, then last night at eleven, then at three a.m., and again while I'd been in the meeting. I hit autodial, but I got his answerphone. I went out to the corridor to leave a message.

'Hey, it's me. I've been at work but I'll be back home in about half an hour.' Hitting the 'end' button, I went back into the office to pick up my keys. Dan was typing.

As I reached for my keyring the latest page I'd done caught my eye. It was the penultimate page. And I knew exactly how the last one would look.

Ten minutes to sketch it out, that was all I needed. I got a fresh sheet of paper and started to draw.

Shadows and darkness and flickers of fading hope. At some point I smelled coffee and I called across to Dan, 'Put on a pot of the hairy stuff, will you?' because I might as well have a cup while I was finishing off this tiny bit, perfecting this panel. I was part way through the next when Dan brought me a mug. I noticed him working beside me as a warmth in the room, a fellow shadow in the story, but then I was back in the caves and this one line wouldn't come right, let's try it again, and again, and that's it. Perfect. That is, it would be if I angled the next panel this way, and let the final one bleed off the page, so –

And then I might as well do the inks, while I was at it. I found a packet of biscuits in a drawer, waved it at Dan, who took one, and then got stuck in with the brush while I was chewing, trying not to drop crumbs on the wet ink.

And then I was done.

I sat up, rubbing the back of my neck to loosen the cricks, and said, 'Hey McKay, guess what?'

But he wasn't there; he must have slipped out without my noticing. To be fair, he could have slipped out any number of times while I'd been drawing and I'd never have noticed. His presence was a constant feeling even if he wasn't in the room. I felt it now, in the open laptop on his desk, the coffee mug, the somehow masculine way his chair had been pushed back.

I grimaced and instead of sharing my triumph, I busied myself clearing biscuit crumbs off the drawing board. The packet was nearly empty, and when I checked, the coffee pot was nearly empty, too, though I had no memory of eating more than one biscuit or drinking more than one mug of coffee.

So where was Dan, anyway? I went to the door and peered down the corridor for him, and then had a look around the archives. I was heading back to the sweatshop, telling myself to stop feeling so crestfallen, that I was still finished even if I couldn't show it to him right away, and that anyway Jim and Digger would be excited for me and they were the ones who counted, when I heard the lift door open and I ran to it.

'I've finished! I finished drawing it!' I cried, and Dan's expression was so delighted and surprised that I was hardly shocked at all when he grabbed me and gave me a big hug.

No, actually that's a lie. I was shocked. My face pressed into the side of his neck, warm and slightly rough and smelling of lemons, and my hands touched the warmth and breadth of his shoulders beneath the cotton T-shirt, and my body, for a moment, moulded against his. I couldn't hug him back, I was so overwhelmed by the reality of being in his arms, and when he let me go I stared at him, with my mouth open.

'That's fantastic,' he said, grinning. 'I've got something for you, too.'

He gave me some A4 paper that he'd been holding in one hand and I hadn't seen as I was too busy being hugged. I read the title page. 'The script for Episode Two.'

'I was printing it out to show to Anthony, but I don't mind showing it to you first. If you let me see your art first.'

'Deal.' We went back to the sweatshop and Dan shut the door behind us. His eyes glinted with mischief.

'What would Anthony think of our clandestine sharing session?' he asked.

Never mind that, what would he think of our clandestine *hugging* session?

'He probably expects it since he's shoved us in together.' Sharing, that is. Not hugging. Stop thinking about the hugging. 'Here you are.' I put the stack of Bristol boards on Dan's desk, and settled into my chair to read.

I looked up, smiling, twenty minutes later. He'd written in monsters, arguments, an underground city and an apparently insane cave dweller named Glypto who, it was hinted, knew a dark secret from Jackson's past. And Girl from Mars and Jackson didn't have a single kiss anywhere.

'It's not ba—' I began, but Dan was poring over my drawings and he was so absorbed that I stopped talking and just watched him.

It seemed a long, quiet time, but it was too short. He lifted his head and met my gaze and my fingers tingled and my stomach twisted in a way that I knew was fear, in case these drawings I loved and had worked so hard on weren't good enough. Something I hadn't felt since showing my drawings at a comics convention to Anthony, years before.

'Fil, these are amazing.'

'You think so?'

'They are incredible. The caves – and the way Girl from Mars reacts to them – I never could have thought that up. It makes me want to change my script now, this is so good.'

I let out a breath I hadn't known I was holding.

'Brilliant. That's – that's great.' Exhilaration filled me, even more than the moment when I'd finally finished. 'Right, we need to celebrate; let's go to the pub.'

'All right.' Dan put my drawings down and went to the door. I followed him.

I seemed to have asked him to the pub, without thinking, as if he were Digger or Jim.

It was sunny outside, and warm but for a small breeze, and I squinted at the sudden change in light. There was a pub next door to UPC, noise spilling out of its doors, and Dan walked straight past it.

'Where are we going?' I asked, catching up to him because I'd veered for the pub door before I'd realised he was continuing onward.

'All the UPC lot go to that pub.'

'Do they?'

'Yes, and they'll be in there celebrating Becca's birthday, so I thought we should go somewhere else.' He paused on the pavement. 'Unless you wanted to celebrate Becca's birthday?'

Who was Becca? 'No, I guess a different pub is good.'

'This one is better, anyway. Friendlier.' We rounded the corner and Dan pushed open the etched glass doors of a Victorian pub. He raised a hand in greeting to the barman, who called, 'Pint of Stella, Dan?'

'Yes please, John, and – what would you like, Fil?'

'Stella's great,' I answered, totally bemused.

'Take a seat, I'll bring them over.'

I slid on to a wooden bench seat, polished from years of backside contact, and stared at the flock wallpaper, listening with a fraction of my attention to Dan's cheerful small talk with the barman while the rest of my brain spun with questions.

Why hadn't I ever been invited to the pub next door to UPC? Did everyone know about it but me?

Normally this sort of thing would not bother me. Normally I would take it for granted that everyone else had a social life in which I was not included. But the situation had become more complicated in the past few weeks. For example, did Stevo know that everyone drank at that pub? Was he there now, celebrating the mysterious Becca's birthday, instead of hanging out with me? Had he introduced Brian to everyone there?

And why hadn't Dan wanted to go there? Was it because he didn't want people to see that I was with him? Sure, he'd asked me on a date ages ago, which should make me think that he wasn't ashamed of being with me, but that was before he knew me.

'Here you go, pint of Stella,' Dan announced, sitting down across from me and sliding across a full pint, wet with condensation. 'John asked if you wanted a half, since you're a lady, but I thought you probably deserved a full one.'

I lifted my full one and swallowed four big gulps, as fast as I could, and when I put down the glass the lager was more than half gone.

'I guess you did,' Dan said.

'Thirsty,' I said, though it had more to do with drowning the questions.

'Fair enough. Listen, I'm sorry if you wanted to go to the Feathers, but I wanted to have you to myself to talk about *Girl from Mars*. We can go back there after this one if you want.'

'No, that's okay.' The alcohol had immediately set about warming my stomach and flushing my cheeks. 'You're right, this is a nice pub.'

'It's my local. I write in here sometimes in the evenings. I've got a flat round the corner which I've rented for the duration of my gig with *Girl from Mars.*'

'What, in Suffolk Mansions or somewhere?' I joked. Suffolk Mansions was this stunning Edwardian block of flats; it was made of red brick and had flowerboxes dripping with colour and huge windows through which one could glimpse crystal chandeliers and antique furniture.

'That's right.'

'Wow.' I took another drink, liking how the beer made it even easier to talk. 'Of course, you must be filthy rich from all the films.'

'Absolutely,' he said. 'I'm totally rolling in it.'

'Rich, talented, popular and good looking, you're like the perfect man,' I said, and then covered my mouth with my hand as I realised what I'd said. 'Whoops.'

Dan smiled. 'I'm glad you think so, though I'm sorry it was a mistake for you to say it.'

'It's not – I mean –' I decided finishing off my pint was easier than trying to explain. I drained it, and then put the glass down on the table with a thump that made the barman glance over. 'Right, let's talk about *Girl from Mars,*' I declared. 'Congratulations on managing to avoid the snoggage in this episode. Do you think you can keep up the good work?'

'Snoggage?'

'Lip locks. Kissy-poos. Smackeroonis.' I puckered up and kissed the air in case he'd misunderstood me.

Dan laughed. 'Fil, are you drunk from one pint?'

I considered. 'Maybe a little.'

'When was the last time you had something to eat?'

'I had some biscuits. I think.'

'Other than biscuits?'

'It was . . . well, I had a sandwich for lunch yesterday. What time is it now, like around two in the afternoon?'

He checked his watch. 'More like seven in the evening. You mean you haven't eaten since Sunday lunchtime?'

'I was working. D'you want another pint?' I stood up.

'I think you should eat before you drink any more, Fil.'

'I'll get some crisps or something. Stella again? You'd better drink up, you're lagging behind here.' I headed for the bar. Maybe John would be friendly to me, too. I smiled at John, who was a big-bellied bald guy.

'Hullo,' I said.

'Hullo,' he said back, and smiled, too.

'Can I please have two pints of Stel—'

A hand landed on each of my shoulders. 'We're going to get some food in you,' said Dan's voice behind me.

Lord, it felt good when he touched me. Surprising, alarming, annoying, but good. Nevertheless, I turned round and he let go.

'I want another drink,' I said. 'I want to do an experiment with social graces.'

'If you have another drink, you won't have any social graces.'

'Now, there you're wrong. See, it's like a virus. Before I met you, I didn't have it, so I was healthy, sort of, but now I've caught it, so—'

He frowned at me. 'Are you sick?'

'No, it's a metaphor.'

'You are definitely drunk. Come on. Pizza.' He put his hands on my shoulders again, turned me round again, and marched me towards the door.

'I don't want a pizza, I want lager.'

'Fil, you are far too small to be drinking on an empty stomach.'

I dug my heels into the patterned carpet, to stop our progress. 'Are you saying I'm a lightweight?'

'Well, you're not much above five foot nothing and probably don't weigh a hundred pounds, so yes.'

I realised this was another one of those cross-cultural miscommunications. 'I meant, are you saying I can't hold my drink? Because them's fightin' words, cowboy.'

'I'm sure you can hold your drink all night if you want to, but it'll make me feel much better if you'll come with me to get a pizza.'

I frowned. 'Do you mean I can hold my drink, as in being someone who's hard as nails and can even drink Digger under the table if I set my mind to it? Or do you just mean that I can hold on to my glass?'

'I mean whatever you want me to mean. Come on, Fil, are you going to eat or do I have to pick you up and carry you to the restaurant?'

I was sidetracked from the puzzlement of American versus British English by the prospect of being in his arms again. 'You wouldn't dare.'

'Now that sounds like a challenge.' He reached down and before I knew it, he'd hoisted me up, one arm beneath my knees and the other around my waist. 'See you later, John,' he called as he kicked open the door and carried me out on to the pavement.

Infinite Space

'What are you doing?' It came out as a very un-hard-as-nails squeak.

'The restaurant's only round the corner.'

'I don't want to go for a meal with you!' Oh no, I'd gone through all this trouble and torture to keep my vow and not go out with Dan and now here we were heading for a restaurant. On a date. 'I said I wouldn't!'

'Well, you didn't say it, exactly, as I remember, it was more like you ditched me beside a crack. But don't worry. This isn't a date, it's a refuelling stop. You can even pay for yourself if it makes you feel better. Though I am filthy rich.'

And tall. And strong. And even handsomer than I'd previously suspected, now that I had a pint of lager rolling around inside my stomach and my face was about three inches away from his.

Of course this wasn't a date. He'd asked me ages ago, and he'd no doubt thought better of it. Plus there was the whole wife thing. He was still mourning for her. And since he'd started at UPC he knew loads of people now, and if he did want a date, which he probably didn't, there was Becca, whoever she was, and the other women who worked at UPC, and no doubt everybody he'd met at his local pub, and all the posh birds who lived in Suffolk Mansions. He could choose anyone. They'd all leap at the chance. For instance, look at how great it felt to be in his arms, carried around like a fairy princess or something. It wasn't my thing, obviously, but for a change, it was nice.

More than nice.

London smelled of warm stone. We passed a florist, colours bleeding on to the pavement, and I let my arm rest round Dan's neck.

'You've gone very quiet,' he said, his voice a rumble against my body.

'I was wondering what Girl from Mars would do if a Neanderthal-like male who'd never heard of feminism slung her over his shoulder and attempted to abduct her and take her to a pizza restaurant.'

'In Issue Twelve she used an electronic hairpin to get out of the clutches of the Pordocks.'

'It was a portable microwave emitter.'

'It came out of her hair, and as far as I'm concerned that makes it an electronic hairpin.'

I was being carried down a London street on a balmy evening by a sexy man, arguing about my favourite comic in the universe, and for a split second I forgot about all the reasons why it was stupid for me to appreciate it. 'Oh my God,' I cried in pure happiness to the skies, 'I love Girl from Mars so, so, so, so, *so* much.'

'You're definitely drunk.' Dan kicked open another door gently, and we were suddenly inside an Italian restaurant, full of potted palms and the scent of garlic and wine. A short, goateed man ran up to greet us.

'Daniel! Signorina!' He seemed not at all fazed by the fact that Dan was carrying me. 'Table for two?'

'Thanks, Luigi. How are you?'

The tables were crowded with diners, and the aisles between them were very narrow. 'Uh, Dan, I think you should put me down before I kick someone in the head.'

'Are you going to stay and eat?'

'Do I have a choice?'

'No.' He put me down. Damn.

Luigi cleared a 'Reserved' sign from a little table in the corner by the window and ushered us towards it. I sat in the spindly wooden chair, looked at the menu which was also a place mat, and suddenly was enormously, ravenously, eat-the-whole-world hungry.

My eyes must have gone very large because Dan asked Luigi right away for bread and olives and a bottle of mineral water, and within seconds it was in front of us. I seized the bread and butter and didn't look up until only crumbs were left and Dan was smiling at me with an 'I told you so' expression.

'How big are the pizzas?' I asked.

'Pretty big. But you should order a salad too. I can recommend the avocado and bacon.'

'What is this obsession with feeding females?' I asked, but when Luigi returned I ordered the avocado and bacon salad and an American Hot pizza with pepperoni and jalapeños. It was only after Dan had ordered that I realised two things: one was that he probably had an obsession with feeding females because he'd had to look after his wife while she was sick – cancer didn't improve your appetite; the other was that I'd ordered an American Hot pizza in a Freudian slip because of the hot American sitting across the table from me.

Fortunately, Dan changed the subject. 'So, you came into UPC yesterday afternoon and worked all night?'

'Apparently. It's dark in the sweatshop, I didn't notice the time.' I popped an olive into my mouth.

'Do you usually work like that?'

'Yup. Don't you?'

He considered. 'Sometimes. When I'm getting to the end of a story. In the beginning and in the middle I need to spend time wandering around, doing other things while my mind is working and making up stuff. Figuring out how it all falls together. But at the end, I know what's going to happen and I want to watch it, so I'll write and write until it's done. I've pulled all-nighters and all-dayers, like you. Forgotten to eat. It happened with *Ninety-Eight Point Six*.'

The first one he wrote for his wife. The one he wrote a happy ending for because he was living through the sad ending.

My salad came and I fell on it, because the bread had barely made a dent in my hunger. The avocado was soft, bland and rich, the bacon crispy and salty. Dan, who was less concerned with stuffing his face than I was, kept on talking between bites of his own salad.

'It's ironic, though, because I hate finishing a story. It always starts out with so much potential. It could go anywhere and include anything. And then with every choice you make, it gets smaller and smaller and then it's finished.'

I looked up sharply from my nearly finished salad. 'You feel that way?'

'At first, yeah. The beginning of a story is like meeting someone for the first time. You don't know anything but the surface, but you're interested in digging deeper. And then you dig and dig and there are endless layers and details. Everyone is a universe. "I could be bounded in a nutshell, and count myself a king of infinite space."'

'*Hamlet*,' I said automatically.

'You know *Hamlet*?'

'I'm not a complete heathen, and besides, my parents each have about sixty degrees in literature. I was drilled on quotations as a kid. It counted as a fun game on long journeys.'

'Right,' he said, and he looked at me for a minute before he started speaking again. 'Anyway, a story starts out infinite. And then as you live with it more, it falls into patterns. You form a relationship with it. You set down rules even though you don't know you're doing it. You start making choices that limit everything else that's going to happen. Maybe you realise that this isn't the right story for you. But by then—'

'—You've invested too much time and work to give it up. And besides, you've got a deadline. Yup, I know the feeling.'

'That's how I felt about *Blue-Eyed Daughter*, to be honest. Don't tell anyone.'

'Well, it will be difficult to keep it from the hordes of entertainment journalists who regularly kick down my door, but I'll try my best.'

Our empty salad plates were cleared away and our pizzas set down. Luigi had definitely got the message that he had hungry customers. I cut into mine, but Dan was staring into the distance, evidently thinking hard.

'That film had the right structure, it should have pressed the right buttons, I had brilliant actors and a great team. But it wasn't right. It's like looking at the same person across the table from you every day,' he said.

'Every day, exactly the same. And you hope and hope that one day they'll surprise you. Let you in. Show you a little bit of their infinite space.'

I chomped down on my pizza and yelped, clapping my hand to my mouth.

'What?' Dan was halfway out of his seat in an instant.

'It's – hot.' I swallowed and fanned my mouth with my palm. 'Jalapeño. Sorry.' I gulped down my glass of water and refilled it from the bottle.

Dan sat down, shaking his head. 'I've never met a woman like you,' he said.

'No, I don't suppose you have.' The thought made me feel glum, especially after we'd been having an interesting conversation, an unbelievably *easy* conversation, that I'd obviously ruined. I went back to my pizza and offered up a change in topic. 'Why don't you tell me how much you love my artwork?'

'It's wonderful. But you know that already, don't you?'

I ducked my head. 'The setting was good to draw.'

'It's odd to see my ideas translated so quickly. With screenwriting the story changes, the actors will add something, and the cinematographer, and then there are the costumes, all the music and editing and everything else, but it takes months, and since I'm working on it myself, my ideas have changed with everyone's input and with the practicalities of putting it all together. But this was all at once, and suddenly it's not mine any more.'

'It's yours, all right. I never would have come up with Jackson Silver.'

'It's ours.' He held up his glass of fizzy water. 'You were too busy guzzling your pint to do this before. But here's to Episode One.'

'To Episode One,' I repeated, and clinked glasses with Dan.

We drank our sparkling water.

'You're right,' he said, though I hadn't spoken, 'it's not really a sparkling water sort of toast.' He flagged down Luigi and ordered a bottle of Chianti.

Filled wine glasses in front of us, we tried again. 'To your art, Fil,' he said. 'Great work.'

I wanted to toast his script in turn. He'd been so nice to me this evening, even counting his carrying me around Pimlico on his shoulder. But I wasn't the schmoozing type.

'To your education in *Girl from Mars*,' I said instead. 'And to finding the right story.'

'I'll drink to that.'

The wine was dark, full and delicious. We finished our pizzas and ordered tiramisu and finished off the bottle, chatting mostly about comics and UPC and London, and I thought about asking him why he'd bothered to ask me to show him around the city when it was perfectly clear that he could make friends with everyone he met and therefore show himself around, but I wasn't quite brave enough. Plus by then we'd started talking about *Battlestar Galactica*, to which, it turned out, he was addicted. Then Luigi came over and talked to Dan about his grandchildren in Umbria (not Dan's grandchildren; Luigi's) while I listened and pictured sun-drenched grape arbours. Luigi brought us each a grappa, and then I looked around and the restaurant was nearly empty and there was nothing else to do but get the bill and leave.

I paid half of it. We went outside, and night had fallen while we hadn't been watching. We walked, side by side, while around us the traffic moved and other people walked and the whole city went about its business, but I felt as if we were in a bubble. As if the Italian restaurant had been another planet, with a different atmosphere, and we were still surrounded by wisps of it. Delicate, and prone to blow away.

We walked in silence. I didn't want to talk, in case that burst the bubble. Dan's stride was much longer than mine, but I didn't have to hurry to walk with him, as I did with Jim and Digger. We fell into step together. Every step was another little puff of the atmosphere gone.

There was a pub ahead; the smokers knotted and fumed on the pavement. *Another drink?* I imagined myself asking Dan casually. I didn't need another drink; my fingers and toes were tingling and my stomach was full. But it would be another half an hour where I was allowed to look at Dan's face, full on, as I had across the table, to smile at him and not think about anything else.

We passed the pub.

Silence, which had begun in order to preserve the atmosphere, was starting to wear it away. I wondered why he wasn't saying anything. I wondered why the words, which had come so easily before, weren't coming to me now. I wondered where we were going, apparently together, though we hadn't discussed it. We were heading in the general direction of his posh flat. Maybe he'd invite me back with him.

The thought fizzed with both excitement and anxiety and yet we were both still quiet. I opened my mouth to say something, anything – surely we had talked about a topic in the restaurant that we hadn't exhausted yet? There had seemed so much to say, some of it even clever and witty.

'It's a nice eve—' I began, just as at the same time Dan stopped walking and said, 'Here's the Underground, do you—'

We were next to Pimlico tube. With all my ridiculous fantasies of going to Suffolk Mansions, I hadn't twigged we were also heading that way.

'Oh,' I said. 'Oh yeah. I should be getting home.'

Dan nodded, and I heard and felt something like a sigh as the last shred of the atmosphere drifted away.

Empty House

The house felt empty as soon as I put my key in the lock. 'Jim?' I called when I got in the door, but I knew he wouldn't answer. I checked the downstairs anyway, and then poked my head round the door of his office and his bedroom. He wasn't there.

In the kitchen, I made myself a cup of tea and was very surprised that the clock on the microwave said it was ten past ten. I'd been gone about thirty-two hours, which was probably why the house felt both very familiar and very strange. My mobile didn't register any more missed calls. Jim was probably with Digger, having a drink or watching a movie. Actually, if he were in the cinema it would explain why his phone had been turned off earlier. Except that had been – what? Ten, eleven hours ago?

Well, maybe it was a long movie. I brought my cup of tea into the living room. The Baz barely cocked an eye in my direction, so he hadn't missed me. Though lizards probably had a weird sense of time anyway, measuring days in lettuce and hours of warmth, and seeing humans as odd noisy shadows. I doubted he could tell one of us from the other.

I curled up in front of the telly. If I was going to be alone in the house in the evening, for once, I might as well enjoy watching something Jim wouldn't be seen dead watching. I flicked through the channels.

Ten minutes later I put the remote down. The thing about television was that most of it was only enjoyable if you had another person there beside you with whom to mock it. I rang Jim, but his phone was still switched off, so I rang Digger and got his answerphone. I hung up without leaving a message and went back to the telly.

I thought about the long pause between Dan and me, as we'd walked down the street. I'd felt, for those several minutes, that we were close, both sort of basking in the good, easy time we'd had. But he'd obviously been miles away. Maybe thinking about Elizabeth, and how he wished she'd lived long enough to come to England with him and share cosy suppers in Pimlico restaurants. Or maybe he'd been thinking about his dad, and how Elizabeth's sunny American charm would melt his distant British heart. Or maybe he'd been thinking about getting a new pair of shoes or getting the leaky sink fixed. Whatever it was, it was clear that while my head had been full of Dan, his head had been full of something else.

None of which should surprise me. My past romantic efforts – if you could call them that – hadn't been known for total harmony of thought. I'd never had the first idea of what Pierre was thinking about, my own brain being too full of deluded tosh. I'd admired many men from afar, but their thoughts, like them, were undiscovered territory. The only men I really understood were Jim and

Digger. And my dad, of course, but for a super-intelligent bloke, he was fairly simple to know: all he wanted was his super-intelligent work, his super-intelligent wife and, unfortunately, a super-intelligent daughter. His disappointment with the latter was assuaged by his preoccupation with the former.

I thought I'd understood Stevo, but obviously I hadn't. I remembered his bitterness this morning, and his insinuation that I neglected my friends. Like he was one to talk, running off with Brian with nary a look backwards. No, my understanding of Stevo had obviously been an illusion, like the illusion of meeting Dan's eyes over a glass of Chianti and believing his sudden, bright smile was all for me.

No. Stop thinking of that. I understood Jim and Digger, and that was good enough. Where the hell were they, anyway? I turned off the television, which I was surprised to see was showing *Canada's Next Top Model*, and tried ringing them both again. After getting no reply, I grabbed my keys and left the house.

They were calling last orders at the Swan when I got there, and there was no sign of my friends at our usual table or anywhere else. I went round to Digger's flat, which was in a purpose-built block about half a kilometre from our house, but nobody answered the door. I walked home slowly, thinking that if I took my time the odds would be greater of Jim already being home when I got there, but the house was still empty. I fancied I heard an echo when I closed the door.

There were signs of Jim everywhere. A book lay facedown on the arm of the sofa, as if he'd just left it. But the house felt wrong without him there, and I paced around the carpet, settling on a chair and then getting up again, turning on the radio for company and then turning it off, going up to my studio to do a few sketches and then abandoning them, wondering where he was and if he was all right and why didn't the call me? It was well past midnight now.

Jim never just disappeared. He always told me where he was going. He always invited me to go with him. Like Laurel and Hardy, Batman and Robin, Mulder and Scully. Half of myself.

I was halfway down the stairs again when the front door opened and Jim walked in. He had a paper parcel that smelled of chips and vinegar and he had changed clothes from when I'd seen him yesterday but otherwise he looked the same as usual, except different, because he'd been gone when I'd wanted him.

'Where have you been?' I demanded immediately.

'Oh, you're home,' he said, and went to the kitchen. I followed him.

'I've been calling you and calling you and you never answered. I went to the Swan and you weren't there.'

'That's because my phone's switched off and I wasn't at the Swan.' He unwrapped his chips, put them on a plate, and began rummaging in the cupboard for ketchup.

'I've been pacing around the house wondering where you were. The Baz is no company whatsoever. Do you know how empty this house feels when you're not here?'

The ketchup slammed on to the counter with a bang. 'Yes, I do,' Jim said, and his eyes were hard with anger, 'because that's what it's been feeling like to me all the time lately.'

'What do you mean?'

'You're never here! And when you are here you're in another world somewhere. I might as well be living alone.'

'I've been working. You know what it's like when I'm working. It's always like that.'

'Yeah. It is.' He didn't seem to be agreeing with me.

'And it's not my fault that Anthony is forcing me to work at the UPC building.'

'Not twenty-four hours a day, he isn't.'

'I've got to get the comic done, Jim!'

'Yeah. That's the most important thing, isn't it?'

I'd heard his sarcasm aimed at a thousand people and things but so rarely at me that for a moment I was lost for words.

'Hold on,' I said. 'We're not talking about me, we're talking about you. You're the one who disappeared off for hours without telling anyone where you'd gone, and turned off your phone so nobody could get in touch with you.'

'Oh, I'm the only one who did that, am I?' He turned away and brought his plate into the living room and I stood there with the echo of his words and the smell of vinegar.

'But I was—' *Working*, I meant to say again, but I stopped because that wasn't true, was it? Not wholly. Because I'd been with Dan, instead of coming home to Jim, who'd missed me.

I'd been neglecting my friend. Like Stevo said.

How'd he know – unless I'd always done it?

I went into the living room. Jim had put his chips on the coffee table but he hadn't touched them. He was sitting on his side of the couch, his arms folded, his mouth set in anger.

I sat down on my chair. The silence settled into the room. This wasn't one of the good ones. It weighed on my chest and made it difficult to breathe.

We didn't fight, me and Jim. We'd argue, we'd bicker, we'd pick at each other, but we didn't fight. We didn't need to. We were friends. We always did whatever we could for each other and put each other first.

But I hadn't put him first.

'I'm sorry,' I said quietly.

He grunted. He wouldn't look at me.

'I mean it,' I said. 'I shouldn't have disappeared yesterday without telling you how long I'd be. And I should have rung again as soon as I knew I was going to be longer than half an hour.'

The silence came back and now it was weighing heavily on me, on my whole body, everything was feeling so wrong and stupid.

I needed to do something to make things better. So I leaned forward and stole a chip. I dipped it in ketchup and I ate it. Then, because he hadn't said anything yet, I stole another. I chose Jim's favourite kind, a long one with crispy edges.

'Hey, get your stinking hands off my chips,' Jim protested.

I reached out to nick another one and he grabbed the plate away. 'If you want chips, go get your own,' he said, and he sounded like how he sounded every time I nicked his chips so I sat back in my chair, chewing and licking the salt and vinegar off my fingers.

'You're a menace,' he said, and I knew I was forgiven.

'So where were you?' I curled up in my chair, smiling.

'I went to the pub.'

'But I looked for you, you weren't there.'

'That's because Rachel needed someone to help her with her moving.'

'Rachel? Oh – is that the barmaid?'

'Yeah. She's moving out of her flat and asked if I'd help her carry some boxes. So I did.'

I considered Jim, wiry rather than bulky, in his spotless T-shirt and jeans. 'You've been carrying boxes for hours?'

'Well, not for hours. We got them shifted and then I helped her unpack a bit. She used to live with her boyfriend but she's got a flat of her own now. I think it was a bad sort of break-up and she wanted some company and that.'

His cheeks were tinged a little with pink.

'Oh. That was . . . sweet of you.'

I looked at him, but he was concentrating on his chips, picking out the best ones and dipping them in ketchup.

'What did you do?' I asked carefully, not sure I wanted to know. I remembered the time I'd seen Rachel crying on the Underground. Jim had probably been consoling her. Telling her jokes, like he did with me. Laughing in his own special Jim way.

I shifted in my seat. Why would this bother me? I'd just spent several hours in the company of a man, after all. Jim had been hanging out with Rachel like I'd been hanging out with Dan. No big deal.

It bothered me.

'We just unpacked towels and CDs and stuff. Some of the boxes were too heavy for her to lift on her own.'

'I'm surprised she didn't ask Digger.' Digger could lift almost anything and was very handy to have around when you were moving. He'd got the couch Jim was sitting on into our house nearly single-handedly.

'It's Monday night, Digger's at his sister's.'

'Oh, yeah.' I felt a bit of relief. Rachel had probably asked Jim because he was the nearest male. And after all, I'd driven Jim to it, being gone all the time. I'd been working too hard. I'd been neglecting my friends. They deserved better.

'I finished drawing the issue,' I told him, 'so I'll have a rest now. And I shouldn't be working so much anyway. That's what the office is for, right? So I can be at home with my mates without needing to worry about work.'

'Presumably,' said Jim, and it was so dryly said, so typical of Jim, that I wanted to run over and hug him. But he wasn't a huggy type, Jim. Neither of us were.

'I'm going to take it easy on *Girl from Mars* for a little while and spend more time with you and Digger,' I said. 'I promise.'

21

Know Your Enemy

And I did. I was sensible. After all, the point of an office is that you can leave it. I limited my work to sweatshop hours, ten till six, and decided I wouldn't work at all on weekends, and that I would spend my ample free time with my friends.

It wasn't easy. Dan did some revisions to his script, to incorporate the darkness I'd drawn into the caves. He'd made Glypto, the villain, even more seductively insane. And there were other, more subtle changes, to the dialogue and the action, things I didn't quite understand yet, but which had what my parents would call a sub-text: a hinting at symbolism and significance that was not yet clear. As if Girl from Mars and Jackson Silver were searching for more than a way to get back to Mars; they were following clues to something they were not sure they wanted to discover. If I gave the script to my parents, they'd instantly be able to figure it all out; but I was enjoying being mystified.

It was a wrench to go home every day and not draw any more.

And of course then there was Dan. He spent the mornings reading and the afternoons writing. It was as if our dinner had never happened. No more spontaneous hugs, or picking me up and carrying me down the street.

Time spent with someone teaches you about them, though. I learned how he ran his hands through his hair and chewed on his pen while he was thinking. How, when he was really into his writing, he muttered to himself and laughed aloud, and then, remembering I was in the room too, shoot me a rueful look. I learned he wore lucky socks to all his film premieres and that he rang his mother every Sunday so she could tell him about the charity committees she chaired, and that his father, an investment banker, had little interest in cinema and none in comics. Dan went for a run in St James's Park every morning and I couldn't decide which scent I liked better, how he smelled in the mornings, fresh from his shower, or in the afternoons, when he smelled more rumpled, worn-in and warm. I learned which sports the Philadelphia Phillies, Flyers and 76ers played, and that his mother was from old Philadelphia money (whatever that was) and that she and his father had been considered a perfect match for each other until after they married and discovered they had nothing in common.

I learned nothing about his wife, except what I knew already, which was that everything was about his wife. We talked about lots of things except ghosts and regret, or my best friends I was spending all the rest of my time with, and then we would go back to work on the caves.

In short, I was keeping everything separate, which was just how I wanted it.

One Saturday we played *Dungeons and Dragons* at our house, and then on the Sunday Jim and I went for our parental visit. I met him in the Mitre afterwards to recover.

'Dear God, I'm glad that's over,' I said, flinging myself on to a bar stool. I wrapped my hands around the pint waiting for me and gulped it down gratefully. 'Thanks for that, mate, I needed it.'

'Tough one?' he asked.

'My cousin Phoebe is pregnant. Again.'

'Ah.'

'And it's my father's birthday on the same day I'm supposed to be at ComicsCon and my mother laid the biggest guilt trip on me and I might have pointed out that they both went to Rome for a convention on the day I turned sixteen which sort of led to a bit of an argument.'

'Ah.'

'And they wondered what I thought of the Booker shortlist.'

'Ah.'

'On the bright side, my father has been given a renaissance cookbook and so we spent much of our time hacking away at pheasant legs.'

Jim drank from his pint, which was nearly gone. 'More cats?' I guessed. The sleeve of his grey jumper was showing signs of claw damage.

'At least two, though they move around fast so it's hard to tell. She's given me another pamphlet about RSI from computer use. And she still refuses to get the hearing aid.'

We both sighed.

'I swear it's a mistake of nature,' I said. 'There is some chemical residue caused by the act of having children, that tragically renders you incapable of being a normal human being ever again.'

Jim tapped his fingers on the rim of his pint glass. 'It's

an interesting theory, though in my opinion, the damage sets in earlier than that, when—'

He stopped dead, his eyes staring at a point behind the bar.

'What?' I asked.

'Don't look.'

I hated it when people say 'don't look' when clearly that is the only thing you are dying to do. 'Don't look where?'

'Shh.' He pretended to be looking at his pint, but I could see he was watching the mirror behind the bar. From my vantage point, it only showed us: slim, neat Jim and messy, blue-haired Fil. I leaned round, trying to see what he could see, but he stopped me with his hand on my arm. 'I think Demon McKay just walked through the door,' he said in a low voice.

'Here? In Wimbledon?' My heart thumped a little.

'I recognised him from that photo. He's with some guy with a goatee and a skinny blonde. Look, quick, now.'

I did. Dan was wearing a V-necked jumper and jeans and he was holding the lounge bar door open for an improbably tall slender woman with long golden hair and big sunglasses.

'Is it him?'

'Yeah.' I hunkered down over my pint. 'It's okay, they didn't see us.'

'That's Carmen Clare with him, isn't it?'

'Oh.' That was why the blonde looked familiar – she was only a bloody film star. 'Yeah, probably.'

'Swanning around with the rich and famous. What a twat.'

'Well, I guess you meet people like that in the job he does.' He also met people like me, who at the moment felt like something scraped off a shoe. As if it weren't enough trying to compete with a dead wife, did I now have to compete with film stars?

Hold on, what was I thinking? I wasn't competing with anybody. Dan wasn't interested in me, I wasn't interested in him. We worked together. I wasn't even supposed to like him very much. Jim, for example, thought that I hated him.

And I hadn't seen fit to inform my best friend otherwise.

I bent my head down further, as if I were examining the beer mat under my pint glass. There was only one problem with this desperate ploy to avoid Dan, which was that—

'Fil? Is that you?'

– which was that blue hair is very recognisable, even at a distance. I straightened up.

'Dan!' I said, giving an impression of surprise that I doubted convinced anybody. 'What are you doing here?' I sat up on my stool and faced Dan and his friends. The goateed guy looked a little familiar, too.

'I'm visiting Reuben, who's doing a little pre-production work here for his next film, *The Throbbing Member of Parliament.*' Dan gave me his white American smile, the smile I'd almost become used to, and I instantly wondered what Jim would think of it. 'This is Reuben Rogers,' he continued, presenting the other man, 'and Carmen Clare. Carmen, Reuben, this is Fil Brown, who's the artist on the comic I was telling you about.'

'Oh,' said Carmen, 'that space comic. It sounds so cute.'

I'd never met a film star before and certainly not a film star who'd just called the major passion of my life 'cute'.

I stared at her. She was beautiful, all right. Not a hair out of place. I wondered what she'd look like if I kicked her in the nose.

'I'm James Lousder,' Jim said beside me. He'd stood up from his stool. 'I live with Fil.'

'Oh, you're Jim.' Dan took Jim's extended hand. 'Nice to meet you at last.'

I watched them shaking hands. I half expected an explosion, matter meeting antimatter. But nothing happened. Jim was standing straight and looking gravely at Dan, as if they were meeting at a World Summit of Seriousness. Dan was smiling in his usual way. Their grip was firm and neither one seemed quite ready to be the first to let go.

'I've heard lots about you,' Jim said, friendly enough. But I knew him too well.

'Really? All good I hope.'

Jim let go of Dan's hand at last and smiled. It was a smile I saw rarely, only in the heat of role-playing battles, or once or twice long ago, in the school lunch room. I had a sudden fear he was about to break into a Klingon war chant, rush forward, and try to snap Dan's neck like a twig.

'I heard you came over here from Hollywood to shove a stick of dynamite up *Girl from Mars*'s arse,' he said.

Oh dear God. I was not good with social situations at the best of times, and this one was rapidly sliding out of control. 'Jim, I think we need to get going.'

'Not a stick of dynamite, exactly,' Dan said to Jim, as if I'd never spoken. 'Just some changes here and there. I'm sure Fil's told you about the scripts we're working on together.'

'Yes, she's told me quite a bit about them.'

I looked at my watch. 'Gosh, is that the time? We'll miss our bus.'

'Have you seen her drawings yet?' Dan asked.

Jim frowned. 'No.'

'So, what brings you to Wimbledon?' asked the man called Reuben, whom I vaguely recognised now as some sort of famous movie director. Apparently he was oblivious of the mighty battle going on beside him.

'My parents live here. I don't live here, though, I live quite a long bus ride away, right Jim?' I nudged him.

'Would you like to join us for a drink?' Dan asked.

'Oh, thanks, but—'

'Sure, I'll have a pint, thanks,' Jim said over my refusal. 'It looks like there's a table over there big enough for five.'

'Great. What would you like, Fil? Pint of Stella?'

'Half. Only half a pint.'

'I thought half-pints were for lightweights,' Dan said.

'It's just that – we really can't stay for very long.' I glared at Jim and tried to get it to sink through his thick head that I did not want to do this, but he merely put his hand on my shoulder and guided me to the table he'd selected in the corner, while Dan went to the bar and the other two followed us.

'What are you doing?' I whispered furiously.

'Know your enemy, Fil,' he reminded me. 'I want to meet this guy who's been making your life hell.'

'It's really not a good idea. I mean, I have to work with him.'

'Don't worry, I won't do anything to embarrass you.'

'It's not that, it's—'

I stopped. I couldn't possibly explain, not in whispers in front of a film star, and probably not anyway. I'd made such a big deal about hating Dan and him being evil and bad for *Girl from Mars*. And I'd meant to let Jim and Digger know I'd changed my mind. It was obviously the right thing to do, now that I was putting my friends first. I just sort of hadn't really ever found the perfect time to do it.

We reached the table and I sat down, chewing my lip. I could have avoided all of this, merely by opening my mouth. Instead, I'd got myself in this mess. Again. It was the same thing as had happened all those years ago with Pierre, except, of course, that I wasn't sleeping with Dan, I wasn't stupid enough to be in love with him, and it was unlikely that there were going to be any threesomes suggested today.

I glanced over at Carmen Clare, who was sitting across from me, casually tossing a perfect lock of perfect hair over her perfect shoulder. Definitely no threesomes, not including me, anyway. Thank God, because if I were required to discuss sex in general, or my lack of a sex life in particular, in front of these people I would probably keel over and die of mortification.

'Of course,' Carmen was saying to Reuben and anyone else who could hear her bell-like voice, 'I loved working with Stephen, he's a legend and I was *so* thrilled to have been asked, but it's so good to escape from LA every once in a while, England is so sweet, and the script you're directing is so *thrilling*, Reuben.'

'Thank you, I'm lucky to have got it, it was ... unexpected. What do you find so sweet about England, Carmen?'

'Oh, the pubs like this one! And then Daniel was showing me his apartment, oh, I mean his flat, and that's so adorable—'

'Here we are,' Dan said, appearing with a tray of

drinks and handing them round: pints for him and Jim, half a pint for me, a mineral water for Carmen, and some kind of short for Reuben. I watched Jim watching Dan and suddenly I knew that even if I had told him that I didn't think Dan was that bad after all, he'd never like Daniel McKay in a million years anyway. I could see it in the way he took in Dan's wide, easy smile, his casual, expensive clothes, his friendliness and confidence and almost inadvertent success.

Daniel McKay had never been an outsider in his life. He'd been popular from the moment he'd been born. People probably fought for seats at his table at lunch.

'Thanks,' said Jim, accepting his pint. Dan sat down, to my horror, right beside him. Reuben and Carmen were chatting away to each other about Reuben's latest project, so Jim and Dan were going to have to talk to each other. Or I was going to have to talk to them both, and I wasn't sure I could handle that kind of balancing act.

'How do you know that Fil thinks half-pints are for lightweights?' Jim asked him.

'She implied as much the other day when—'

'—We had a swift drink while we were discussing work,' I interrupted, because of course I hadn't got around to telling Jim I'd been out with Dan that night. Dan gave me a surprised look, and then he nodded.

'Yes, while we were working. What do you do, Jim?'

I worried my lip and sat on my hands until I realised that I couldn't drink my drink that way, so instead I wrapped them both around my half-pint and took a big gulp.

'I'm a Consultant Software Engineer specialising in developing open-source device drivers and Linux kernel porting.'

'Sounds like something out of a science fiction movie,' Dan joked, and Jim merely regarded him, deadpan, the expression of a fan whose genre is being mocked.

'Really?' he asked. 'Which one?'

'Dan loves *Battlestar Galactica*,' I said quickly to Jim.

'Is that so?'

'Yes, totally. I got to go on set when they were filming some of the Caprica sequences, it was amazing.'

'Wow.'

Rarely have I heard such an unenthusiastic 'Wow'. Dan didn't seem to notice, and started telling Jim about what he'd watched being filmed and some of the problems the director had overcome. I'd heard some of this before, over pizza in Luigi's, and it had seemed like fascinating insider information. Now, filtered through the way I knew Jim was perceiving it, it sounded like name-dropping.

I couldn't listen. Instead, I drank my half-pint, wishing it were a teleporting device, and tried to direct my attention to Carmen and Reuben's conversation.

'And the cab scene, it's so cute! It's such an adorable script, Reuben, and you are a genius director, though as I said my agent was worried about the amount of nudity, especially at this stage in my career, you know?'

'Don't worry, it will all be very tasteful.'

'But the sex scene on the London Eye, I mean that's all glass, isn't it? It's a really sweet thing, like a giant carnival ride, I love it, but if you film that on location it's all going to get a little exposed, isn't it?'

I thought suddenly of a vast space full of nude sculptures. It wasn't just the conversation that reminded me of that nightmare moment with Pierre and Marie, but the sense of everyone else understanding something that

I couldn't comprehend. On my right hand, the world of sex scenes and agents and filming on location. On my left, the world of two males head butting over something when they didn't need to. I wasn't sure which one was worse.

'What about you, Fil?' Reuben asked beside me. 'What do you think it's like, having sex on the London Eye?'

Enough. I stood up.

'Jim, I think we really need to catch our bus now.'

Calmly, Jim took another drink from his pint and then he stood. 'Thanks for the drink,' he said to Dan, and nodded to Reuben and Carmen. I grabbed his wrist and dragged him out of the pub as fast as my legs would take us.

'You were right,' Jim announced as soon as we hit the pavement outside. 'That guy is a total wanker.'

'I never said that.'

'You didn't need to, he's self-evidently evil. I've never met anyone so pretentious in my life. Did you hear him trying to impress everyone about watching *Battlestar* being filmed?'

Yes, and did you hear yourself stonewalling him, Jim?

'Maybe he needs a bit more of a chance,' I said.

'A chance to do what? Ruin your career? We need to do something to get rid of Demon McKay.'

'I don't want to talk about it, Jim.'

'Can we start a petition? Or steal his computer? Maybe get his visa revoked some way?'

'I said, I don't want to talk about it.'

'I know it's painful, you're stuck in an office with him, but come on, we can think of something. Kidnap him and stuff him in the cargo hold of a plane back to America?'

'I *don't want to talk about it!*'

We'd reached the bus stop. I kicked it.

Jim stepped away from me. 'All right, I was trying to help you, that's all.'

'Believe me, Jim, I don't need your help with this. I didn't want you to talk to him in the first place and the last thing I need is you going on about how much you hate the person I'm working with.'

And a little more than working with. In my dreams, anyway.

I stared at the pavement, furious and guilty and embarrassed, my face flaming and my stomach sick.

And the worst thing was, it was my own damn fault.

'I just don't want you to be hurt,' Jim said to me. 'I never want you to be hurt.'

I rubbed my face with both my hands, as hard as I could. Suddenly I wanted to be at home, in the sweat-shop, anywhere, as long as I could draw and not have to think.

'I know,' I said. 'Look, can we get a cab home?'

Women Are From Venus

I sat in my usual seat in the Swan, drawing big, hairy, bloodthirsty wolves on the quiz sheet.

On the one hand, we had to beat those accountants. They gloated like nobody's business, and they deserved to be taken down a peg or two.

On the other hand, I'd always believed Jim and Digger were men of stiff moral fibre.

'It's cheating,' I whispered to Digger.

'It's not cheating if she's part of our team,' he said placidly, sinking the rest of his pint.

'But she's not.'

'I hate to contradict you, but it appears that she is. Besides, she knows her Eurovision. And we need her.'

Jim returned to the table, his hands full of pints and his face wreathed with smiles. 'It was Estonia.'

I wrote it grudgingly in the blank space. Then I drew a big Estonian wolf eating it.

'Is Rachel officially on our team now?' I asked. 'Because we should put her name down if she is.'

'Put her name down, then.' Jim settled back with his pint and the picture round.

I looked at Rachel, where she stood behind the bar pulling pints for some of the accountants. She was wearing a T-shirt that clung to her figure and her long curly hair was piled up on top of her head.

'Can we even have someone who works in the pub on our team?'

'I told you, I checked and it's no problem.' Jim took my pencil and wrote an answer down underneath a photo. 'We are going to win. I can feel it in my bones.'

'Actually,' I said, 'it was my idea in the first place to ask Rachel to join the team, but *you* said we didn't need any new friends.'

'Well, obviously you were right. Don't enjoy it too much.'

I sighed.

'Next question.' The quizmaster's voice boomed and crackled through the inadequate pub PA. 'What girly film featured Lisa Kudrow and Mira Sorvino claiming they'd invented Post-its?'

I looked at Jim. Jim looked at Digger. Digger looked at me.

'*Casablanca*?' I guessed.

Something strange happened. Jim put his pint down on the table and sat up straighter. Beside him, Digger did the same thing.

Rachel appeared by my elbow. '*Romy and Michelle's High School Reunion*,' she whispered.

Jim and Digger erupted into smiles. 'Excellent,' Digger said. 'Write it down, Fil.'

They were sitting up straighter when Rachel came by? What was going on here? Was it because she was so obviously female? I watched her go to the next table and collect glasses. She was wearing a short-ish denim skirt and patterned tights. She walked with a sway to her hips. Her hair bounced.

'This is really not fair,' I muttered, writing down Rachel's answer.

I'd always been the girl, the only girl, even though I was one of the boys. They didn't treat me differently – I wasn't expected to do the washing-up any more than my fair share, or to know about curtains, or to drink girly half-pints or white wine spritzers. Digger and Jim didn't slow down their long-legged paces for me, or hold doors open, or put down the toilet seat after they'd used it, or let me get out of buying rounds.

In fact, the only concessions I got for being female were that I got my own chair in the living room and that whenever I was cranky they would assume it was the result of mysterious female hormones, even if it was clearly the result of something glaringly non-hormonal such as having sat down for the millionth time on a loo whose seat was up.

The day Digger and Jim sat differently because of me would be the day I put drawing pins on their chairs. Actually, I was considering it.

I glanced at Rachel and thought about a few other uses for drawing pins.

'We're going to bury those accountants,' said Jim, rubbing his hands.

All of this got me thinking about being female, which prompted yet another dig around inside my wardrobe. The results were depressing. I had far too many pairs of boy-fit jeans, and exactly two skirts. The first, I had purchased, and worn, for a distant cousin's wedding in Ireland, after being informed in no uncertain terms that I would not be allowed through the doors of the church in a pair of trousers. It was denim, and as close to boy-fit jeans as I could possibly make it.

The second, my mother had bought for me. Long ago, in the turbulence of my teenage years, she had thrown up her hands in despair and sworn never to attempt to dress me again, so I wasn't sure why she'd braved giving me a skirt as a Christmas present. I took it as a last-ditch attempt to plant a seed of femininity in me: first the skirt, then maybe a touch of perfume, then possibly a little discussion of third-wave feminism and then bang! I'd be giving her grandchildren.

I'd never worn it. But I actually liked it, as an abstract object, which was why I hadn't thrown it away. It was brown (of course) but it had orange retro-style flowers on it, and a slight flare at the bottom, and it could be rather funky, I thought, on the right person, on the right occasion. For example, if the person were doing a panel discussion, along with a Hollywood writer, in front of a lot of comics fans at a convention.

I tried it on and stared at myself in the mirror. I didn't have a full-length mirror, just the one on top of my chest of drawers, so I had to climb up on the bed to see the outfit, twisting round to get a view of all angles. It looked stupid, but maybe that was because I was wearing trainers and a green T-shirt. I rummaged around until I came up with some black boots and a black T-shirt, and tried that combination instead.

It didn't really work either. The part of me that was covered by the skirt looked like a girl, but from the waist up and the calves down I looked like me. I tried other combinations, with different tops and shoes and with jeans underneath, but none of it produced that mystical 'Fil as a woman' image I had been hoping to create.

How did other women do it, anyway? Presumably they went shopping in packs. They asked each other's opinions and borrowed each other's clothes. This option wasn't available to me; I didn't have any female friends to ask and it would be a cold day in hell before I went shopping with my mother again. I remembered my teenage years far too well.

I put away the skirt and my inadequate accessories, got dressed as myself, and went downstairs. Jim was washing up and listening to the radio.

'Have you been moving your bedroom furniture around?' he asked me.

'Trying on clothes,' I told him. 'I need to go shopping.'

'What do you want to do that for?'

This, again, was a place where my life was different from most females'. I assumed that if a normal woman told her best mate she needed to go shopping for new clothes, the two of them would immediately start frothing at the mouth in a frenzy of joyous fashion-lust, and would stampede a path to High Street Ken.

Jim, on the other hand, approached shopping in the following manner. He would find a pair of jeans or trousers that he liked, which he felt suited him, and which were comfortable. Then he would buy several pairs of them, in different colours if they had them, but otherwise several identical pairs would suffice. I suspected identical clothes were easier for him, with his colour blindness. Ditto for shirts, socks, jumpers and, I presumed, underwear, although I had never witnessed this particular act of shopping. He would wear these items and wash them on a rotational basis, essentially wearing the same outfit in different permutations every day. In this way, he only had to shop once in a blue moon, when a set of clothes wore out.

He always looked fine to me. Of course I had a limited knowledge of fashion, but he was at ease in his clothes, and that seemed better to me than being trendy. This was a change from when he'd been a kid, when aside from the omnipresent cat hair, even his non-school-uniform clothes had been stiff from ironing and not really age-appropriate. His mother used to put him in button-down shirts and ties, even for a trip to the swimming pool, and it was a daily ritual for Jim to remove his tie and stuff it into his big bag as soon as he was around the corner from his house.

About the age of fifteen he broke free from this mother-dressing, started growing his hair, and instantly (in my opinion, anyway) became one hundred per cent cooler in appearance. But of course by then the damage to his reputation had been done. He was the geeky kid, the weird kid, the one who survived being bullied only because of the sharpness of his wits and the fact that he never appeared to care.

He still got his share of it, though. School wasn't easy for me, but I, for some reason, floated below the radar of most people. If I'd had to deal with the taunts and threatened violence that Jim dealt with every day, I'd have cowered underneath my bed rather than getting up and shouldering a huge backpack of schoolbooks and science fiction novels. And it wasn't even as if it were from a few particular individuals who Jim could avoid. Every single student at that school, aside from me, called my friend Jim Lousder 'James Loser'. Casually, laughing, as if they thought that was his real name, as if they had no idea how every single time they did it they tore another little hole in Jim. Because he never showed it. Not even to me.

He was the bravest person I knew.

Now, watching him wash out mugs, his hair neatly tied back, a grown-up person who'd survived the torture of being young, I felt a great rush of affection for him.

'D'you want to come with me?' I asked him. 'I need something to wear for the conference panel discussion.'

'Black,' he said immediately.

'No.'

'Can't go wrong with black.'

'I want to make a statement, not hide.'

'Paint your face green,' he said, but he dried his hands and came along with me.

However fond I was of Jim, though, I couldn't help but wish, as we walked into the Oxford Street H&M, that he was a woman.

'Blimey,' he said, stopping stock-still and gazing around, 'why wasn't it on the news?'

'Why wasn't what on the news?'

'The zombie epidemic.' He pointed to the heaving clusters of women around the dress racks and handbag shelves.

'Just smile and mutter "Braaaaaainnnns", you'll fit right in,' I said impatiently. I wanted to get this over and done with, not stand around commenting on the shops and their customers. I tugged on his sleeve, trying to make progress into the shop. He came, but with limbs stiff and eyes glazed.

'Braaaaaainnnns,' he crooned under his breath as I rifled through racks of clothing. Some of it looked all right to me, but how was I supposed to know? If it was on sale here it must be fashionable enough, right? But then how would I know if it suited me?

There were frocks, smocks and trousers; tights, blouses and belts and little flimsy flat shoes and strange drapings of crocheted stuff without obvious armholes or purpose. There was a whole wall of bangles and hair slides and socks. 'What do you think of this?' I asked Jim, holding up a bright red jumper/dress-type thing, but he was still muttering about eating living flesh, so I loaded my arms with things to try on and went to the dressing room with him trailing after me.

The dressing room was packed with women. Mostly model-slim waifs, but a few scattered other sizes and shapes and ages, all of them throwing on clothes and asking each other's opinions. Saying things like 'Does it make my boobs look huge?' or 'Didn't Cheryl wear something like this?' or 'I don't know, I've got two pairs like these already' or 'Nip out and get me a size eight, will you, hon?' All of it said with the air of confidence and joy. They liked doing this. They thought it was normal and fun. Ever since they'd been old enough for pocket money they had spent their time and cash on glamour.

You know that book, *Men Are From Mars, Women Are From Venus*? I stood there in that changing room, surrounded by women, and I didn't feel like I was from the same planet as any of them.

But I wasn't a man, either. I wasn't even Girl from Mars, who had the strength of a dozen men and the sex appeal of a goddess. I was floating in space in between, not really from anywhere.

The first thing I tried on was too tight, the second too big, although they were supposedly the same size. This seemed to be one of the many conspiracies on the part of clothes manufacturers to test whether you were truly a woman, by requiring you to try on everything before you bought it. Digger, I knew, would go to a shop and pick up something off the shelf in extra large and buy it and take it home and wear it.

The third thing, the dress/jumper, fitted me around the chest and hips, but it was tight, painfully so, around the elbows. The *elbows*. What the hell?

'Is someone trying to tell me I have fat elbows?' I muttered, and threw the garment aside to try on something else.

This was a blouse with some sort of tie at the waist and puffed sleeves, like nothing I'd ever even touched before, and a narrow skirt which gave me oh, about two spare inches around the knees to use for walking. I hobbled out to find Jim. I felt ridiculous but at least I'd found an outfit.

He was leaning against a wall, acting for all the world like he was conducting an anthropological study. It was a couple of moments before he noticed me, but when he did, his expression changed.

'What does that mean?' I demanded.

'What does what mean?'

'The way you looked at me just now.'

'How did I look at you?'

'Like –' I couldn't define it, so I tried to show him. His eyes had widened a bit, his eyebrows quirked up, his mouth tightened.

'I've never looked like that in my life,' he said.

'You did, just now.'

'I assure you I didn't, unless I suddenly changed into a startled budgie.'

I was getting nowhere. 'What do you think, then?'

'About startled budgies?'

'About the outfit.'

'You look . . . different.'

'Different good, or different bad?'

He inspected me. 'Is it meant to be so tight around the knees?'

'How am I supposed to know? Maybe I have fat knees, like I have fat elbows.'

'What?'

I gave up and went back to the dressing room and tried something else on, a wrap-around dress I'd thought might make me appear sophisticated but more likely made me appear to be a boy-shaped boiled sweet.

When I emerged Jim got The Look again. I didn't bother to replicate it this time.

'No good, huh?' I asked.

'I didn't say that.'

'Well, what did you say?'

'I haven't said anything yet.'

'You –' I decided not to argue that an expression was worth a thousand words. 'What do you think of it?'

'It's . . . different.'

Around me, dozens of women talked to other women, exchanging easy opinions and commentary about fashion. It might as well have been in Venusian.

'Different from the other different, or the same?' I asked, clenching my fists.

'What do you mean, the same?'

'Oh for God's sake, Jim!' I exploded. 'All I want is to wear something that makes me look like a damn woman for once in my life. Is it so hard to say whether something looks okay or not?'

'I—'

The women were staring at us.

'Forget it,' I said before he could start going on about zombies again. 'It was a stupid idea.' I stormed back into the changing room, flung off the dress and dragged on my own clothes. Jim was waiting for me when I emerged empty-handed, and he walked beside me out of the shop on to Oxford Street. We didn't say anything as we got on a bus and found two adjacent seats upstairs.

It would have been more productive to go shopping with my mother. It would have been torture, yes, and I would have ended up with something brown, but I actually would have bought something for my trouble. But what had I expected from a man who kept his *Star Trek* T-shirts for Sunday best?

I stared out at the hundreds and hundreds of women walking around London looking like women, and fumed. Even the damn old ladies were better dressed than I was. I was an awkward, unattractive tomboy and I might as well wear a sack for all Jim, or anyone else, cared.

'I think you look beautiful in everything,' he said quietly, beside me. When I whipped my head around to stare at him, he was blushing furiously.

He was embarrassed to tell such a bare-faced lie. But it was to make me feel better, so I softened.

'Shut up,' I said affectionately.

He regarded me for a good long time, with the redness hovering on his cheeks.

'It's all right,' I said. 'I'm over it. Who do I want to dress up for, anyway? You and Digger? You two would just about have a heart attack if you suddenly discovered I was female.' I laughed at the prospect of it. Jim didn't laugh. He didn't say anything.

Comics Con

I got to Victoria with enough time before my train to buy a coffee and croissant, but the barista fumbled my change and so in the end I had to rush to get on board, pushing through the morning crowds and blurry train announcements, dragging my suitcase with one hand and balancing my food and drink in the other. As the 9.06 to Brighton pulled out of the station I tugged along the aisle past other passengers, looking for an empty pair of seats where I could spread out a bit and do some sketches.

'Fil,' said a voice ahead of me and I saw Dan, in sole possession of a table, his laptop and a notebook already open in front of him. He had a coffee from the same café I'd bought mine from. My insides leapt at the sight of him, which was silly for all sorts of reasons including the fact that I saw him almost every day.

'I – thought you'd be taking the later train to the convention with the others from UPC,' I said.

'No, I wanted to do some work, so I thought I'd come down by myself and maybe get in half an hour at the hotel before the convention. Looks like you had the same idea?'

'Yeah, I've got some stuff to do.' This was true. The main reason I'd chosen an earlier train, though, was to avoid making conversation with people I didn't know very well. And because I thought Stevo would probably be on the later one.

'Are you going to join me?' Dan asked, and I realised I was standing blocking the aisle with my coffee about to tip over the side of the cup. I set it down on the table and before I could do it myself, Dan hoisted my overnight bag up on to the overhead rack for me.

'I thought Jim would be with you,' he said, sliding back into his seat.

'No, he's had his fill of comics conventions,' I said. Jim had, in fact, volunteered several times to come. Digger had offered, too. But I'd said no. Partly, yes, because Jim and Digger had been to ComicsCon before. But also to avoid, once again, the issue of my friends not liking Dan. I was living in two worlds, one at home with my friends, and one at work with Dan and Girl from Mars, and I didn't really want them to collide. In some ways I resembled Clark Kent and Superman, except without the pesky phone booth transition, or the super powers.

I unpacked my sketchbook and pencils from my shoulder bag and arranged them next to my snack on the table. 'Usually I do these things with Stevo,' I admitted. 'It's easier if you have someone with you. It can get a bit overwhelming.'

'I'm glad I've got you to talk me through it, then.' Dan sat back in his seat in that easy way he had, the way that could make it easy to talk to him. 'Have you been to lots of them?'

'Lots. That's how I got the gig with *Girl from Mars*, actually. I kept going to conferences and thrusting my artwork underneath Anthony Alwards's nose, hoping he'd look at it.'

Dan laughed. 'You stalked Anthony?'

'Well, everyone does some stalking at the beginning. Most publishing houses don't have open submission policies these days and *Girl from Mars* is one of the hardest to break into because a lot of established artists want to do it. The only way you can get your art seen is to show it to an editor at a convention.'

'How did Anthony react to that?'

'He told me to fuck off after about two seconds. Every convention it was the same; I'd get my chance, I'd show him my work, he would glance at it and tell me to fuck off. So I'd go home and work on it some more until the next convention.'

'Harsh.'

I shrugged. 'I deserved it. I knew I was getting better when he gave me half a minute one time before he told me to fuck off. And then the next time, he gave me a whole minute, and then he told me to call him. The next week I had a trial story to draw.'

'So you must love these conventions,' Dan said.

'Not so much.' I set my croissant on top of its little bag and pulled off a corner.

'Really? You're such a comics fan, I'd think you'd be right at home surrounded by people who love them as much as you do.'

'You'd think that. I sort of expected that, the first one I went to. But actually it's –' I tried to think of how to explain it, because I'd never had to explain it to Jim and Digger, who immediately felt the same way I did. 'I've always felt that *Girl from Mars* was mine. Even when I was a fan, I didn't love her because other people loved her or because loving her made me popular. I loved her because the stories said something to me. So when I'm surrounded by fans, all of them thinking they love the comic as much as I do, I feel sort of jealous.'

Dan laughed, though I didn't feel he was laughing at me. 'I can see how you'd be a little possessive. So what do you do, if you're not communing with fans?'

'I walk around, look at the stuff on display. I buy a bunch of comics. I go to the panels and the events. Mooch around. Watch some of the other artists drawing.'

'You don't usually speak? Or draw?'

'I, er, like to keep a low profile.'

What I meant was that I'd rather pull all my fingernails out than speak or draw in front of a bunch of people. Anthony expected us to talk on a panel tomorrow and my guts had been twisting themselves into knots for days just thinking about it. The shopping had only been the first symptom.

I'd done some sketching at a conference, once, a couple of years ago for charity. Stevo was doing it and I'd thought, how bad could it be to sit in the exhibition hall and draw some stuff to sell for a good cause? I learned quickly how bad it was when the punters, without exception, all stared at me and said, 'You're Fil Brown? But you're a *girl*!'

But I wasn't going to tell Dan about that. He was used to giving interviews, dealing with strangers and crowds. He could do all of that with the same charm he was using on me right now, and he wouldn't understand how it made me feel so foolish that I clammed up.

'If it's anything like film festivals, all the action happens late at night in the bar,' Dan said.

'Something like that,' I agreed, though again, I wasn't telling him the strict truth there. I knew that all the attendees went to pubs and bars after the con finished every day, but I couldn't tell you what went on there because I generally hung out in a little knot with my own friends or friend.

'I'm really looking forward to it,' he told me. 'I like learning about the comics world. And I think it's about time I started up my own *Girl from Mars* collection.'

'Did your grandfather sign any of the ones he gave you? They'd be worth a bomb.'

'I wouldn't sell them for the world,' he said and I nodded approvingly.

As the train nosed through London and outwards, we drifted into mutual work in the way we'd become accustomed to, every now and then exchanging some words or a joke, sipping coffee in tandem. Once or twice his legs bumped against mine and my heart knocked against my ribs.

Here was another reason to keep Dan and my friends apart. They'd see this reaction. I didn't go brushing legs with Jim and Digger as a rule, but when I did by mistake, I didn't nearly have a heart attack. And annoyingly, it was completely involuntary. Dan, though, didn't seem to notice me or my reaction. After a while he straightened up and pushed his hair back. 'I've got a present for you if you can answer a question.'

'Shoot.'

'Do you know the name of the colony that Kingsley the Talking Ant came from?'

I thought, hard. 'No. But I know where the issue is on the shelf in the archive. I can picture it. Yellow cover, big action shot of a crashing meteor. Ants everywhere.'

'That's not much help to me, since I can't get to the archive for a few days.' He gestured to his notebook. 'I've just put "XXX" in here, but it would be cool to fill it in. And of course you won't get your present without it.'

'Tell you what you can do,' I said. 'Can you get online from here?'

'Think so.'

'Look at the *Girl from Mars* fan boards on the internet. If you post a question there you'll generally get a response within half an hour or so, and those guys know everything. I've used them for continuity when I couldn't find something in the archives.' I gave him the address and he typed it in. 'So where's my present?'

He flipped back several pages in his notebook and slid it over the table to me. 'It's Episode Three. If you don't mind reading my handwriting instead of a typed copy.'

I snatched it from him. 'Handwriting's okay,' I said, which wasn't quite true because reading his handwriting with him here sitting across from me felt too intimate, nearly as flustering as bumping his legs. But the story was way too important to miss. I settled back with the precious notebook and began to read, as I heard Dan tapping and browsing on his computer.

He'd called it *'Electric'*. From page one panel one in Dan's bold black letters I was back in the caves and this time the shadows had greater definition and menace. In contrast, Girl and Jackson's banter was becoming distinctly more flirtatious.

I glanced over at Dan, about to call him on it, but he was absorbed in his laptop screen and I decided to let it rest for now. Maybe they were acting this way under the pressure of the moment, to raise their spirits, and it wouldn't lead to anything. I went back to the script, which wasn't difficult because, despite the bothersome flirtation, Girl from Mars and Jackson were getting very close indeed to finding the Tachyon Intercept Manipulation Engine, which was a localised time-shifting device Jackson had invented in theory two years before, and which had had all its documentation and research stolen by Glypto who turned out to be Jackson's former lab assistant, and who had built the device in secret for his own, as yet unclear, nefarious purposes. The TIME device, of course, was the key to Girl from Mars's overcoming the many biological and astrophysical obstacles preventing her from going home. And it was, as Dan's panel descriptions made clear, resting down a short passageway from where Girl and Jackson traded witty, sexually charged comments.

It seemed far too easy. And this was only Episode Three. Then again, as brilliant as the caves were, it was about time for another setting, to make things visually interesting, so if they got the TIME device they could go above ground and maybe into space.

Still, it seemed like Dan was making it happen too quickly. I looked up, again about to say something, but he was reading his screen intently, a small frown line between his eyebrows. So I went back to the story. There were only two pages left.

They crept down the passage and rounded the corner to a vast cavern where, according to the panel description, the TIME device sat on a specially formed stalagmite, its glowing gauges creating a soft blue light in the darkness. The drawing was to take up half a page.

PANEL TWO: GfM and Jackson turn to each other, joy on their faces.
GIRL FROM MARS: WE'VE FOUND IT!

PANEL THREE: A close-up of their profiles. They have embraced in their excitement, and their lips are a hair's breadth apart.
GIRL FROM MARS: OH.

PANEL FOUR: The same close-up. A long moment.

PANEL FIVE: The same, but Girl from Mars has a slight smile.
GIRL FROM MARS: WE'LL HAVE TIME FOR THIS LATER, JACKSON.

Okay. I hated it, of course. It was romantic tosh, but Dan had written it, and I couldn't help but imagine Dan and me in the pose he'd described, embracing each other in our joy at finishing Episode One.

The memory made my skin flush, and I took a deep breath to cool down before I turned to the last page.

PANEL ONE: Girl from Mars steps into the room and a blue arc of electricity shoots from the TIME device to her forehead.
SFX: *ZZZZT!*
CAPTION: WE THOUGHT WE HAD *TIME*.

PANEL TWO: Girl from Mars falls to the floor, her body limp, her eyes pure, opaque white.
CAPTION: WE WERE *WRONG*.
JACKSON: *NOOOOO!!*
CAPTION: *NEXT EPISODE: GHOSTS*

I stared at the page. 'You have got to be kidding,' I said. He'd killed Girl from Mars.

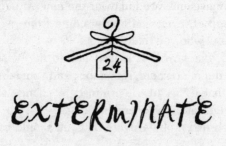

EXTERMINATE

'Philomena, what the hell is this?'

I dragged my gaze away from Dan's writing and looked at his face, which was stormy.

'What are *you* angry about?' I asked. 'You're the one who killed her.'

'And you're the one who's been posting about me on this fan forum. Or is there another Desdemona out there?'

Oh. I'd forgotten about those posts. 'I was just polling opinion. These people know a lot.'

'One question would have been polling opinion. You've got a dozen posts here, every single one of them insinuating that I'm some Hollywood big shot who's only in it for the cash.' He turned the screen round and pointed to one of my Desdemona posts.

He was understating it. 'Hollywood big shot' were the actual words I'd used.

I hadn't meant to post more than once or twice, but it's easy to get carried away on the internet. Especially late at night, when you're lying awake worried about your comic and your job, and you feel that everyone at UPC is conspiring against you to favour the new guy. You sort of want support, even if it's only online from people who don't know who you really are.

'Well, that's what it looked like to me,' I said. 'You burst in out of nowhere, remember, and you were writing scripts that didn't fit, determined to change *Girl from Mars* even if it didn't need changing.'

'If you had problems with that you should have come to me.'

'I did. I waved a script in your face and told you that you didn't know jack about writing for comics, or did you miss that part?'

'And then you went straight out and complained about me in public, behind my back.'

'Nobody knows who I am.'

'But what if they find out, Fil? It can't be hard to make the leap if someone happens to know your name. Can't you see how that could kill this project stone dead if people think the artist doesn't have faith in the material?'

'Right, so I'm supposed to pretend I don't have reservations about what you're doing? About this, for example?' I held up his notebook.

'You're not supposed to sneak around and air your reservations in public under a pseudonym.'

'You're overreacting. All I did was post a few comments. And it was weeks ago, anyway.'

'Did you listen to Anthony in the meeting? If this project doesn't succeed, *Girl from Mars* is going to sink. And it can't succeed unless we collaborate.'

'Collaborate!' I burst out. 'How the hell can you talk about collaboration when you go and kill Girl from Mars!'

'Now who's overreacting?'

'I'm not overreacting. She's dead. Her eyes have gone white. It's Arcturan electricity, isn't it? Someone set it up as a trap.'

'Girl from Mars has died before.'

'Not from Arcturan electricity! That's mental stuff, that's *dead* dead, you've read *Arcturan Anarchy*, you know what it does to Martian insides! She's a shell of green skin!'

'She's a fictional character, Fil, and besides, she'll come back.'

'I know she'll come back! Jackson will use the TIME device to get her back, it's bloody obvious, but that's not the point! The point is that you can't kill off Girl from Mars and bring her back because *you* need to tell that story to make yourself feel better! She's bigger than that, she's more important than that, she's not one of your bloody films and she's not your dead wife!'

The carriage went very quiet, except for the clunking of the train on the rails.

'What do you know about my wife?' Dan said, in a low voice.

His face, white and cold like Girl from Mars's dead eyes, told me I had made a mistake but there was nothing for it now but to go on.

'I know all your movies are about her. I know you keep on writing stories about love and bringing people back from the dead because you're still mourning her. And I know you're trying to do the same thing with this comic.'

'And how do you know about all of this?'

He scared me a little. He'd been angry when I'd confronted him about his first script, but that was nothing compared to this. He was utterly still, boring into me with his eyes, his hands fisted on the table, dangerous.

'I read about it,' I said.

'You read up on me behind my back, too?' His voice was raised.

I held up the notebook. 'You can't hijack Girl from Mars and use her to help you sort out your personal issues.'

The train stopped and the PA system announced, 'We have now reached Brighton where this train will terminate.'

Dan stood up. He grabbed the notebook from my hand and he reached up and swung down his bag from the overhead shelf where it had lain next to mine.

'You need to think about who's hijacking Girl from Mars for personal reasons,' he said, and he turned from me and walked off the train.

I sat there, my own fists clenched on the table, with every passing passenger staring at me, the strange girl who'd had a loud and public argument on a train for the whole carriage to hear, and I thought, *How dare he*.

He was the one who was twisting everything. I hadn't posted as Desdemona for weeks, not since I'd read Episode Two, and besides, the fans were entitled to have an opinion about what was going on. And I wasn't hijacking Girl from Mars. I loved her, just like I always had. I was being loyal.

I hauled my own bag off the shelf and lugged everything through the station to a taxi queue. I didn't see any sign of Dan. We were staying at the same hotel, but he must have got a taxi before me. I didn't know why I was looking for him anyway because I didn't want to see him and his righteous American attitude.

I fumed all the way to the hotel, which was the same one I always stayed in for ComicsCon, booked by UPC and far from exclusive. When I checked in I found I had the same single room I'd had last year, despite Anthony going on about how essential my presence was and how the future of the comic was riding on it. Obviously he wasn't into coddling the talent.

After throwing my bags on the bed, which bowed under their weight, I paced around the room, even though I had stuff to do. I kept on seeing Girl from Mars, still and hollow, lying on the rock floor of the cavern. It made me feel as if my own guts had been vaporised by Arcturan electricity. I wanted to cry.

Mid-pace, next to the little MDF dressing table, I stopped because I realised why I felt so awful. I was mourning Girl from Mars's death. Actually mourning it, even though I knew she'd come back, as if she were a real person.

And quickly on the heels of that realisation came the awareness that I'd argued with Dan about his wife, who really was dead.

My guts didn't feel vaporised any more, because hot shame flooded through them.

'Oh, shit,' I said, and fell back on to the bed next to my bags.

I was not socially adept, not by a long shot, but even I should know better than to argue publicly on a train with a man about his dead wife without even expressing an iota of sympathy. No wonder he was angry at me. I'd hurt him badly. He'd probably felt like zapping me himself.

I covered my face with my hands. I should go and find his room and apologise. The thought filled me with dread and embarrassment.

I got up off the bed and took the lift down to reception to ask for his room number. In the split second between

the lift arriving and the door opening I imagined Dan
standing in reception making some query at the desk,
glancing over when the lift opened and spotting me and
setting his jaw again in anger, and the prospect was so
horrible that when the lift door did open and Dan wasn't
actually there at all, I went straight past the desk and ran
out of the hotel.

The sun was out, gulls wheeled in the sky and I could
smell the sea on every breath I took. I went down to the
seaside and marched around, the gravel crunching under
my trainers. The pier looked like a white city floating on
black spider's legs. There were a couple of children and
a dog racing back and forth where the waves hit the
shore. I stared at the grey sea and realised that none of
this was helping.

What I needed was comic books.

I checked my watch. By the time I walked to the
convention centre from here, the exhibitors should be all
set up and the convention would have just begun. The
panel wasn't until late this afternoon, so I had plenty of
time. I hiked up the beach towards the concrete block of
the exhibition centre.

But when I reached it, I hesitated by the entrance
door. The con had started. People, mostly male, streamed
in, eager and excited, practically rubbing their hands in
anticipation. I could tell from the noise and the warmth
pulsing through the door that it was crowded already. I'd
never been to one of these things by myself. And here I
stood, without Jim and Digger, without Stevo, without
Dan. About to plunge in alone.

I peered in. Superhero posters soared, bigger than
life, on the walls. Tables groaned with comics, music
blasted, screens flashed. I wondered what Dan would

make of the Goths, of the artists huddled over pads, of the cosplay people dressed up as Batman and characters from *Star Wars*. Of the punters milling about in packs, exclaiming over their finds. It was certainly different to Cannes, I thought.

Someone wheeled past me in a Dalek costume, buzzing 'EXTERMINATE', and I took a deep breath and slipped into the room in their wake.

It's Always the Same Stormtroopers

Two hours later I was adding yet another comic book to the stack under my arm when someone said at my elbow, 'Hey, Fil.'

It was so familiar that for a second I didn't register why it was strange. I turned and said, 'Hey, Stevo.'

'How are you liking the Con?'

'Fine. I'm picking up some good stuff. You too?' The stack under his arm was nearly as big as mine.

'I found a bunch of Dredd.'

I nodded. He shifted from foot to foot. Normally I would have asked him about his Judge Dredd stuff, but nothing about this day had been normal. 'It's weird being here and not hanging out with you,' I said.

Relief swept across his face. 'I was just thinking that.'

'You want to get a coffee?'

'Yeah.'

In the café, we found a table next to four guys dressed as *Star Wars* Stormtroopers. 'D'you think they're the same ones?' I asked Stevo, because I'd asked him that question many times before.

'It's always the same Stormtroopers,' he said. 'Jim and Digger didn't come with you?'

'They were busy. You're not here with Brian?'

'He had to work. I'm only down here for the day anyway. Listen, Fil, I –' He took a deep breath. 'I'm crap at this emotional stuff.'

It's not hard, all you do is say you're sorry, I thought, and then I remembered why I'd run away from the hotel. So I shut up.

'I didn't mean for things to turn out like this,' he said. 'I didn't want to fight with you and not be friends. It's just – it's like I said, I'm not really good at explaining stuff. And then whenever I do you get all pissed off.'

He looked miserable. But I couldn't let him off that easily. He'd dropped us.

'Well, you've got to admit I've had a reason to be pissed off. You got a boyfriend and suddenly we're not good enough any more.'

'That's not what happened.'

'Yes it is. It's like—' Oh, what did I have to lose. I said it. 'It's like you're embarrassed by us or something.'

'Embarrassed by you? Fil, I'm not embarrassed by you. You and Jim and Digger are awesome. You'll think up something to do and then just go and do it. I tell Brian about the fun stuff we used to do all the time.'

I processed this. 'But – why then?'

'I was scared the three of you wouldn't like him.'

'What? Why wouldn't we like him? You like him, right?'

'I love him.' This was said with so much certainty and force that for a moment, it seemed to transform Stevo's face into something rare and beautiful. 'But I think you've forgotten what it was like when you and I made friends and you introduced me to Jim and Digger.'

'They thought you were great and you fitted right in.'

'No, they didn't, Fil. That might be how you remember it now, because that's how it turned out eventually. But I spent a lot of time being on the fringes. Jim didn't really speak to me at first. I got this strong vibe that he thought I was trying to steal you away or something. And Digger, well, Digger doesn't say a word unless he knows he can trust you. I was pretty miserable for a while, but I didn't know anyone else, so I stuck with it and it was worth it in the end.'

I frowned. Stevo had no reason to lie to me, but if this was true, how had I missed it completely?

'You were working a lot,' Stevo added. 'In *Girl from Mars* land. Sometimes I wondered if it was because you didn't want to get involved in the atmosphere.'

'Stevo, if I did that it wasn't intentional. I thought you were fine, really I did. Jim and Digger are the kindest people I know. They wouldn't freeze you out on purpose.'

He shrugged. 'Whatever. Anyway, kindness doesn't have anything to do with it. I think Jim and Digger are great blokes. It's just the way the three of you work together. There's this insider world, and when it looks like anyone's going to touch it, you close ranks before they can shake things up.'

'We're friends, we don't need anybody else,' I said promptly. The mantra.

But if that mantra was true, why was I living a double life? Home and work, with the two never touching? If I didn't need anybody else but my friends, I wouldn't care about Dan. Or need Girl from Mars.

Maybe Stevo was right, and I worked hard to avoid what was going on at home. Maybe I used Girl from Mars as a way of escaping from doing the same thing, day after day. Because really escaping was far too frightening.

'We're friends, anyway,' I asserted. That much was definitely true.

'Yeah. But it's like a perfect closed circle,' Stevo said, tracing lines of sugar on the table. 'It seems to me sometimes that it's more that you have to get in there quickly and judge people before they can judge you. Not that there's anything horribly wrong with that, y'know, we all do it, but I saw how the ranks got closed on me, so I noticed it happening with other people. And I didn't want to put Brian through it.'

'What other people?'

'Oh, you know, it happened all the time – in the pub, for example. Someone would come up to chat and zing, it all reverted to Fil-and-Jim-and-Digger land. Like an instant wall coming up.'

I opened my mouth to deny this always happened, but all of a sudden I thought of Rachel. How she'd talked to us for ages, and we'd never even known her name. She'd come over and say something and we'd basically ignore her. Actually, I'd been doing the same thing, more or less, even since she'd joined our pub quiz team. And then there was the way Jim had stonewalled Dan, while pretending to be friendly, as if he were drawing a line in the sand.

Maybe we'd done that with other people, who weren't as persistent. And I'd never noticed because our walls were so automatic.

'We're just being loyal,' I said, though it wasn't with conviction.

'Okay. But you can see it's hard to break into. The dynamic is so tight.'

'What – what do you mean, dynamic?'

'Oh, you know. This big tension between you and Jim, and Digger there to break it, all surrounded by private jokes.'

'There's no tension between me and Jim. We've known each other for ever, and we like arguing for fun.'

'Whatever,' Stevo said, shrugging again. 'You know best. Anyway, the point is that I still want to be friends with you. But like I said, maybe introduce you to Brian first, and then maybe the next day to Jim and Digger. But we can do it all at once, I don't care. I miss you guys.'

'And we miss you, Stevo,' I said, and we smiled at each other, and the sight of his neat, bespectacled face looking as he used to look made me realise just how much I had missed him.

'Cool.' He stood up. 'Look, I've got to go and sketch for a couple of hours before I head home. You want to come?'

I checked my watch. 'I've got to do some stuff before our panel.'

'Okay. I'll call you.' He hugged me, an awkward bony Stevo-hug, something I'd never had before, and then dodged around the Stormtrooper table and disappeared in the crowd.

A New Story

I opened the hotel-room window, cranked the fan in the bathroom, and spent a couple of hours dyeing my hair bright pink. After my squib of a shopping trip with Jim I'd figured that pink hair was the only way I was going to get myself to look feminine at all.

I hummed and even sang, though my singing was appalling, because my conversation with Stevo had made me feel light. I hadn't known how much missing him had been weighing me down until those weights weren't there any more. And I still had to speak in public, and I'd still hurt Dan badly, but I had new comics and new hair and I had my friend back. I wrapped my rinsed and pink hair in a towel and perused my fashion choices for the panel discussion.

Black. A bit more black. A Girl from Mars T-shirt I'd picked up at the Con, with a print of Wayne Jayson's *Betelgeuse Bonanza* cover. They'd only had a small size. And the orange-flowered skirt, shoved in the corner of my bag on the off chance.

I looked from the T-shirt to the skirt. There was a big

orange starburst on the T-shirt. And quite a lot of brown, actually. In fact, colour-wise, the two went together quite well. It was almost like fate.

T-shirt, skirt, black tights, black boots. I surveyed myself in the full-length hotel-room mirror, and I sort of looked funky. Like a girl, but a comicked-up girl. I messed up my hair into a passable state and left the room, locking the door behind me before I had the opportunity to change my mind.

The Con was even busier when I got there. Maybe it was the outfit, maybe it was the conversation I'd had with Stevo, hell, maybe it was the hair dye chemicals seeping into my bloodstream, but I felt completely different when I stepped through the door to how I had several hours before.

I was in a room full of strangers, and I was alone. But the posters, the displays, the costumes, even the ubiquitous casual-wear uniform of the punters, all created a vibe that buzzed on my skin.

I might have nothing else in common with any of these people, but we shared something: we loved comics and we loved escape. Maybe in the real world that made us a bit weird, and possibly more than a bit obsessive.

But for this one weekend in this one room, we were all completely normal.

I smiled, and although I wasn't smiling at anyone or anything in particular, a pierced-lip girl dressed in a short skirt and clutching stacks of manga caught my eye and she smiled back.

It made me want to giggle. I kept walking. I smiled at a balding guy with a baseball cap who was selling photocopied copies of his indie comic. I'd looked at it before; it appeared to be strident political satire of figures

I hadn't really heard of. From the size of his pile of books a lot of the Con found it as incomprehensible as I did. But he saw me smiling at him and the glum expression on his face disappeared. 'Cool T-shirt,' he said. 'Love Jayson.'

'Me too,' I said, and moved on, leaving a spark of brightness behind me.

It really was like a virus. You could catch a smile like a cold and pass it around with less effort than a sneeze. I smiled at the two guys arguing over a copy of *Daredevil*; I smiled at the man dressed as Wonder Woman; I smiled at the guys manning the UPC table and exchanged a few words with them; I smiled at the father there with his toddler who wanted to grab all the action figures off the tables. I smiled at everyone I encountered and they all smiled back at me, all different smiles but every one of them acknowledging that yes, we had our differences and our jealousies and our fears but we were the same.

I was just wondering how I could tell whether the Dalek was smiling when someone tapped me on my shoulder. 'Excuse me,' said a female voice, 'aren't you Fil Brown?'

It was a girl, about sixteen or seventeen, with long dyed-black hair and semi-Goth make-up, dressed in camouflage trousers and a hoody. She held a portfolio of drawings.

It was my cue to make an excuse and dodge out of there. I smiled at her. 'Yup. What's your name?'

'Georgie Marlow. Oh my God, I love your stuff so much, I have everything – especially since I found out you were a girl; I think you are totally amazing and I want to be just like you.' She blushed bright red underneath her pale powder. 'Uh, that was cool. Not,' she said.

'It was pretty cool to hear,' I told her. 'Want to show me your drawings?'

We found a corner and she spread out her portfolio. She wasn't kidding when she said she wanted to be just like me; I saw my style stamped all over her work. But I also saw her face, which was worried and elated and I knew the rush of excitement and fear she was experiencing, the feeling that this could be the most important moment of her life.

'You've got talent,' I said. 'But you need to find your own style. Learn from the artists you admire, but put yourself into it. Draw with love.'

She nodded, but I could tell she couldn't really understand what I was saying.

'Keep drawing and you'll figure it out.' I laughed. 'Listen to me. Most of the time I'm stumbling around without a clue about anything and here I am acting like some sort of a guru.'

'You are,' she said fervently.

'Nobody is,' I told her. 'You've got to find your own place in the world, or even better, make your own world for yourself. Good luck with it, though. Come and see me next year.'

I signed some books for her and then saw the time and had to run for the lecture theatre at the far end of the conference hall because the panel discussion was about to start. Dodging through people and around stalls and Stormtroopers, I felt as if I could fly.

And then I got to the lecture theatre and it was packed, absolutely full. Stupidly I'd come in from the back and from here the table in the front of the room looked tiny, punctuated with puny glasses of water and even punier name tags. Anthony stood there already, and so did Dan. He wore jeans and one of his white shirts, rolled up to his elbows. Even from here I could see how it made his black hair and blue eyes stand out, how it exposed his masculine throat and sexy forearms, and I knew how he smelled after his shower, and he glanced up and met my gaze and though he didn't smile, of course, my hands ached and I had to catch my breath because he was so, so, so, so, so lovely.

I wondered if I'd ever stop seeing him anew every time, and barely look at him, as I barely looked at Jim and Digger. I didn't think so. I didn't think he'd let me.

And of course, he probably wouldn't stick around long enough anyway. Especially if I kept on pissing him off at every available opportunity.

'Brown,' bellowed Anthony from the front of the room, his voice seemingly covering the miles without any effort at all. I didn't wait for him to swear, but hurried down to join him.

Dan watched me all the way; I wasn't looking at him, but I could feel his gaze. He was probably mentally cursing me.

As soon as I seated myself, next to Dan as it happened, the moderator hushed the room and introduced us by presenting summaries of Anthony's, Dan's and my career.

I tried smiling at one of the strangers in the front row. He smiled back, so I tried another a little further back. He smiled back too. All the time I could feel Dan next to me, hear his soft breathing.

The moderator mentioned the name of our six-part series and that Episode One would be out next Thursday, and he said we'd be open to questions from the floor, but right now he was going to turn the spotlight over to Anthony Alwards who could tell us a bit more about the project.

Before I could think twice, I stood up.

'I don't think Anthony will mind if I say a few words first,' I said. Anthony blinked, but he didn't say anything, so I carried on.

'I have loved Girl from Mars since I was a teenager. I don't know about the rest of you in this room, but I wasn't very popular or happy and I didn't know how to find a world where I could fit in. Girl from Mars helped to give me that world. I wanted to be just like her. Hell, I still want to be just like her.'

A ripple of laughter went through the room. It didn't touch Dan. I didn't see whether he was smiling or not because I still wasn't looking at him.

'What I'm trying to say is that I'm possibly the biggest Girl from Mars fan in the universe, and I know that she's ready for a change. Nobody can stay the same for ever, even aliens from outer space. She's ready for new challenges and new experiences and maybe even ready to get close to someone else. And Daniel McKay is the best person I know to take her there.'

You'd think this would be a good time for me to look at Dan, but I knew if I did that I would lose my nerve. So I focused on the middle of the crowd – all of whom were totally silent, listening to me, of all people – and kept going.

'I don't know how this story is going to end yet,' I said, 'I only read Episode Three this morning. But I can tell you that Dan's writing has prompted me to do what I reckon is maybe the best drawing I've ever done. Working with him is a true collaboration and I can't wait to see what he comes up with next.'

I sat down. There were some murmurs from the audience and I dared to glance at Dan. He was staring at me. I smiled at him and for a moment I thought he was going to say something.

But he didn't, because by now Anthony was speaking, and then the questions started.

'Bloody good job, you two, drinks on me,' said Anthony when it was all done, when both the panel and the post-panel questions and the requests to look at work were over. I'd spoken to some more artists, and heard Anthony tell many more of them to fuck off, and now the room was nearly empty, the last stragglers filing out to find a pub.

'Wow,' I said to Dan, watching Anthony go, 'did I hear right or did he just offer to buy us a drink?'

Dan didn't answer. When I turned to him he was looking at me in that same intense way he'd been looking at me when I'd first come into the theatre, and probably while I was giving my big speech, and at any available intervals after that.

And that probably meant that he hadn't forgiven me so I launched into it now that we were alone. 'Dan, I'm sorry for what I said about your wife. I don't know anything about her and it was out of order. As far as I'm concerned you can tell whatever damn story you want. I trust you.'

'Turn round,' Dan said.

I frowned, puzzled, but like him, I was in a swivelling chair so I pushed it round so I was facing away from him. I heard and felt him scooch himself over on his own chair and then his fingertips were on my neck, just behind my ear, searching, gentle and warm on the skin there in a way that made me shiver.

Then he turned me back round, though he didn't move his own chair back so we sat, knee to knee, facing each other. 'No nodule,' he said, a hint of a smile touching the corner of his mouth, 'that's a relief. For a minute there I thought you'd been reprogrammed.'

I grinned. He was referring to *Girl from Mars* issue 417, *The Cyborg Sacrifice*, where the only hint of whether robots had taken over a human's mind was a small metallic nodule implanted in the back of the head.

'No,' I said, 'I'm myself. I meant what I said. All of it.'

Dan nodded. 'Thank you. I shouldn't have stormed off and left you on the train. It was rude.'

'I'd been rude and I deserved it.'

'Well, I'd killed Girl from Mars.'

'She's tough enough to take it.'

'And so are you.' He laughed, but it was half a sigh. 'You were right, though. I've been thinking about it all day. I am telling the same story over and over. My reasons aren't as simple as you implied they are, and I'm not doing it without a certain awareness of the commercial appeal of that story, but it's the same story in the end. I keep on bringing people back from the dead. And when it comes down to it, I'm doing it to try to make myself happier.'

'And does it make you happy?'

'No,' he said thoughtfully. 'It doesn't. Lots of things do make me happy these days. But not that story, not any more.'

'Maybe it's time for a new story,' I said. Something about this conversation, maybe the subject, maybe Dan's closeness and the way he was looking straight into my eyes, maybe the way we were all alone in a very big room, was making it difficult for me to catch my breath properly.

'It's time for something new,' Dan said.

'Like what?'

'Like something I've been wanting to do for a while, and you'll have to tell me if it's not okay.'

'Me?'

'Yes. Okay?'

I wondered what the hell he was talking about. Maybe I'd missed it because his closeness was messing with my brain.

'Sure,' I said.

He leaned forward in his chair and kissed me on the lips.

It was a brief kiss but it tilted my world at a crashing angle and when it was finished I stared at Dan.

'Oh,' I said.

'Is it okay?'

'It's –' I touched my lips, which were very warm. 'You've wanted to do that for a while?'

'Yes.'

'Really?'

'Really. So is it okay?'

I leaned towards him experimentally, to see if it would happen again. Incredibly, it did.

Dan's lips fitted mine perfectly, strange and yet familiar from dreams. He cupped the side of my face in his warm hand and I put my fingertips on his shirt, above where his heart beat. He seemed calm and in control but his racing heart told a different story.

He wanted to kiss me. He'd wanted to for a long time. Maybe even half as much as I'd wanted to kiss him.

I wiggled forward, pressing closer, opening my mouth to him, and with a swift movement that made my world tilt even more, Dan pulled me off my chair and on to his lap. My legs curled round his and his arms held me very tightly and now it was nothing like I ever could have dreamed. In my dreams I'd seen him kissing me, seen how our bodies came together and how our eyes closed and lips met, but I hadn't heard the rustle of his clothes and the quickness of his breathing. I hadn't felt the shocking intimacy of his tongue and the smooth perfection of his teeth, or even the feel of his hair wound round my fingers. Or how his whole body and every motion told me that he wanted this, he wanted me. A moan escaped me and he held me even tighter, kissed me even harder and yet still with that gentleness, with that wonder that was Dan.

Two things happened at once: my mobile phone rang, and the door to the theatre opened.

'Oh, sorry,' someone said. Dan and I broke apart from each other in time to see a person leaving, closing the door behind him. It was someone vaguely familiar, though in my dazed and passionate state I couldn't place him.

'Your phone,' Dan said, just as it stopped ringing.

I was still in his lap, his hair was wound in my fingers and his face was inches from mine. My lips burned, and my chin burned in a different way from rubbing against the slight roughness of his chin. I hadn't been kissed in so long I'd forgotten that feeling. And I'd never been kissed by someone like Dan, someone who kissed as if he meant it. His lips were pinker too, and moist, and his black eyelashes were very long. I rested my cheek against the side of his face so I could feel his eyelashes brushing against my skin as he blinked. He ran his thumb up and down the side of my thigh, through my skirt. Little movements of desire, not as obvious as the kissing, but as important.

My phone began ringing again.

'Are you going to get that?' he asked, his voice rumbling against my chest.

'I can't imagine anything more urgent than this,' I said, and this time I kissed him. And sank into the pleasure of it.

My phone stopped, and then started up again immediately.

Dan pulled his head back a little and with one hand, the one that wasn't actually holding me, he reached into my open bag and found my ringing and vibrating phone. He glanced at the screen. 'It's Jim,' he said, and handed it to me.

Jim, three times in a row without leaving a message. I slid off Dan's lap back on to my chair, and answered the call.

'You've got to come,' he said, without waiting for me to say anything. 'Digger just called me from the hospital.'

What Are You Going to Do,
Hold Him Down?

The man in the hospital bed was a slack parody of what he must once have been. Skin fish-belly pale, hair sparse and brittle, a large frame shrunk down to a lump underneath the blanket.

Digger slumped beside him in a plastic chair. He glanced up when I arrived, his face hardly more alive than the patient's. Then his attention focused again on the man in the bed.

Jim, who'd been standing behind Digger, rushed over to me. 'I'm glad you're here,' he said, his voice hospital-hushed. 'How'd you make it so fast?'

'Got lucky with the train,' I said. 'Is Digger all right?'

'I'm not sure.'

'Who's that in the bed?'

Jim steered me out of the room and down the corridor to a little waiting area, with a few plastic chairs and some magazines. 'You know what he's like. He rang me and said he was in the hospital, and could I ring you and come. I thought he'd had an accident or something. But I found him here with his dad.'

'That's his dad? I didn't even know Digger had a dad.' His mother was dead, and he had Billy and Alice, his younger brother and sister, twins. He'd never mentioned his father.

'Apparently he's had a massive stroke. He's probably going to live, but they're not sure how much brain damage he's got.'

'Digger told you this?'

'A nurse. Digger hasn't said anything except that it's his dad. He's just been sitting there staring at him this whole time, since I got here anyway. I bought him a sandwich and he hasn't touched it.'

Digger not talking was not so unusual. But Digger not eating . . .

'How'd he suddenly get a dad?'

'I don't know.' Jim looked as worried as I felt.

'Should we be in there with him?'

'I think he just wants to know we're here.'

I nodded and sat down on a chair, which squeaked under my weight. 'Well, at least he's not all busted up from a car accident. I thought he'd be in traction at least.'

Actually my imagination during the entire journey had been filled with mental photographs much more gory than that, but there wasn't much point in going into that now.

Jim sat beside me. 'You're wearing a skirt,' he said. 'And you've changed your hair.'

'Oh. Yeah.'

'How was the Con?'

The Con. Dan. I blushed and dipped my head to hide it.

'Oh, you know, it's the Con. I got a bunch of indies, but they're in my hotel room with all my other stuff.'

'Were the Stormtroopers there?'

'Of course.'

'How did the panel go?'

'Great.' I blushed harder. 'Actually, I – I'm liking Dan's story, you know.'

Jim snorted. 'Well, that's something.'

'I think he's – you know – becoming a bit more human.'

'Ugh, I don't want to talk about it, I've had enough bad news today.'

'Right.' Relief mixed with guilt felt a bit weird, but at least I didn't have to talk to Jim about kissing Dan. It wasn't the time or the place for snog-talk.

'Something else happened, though,' I said. 'I had a chat with Stevo, and he wants to meet up.'

'Yeah, I'll believe that when I see it.'

'No, he means it, Jim. He said he was worried that we wouldn't like Brian.' No need to go into all the other stuff about this, either, how Stevo had felt left out at first, or how he said we closed ranks on strangers. We could discuss it later, if we wanted. Today was a day for slanting things towards the positive. 'He's missed us as much as we've missed him.'

'Hmmm.'

We lapsed into silence, punctuated by the noise of nurses walking past in rubber-soled shoes. I got us some coffee at one point and brought Digger a cup, though he didn't look up when I put it down beside him. The man in the bed didn't have a beard, and his eyes were closed, but I could see that he was tall, and had Digger's broad shoulders and straight nose. I sat with Digger for a while, and then went back to Jim.

He was reading *Hot! Hot!* magazine, which meant that he'd exhausted all other reading material in the room. He looked up when I sat down.

'Says here that Carmen Clare's gone back to LA. Strange, I thought she said England was *so cute.*'

'Maybe she couldn't deal with the cuteness.' It occurred to me that maybe Dan had kissed me because Carmen had left the country. But then I pushed the thought out of my mind. There was enough to worry about without spoiling that one good thing, too.

'Probably she's gone to hang out with *thrilling Stephen* again. Can you believe she's going to be the lead in *Star Pirates*? I was looking forward to that film. Now I'll have to bring tomatoes to throw at the screen. In fact, I'm not sure I can ever watch any movies again, the people making them seem so annoying.'

'I don't think they're all like that, Jim. For example—'

Digger appeared in the waiting area and I jumped up and hugged his arm. He looked smaller than usual, though he felt as huge as always.

'Visiting hours are over,' he said.

'Are you okay?'

'Pub.'

The closest one to the hospital was a chain pub, dominated by fruit machines and posters about cheap alco-pops. I waited for Jim to make a comment about these places being the McDonald's of drinking, but he didn't say it. I wished he would. We could all do with a little crumb of normality today.

We were well into our second pints when Digger finally spoke. 'You're wearing a skirt,' he said to me.

'You've got a father,' I replied. I wasn't sure if it was safe, but somebody had to say something sooner or later.

Digger lifted his glass to his lips and swallowed the rest of his beer. The pint glass was tiny in his hand. He put it down on the table and said, in an everyday voice, 'He used to beat the shit out of me.'

Jim put down his glass, too. So did I.

'Whenever I did something wrong,' he said. 'Or when I did something right, but not enough of it. Sometimes when I didn't do anything and he just felt like it. He used a belt and his fists. Or whatever he could find. I thought it was because he had a temper but then when I got older I noticed he never touched my face. Just my body where it could stay hidden.'

'Oh,' I said.

'I didn't tell anybody. Nobody knew.' Digger lifted his glass, seemed to notice for the first time that it was empty, and stood up. 'Another beer?'

'I'll get them,' said Jim, and hurried to the bar, his hand in his pocket.

Digger sat stroking his beard, waiting for his drink. He didn't say anything. I tried to take this in. Picturing him younger and bruised. The idea was too unbelievable until I suddenly remembered how Digger left the room during NSPCC advertisements and all at once I could see him as if on a television screen, small and skinny, baggy clothes covering his hurt, and a pale, bare, unmarked face.

When Jim came back Digger took another massive drink and then continued in his normal, conversational tone. 'I didn't mind, though. As long as it was me and not Billy and Alice. They were smaller. I could take it. And if I was around, he wouldn't touch them.'

'Jesus Christ,' exploded Jim, 'do you mean you *asked* him to hit you instead of your brother and sister?'

'Only until I got taller than him. Then he stopped. But he still got angry.'

Digger looked away from his pint, at a flashing fruit machine. He seemed mesmerised by it. I realised he hadn't once met my eyes, or Jim's, since I'd shown up. But he seemed to need us here, seemed to need to tell us about what had happened.

'Did it work?' I asked. 'Did he beat them up too?'

'Not so much. Not much at all, I don't think. I waited to start university until they were ready to move out. That way I knew they were safe.'

'Do they know you took it instead of them?' I'd met Billy and Alice; he was an electrician and she worked in a café and was engaged to be married. Both of them were quite chatty and seemed normal enough.

'I – I'm not sure,' Digger said. 'They're okay, though.'

'Why weren't they at the hospital?' Jim asked.

'I didn't tell them. They don't like him. We haven't talked to him in years.'

'But you felt the need to come down here and sit by his bedside all day?' Jim was so angry that his lips had gone white. He looked as if he might punch something.

'The hospital called me. I'm the oldest.'

'Why didn't you tell us?'

'I don't like to talk about it.'

'But for Christ's sake, we're your *best friends*!'

'There are things you don't say.'

'Not things this big. You can't hide stuff for years.'

'Are you sure about that?'

Jim didn't reply to that. He clenched his fists on the table, and I noticed his pint had gone down quickly.

I stood up. 'I'll get another round,' I said. Digger was still strangely calm, but Jim needed another drink.

I was waiting for the barman to pour us all a whisky chaser when Jim joined me at the bar. 'He says he's going to take care of his father,' Jim hissed, his eyes aflame. 'He's going to give up his fucking life to look after a bastard who used to beat him to a pulp.'

'He's upset,' I said. 'He doesn't know what he's saying.' But privately, I thought that sounded exactly like the sort of thing Digger would do.

'We've got to talk him out of it, Fil.'

'We can try.'

'I won't let him do it.'

I paid for the drinks. 'He's six inches taller than you and weighs twice as much as you do, Jim. What are you going to do, hold him down?'

'I can give it a go.' He flexed his hands as if to practise for a wrestling match, but I shoved three pints into them and we hurried back to the table as if Digger were going to disappear to look after his disabled father at this very minute.

But Digger was still there, still staring at the flashing lights. When we put the drinks down in front of him he drank steadily and quickly, as if he had a hole inside him that he needed the alcohol to fill. Jim and I, on the other hand, didn't touch ours. I still had half my pint left over from the last round. I hadn't eaten since a grabbed sandwich lunch at the Con and the beer I'd drunk was sloshing around in my empty stomach.

'Doesn't seem right to sit here without the two of you arguing,' Digger said.

'Unfortunately we both agree that you should think about it before you decide to nurse your father back to health,' I said. 'You've had a big enough shock today and you shouldn't be jumping into things. Besides, he might get completely better and not need you anyway. He probably will.'

'He won't,' Digger said. 'And I'm the only one he has.'

He drained his pint and then knocked back his whisky in one. Usually four pints and a shot were hardly enough to touch the sides of Digger's sobriety but maybe events had made him more susceptible because when he stood he had a distinct sway.

'Same again?' he said, seemingly not noticing our full pints and our two full whiskys on the table.

'I think you need to go home and get some rest, mate,' Jim said.

'Yeah. Maybe I do.' Digger drew in a big breath and slowly let it out. Then he actually looked at me and Jim.

'Will you two do me a favour?' he asked. 'Will you talk to each other? Sort things out between you? You need to.'

'Sure, mate,' said Jim. 'We'll do that. Come on, let's get you home.'

We dropped Digger off in a cab and went back to ours. As soon as I'd shut the door behind us I thought about what Digger had asked us to do. The house felt quiet, as if it knew and was waiting for a conversation.

I made us cheese on toast and tea and we sat in front of the television watching whatever was on until we were both yawning and then we went to bed, parting on the landing. 'Goodnight,' Jim said to me, and 'Goodnight,' I said back, and that was all we said.

That Gap Between Us

S ome time later, I was woken up by the noise outside. It was a swishing and a cracking, interspersed with violent breaths. I crept out of bed and went to the window, which was open a little bit to let in the cooler night air, and looked out on to the back garden.

Jim was out there. He wore blue pyjamas. He had a board in his hand; it was a piece left over from when we'd put in some new kitchen units. He gripped it with both of his hands and he swatted, with a hard chopping motion, at a butterfly bush. Leaves and purple flowers littered the grass around him.

His face was twisted in a way I'd never seen it before, like anger and pain all mixed up into one expression. He slashed and slashed at the bush. The muscles in his shoulders strained against his pyjamas and his hair flew around his face. His breath came in pants and grunts and half-formed sobs.

I bit my lip.

Who was he fighting? Digger's father? Digger's own grief? Or was it something in himself? The kids at school who'd always laughed at him? The guilt because he'd needed to break away from his mother, the fact that Stevo had left? Everyone with the power to mock and scorn and hit? Or the fact that with all the enemies in the world, he could only hit a butterfly bush?

Was he striking out at me?

The truth was that I could guess but I could not know. I watched Jim battle with the butterfly bush; I held my breath with every blow and I felt the depth of everything inside him that remained a mystery despite all of our years together. Or maybe it was a mystery because of all our years.

I pictured myself going downstairs and out into the cool garden, stepping on twigs and broken flowers, and holding out my arms to Jim. I stepped back from the window, wondering if I was brave enough to leap over that gap between us. To find out what he'd feel like as I held him, what we would say to each other if we could talk.

I stood there, motionless, because to move forward would be to change everything.

Jim stopped slashing. He stood there for a moment, breathing heavily, his eyes glittering like a warrior's in the moonlight. Then he stooped and carefully began to gather the shattered pieces of the bush. As I watched, he picked up every leaf and every blossom and put them behind the bush's stem, where they wouldn't be visible.

I waited until he had finished and heard him coming through the kitchen door into the house. Then I climbed back into bed and breathed as if I were asleep.

*

The next morning I was brushing my teeth with my spare toothbrush, since I'd left my usual one in Brighton, when there was a knock on the door. 'I'll get it,' I called, and clumped down the stairs in my bare feet, T-shirt and tracksuit bottoms, figuring it was probably Digger.

It was Dan. He was wearing jeans and a grey T-shirt and had his own bag slung over his shoulder and mine in his hand.

The idea of Dan here at my house was so alien that I stood there blinking at him, my toothbrush still in my hand.

What should I do? Should I slam the door and run away? Should I launch myself into his arms and kiss him? The thought brought back a full-body memory of what we'd been doing the last time we'd been together and with that came a punch of guilt. A slash at the butterfly bush.

'Hi,' Dan said. He smiled at me, that make-Fil's-insides-melt smile. He looked so glad to see me.

'How do you know where I live?' I asked him. Grace and charm, that's me all over.

'Anthony found out so I could bring your stuff back for you.' He held up my bags. 'And so I could see how you're doing. Are you okay?'

'Um. Yeah. I'm fine.'

'How about your friend?'

'He's – not so good.' And at the very moment Digger had been not so good, I'd been at the ComicsCon snogging Dan. That whole vow thing had been Digger's idea, and I'd trampled all over it while Digger was rushing to the hospital.

God, what sort of a friend was I?

'I'm sorry,' Dan said.

'Yeah, me too.'

He paused. 'Can I come in?' he asked.

Duh. The man had brought my bags all the way back from Brighton for me, he'd given me the best kisses I'd ever had in my life, and he deserved at least to be asked in for coffee.

But then he'd meet Jim, who was probably in the kitchen making breakfast right now. And how was I supposed to explain to Jim now that I'd betrayed him and Digger, too?

'I don't think that's a good idea,' I said.

'Oh.' His face fell. 'Well. Okay. I understand.'

'No, you don't.' I heard movement behind me somewhere, in the house, and I quickly went on to the doorstep and closed the door most of the way behind me. 'I'm sorry, Dan, I can't really explain it. It's just not a good time right now. My friend's father is very sick and we need to look after him.'

'Right. Okay. Well – here's your stuff.'

I took my bags from him. The handle of my overnight bag was warm from his skin. I thought about his hands on my legs and my face.

'Thanks,' I said. 'I'll see you at the sweatshop, all right?'

'Yeah. I'll see you. Bye, Fil.'

He turned away and I watched him walk down the street, until Jim called out, 'Do you want toast?' and I went back inside the house.

The Dead

Episode One hit the stands that Thursday, but I didn't really notice. Jim and I spent time down at the hospital whenever we could, with Digger. Not that we could do anything; his father had regained consciousness within twenty-four hours but he couldn't talk or walk, and had no use of his left-hand side. Most days he stared at Digger through his one good eye.

Digger seemed barely conscious himself. He walked and sat through the days. But we both felt that we needed to be there for him, in case he suddenly wanted to talk some more.

It was better to be at the hospital, anyway, because our house seemed to get quieter every day.

'Come and stay with Jim and me,' I said to Digger one day as visiting hours drew to a close. His father had been moved the day before to a rehabilitation unit, though nobody knew for how long. 'I know the couch is too small for you, but you can have my bed and I'll sleep in the studio. Then you won't have to worry about food or laundry or whatever.'

'I've got things to do at home,' Digger told me, and he went back to staring at his father, who, with the nurse's help, was attempting to drink a glass of water with a straw. I couldn't imagine what Digger had to do at home. Somehow I doubted it was making food and doing laundry. Digger's wardrobe was not varied at the best of times but he'd been wearing the same sweatshirt for days.

His father dropped the straw out of his mouth. His lips twisted and his tongue thrust at his crooked teeth. 'Dugls,' he said, 'whyeroo ere?'

The words were mangled but Digger took them as if they were perfectly normal.

'I'm going to look after you,' he said.

The corner of Mr Mann's mouth drooped. 'Go,' he said. Crystal clear.

Digger didn't move from his chair.

In my spare time, I avoided UPC. For one thing I didn't want to be in the sweatshop in case Digger needed me. Largely, though, I was avoiding Dan. The situation was complicated enough.

Stevo rang, as he'd said he would, and when he heard the news about Digger's dad he came to the hospital to visit. He didn't bring Brian, but he promised that he would when we weren't spending so much time at the hospital. Afterwards we all went to the chain pub, which was becoming perforce a regular haunt of ours, and sat together over pints and crisps. I'd bought the crisps as a temptation to Digger, but he didn't touch them.

It was awkward. Digger wasn't talking, just sinking his pints, and Jim was radiating distinctly hostile vibes. I remembered what Stevo had said at the conference, how I hadn't been there when he'd first become friends with us, and I did my best to smooth things along. Eventually I got Jim and Stevo talking about a programme they'd seen on meerkats on Animal Planet, and then about animal social systems in general, and soon they were chatting along, almost as if they'd never stopped.

Almost, but not quite. But I thought that in time, it would get better, especially after we'd met Brian and felt more involved in their life together. And, of course, Digger would be back to being himself soon. Wouldn't he?

In between hospital visits and sitting in the pub listening to the fruit machines, I had to get on with Episode Three. So after about a week of avoiding the issue I took the tube to Victoria and walked up the road to UPC. I managed not to take a short detour to look at the outside of Suffolk Mansions, where Dan lived. I was jittery enough, wondering what I was going to say to him if I saw him in the sweatshop. I'd have to . . . what? Kiss him? Tell him I couldn't kiss him? The whole prospect made me feel like hiding somewhere.

I showed my badge to the receptionist at UPC and she said, 'You don't need to do that, you know.'

She'd never spoken to me before, so I regarded her with some surprise. 'I thought we needed to pass security,' I said.

'Yes. But I know who you are. You've been working here for years and you're pretty distinctive looking.'

I tried to remember if I'd ever seen her before. I must have done. Dozens, if not hundreds, of times, from what she'd said. She had golden-brown skin and straightened black hair and a slightly exasperated expression.

'Oh,' I said. 'Okay, I won't show my badge.'

'You can just say hi instead. "Hi, Becca." It's easier.'

'Right. Sure. Uh – hi, Becca.'

'Hi to you too,' she said.

By the time the lift reached the fourth floor my palms were sweating and I felt like crawling down the lift shaft, no doubt leaving a trail of nervous slime behind me. But as soon as I approached the sweatshop I saw that the lights were off and that I was safe.

It had a deserted air about it. There were dirty coffee cups on my side of the room, and biscuit packets, and scattered sketches – exactly the way I'd left it before the convention. Dan's desk was absolutely clean, and there was no sign of his laptop or notebook. I quickly checked his top drawer, which was empty.

So he was working from home today. No big deal. But there wasn't a feeling of him in the air, and I couldn't help but suspect that he hadn't been here since the Con, either.

'You'd have thought he'd have called me, when his first comic book ever came out,' I said aloud to the empty room, but I knew why he hadn't. He was avoiding me, too. I could ask Becca when I went downstairs to confirm it, but I didn't need to.

I gathered up my supplies and my favourite mug and slung them all in the big bag I'd used to bring them here. Who'd have thought I would be sad to be going back to work in my own space?

Drawing Episode Three was a welcome escape, but I couldn't seem to do it while visiting the hospital with Digger, and not for very long at home, either. Though I was as absorbed as ever in the story and the setting (the TIME device was particularly challenging and fun to draw) I found thoughts of the real world interrupting. I ended up developing a routine of drawing in two-hour chunks when I was home. Two hours in her world, and then a long stretch in mine until I had another two hours free.

The two hours drawing raced by all by themselves, and the rest of the time dragged. I wished I had a time distortion device myself so that I could make it happen the opposite way.

Digger's father began eating solid foods, having re-learned how to swallow. Digger had lost weight, and though he had a bit to lose before it became dangerous, the speed at which he was dropping it made me and Jim worry. I consulted with one of the nurses and she gave me some recipes for high-protein shakes. The problem was getting them down Digger when all he seemed interested in was something with an alcohol percentage of five per cent or greater.

I got Episode Four via email from Anthony. Typically, he hadn't included any personal note with best wishes for me or my friend, but he had sent it by attaching Dan's original email to him on the bottom. 'Hi, Anthony, here's Four, hope you like it, Dan,' it said, and I read that sentence over and over again, trying to figure out any deeper meaning, possibly meant for me, but reluctantly I concluded it was just a note to Anthony.

The script was a little bit of a surprise. As I'd expected, Jackson Silver grabbed the TIME device and used it to change the order of events so that Girl from Mars avoided the Arcturan electricity. But the mere act of him using such a device flooded the caves with a strange energy, which quickly coalesced into the shapes of ghosts from Girl from Mars's past.

You can't be a comic-book heroine for over fifty years

without ending up involved in a lot of death. In my career drawing *Girl from Mars*, I, personally, had depicted splattered civilians, blasted villains and countless vanquished aliens. But I could see where Dan's hours in the archives had paid off, because the ghosts he had chosen were those of the beings whose deaths Girl from Mars had in some way caused or failed to prevent.

There was her sidekick, Berger, who fell out of an airlock while Girl from Mars was engaged in battling the evil Wartan, back in 1972. The six virginal Goolat sisters, killed in 1986 by a venomous egremort worm before Girl from Mars could find the cure. Nancy, the young stalker who Girl hadn't been able to stop from plummeting to her death in 2006. A sentient cloud dispersed in 1998. Girl from Mars's own mother, who died while her daughter was in exile. And, of course, Kingsley the Talking Ant, crushed in 1959.

I read it tucked up on the couch in my attic studio and shook my head in admiration. However ignorantly he might have begun this project, Daniel McKay now knew his stuff. He'd used over fifty years of comic-book history to choose the figures most likely to inspire remorse, guilt and soul-searching in Girl from Mars. And the man could write. Even with the small amount of words that would fit into a speech bubble, he could create a rich well of emotion. I knew, reading his script, that Girl from Mars had thought about these dead every single day of her life; she never stopped blaming herself. And that these ghosts, inside her Martian soul, were a big part of what kept her from going back home.

It was the best comic-book script I had ever read.

And of course I read into it. If Dan's message to Anthony had yielded no results, this script gave me plenty. Daniel McKay, once again, was writing about his wife. But this time, instead of creating a fantasy where Elizabeth could come back to life, he was writing about his own grief. How even though it couldn't possibly be his fault that she had died, he felt responsible all the same.

Had he done this because I had confronted him about it? Or had he planned for the story to go this way all along? I didn't know, but I paced around my studio and thought of him writing it and felt so, so sorry for him. I read through the script yet again and I wanted to go straight to Suffolk Mansions and give Dan a massive hug.

But I couldn't do that, of course. Because if this script was an expression of the pain Dan felt, then it was also a message to me that the past was much more powerful than anything in the present. Next to this emotion, our kiss meant nothing. A little blip of momentary lust.

Help

I was pacing gloomily around my studio mulling over all of this when Jim came up with a couple of copies of the new *Girl from Mars*. Though normally I would joyfully grab them from his hands, this time I stayed on my couch and thought. Had another month gone by? It seemed both the quickest and the slowest month of my life.

'Your Episode Two is out,' Jim said unnecessarily, standing in the doorway without coming in. I nodded.

'It's really good,' he said. 'Really good, Fil. I read it in the shop. Then I had to read it again as soon as I got home. I think it's probably the best thing you've ever done.'

He seemed proud, as usual. But there was something else, almost a note of disappointment.

'Told you,' I said.

'Yeah. But I thought – anyway, it's different. You've changed your style.'

'Have I?'

He nodded.

'Huh,' I said. 'That's interesting. It wasn't intentional.'

'I brought you an extra one to bring to Digger. I've got to work on this systems upgrade this afternoon if it's going to go ahead.'

He'd been working a lot. Sometimes he even went into the office at Compugist. The empty house made the time drag more.

I decided to try a slightly different tack: I went to Digger's flat to pick him up and go to the unit with him, instead of meeting him at the hospital as we usually did. Even though I'd texted him to tell him when I was coming, I had to knock four times before he answered the door.

He didn't say anything, just shuffled backwards out of the way so that I could come in. Digger's flat was always tidy, much tidier than our house was; sometimes when he thought we weren't looking he surreptitiously put our stuff away. The first thing I noticed when I walked in was the line of Glenlivet bottles by the side of the couch. Each of them neatly placed next to its neighbour, and each of them empty.

'Um, my comic came out,' I told my friend. 'You know, the big "new direction" thing. Episode Two.' He turned away to get his house keys, so I put the comic on the coffee table, being careful not to knock over any of the bottles. There was a stack of books on the table, all from the library. The top one read: *Coping with a Stroke Victim: Rehabilitation and Physical Therapy.*

Should I say anything about it? Should I just carry on? If I confronted him would he withdraw more?

'So Jim's making his curry, and said you should get over to ours for seven.'

'I'm busy,' said Digger, going to the door and pausing to wait for me.

It was too much. 'Are you doing all this research so that your father can come and live with you when he gets out of hospital?'

'Probably I'll live with him. Too many stairs here.'

'Digger, you can't just sit in this room and drink and plan to throw your life away on a person who made your life hell.'

'Fil,' he said, 'I am twenty-eight years old. I'm the only person in my family to have gone to university. I live on my own. I don't have a career. I don't have a girlfriend. I haven't achieved anything except for a degree I don't use. What else am I going to do?'

It was the most he'd said in weeks and his voice sounded rusty.

'You have us,' I told him. 'You've got your friends.'

'I want more than that. And my father needs me.'

'At least get your brother and sister to help you.'

'Billy and Ally are better away from it.'

'At least get us to help you. Stop shutting us out. Let us share some of it. Like we could have a rota system or something, you could go round on Mondays, I could do Tuesdays, Jim could do Wednesdays, like that. And there must be carers and things you can get, people to help. It can't all be on you.'

'He's mine,' Digger said, and he went into the corridor and waited for me to come out.

'Please let us help,' I said. He shut the door behind us and trudged ahead of me.

As we rode the tube in silence, along with all the other silent people, I thought of Dan. I usually did these days when I was on the Underground. He had a talent with words, he could talk about feelings, he knew what it was like to have ghosts. I wondered if he'd know what to say.

Unfortunately, it didn't look as if I'd be able to ask him any time soon, if ever.

When we got to the rehabilitation unit, Digger stopped short just within sight of his father's door. A man and a woman stood outside it, looking through the little window. They both had curly brown hair, but that was the only way you'd know that they were related to Digger. Alice was five foot six or seven, pretty and curvy; her twin Billy was wiry and well under six feet.

When they saw Digger, Alice lifted her chin. The siblings might not share the gene for height, but they shared one for stubbornness. 'We want to see him,' she said.

Digger hesitated.

'We're grown up now,' Billy said. 'We don't need you protecting us. We need to face him sooner or later.'

'Let us, Doug,' added Alice quietly.

I nudged Digger's arm. Then he opened the door, and the three of them went in.

Headline News at the
Water Cooler

'And in final news, the Peregrine Award nominations are announced next week and I'd be very surprised if we didn't scoop a few. Sales on *Girl from Mars* are incredible. Just incredible.'

What was even more incredible was that Anthony hadn't sworn for an entire editorial meeting. He even nearly achieved a smile.

'The Peregrines will go to indies this year,' I murmured to Stevo, who sat beside me, perched in the back as if the past few months had never happened. '*2000AD* and Marvel bagged the big ones last year and they'll have had enough of the mainstream publishers. They feel it's their job to encourage grassroots development.'

Quite frankly I had too much to think about to care who got the Peregrines this year, but I was talking about it to keep up some semblance of normality, much as how Jim and I had gone to the pub quiz by ourselves. Without

Digger we did worse than ever, even with Rachel feeding us answers whenever she came by to pretend to clear glasses. As with all our other attempts at normality, it only served to highlight how different everything really was now.

Even UPC was feeling weird. I'd been expecting Becca's cheery 'Hi, Fil!' when I came in, and even rehearsed a reply, so that wasn't surprising. But other people were smiling at me, too. Some of them even said hi. Maybe it was that virus theory at work, but it was definitely strange.

'I'm not sure the awards work like that,' Stevo mused. 'Surely they can't do it according to a quota and politics. It's for the best comics, no matter who publishes them.'

'Being in love has erased all your cynicism,' I told him. 'If it were awarded to the best comics, *Girl from Mars* would win it every single year because it is self-evidently the best comic on the planet. In reality, it hasn't won a Peregrine since Wayne Jayson in 1984.'

'What about Buster McMahon in 2006?'

'He got it for writing *Death Stare*, not *Girl*. An indie. I'm telling you, UPC hasn't got a chance in—'

'Brown and Ng, as glad as I am to see you on speaking terms again, I suggest you save the school-yard gossip for after the meeting. As I was saying, I have the greatest hopes for our *Girl from Mars* twosome.'

There was a low buzz of laughter and chatter in response to this, and several heads turned to look at me. My face flushed, and it didn't stop until Anthony had moved on to discussing something else.

Where was Dan, anyway? I'd checked the sweatshop and the archives before coming to the meeting, and there was no sign he'd been anywhere near the building for the past few weeks.

I missed him. I also missed Digger. Even though I saw him every day, I missed Jim, too. Our conversations, naturally enough, tended to focus around Digger and what we were going to do. We hadn't had a single good knock-down argument about science fiction for weeks now. Or anything else.

It was ironic that not long ago I'd been thinking about how I was balancing myself between two different worlds. Now I barely had enough world to wrap around me.

Stevo, though, was back. We'd probably go to O Solo Mio for coffee after this. The old habit only emphasised how much everything else had changed.

The meeting finished with Anthony's customary 'Now get the hell back to work', and I craned my neck round again in case Dan had come in while I wasn't paying attention. He hadn't. I did spot Bradley the letterer, though, and remembering that he'd seemed to be chummy with Dan earlier, I touched his shoulder.

'Hey,' I said. Though we worked on the same title and often on the same issues, I was pretty sure this was the first time I'd instigated a conversation with him in my life. I'd talked with him, of course, but mostly by email and mostly because he'd said something first.

'Fil,' he greeted me. 'Loving Episode Three.'

'Oh, are you lettering it?'

'Surely am. You and Danny-boy are hot stuff.' He raised his eyebrows in a way I didn't quite know how to interpret.

'Oh, well, speaking of that,' I said, trying for nonchalance, 'have you spoken to Dan lately? Any idea about how he got out of coming to the meeting?'

Bradley's eyebrows went even higher. 'You're the best person to know about what Dan's doing, I'd have thought.'

'What do you mean?'

'Well, after what we all heard about the two of you at the Con—'

Oh, shit. 'What did you all hear?'

I must have sounded as alarmed as I felt because Bradley held up his hands to placate me. 'Don't worry, Fil, everybody's really happy for you. This place isn't exactly seething with sexual activity so every little bit is headline news at the water cooler.'

'Who saw us?' I asked, resigned.

'Who saw who, doing what?' Stevo asked at my shoulder, hugely interested. He was evidently as out of the gossip loop as I was, even though I was the subject of it.

'It was Mike Hammell, from RDR,' Bradley told me. I had no idea who Mike Hammell was, but RDR was a company that made interactive computer games with comic-book-type superheroes. Digger had a couple of them. 'Apparently he forgot his glasses in the theatre so he went back and saw the two of you with your lips—'

'Please, please stop,' I said, burying my face in my hands. So it had gone through RDR, and then UPC, and probably through every single comics pro and fan in the country that *Girl from Mars*'s writer and artist had been caught in a public lip-lock.

No wonder everyone had been smiling at me today. They were laughing their arses off at me and my supposed love life.

'Nobody's seen either of you since the Con so we all assumed you were all loved-up together somewhere,'

Bradley continued. 'Collaborating.'

'Oh, God,' I said, and bolted from the room. I could have sworn I heard Bradley chuckling behind me.

I took the stairs, not wanting to risk running into anybody else who was going to laugh knowingly at the sight of me and my loose lips, and charged through reception with an embarrassed half-wave to Becca. I was several metres down Vauxhall Bridge Road before Stevo caught up with me.

'You were kissing Daniel McKay?'

'Please, Stevo, I don't want to talk about it.'

'It's fantastic, though! He's really cute. Is he a good kisser? I bet he is. Have you been seeing him?'

'Stevo, just because you're all in love doesn't mean everyone else has to be walking in sweetness and light. It was a mistake and a one-off. I don't want to talk about it.'

'What did Jim say? And Digger?'

'They don't know. And if you mention it to them I will personally rip you apart limb from limb. They have enough to worry about without knowing about a single, isolated kiss that will never happen again in a million years. Now can we go for coffee and talk about something else?'

'Sure,' said Stevo, but within thirty seconds he was whistling. After a few bars I twigged the tune as Prince's 'Kiss'.

I punched him on the arm as hard as I could, but he only laughed.

My Name is Fil, and I'm a Snogaholic

On the following Thursday Jim and I were approaching the doors of the rehab unit when we saw a familiar red-haired figure walking past the other way. She changed her course when she saw us. 'Hi,' Rachel said. 'What are you up to?'

'Oh, we're visiting Digger's dad,' Jim said.

'Digger's dad?' Her eyes widened in concern. 'What's wrong with him?'

I shoved my hands in my pockets.

'Well, really we're seeing Digger,' Jim told her. 'And he's visiting his dad.'

'Can I come?'

'I don't—'

'Please? I haven't got anything to do and maybe I can help.'

I remembered what Stevo had said about us closing ranks on new people.

'You might as well,' I said, though I couldn't muster any enthusiasm for it.

Rachel smiled. She fell into step with us and chattered easily all the way across the lobby and up in the lift, about her day, her flat, the lateness of her bus and the great book she was reading. I tried not to listen, especially when Jim answered her, because it felt like Jim and I hadn't had an easy conversation like that for longer than I wanted to think about.

How come she could breeze in, when I felt like lead?

When we got to his father's room, Digger was in the chair that seemed by now to be permanently welded to his body. He actually looked up when he heard Rachel's voice and nodded to her, which was more than I'd got in days. 'Hello, Mr Mann,' she said cheerily to his father and he smiled at her with half his face.

My mouth dropped open. It had never occurred to me to speak to Digger's father. Mostly because of what he'd done to Digger, but also because of what he was going to do. But Rachel, obviously ignorant of his past, asked him questions, coaxed answers from him and generally treated him like a human being.

I sat in a chair, useless, while Rachel talked to Mr Mann and Jim stood beside Digger.

Nearly an hour later a pretty, buxom woman with neatly corn-rowed hair bustled in and said in a musical West Indies accent, 'Afternoon, Mr Mann, it's Angelique. Time for your therapy now. You staying to help us, Douglas?'

Digger nodded for the second time that afternoon and we took our cue to leave. As we left I thought I glimpsed him smiling through his beard at Angelique, but I thought surely that had been wishful thinking.

Or maybe not so wishful. Because if I were indulging

in a fantasy, surely I'd imagine that Digger had smiled at me and at Jim. That I'd been the one to bring a bit of sunshine into the room, not these strangers.

Rachel grew silent as we walked out of the building. She walked with us to the bus stop, and got on the bus with us, sitting in front of us and turning around to face us.

'Digger's dad reminds me of my uncle,' she said. 'He had a stroke about a year ago and he was a lot like that in the first few months afterwards. He really recovered, though, with therapy. He's nearly back to normal now. He forgets words sometimes but that's about it.'

'You should tell that to Digger,' Jim said.

'I will.'

I wished I could say something, do something, be something other than a helpless lump. No wonder Jim liked Rachel. No wonder everyone liked her, except me.

She got off the bus with us and walked with us to our house. I kept on waiting for Jim to make an excuse, to signal that she should go away, but he didn't, and I couldn't quite say it myself. She'd helped Digger to smile. I owed her something.

'God, you're so lucky to live in such a big house,' she said. 'My flat is the pokiest little thing, isn't it, Jim? But working in a bar while you get your MA doesn't really get you a Central London penthouse.'

She was at our front door. I kept my hands in my pockets, not getting out my keys to unlock the door. Couldn't this woman take a hint? I saw Jim hesitate, and then he put his own key in the lock.

Rachel stepped into our hallway and just like that, I saw our house through new eyes: the carpet we'd never bothered to replace, the doodles on the wallpaper, the lightbulb I'd neglected to change. It seemed dark and cramped and prosaic and I gritted my teeth at this perception of my own life.

'Whoa, how many *Star Trek* videos have you got?' she said as she came into our front room.

'All of them,' Jim said quietly.

'Oh. Cool.'

Automatically I went to my flowery girl chair and Jim sat on his side of the couch. Rachel sat beside him, in the big dip in the middle.

'That's Digger's seat,' I said.

'Oh.' She moved over a little, to Stevo's side of the couch.

'Do you want a cup of—' Jim caught my eye, and his voice died out.

Silence. I watched her looking around. The mismatched furniture, the shrine to The Peregrine-That-Has-Not-Yet-Been-Won on the mantelpiece, the crooked candles.

'What's—' Rachel cleared her throat. 'What's your lizard's name?'

'The Baz is an iguana,' Jim told her.

'I used to have a cannibalistic hamster,' she said, and my mobile phone rang.

It was Anthony. 'Brown!' he said as soon as I answered. 'Get down here, now!'

Yikes! The problem with Anthony's vernacular was that you never knew whether he was actually angry or not. 'Am I in trouble for something?'

'You are if you don't get down here sharpish.'

I checked the clock. 'It's nearly six.'

'All the more reason to put your skates on.' He rang off.

'What is it?' asked Jim.

I stood up. 'I've got to go down to UPC, and God knows how long it will take. Maybe he needs Episode Four done early.'

'Oh.' Rachel looked from me to Jim. 'I should probably be going too, then.'

'Probably,' I muttered, though I couldn't tell if she heard me. I ran upstairs and grabbed some art supplies, in case Anthony was indeed sending me to the sweatshop for the night. Rachel was still sitting on the couch when I came back downstairs.

'I'll text you if I end up working all night, Jim,' I said. He nodded, and I hesitated. It seemed wrong to leave Rachel here. But Anthony expected me to jump.

God, what was wrong with me? Rachel was nice. She wasn't going to trash the place. 'See you later,' I said, and ran for the tube.

Becca had knocked off by the time I got to UPC so I swiped my ID. Any worries about Rachel had been totally obliterated by my growing worries about what Anthony wanted with me at this hour. Did he have a problem with the art for Episode Three? I personally thought it was pretty good – well, more than pretty good actually, I thought it was nearly even as good as I wanted it to be – but maybe I'd let too much of my gloom show through.

Maybe he was going to tell me off for not spending enough time in the sweatshop, after he'd gone to all the trouble of half clearing it out for us. Or maybe—

I went cold and hot all at once. Or maybe he'd heard the rumours about me and Dan kissing at the Con, and he wanted to yell at me for being an unprofessional snogaholic.

I swallowed as I went down the corridor to Anthony's office. Through the glass door I could see two figures, and I didn't have to look twice to know that one of them was Dan.

Oh, God. We were going to be chewed out for kissing.

Could I run and hide under a rock somewhere?

'Brown!' thundered Anthony, sticking his head out of the door. 'Took your time, didn't you?'

I scampered into the office, my heart pounding. 'Hi,' I muttered. I didn't dare to look at Dan, but I felt him in the air.

'Right,' Anthony said, 'you are probably both wondering why I called you here so urgently, at a time when any sane person would be down the pub, but this is something that needs to be dealt with in person and with both of you present.'

It was the kissing. And even more terribly exquisitely humiliating, I was going to have to hear Dan apologising for it too.

'I didn't mean for it to happen,' I said quickly, so I could get in there first.

'Shut up,' said Anthony, and I glanced at Dan. He looked gorgeous and sexy and a little bit sad. Like he'd looked on my doorstep weeks earlier when I wouldn't let him in.

Anthony opened a drawer of his filing cabinet, put his hand in, and paused. 'I had some news today,' he said, and paused some more, as if he were getting ready to pull out a rabbit or something.

Dan broke the pause. 'What's the news?'

'*Girl from Mars* has only bloody been nominated for three Peregrine awards.'

My mouth dropped open. 'But—'

Three! Three Peregrines! It couldn't be true.

'But they don't announce the nominees until Friday,' I managed.

'Tomorrow.' Anthony tapped the side of his nose with a finger that was not in the filing cabinet. 'But I've got my sources. It's all for *The TIME Temptation*. Daniel McKay for best writer, Episode One, Fil Brown for best artist, Episode Two, and Episode Two for best colour comic of the year.'

'It just came out last week!' I gasped.

'Right in time to pull a last-minute nomination. Looks like a certain editor is shit-hot, doesn't it?'

Anthony pulled out not a rabbit, but a bottle of champagne. He popped the cork and poured the wine into three coffee mugs he had lined up and ready on his desk. He passed one to me and it was tannin-stained and chipped, but I didn't care.

Three Peregrine nominations! And one all for me!

'To Girl from Mars and her sweet green arse,' said Anthony, and as we clinked mugs I dared to look at Dan again. He was smiling.

'To Girl from Mars,' we both said, and drank.

'With that in mind, this means I expect the two of you to devote every waking hour to making the rest of this story the best it can possibly be. I'm looking for a nomination for every episode in next year's awards. You've raised the bar and now you have to keep on raising it.'

'The script for Episode Four is amazing,' I said, and I was rewarded by Dan's smile growing wider. Sparkle in his eyes and everything.

'You and the archives gave me the idea,' he said.

'I need you to keep schtum about this until tomorrow,' Anthony said. 'And when it is announced, you're going to act so surprised people will think you've just been kicked in the balls. Or wherever,' he added for the benefit of my gender.

'No problem.'

'Sure.'

'Be around tomorrow. You two have a perfectly good office, I'm going to start getting even more complaints if you're not using it.'

'Okay.'

'Will do.'

'And please feel free to kiss each other in public all you want. Stuff like that can only give the comic more publicity.'

My face went hot. Anthony tipped back his head and downed his mug of champagne.

'Now get the hell out of here,' he said, 'I need to go home before my wife cuts off my dick and uses it to clean the windows.'

I was so stunned by the image that I put my champagne down on the desk without drinking the rest of it. Dan set his down next to mine.

'Let's go,' he said in a low voice to me, and 'Thanks, Anthony!' louder to our editor.

'Th-thanks, Chief,' I stuttered and was rendered even more speechless by Dan taking my hand and pulling me out of the office. We speed-walked down the corridor to the staircase and down as fast as we could.

Outside, Dan dropped my hand and stared at me. 'Uses his dick to clean the windows?'

I clapped the hand he'd been holding to my mouth, but I couldn't stop myself letting out a torrent of half-hysterical giggles. 'Please don't make me imagine it,' I said.

'I already have.' He grimaced.

'Did you notice he only poured out about a third of the champagne and then rushed us out of there? Do you think he's bringing the rest of it home to his wife?'

'I don't want to think about that relationship any more

than I already have, thank you.' Dan shook his head as if to clear it. 'Three Peregrines, though.'

'Unbelievable.'

'It is.' He scratched his head. 'What's a Peregrine?'

'It's the UK's biggest comic award and it's chosen by readers, so it's – just – amazing. But it's not only for UK comics, it's for all comics, American too, Japanese, everything.'

'So pretty damn good.'

'You could say that.'

We stood on the pavement and smiled at each other.

My God, I had missed him.

'Listen, Fil,' he said, 'I'm sorry about what happened at the Con.'

My elation deflated.

'Oh. Well, that's okay. I mean, we didn't plan to do it, it just happened.'

'But I shouldn't have let it. I got carried away by the moment and how you looked and what you'd said, and I forgot all about you and Jim.'

'What do you mean, about me and Jim?'

'I'm not the kind of guy to break anything up. It's just that I like you, and—'

'Wait a second,' I said. 'Jim isn't my boyfriend.'

'He isn't?'

'No. He's my best friend. We have a house together. But there's nothing going on between us.'

'So why wouldn't you let me into your house?'

'Um. It's complicated. But it wasn't—' I took a deep breath and plunged in. 'It wasn't because I didn't want to kiss you again.'

Then You Turn the Page

As soon as it was out, I couldn't believe I'd said it. It must have been the good news and the half a mugful of champagne and the relief of knowing that Dan had been avoiding me not because he was regretting kissing me but because he thought I already had a boyfriend.

Dan gazed at me. I gazed back. It was almost as if we were kissing again already.

'If that's the case,' he said, 'I have a full bottle of champagne at my flat. And real glasses. And some pasta I was cooking when Anthony called.'

I pretended to consider. 'Is it posh champagne? Since you're so rich?'

'Posh champagne and cheap pasta.'

'Just how I like it.'

We started walking towards Suffolk Mansions. I hoped he would take my hand again, this time for its own sake rather than to get me out of the UPC building quickly. But maybe that was a bit much. We'd been avoiding each other for weeks, after all.

'Where have you been?' I asked him.

'Working at home, mostly, though I've spent some time with my dad. I thought it was best to keep out of your way.'

'Because of Jim?'

'Because of how much I liked kissing you.'

His words gave me a warm glow that was much better than any champagne, posh or otherwise. I didn't say anything for a few minutes, so I could savour it.

Suffolk Mansions was built of cream and rosy brick and had elaborate art nouveau tiles in the entranceway. Dan let us in with his key and we crossed a rather grand foyer to a curly banistered set of curving stairs. Our footsteps echoed.

I shouldn't be here.

But three Peregrine nominations deserved proper champagne, didn't they? And there was nothing saying that Dan and I were going to do any more than just drink champagne and eat pasta. It wasn't even a date, not properly. A date was going out together, not staying in. Or so I assumed; my experience was not exactly comprehensive.

We walked along the first-floor corridor and Dan opened his door and stepped back to let me in first. And as soon as I set foot inside Dan's flat I knew I was kidding myself. I wasn't here because I wanted to celebrate the Peregrines. I was here because I wanted Dan.

In the throes of this realisation I paused and, to distract myself, checked out the sitting room of Dan's flat. He had high ceilings, vast windows, Turkish rugs, lamps in strategic places, and soft leather sofas – three of them. *So adorable*, I remembered blond, famous Carmen Clare saying.

'Posh is right,' I said.

'I didn't furnish it,' he told me. 'It came this way. My own taste runs more to normal.'

I caught a glimpse of myself in a gilt-framed mirror. My pink hair clashed rather badly with the cream walls and tasteful landscapes.

'Then again,' Dan said, 'normal is pretty overrated. Choose a couch and I'll grab us some champagne.'

I sank into the nearest one and tried not to think about the fact that I was here, with a man I fancied like crazy, and who, unbelievably, was attracted to me too. And that for the first time ever, we were properly alone. Nobody was going to interrupt us, nobody was going to be able to know anything that we did or said.

I whipped out my phone and texted Jim. *Will be here quite late, don't wait up.*

I turned my phone off and shoved it into my bag and then pushed my bag as far away as I could with my foot, to isolate the guilt.

Dan returned with two sparkling-clean glasses and a bottle of champagne. 'Have you been expecting to celebrate?' I asked him.

'It was left in the refrigerator for me when I rented the flat, and I was waiting for someone to share it with.' He twisted the cork expertly and it popped out with a loud sound and a small drift of vapour. He handed me a slender glass of golden liquid and then he sat down on the sofa beside me.

I twisted the stem in my fingers. I really was more suited to a tannin-stained mug. 'You didn't want to share it with Carmen?'

'Are you joking? It would've sent her straight back into rehab.'

'Is that why she went back to LA? For rehab?' That perked me up.

'Why do you care about Carmen?'

'Because, uh, I thought that maybe like you and she might have had, you know, something.'

He laughed. 'Believe me, I'm not that stupid. Anyway, she went back to LA because she got chicken pox.'

'Please tell me it was all over her face.'

'It was all over her face.'

'I so have to tell Jim.' And then I shook my head, because Jim was for later. Right now was for celebrating, and maybe being a bit of a new Fil, a Fil who drank champagne and hung out in posh flats and had been nominated for a major award. I looked at Dan and his red shirt and combat-style shorts, which should have been too scruffy for this room but somehow fitted right in. Maybe that could be true of me, too.

'Anyway,' I said, 'to the Peregrines.' I raised my glass.

He shook his head. 'To collaboration.'

'To collaboration,' I agreed.

We clinked glasses and I tasted the champagne. I don't know much about these things, my usual tipples being the boy-drinks of lager and whatever spirits we could get hold of, but it tasted clean and biscuity and it warmed me all the way down to my toes, which meant, I assumed, that it was quality stuff.

'I really love Episode Four,' I said. 'It totally blew me away.'

'I'm surprised you're not accusing me of writing it about Elizabeth.'

The name hung in the air between us. I took a sip of champagne and I tasted it. Elizabeth. The person always here and never here.

'It's a different story from your other ones,' I said carefully.

'Yes. It is different. It's darker. It's something I trust you to draw for me.'

I nodded. I thought about asking him whether I'd been right in what I'd read between the lines, but I wasn't sure I was ready yet to hear it. I'd only been this newish Fil for five minutes. 'What's going to happen in Episodes Five and Six?'

'I'm not sure yet. I keep on changing my mind.' He grimaced. 'That's why I've used up half a forest drafting it.'

'Well, Episode Four is going to be great to draw. I'll need to spend some time in the archives to make sure I get everything right. I mean, obviously I can draw Kingsley the Talking Ant, everybody draws him from about the age of five, but the Goolat sisters are a little trickier.'

'I've still got your collection, do you want it back?'

'No, not if you're using it. I've pretty much got all the issues I own memorised anyway. But I haven't got the Goolat sisters.' Though time in the archives meant time away from Digger.

Dan rose. 'Okay, you've got a frown starting between your eyebrows and that's not allowed on a night when we're celebrating. Want something to eat?'

'Yes, please.'

He refilled both our glasses. 'It won't be a minute. Wait here.'

But of course I couldn't just wait here, not when there was Dan's flat all round me. I got up from the couch and wandered to the window to look at the view of other expensive buildings, and then surveyed the room. I half expected to see a photograph of Elizabeth framed somewhere, but I didn't. In fact, there were very few personal items, which made sense if the flat was fully furnished and Dan only intended staying here for a few months.

However, there was one thing I was pretty sure hadn't come with the flat: by the wide-screen plasma television on one wall there were three stacks of DVDs, each one so tall it was in danger of falling over. Browsing through their titles I saw every genre: romantic comedies, sure, but also action, sci-fi, dramas, foreign films and art-house pics. I didn't recognise several of them, but I did recognise an obsession when I saw it, and I smiled and then wandered into the kitchen.

It was all granite and steel, with hand-thrown tiles and sleek inset lighting. Dan stood at the shining cooker, stirring a boiling pot.

This was where his photographs were. They were tacked on to the stainless-steel refrigerator with magnets, and there were nearly two dozen of them. I gravitated towards them as if I had a magnet attached to me too.

'That's my sister Di and her husband,' Dan said, appearing at my side smelling faintly of pasta, and pointing to a photo. 'And there's my mom. And these are my friends Boris, Georgia, Mavis and Martin at the Grand Canyon a couple of years ago. That's my cousin Eric, and his kids, and this one, forgive me, is of me at Cannes with Francis Ford Coppola.' He looked a bit sheepish in real life, though in the photo he looked amazing, wearing a dinner jacket and a thrilled expression.

There was a very recent one, blurred as if it had been taken on a mobile phone, of him and an older dark-haired man – his father, I guessed – standing next to the prime meridian at Greenwich. There was a snapshot from the theatre at the Con, taken from the audience's perspective. Anthony, Dan and I all stood together, and I was smiling like crazy, my pink hair the brightest thing in the photo. And an older one, a Polaroid of him, very skinny in a dinner jacket which clung to his teenage shoulders, holding hands with a blonde girl in a formal dress.

I stared at the blonde. This was Elizabeth.

'I like to feel surrounded by friends when I eat,' he said, sounding a little sheepish still.

I dragged my eyes away from comparing the prom Elizabeth and the Con me, and surveyed all the other photos. Group shots, solo shots, posed family pictures and blurry mid-action scenes. Dan was in some of them, and not in others.

'You've got a lot of friends,' I said.

'Yeah, I'm lucky. Hold on, I think that pasta's about done.'

I bit my lip, looking at the refrigerator. I was glad I was included there. But there were so many other people, so many with special places in Dan's life, it seemed impossible that there could be room for all of them. I also couldn't help being aware that if I had a refrigerator display of friends, it would be pretty unvaried in comparison. I could put my mum and dad on there, and that would bulk it out a bit, but otherwise it would be Jim, Digger and Stevo, over and over again.

Of course I'd probably put Girl from Mars on there too. But fictional friends didn't really count.

'The one at Greenwich is my dad,' Dan called over to me (the kitchen was, in fact, big enough so that calling was necessary). 'He's the one who sorted out this flat for me. I mean, I pay for it, obviously, but he found it.'

'That was nice of him.'

'It's my father all over.' Dan poured the pasta into a colander in the sink. 'He likes solving problems and buying things. He shows his feelings through material objects, always has. But it's one way of showing them, at least. I'm working on other ways, but meanwhile' – he shrugged and looked around – 'this flat is my father saying he loves me.'

He put the pasta in bowls and ladled sauce from another pot on top. Then he took out cutlery and led me back into the living room.

'I didn't think you'd mind eating here instead of the formal dining room,' he said, taking his place again on the couch where he'd sat before.

'There's a formal dining room?' I settled down next to him, and he passed me a fork and one of the bowls. It was full of pasta with bright red tomato sauce, smelling of basil and oregano.

'Well, it's meant to be. At the moment it's my office. I've got stacks of paper everywhere.'

I wound spaghetti round my fork. 'I never thought I'd say it, but I've sort of missed the sweatshop.'

'I've missed you,' he said quietly.

It was a good thing I hadn't put the food in my mouth yet, or I would have choked.

'I missed you too,' I said.

He met my gaze for a moment, during which I felt zings of electricity down my spine through my arms to my hands, and then went back to his spaghetti. 'How's your friend with the sick father?'

'His father seems be getting better. But I'm not sure about my friend.'

'Are they close?'

I snorted a derisive laugh. 'Not exactly.'

'It sounds like you have some opinions about this.'

I hesitated, but then I thought about Dan's refrigerator full of friends, and Elizabeth. He'd worried about the people he loved, too.

I took a gulp of champagne, and then, between bites of what was really quite delicious pasta, I told him about Digger. His childhood, how he'd protected his siblings, how he'd had no contact with his father until the stroke. How he wasn't eating, was drinking too much, wouldn't speak. And how he was determined to take care of the man who'd done this to him.

Dan listened in silence, eating his meal. When I was finished, he asked, 'And how do you feel about all of this?'

'I think – I think different things. See, Digger has always been the kindest person I've ever known. He volunteers at cat shelters and places like that. And he's always looked out for me, and for Jim, it's like when he's around things are always calmer and mellower. He's huge, you know; if you saw him you'd think he might be scary, but as a matter of fact he's very soft inside. I hate so much to see him get hurt. But at the same time, I can see that if he didn't take care of his father, despite how his father hurt him, he wouldn't be Digger.'

Dan nodded. 'I can see that. But how do *you* feel about it?'

I blinked at him. This was something I'd never considered. Certainly nothing I'd ever discussed.

'I feel . . .' I thought about it. 'I feel sad and scared that things are going to change. I'm angry at Digger's father for what he did, of course, but also for taking him away from us. And I'm – I'm angry at Digger, too, for not being around in our lives any more. For not letting us help. For choosing his father over us.' I frowned, almost frightened, because as I said all the reasons for my anger, I felt it, bubbling up hot inside me. 'But I shouldn't feel that way.'

'You can't control how you feel.'

'Sure you can.'

'How?'

'You never talk about it and you ignore it, and it goes away.'

He put down his empty bowl, and then he refilled both of our champagne glasses. He did it very slowly and deliberately, as if he had to concentrate on every movement.

'Can I tell you something I've never told anyone?' he asked me.

'Shoot.'

'When Elizabeth got ill, I was so angry with her I could barely look her in the face.'

I leaned forward, wanting to know more, although knowing more would hurt. 'What did you do?' I asked.

'I didn't show her. I tried to ignore it. It wasn't her fault she got cancer. I thought it was a stupid, selfish emotion for me to have.'

'Did it go away?'

He smiled sadly. 'I spent one night tearing out every page in all of my journalism textbooks and ripping them to pieces. That helped.'

'I guess it makes sense to be angry at someone because they're going to leave you for ever.'

He looked at me in a funny sort of way. 'That was part of it,' he said.

'Are you still angry?'

'No. That went away when she got really sick. I couldn't be angry at her then.'

'What do you feel now?' I was frightened to ask it. But I wanted to know.

He tipped his head back to look at the ceiling and he took a deep breath, so deep I could feel the couch cushions moving beneath us. Then he let it out in a long sigh.

'For a very long time I felt guilty,' he said.

'Dan, you couldn't do anything to keep her from dying.'

'I didn't feel guilty because I didn't stop her dying. I felt guilty because I didn't love her enough.'

It hurt him to say it. I found myself reaching my hand out and touching the back of his, my fingertips resting between the hills of his knuckles.

'I'd known Elizabeth for ever,' he said. 'Our families were close. We decided we would get married when we were about five years old. We dated all through high school. We did everything for the first time together. I loved her very much, Fil. Don't get me wrong on that. Not just as a sister, though she was like that too. She was beautiful and I loved her as a woman. I loved her the most I thought I could ever love any person.'

For some reason his words hit me like a series of light but devastating hammer blows in the chest.

'It sounds like you loved her enough,' I whispered.

He shook his head. 'We never told anybody this – we pretended to forget it as soon as she got the diagnosis – but when I went to college, we'd decided to take a break. I wanted to leave Philly and meet new people and do new things. I was planning to go overseas to work. Elizabeth didn't want to. We were still engaged but we'd put it on hold, to wait a little while to see if with distance we still wanted each other. I thought when I got to college I'd miss her like crazy. Instead I felt – relieved.'

He took a drink of champagne. So did I.

'I wanted to change,' he said. 'To find out who I really could be inside. Elizabeth – well, she was happy with what she was and what she had. She said I'd go away and eventually I'd realise that deep down I really wanted a house in the suburbs with her and our children. And I might have chosen that, eventually, on my own.'

'But when she got sick you felt like you didn't have a choice any more.'

He nodded. 'When she got the diagnosis the lymphoma had already progressed pretty far. She had aggressive treatments, but we all knew that it was about prolonging her life for weeks or months, not years. I couldn't deny her what she'd always wanted. What *we'd* always wanted. So we got married.'

You know when you see a drawing of something from one angle, close up in one panel? It makes sense to you, you anticipate where the story is going. Then you turn the page, and the next drawing is a splash over the whole spread. The viewpoint is different, the perspective is wider, the detail finer, the inking sharper and the colours more varied, and suddenly you see the whole thing and you realise you hadn't understood the story at all.

'You made the movies out of guilt?' I asked.

'I made them out of loss, and love, and grief, and anger and guilt. All of it mixed together.'

'Everything Girl from Mars is feeling in Episode Four,' I said.

'Episode Four is about facing the past. Episodes Five and Six are going to be about moving into the present and future.'

'So you are using Girl from Mars to sort out your personal issues.'

'Sure, I am. Just like you are.' His sudden smile was

like the sun coming out after the rain. 'She's pretty amazing for an alien, isn't she?'

'Told you so.' I finished the champagne in my glass and Dan poured us another. I knew the question I wanted to ask next, and it made me fidget in my chair.

'Out with it,' Dan said.

'What is the present and the future?' I asked.

'Do you mean in the comic?'

'I mean in real life.'

Dan put down his glass. 'Fil, do you know that you are the first woman I've asked out on a date since Elizabeth died?'

Which I guessed meant that I was the first woman he'd asked out on a date at all, because he and Elizabeth had always been together before she died. The thought made my head spin.

'You haven't been out with anyone? For five years?'

'That's not what I said. I've been out with plenty of women. My friends set me up with women every chance that they get. But standing in Tate Modern with you was the first time I was inspired to do the asking myself.' He paused. 'And then, of course, you ran away.'

I could tell him about the vow, but it still sounded too weird, and besides, that wasn't the real reason I ran away from him anyway. 'I was scared to death. Nobody has ever asked me out on a date before.'

'I'm not that scary, am I?'

'You're extremely scary. You're so friendly and confident and open. I don't know anybody like you.'

'I don't know anybody like you either.'

Our gazes met and the air went all hot and soupy. And at the same time there seemed to be very little oxygen in it.

'You know what I think?' I said for something to say, to keep my mouth working so I didn't either make an undignified lunge at Dan or else faint. 'I think that Girl from Mars would never hide in a toilet and then run off if an Earthling asked her out on a date.'

'Fil,' Dan said, 'don't you know yet that you are so much better than Girl from Mars could ever be?'

And because he was a writer, he knew that that was the perfect moment to lean towards me and kiss me.

A Whole Different Universe

He tasted of champagne. His mouth was warm. The first kiss was a quiet moment of recognition. Yes, it is this good, yes, it does feel right, yes, just plain *yes*.

'Anthony said we should do this all we wanted,' he whispered against my lips.

'In public, he said.'

'We can go out to the balcony in a minute.' But we didn't move.

The second kiss deepened and made me hungry. I opened my mouth to Dan and pulled him backwards with me on to the couch, so he lay half beside me and half on top of me, our legs tangling together at the knees. He was so solid and real. His body pressed me into the soft leather and I clung to him, digging my fingers into his back through his cotton shirt.

Nobody was between us. There was only me and Dan and all of these feelings, with my hands aching and aching.

Slowly, we explored each other's mouth, lips, teeth and tongue, and then Dan dipped his head to kiss the side of my jaw, my neck, the rim of my ear. He kissed the line of my eyebrows and ran his fingers over my collarbone, bare above the V-neck of my T-shirt. I smoothed my palms down his bare forearms. The luxury of skin on skin, even these little bits.

'You're beautiful,' he said, and though I'd been in a kiss-induced trance of bliss, that brought me out of it enough to laugh.

'That's nice of you to say so, but you are so lying,' I said. 'I'm not beautiful. I don't even look like a girl.'

'I'm not lying. And of course you look like a girl. A woman.'

'Dan, I do look in the mirror every morning.'

'Are you calling me gay?'

'No, of course not; well, I really hope not, but—'

He chucked me on the chin. 'Shut up, Fil. Believe me, you're a woman. I've seen a few and I know.' He stroked his hand down the side of me that wasn't pressed into him, over shoulder and ribs and waist and hip and thigh.

He certainly made me feel like a woman. 'Okay, but—'

'And you're beautiful. I thought you were beautiful from the minute you walked into that café and started staring at me.'

That shut me up. He smiled at my evident surprise. He kissed me on the chin, and on the corner of my mouth.

I could melt into this. The couch squeaked and settled with the little movements of our bodies. His breathing so intimate with mine.

I needed to know, though. 'How?' I asked, though I could barely summon the voice.

He stopped and looked at me. 'How what?'

'How did – do you think that I'm beautiful?'

As soon as it came out it sounded like a plea for flattery, but Dan's blink and his half-smile showed me that he understood that it was a simple desire for a change in perspective. I needed to know how he saw me, before I could wholly believe what was happening between us.

'At first it was your eyes,' he said, touching the corners of them with his fingertips. 'They're the colour of moss in summer, but what I noticed first was how big they were, big and clear and seeing. You looked at everything in the room and then I saw you translating it with your fingers into your book, like the café was flowing through you, somehow. Like everything was more real because you were there to see it.'

This was not what I was expecting. 'Go on.'

'You've got a perfect heart-shaped face.' He ran his thumb around the outline of it. 'And innocent skin. You blush at the drop of a hat. And yet you dress so tough and walk so alone.'

'Oh,' I said.

'And your neck is about the most feminine thing I've ever seen.' He stroked it. 'It's vulnerable and pale and graceful. I would watch you bent over your drawing in the sweatshop and sometimes I had to turn away before I got up and went over to you and kissed your neck. Like this.'

His kiss on my neck sent shivers down my entire body.

'So not your normal type of beautiful then,' I said.

'No. More beautiful than that.'

He kissed me on the neck again and this time I let myself relax into it. In fact, I let myself do more than that. I touched him, learned the soft thickness of his hair and the breadth of his shoulders as he kissed me. I ran my fingers over his neck, the strong cord at his nape and the way his hair curled in the back where it was growing out of his haircut. I lifted my leg so I could wrap it tighter round his and I took one of his hands and brought it to my mouth so that I could rub my face against it and kiss the palm. That long lifeline, the broken love line. He tasted of salt. I took the tip of his thumb in my mouth, because I wanted him there.

Dan groaned and kissed downwards. I felt his hot mouth and breath on my clavicle, the hollow of my throat, and then, thrillingly, through the cloth of my shirt on the upper slope of my breast, and his free hand clasped around it.

'Oh God,' I breathed on an exhalation of joy. Dan raised his head to meet my gaze. His blue eyes were smoky, his hair in disarray. I felt his erection against my thigh and I wanted him so much that it hurt.

'I didn't expect this tonight,' he said, his voice low and rough and sexy. It rumbled against my belly and my extra-sensitive nipple where he held it.

'Me neither.' I kissed his hand again, and then his lips. Losing myself in his mouth and his hand and his body.

'I don't want to make love to you for the first time on a couch,' he said between kisses.

Make love to you echoed in my head. 'Let's go to the bedroom then,' I said, my heart in my throat.

His expression of pleasure and plain lust at my suggestion made me laugh.

'In fact,' I said, struggling to sit up, but not that much, because being beneath him was really very nice, 'I am a Peregrine nominee and therefore I command you to take me to your bedroom! Now!'

'Yes, ma'am,' Dan said. He rolled off the couch, and before I could feel lonely he picked me up in his arms like he had that time he'd carried me to the restaurant. I wrapped my arms round his neck and kissed his forehead, his cheek, and nibbled on his ear.

'You're going to make me run into the wall,' he told me, and I tried to stop, but I couldn't. It was taking so long to cross the room, and there was so much of Dan that I wanted to touch.

But we did finally get to his bedroom. It wasn't as big as the main room, but it was big. The bed was big. The mirror on the wall was big. There was a chandelier.

'Holy cow,' I said. I wondered if he was going to throw me on to the vast bed like some sort of alpha romantic hero, but instead he put me on my feet beside it. The carpet was so soft that I felt like I sank down a couple of inches.

And there we were. Me and Daniel McKay, in a bedroom on our own. For all my bravado and desire I suddenly did not know what to say or do.

'Um,' I began, and felt myself flushing all the way down my kissed and caressed skin. 'Do you have any, um, c-condoms or anything?' I stumbled over the words like a teenager.

'Yes.' He touched my shoulder, my cheek, my hair, but my ease was gone. Of course he had condoms. Sex was probably a part of his life. All those women he'd been set up with by his friends. He was so good looking some of them were bound to have wanted to sleep with him, and just because he was a widower he wouldn't lead the life of a monk.

'I – haven't done this for ages,' I said. There. It was out. 'Actually, I'm not sure I was any good at it in the first place.'

'Well,' said Dan. He unbuttoned his shirt and dropped it behind him. His chest was all luscious planes, firm belly and the most delicious-looking trail of hair. I flattened my palm against his ribs and could feel his heart beating, very strong and fast.

He pulled off my T-shirt, gently unfastened my bra, and then he took me into his arms. My flesh pressed against his and I felt as if I were stepping into an entirely different universe to any I'd experienced in my life.

'There's only one way to find out,' he said.

Earthling Reproduction for Fun and Pleasure: A Refresher Course

It turned out I was pretty damn good at it.

Walking Around Naked

Morning sunlight glistened off the chandelier and Daniel McKay stood in the doorway, naked and holding two mugs of tea.

I pushed myself up to a sitting position on the great mounds of pillows and stared. There he was, a delicious, sexy, grown man. And I, me, Philomena Desdemona Brown, was allowed to touch him as much as I wanted, wherever I wanted. In fact, I had spent most of the previous night doing just that.

'You are the most gorgeous thing,' I told him. 'I don't think you should ever put clothes on, you should just walk around naked all the time.'

'That could get cold in the winter.'

'We'll stay inside. I'll walk around naked too. Hey!' I threw back the covers and jumped out of bed. 'I've never walked around naked before!'

'You haven't?'

'I live with a bloke.' I walked around the bedroom, feeling the air on all of my skin. 'This is pretty cool.' I marched to the doorway, getting a little distracted by having to touch Dan's touchable bum on the way past, but then made it successfully into the corridor, and I marched naked down to the kitchen. I paraded around the kitchen table, my bare feet slapping on the tiles, and went into the living room where the huge windows were also unclothed, giving a view out on London and also into the flat. After a moment's hesitation I sprinted across the room in a circuit, then scampered back to the bedroom.

Dan was still in the doorway, cups of tea in his hands, watching me. 'You're crazy,' he said.

'It feels great.' Both being naked and having Dan watch me being naked. I kissed him swiftly on the cheek, took one of the cups of tea, and brought it back to bed.

'Feel free to do it whenever you like,' Dan said, joining me. The bed dipped slightly when he got in and I cuddled up next to him, enjoying the heat of his body and how I fitted perfectly into his side. 'In fact, I'd advise that whenever you feel the urge to strip and run around that you come straight here.'

'That's good advice,' I said happily. Because if that wasn't an invitation for me to come around for more sex in the future, what was? I put my tea on the bedside table to free my hands for what they really wanted to do, which was to touch Dan all over. His long thighs, his firm stomach, the ripple of his ribs, his muscled arms. I'd drawn a lot of buff superhero types, and I had, in fact, seen quite a few naked men – granted it was in life-drawing classes and not in bedroom situations – and Dan's body was by far the best out of all of them. He was strong, but not steroidy, and lean and gloriously imperfect. He had a circle of freckles on his hip and a puckered scar from a bicycle fall on one knee. He was circumcised, which he assured me was normal for

American men but was slightly, pleasantly shocking, as if he were extra bare. I slipped my hand downwards to explore that particular part and felt him growing rapidly from soft to hard in my palm.

It was a miracle. It was a celebration. A man like this, *this* man, could be attracted to me. So attracted that we'd been doing it all night and he couldn't wait to do it again.

'Do we have another condom?' I asked, stroking him upwards, circling my thumb around the tip.

'One more, I think. I'll have to buy some.' I felt him reaching over to his bedside table.

I pictured him going into a chemist's and picking up a packet of condoms, smiling because he was thinking of having more sex with me. Brilliant as the picture was, it did bring up the question of how and why he'd bought the ones we were using now.

'So you've, uh, slept with some of these women you've been dating,' I said, accepting the condom from him and beginning the enjoyable task of rolling it down over the length of his penis.

'It seemed like something I should do,' he said. His voice was a little breathy because of what I was doing to him, and his hands were caressing my shoulders and breasts. 'To get back on the horse, as it were.'

'Was it . . . all right?'

He pulled me up to him so we were face to face and he kissed my lips. 'Pretty disastrous, if you want to know the truth.'

'It – didn't work?'

'Oh, everything worked the way it's supposed to. But it felt like going through the motions. It wasn't –' He clasped my hips and rolled me over so that he was on top of me, his body a wonderful weight on mine. I wrapped my legs around him because I was ready and impatient.

'It wasn't like this,' he said, and slid inside me and began to move.

Nothing was like this. Dan's body around me, inside me, his mouth next to mine, his blue eyes looking at me, his hands on my skin. His smile and his voice and the way he breathed and moved. The taste of his sweat and the way his hair smelled, how my little noises of pleasure drove him crazy. Our new world together, a special atmosphere and a unique gravitational force.

I laughed, this time, when I came because I couldn't imagine anything that could make me happier, and Dan held me so close to him I could see his orgasm behind my eyelids as starbursts and explosions.

Afterwards was just as good, in a different way, lounging in bed together drinking our tea, my head on his chest and our fingers playing tangling games. I felt like I could say anything, feel anything and it would be okay. That I could become whoever I wanted to be.

'What do you have to do today?' I asked lazily.

'I seem to remember Anthony ordering us to be at UPC for the award nomination announcements.'

'Oh, yeah.' I sat up and checked the clock. 'Oh, shit, I have to go if I'm going to get home and change in time.'

He curled his hand round my wrist. 'You can shower here.'

I could. Then Dan could join me in the shower. Then I could put on my clothes, which had spent the night on Dan's floor, and go into UPC hand in hand with Dan, rumpled and exuding sex.

There were enough rumours already. 'Nope, I want clean underwear,' I said, and freed myself and slipped out of bed.

Dan sighed and rolled out of bed too. He pulled on a dressing gown as I put on my clothes and ran my fingers through my hair to make it look messy in a way that wasn't necessarily bed-messy. He walked me to the door, past our abandoned champagne flutes and empty bowls, and kissed me with it open, halfway out into the corridor. 'I'll see you later,' he murmured, and I skipped down the stairs, singing under my breath.

Reality sank in as I got off the tube at the other end of the Northern Line. Because this was more than a date, more than a kiss, and I was going to have to tell Jim about it.

My stomach and lungs felt as if they had contracted into very small stones. My footsteps dragged. What was I going to say? *Sorry I've been out, mate, but I've been shagging my former enemy all night?* I turned on my phone and checked it, but there were no messages or missed calls. At least that was a relief. I delayed for a little bit, going into a newsagent's and buying a Coke that I didn't want, but in the end I had to go home.

'Hello?' I called when I opened the door, but I didn't get a reply. The house didn't feel empty, though, and when I went through to the kitchen I saw the remains of Jim's breakfast toast on the table. Clean pots and pans and dishes were stacked on the draining board – from last night's meal, I assumed. There were two dishes, two forks. He'd eaten with Digger. Or maybe Rachel.

Suddenly I realised the impact of all those hours apart. That things might not have just been happening to me.

I popped open my Coke and walked slowly up the stairs to the spare bedroom that served as Jim's office. One of my cartoons was on the closed door, of Jim dressed in a Star Fleet Captain's uniform above the caption: James T. Lousder's Ready Room, Enter At Peril. From inside, I could hear the clicking of computer keys.

I knocked. The clicking stopped and Jim said, 'Yeah?'

The spare bedroom was pretty small, but Jim had organised all of his stuff neatly on shelves lining three of the walls. The other was taken up by his desk and all his computer equipment, which was laid out as precisely as a surgeon's instruments. By his monitor he had a framed photograph of me and him, taken at arm's length with Jim's camera one day when we'd gone to London Zoo, seven or eight years ago. Our heads were together and you could see an elephant over my right shoulder.

Jim sat at his monitor, his hands on his keyboard, his hair in a neat ponytail. 'Hi,' I said to him, and stepped fully into the room. I'd hardly ever been in here; it was his domain, as my studio was mine.

'What's up?' he asked me.

Couldn't he tell? From my hair, my kissed lips, my bedroom-floor clothes, the way my whole body was beaming light?

'I've, uh, got to tell you something, Jim.'

What was I afraid of, anyway? Surely my best friend would be happy for me. Surely our friendship was big enough to accommodate another person in the mix.

Or two.

The shelves round the walls muffled noise and made the room seem small and crowded.

Jim swivelled his chair so that he faced me, and he put his palms on his knees. 'I've got something to tell you, too.'

'You first,' I said quickly.

'Okay.' He breathed in deeply, while I held my breath. 'Last night, Rachel asked me out.'

I let out a little cough of relief. 'That's it?'

'Yeah. She ended up staying for something to eat and we got talking, and she asked if I wanted to go to a movie or something with her sometime.'

'Well –' A movie or something. That seemed so minor, next to what I'd been doing. And if Jim went out with Rachel, then he could hardly mind what I was up to with Dan, right? I liked somebody, he liked somebody. No big deal.

Things would change. But not . . . as much as they could have done.

'That's great,' I said.

'Is it?'

'Yeah. She's really nice. Actually I think she's liked you for a while.'

And why wouldn't she like him? Jim was great, and he was good looking in his own special Jim way, and now finally, finally, someone was seeing him properly and understanding his worth. 'Actually that's fantastic, Jim.'

I smiled. I could cope with Rachel. With the way I felt about Dan, I could cope with anything.

'I said no to her,' Jim said. 'Of course.'

'What? Why?'

He fisted his hands on his knees. 'We took a vow, Fil. Don't you remember? Death before shame?'

'But – listen, Jim, I'm sure it will be fine. We'll talk to Digger. He likes Rachel anyway. And besides, we were all drunk and—'

'Being drunk doesn't matter. I meant what I said. I'll always mean it. Real friendship is more important than anything or anybody else. I'm not going to just dump that because a girl happens to like me.'

'But she's not just any girl, Jim, and besides, we didn't know about her when we took the vow.'

'Fil, you're talking like Rachel is the only girl who ever liked me.'

I'd been planning on saying more, but that shut me up. I had thought that, to be honest. I'd believed it was unfair and a symptom of everything wrong with the women of the world, but I had assumed that Jim was still single because he hadn't had any offers.

Which was, I saw now – with Jim slender yet strong in his chair, his grey eyes snapping with anger – horribly, horribly condescending. I'd undervalued and under-estimated him.

'Of course not,' I said quietly. 'You deserve to have every girl in the world, Jim.'

'But I don't want them. I don't want to go out with Rachel. Is that so hard to understand?'

'No, but—' I pinched the back of my neck. 'No.'

'It doesn't even have anything to do with the vow. I'd still say no.'

'Okay.'

'Okay,' Jim said. He uncurled his hands and flexed his fingers, and sighed.

'Now what was it that you had to tell me?' he asked.

'Oh – I – um.'

With my finger, I touched my mouth. My mouth that had drunk champagne, laughed and kissed. Made love to a man and told him my feelings.

'Oh, yeah,' I said. 'Well, it's that *Girl from Mars* is up for three Peregrines.'

Immediately Jim jumped out of his chair. 'Three? Are you kidding?'

'No, it's going to be announced today. One for best comic, one for best writer, and one for me.'

'Fil! That's fantastic!'

'Yeah,' I said. 'It really is.'

He rubbed the side of his cheek. 'Wow, I wasn't expecting that at all. Not that you don't deserve them, you've been due one of those for years now, but it's just that when you came in I thought you had something different to tell me. From the way you were acting.'

'No,' I said. 'No, that's it. That's all I need to tell you.'

Panels

Sometimes it's useful to show time passing by drawing a series of still panels, each disconnected, leaving the reader to draw the thread between them. You choose the beginning point – for example, the moment I didn't tell Jim about Dan – and the end point, the day before the Peregrine Awards. Between those two points you have a few chosen moments.

And in between those panels, you have the white spaces, that magical little bit of comics which is known as 'the gutter'. The blankness that indicates time and space and change.

I did, in fact, draw some of the highlights of these past weeks. I drew a few of them at the time, at home in my bed thinking through the days, though of course those were destroyed. I drew some of them later, too, when I was alone.

In them the time is always now, the colours are always true.

Close-up: between two chairs, Dan taking my hand in secret as Anthony announces the Peregrine nominations.

In a vintage clothing shop: I stand in front of a mirror, wearing a fuchsia satin dress from the fifties. It flares out from the hips and sits delicately on my shoulders. I am someone familiar, someone strange.

A long shot: Jim and I sit in the Swan, pints in front of us, puzzling over the picture round. No need for speech balloons. Far away at the bar, Rachel polishes glasses.

Close-up: in the dim light of the sweatshop, I am surrounded by drawings and Dan stoops down and kisses the back of my neck.

Digger in a green-painted physical therapy room, holding his father's sock-clad feet as the old man struggles to lean forward and touch a bony, sparsely haired shin. Digger's hair is falling around his face and the expression in his eyes is either triumph or anger, hatred or love.

Late one night, the only light from an almost unbelievably full moon, I sit in Dan's bed with the blankets pooled around me. I hold a pencil, but at this moment, I cannot draw because I am too busy watching his face while he sleeps.

In between those panels lies the gutter. White space. Where you don't have to draw anything, because things change all by themselves.

A Big Old Betelgeusian Ray Gun

The day before the Peregrine award presentations, I was upstairs in the bathroom in my dressing gown, a plastic bag tied round my head to help the hair dye work, practising my acceptance speech into the mirror. Not that I was certain I'd win; just because *Girl from Mars* deserved a Peregrine didn't mean I deserved it myself. But, on the off-chance that I did, I didn't want to get up there on the podium in front of the entire British comics industry and choke.

Who should I thank? Daniel, obviously, and Anthony. And Jim and Digger and Stevo, all of whom would be there. But my parents would be there, too – I'd invited them over the marmalade-glazed lamb one Sunday lunchtime, hardly knowing whether they'd accept, and they'd bemusedly said yes. Should I thank them? Would they even want to be thanked, disapproving as they were of the whole medium?

'Thanks to my mother and father, for giving me something to rebel against,' I said to the mirror, creating mist on its surface.

I frowned. It didn't do justice to my feelings: how surprised and pleased and nervous I was that they wanted to be there for me. The emotions were too mixed up to be put into words, and language was never my strong point anyway.

There were some definite downsides of this trick Dan had shown me, of thinking about how I felt. All in all it was easier to stick with the comic book staples of ZAP! and POW! and ZOWIE!

I didn't think that would quite do it either.

I heard a muffled knock on the door downstairs, and I yelled out of habit, 'Jim! Door!'

It took a few moments' silence before I remembered that Jim wasn't in. He was at the office of the company he was contracting for, sorting out their software issues. He'd been there for the past few working days, though I hadn't really noticed since I was in the sweatshop or stealing hours in Suffolk Mansions with Dan. I tugged my dressing gown closed and padded down the stairs.

I should have known Jim wasn't here, from how empty the house felt. But the truth was, it felt that way, these days, even when he was here.

The knock repeated on the door, and this time, unmuffled, I recognised the heavy rhythm, even though I hadn't heard it for ages. 'Hey!' I cried, in happiness, and flung open the door.

And then I stepped back.

The man on our doorstep was tall, very tall, and clean-shaven, with close-cropped curly dark hair. His eyes were hazel. He smiled a half-smile and one of his cheeks dimpled.

'Digger?' I gasped.

'Yup.'

I took in his blue denim jacket, his fresh skin, that dimple I'd never seen before. The eyes were Digger. The shoulders, too.

'Are you sure you're not his clone?' I asked.

'Yeah, I was born in a test tube of a toenail clipping. You going to let me in, or what?'

It was definitely Digger. I stepped aside and let him in. How come, without his beard and his long hair, he even walked lighter?

I followed him as he went straight into the kitchen and poured himself a pint glass full of milk. He took it to his bowed-down centre of the couch. He took up less space than he used to. Although I went to my own girl chair and sat as I had a million times before, everything felt so different I could hardly recognise the feeling of the upholstery on my bare legs. I stared at Digger and tried to figure out what to say.

'Hey, Digger, you got a haircut,' he prompted me.

'I never knew you had a dimple,' I said.

He smiled. It got deeper. He looked so young.

'I need to ask you a favour,' he said. 'It's a bit last minute.'

'Anything.'

'You know the awards ceremony tomorrow night? I wondered if I could bring someone.'

His father? I swallowed. 'Okay. I'm sure we can swing another seat at the table.'

'That's good,' he said, settling back on the couch and laying his arm over the top of the cushions. 'Because I already asked her.'

I nearly jumped out of my seat. '*Her?*'

'Yeah.'

'What do you mean, *her?*'

'I mean that the person who I'm bringing has two X chromosomes. You know, female. Like yourself.'

'But—' I was gaping, but Digger, this new, dimpled Digger, was smiling in a quiet way. 'But – we took a vow. It was your idea. In Klingon and everything.'

'Fil,' Digger said, 'vows are all very well and good, but keep it in perspective. This is a *date*.'

I closed my mouth. I opened it again. I closed it.

'You look like a fish,' Digger told me. 'Who got her head caught in a plastic bag.'

'I feel like a fish,' I said. 'What the hell happened to you?'

'I'm not afraid of him any more, Fil,' he said. 'He's an old man and he can't hurt me. Everything he did is finished and it will never happen again. I don't need to hide. Not from anyone.'

His naked face was young and beardless and, I saw wholly for the first time, handsome.

'You're a good-looking dude, Douglas Mann,' I told him. He blushed a little.

'You and Jim have been good friends to me.'

'We thought we'd lost you.'

'There are some things you need to do on your own.' He drank down his milk in two gulps, an action that superimposed the old Digger on top of this new Digger.

'Where's Jim?' he asked.

'Working.'

'Upstairs?'

'In an office. I thought that hell would freeze over before he did so, but apparently I was wrong.'

He nodded. 'Have you talked to him yet?'

'I talk to Jim every day,' I said quickly, because the question gave me that hard-to-breathe feeling.

'That's not what I mean.'

I shifted in my chair. 'What does it feel like to have your beard shaved off? Is your skin all new? Sort of like a butterfly wing?'

Digger sighed. He got to his feet. 'I'll meet you at the awards. Are you and Jim going together?'

'Of course.' I'd briefly considered suggesting that Jim asked Rachel. But there wasn't much point. 'Can't wait to see the two of you in suits.'

'Can't wait to see that Peregrine above the fireplace.' He strode forward and hugged me into his arms. He'd never done it before but it was a big Digger-hug, warm and bearlike. Then he got a mouthful of plastic bag and pulled away, snuffling.

'What colour are you doing it?' he asked.

'That's another thing you'll have to wait and see.'

He ran his hands through his own short hair. 'Talk with him, Fil. You can't be afraid of things for ever.'

'I'm not afraid of anything except for a big old Betelgeusian ray gun.'

He snorted. 'Tell Jim to come round to mine when he gets home,' he said, and left his milk glass on the coffee table.

A timer went off upstairs. I went up to the bathroom and rinsed the dye out of my hair. Then I stood in front of the mirror again, looking at my brown hair with only a few fuchsia streaks in it, gnawing my lip, and wondering if I was ready, like Digger, to show the world who I really was.

Qamu/s Hey qaq law'
(orv/s y/nqaq puS!

Instead of practising my acceptance speech, which wasn't likely to get used anyway, I should have been practising putting on lipstick. It took me half a dozen tries and half a loo roll before I got it into a shape approximating my lips. I scrutinised it and pursed my mouth.

'Fil! We're going to be late!' bellowed Jim from downstairs, where he had been waiting for me. Like a sensible person it had taken him half an hour to shower, shave, and put on his clothes. I'd been hogging the bathroom ever since. I couldn't figure out how most women ever got out of the house if they did this every day.

I sighed, checked my dress one last time to make sure it was covering my boobs (such as they were), and flew down the stairs. I had considered high heels to go with my dress, for about twelve seconds, until I'd decided to stick with flats. Otherwise I would surely have been dead by the time I got to the bottom of our staircase.

I nearly fell down anyway, because Jim was waiting for

me at the bottom near the front door and as soon as I appeared his eyes got so wide, his eyebrows so high, his mouth so open, that I was struck with a paroxysm of self-doubt strong enough to make me forget how to deal with steps.

'What?' I said, halting stone dead five steps from the bottom.

'You look—'

If he said *different* I was going to scream.

He swallowed. 'Beautiful,' he said.

I suddenly had a huge lump in my own throat.

'Thanks. You scrub up pretty well too.' He did; Jim suited a suit.

He kept on staring. My position on the stairs meant that he was looking up at me, and he could see all of my outfit easily, from my newly dyed hair to my sparkly flats.

'I was a little worried about wearing a dress,' I said.

'You don't have to be. You look absolutely stunning, Fil.'

Jim said it without a trace of irony, and with a total conviction I'd rarely heard from him. He'd spent a great deal of time at Digger's flat the night before, after he'd got home from work. I wondered if Digger had been nagging him, too, to be more open with me.

Well, I could be open back. I walked down the rest of the stairs and I took Jim's arm in mine. 'I'm glad you're my date, James T. Lousder. I've been looking forward to this since I was a little girl and you gave me my first comic. Even if I don't win any awards, this night is a dream come true.'

'Yes,' he said, sounding dazed, and the taxi beeped outside.

'My parents are in it,' I warned him as I grabbed my

wrap (a concept hitherto foreign to me) and we stepped out of the house. 'I thought if I left them to their own devices they'd end up at the Globe again.' They always ended up at the Globe theatre. Every time they went into Central London. It was as if the place had a tractor beam that pulled them to it and made them stand around outside it reciting *The Tempest* to each other. Last time I'd arranged to meet them for dinner in Chinatown I'd sat on my own in Wong Kei's for forty-five minutes before I gave up, got a takeaway, and went down to meet them on the South Bank.

'You're going to have to run interference for me,' I told Jim on the way to the cab. 'I need this time to get quietly nervous in the corner.'

'No problem. Hello, Professor Brown, Dr Brown.' We sat on the jump seats and strapped ourselves in.

'You look nice, Philomena,' my father said.

'You always say that, Dad.'

'And I always mean it.'

'Though that *is* a lovely dress,' my mother added, and stroked her own brown satin and cashmere.

'Thanks,' I said, and I smiled at her. Then I bit my lip, which tasted different because of the lipstick, and looked out the window while my parents bombarded Jim with the usual questions about his life.

As Jim was totally used to this I felt at liberty to leave him to it and I got on with the serious business of worrying.

I'd never been to the Peregrine awards before; I'd had no need to, and I wasn't the sort of person who went to parties for the sake of it. I had very little idea of what to expect. Dan had been to the Oscars, and this, of course, was nothing like as big as that. It was a pretty small ceremony in general and the eyes of the world were definitely not trained on the Park Grove Hotel. There wouldn't be any reporters or red carpets. But even without the entire world watching, the scope was still very large to fuck up spectacularly in front of everyone I knew. Whilst wearing a dress. What if I tripped? What if I had lipstick all over my teeth? What if I didn't win? What if I didn't win and everybody laughed at me for even trying?

'Oh look, there's the Globe,' said my father. 'Look, Philomena, James. I never get tired of seeing it. So small and brave. "The cloud-capp'd towers, the gorgeous palaces, the solemn temples, the great globe itself . . ."'

And of course, there was appearing in public with my family, something I attempted to avoid as much as possible. On the one hand, you would hope that people in the comics business would be relatively tolerant of others' foibles. On the other hand, my mother could start talking feminist theory at the drop of a hat, and tended not to notice others' blank looks. I dreaded what could happen if someone were to bring up Wonder Woman.

The cab pulled up outside the Park Grove Hotel and, to my surprise, Jim scrambled out and held open the door for my mother and me. 'Thanks,' I said to him as I smoothed my dress and, with a rush of relief, spotted a familiar tidy figure heading down the pavement towards us.

'Stevo!' I called, and waved in case he didn't recognise me in a dress. He was wearing a dark suit and a bright tie, and was accompanied by a taller, older man in impeccable beige linen. He was slender, had a chunky silver ring on one elegant finger, and aside from a bit of silver-grey hair at the temples, was completely, shinily bald.

'Fil, Jim!' Stevo greeted us, and shook my hand and clapped Jim on the back, and then gestured to the man beside him. 'This is Brian.'

Somehow I managed to recover a small memory of how to function socially. 'Great to meet you at last, Brian, I've heard so much about you. These are my parents, Linda and Geoffrey Brown. You remember Stevo Ng, Mum?'

While they were all shaking hands and exchanging those words you were supposed to, Jim nudged me in my satin-clad ribs. 'Brian,' he whispered, and he didn't say any more because I knew exactly what he was thinking.

'Jean-Luc Picard,' I whispered back. He was a dead ringer. Put the man in a Starfleet uniform and he could stroll right on to the deck of the *Enterprise* without anyone turning a hair.

'Incredible,' said Jim, and I saw that Stevo was watching us and looking a little apprehensive so I grinned at him and gave him a subtle thumbs-up.

'You must forgive me,' my father was saying, 'but you look extraordinarily like a younger Patrick Stewart. The actor? I saw him as Claudius in *Hamlet* last month.'

'Oh, me too, I loved it,' said Brian, and fortunately his voice was nothing like the starship captain who also happened to be a Shakespearean actor, and we all proceeded into the hotel, Brian and my parents chattering away, while I shook my head. What were the chances of my parents and Jim recognising a resemblance to the same person?

'I'm not going out with him because of that,' Stevo said to me, at my elbow.

'No. Of course not. And you mustn't expect to get your back ripped off about it, either.'

'I'm kind of disappointed you didn't end up with Whorf,' said Jim.

'We've all got a bit of inner Klingon,' said Digger's voice, and I looked round, startled to find we'd walked past him in the hotel lobby without noticing. He was wearing a brown suit and his newfound dimple.

'Digger?' gasped Stevo, and I saw that Jim was enjoying the reaction as much as I was. Though probably not half as much as Digger.

'You've met Angelique,' he said, presenting the woman next to him. She wore a bright red dress, her bosoms attractively plumped out at the top of it, and the top of her corn-rowed head didn't quite reach Digger's shoulder.

'You're the nurse from the hospital,' I said.

'Speech therapist,' she corrected, but she was smiling. She had her arm looped round Digger's. He looked about fit to burst.

'I'm really glad you could come,' I said, and boy, did I mean it. Digger looked so happy, and Stevo too, and all of us were here together, like the old days but completely different, and I was the reason we were here. In our best clothes and manners, with the new people we cared about, because of me and Girl from Mars.

I wanted to hug them all. Jim, so good looking and straight-standing, no longer the skinny cat-haired boy bowed over by book bag and taunts. Digger, smiling for the world and Angelique to see. Stevo blushing, reaching out a hand to take Brian's with easy intimacy. Even my parents smiled and chatted and seemed to take everything in their stride.

And I was in a dress. And not only a dress, but a pink dress, and I was about to go and stand next to a man who, by many criteria, could be considered (don't jinx it, don't jinx it, don't think too much about it) my boyfriend.

Then we started walking towards the function room, and I noticed that our feet trod on a real, honest-to-God red carpet. And then Jim, by my side, said, 'Wow.'

The function room was laid out with round tables, each one streaming silver balloons. On the stage at the front of the room, in front of a blue velvet curtain, perched a giant falcon which looked as if it were made out of silver foil – a huge replica of a Peregrine award. And on the bright television screen next to it, flashed the names of the award nominees.

'BEST ARTIST, Fil Brown,' it said, at the very moment I happened to see it. Accompanied by my first page splash for Episode Two.

But that wasn't the best of it. The best of it was standing at a table halfway across the room, in a black suit and a white shirt, his hands in his pockets as he talked to someone, and when he glanced my way and caught my eye, his face lit up. Enough to illuminate the whole room and make my insides melt with desire and joy.

I turned and ran as fast as I could for the loo.

They were rather nice loos, with big mirrors and shining white porcelain sinks. I locked myself into a cubicle and tried to breathe.

Right there, in that silvery room, all of my worlds were going to collide. My friends, my family, my lover, my work, even Girl from Mars, all the planets that usually spun in separate orbits were lining up together, all depending on me not to wobble them off course.

'Shit,' I said. I thought about sitting down on the toilet, but I cared too much about my dress. I cared too much about everything.

'Shit,' I said again.

'Fil?'

There were brightly polished male shoes visible underneath the cubicle door. Nobody could polish a shoe like Jim.

'You're not supposed to be in here,' I told him through the door.

'There aren't many women in the place, to be honest. I think I'll be okay. Are you having a bladder crisis, or are you hiding?'

'Hiding,' I admitted.

'Why?'

Jim must have spoken to Digger last night; I couldn't imagine him following me and asking me what was wrong otherwise.

'All my dreams are coming true,' I said.

'Isn't that a good thing?'

'It's bloody terrifying. What if it doesn't work out? What if it does work out but then it goes horribly wrong? I had an image of all of this in my head, but I never thought it would really be me it happened to. Or I thought that if it happened to me, I'd be someone completely different by then. But I'm the same as I always was.'

On the other side of the door, he was silent.

'I know how you feel,' he said finally.

I buried my face in my hands. 'Don't say that. Say that everything will be fine.'

'I don't know that. How about I go get you a gin and tonic?'

'That would probably help.'

After I'd heard him leave, I emerged from the cubicle and checked myself in the mirrors again. Miraculously, the lipstick was still intact. A woman wandered in. She looked like somebody's grandmother, the type of person who might not want a man in her Ladies', so I went and sat in a chair outside the door to wait for Jim.

He returned soon with a gin and tonic; he gave it to me and I drank it down. The bubbles tickled my nose and the ice bumped against my teeth.

'You're right,' I said. 'That helped.'

Jim stood straight, thrusting his chest out. 'QamuIs Heg qaq law' lorvIs yInqaq puS!' he spat with his best Klingon scowl.

'What does that mean?'

' "Better to die on your feet than live on your knees." '

'You are seriously weird, you know that?' I stood up. 'But you're right. You're a good mate, Jim.'

I kissed him on the cheek. His skin was smooth and I could smell a hint of aftershave.

'Fil, I want—'

I noticed I'd left lipstick marks on his cheek and I wiped them off with my thumb. I saw his jaw bunch as he clenched his teeth.

'I need a drink myself,' he said.

'Well, let's go get one.'

Better to die on your feet than live on your knees, I reminded myself as we walked back into the function room. Thank God I hadn't worn heels, or I'd be doing both at once.

As soon as I walked in I saw that one bit of world-colliding had already occurred without my having to be there; Dan, accompanied by an older man I recognised as his father, had approached the remainder of my group and they were trading introductions all round. I barely had time to gulp before he finished shaking my father's hand and turned to me.

'Fil,' he said, 'you look gorgeous.'

His blue eyes said more than that. They said he wanted to drag me out of that room and pull my dress off me and do all sorts of wonderful things to me. His quirked-up smile confirmed it.

Against the odds, I restrained myself from flinging myself at him, rucking my skirt up, and wrapping my legs round his waist as he kissed me senseless. I'd been restraining myself in this way most days at UPC, but tonight it was particularly difficult. Instead, I stood on tiptoe and kissed him on the cheek, as I had Jim a few minutes earlier. His hand rested briefly on my satin-clad waist and warmth flooded through me from there and from where my lips had touched his skin.

It was over way too quickly but I didn't trust myself for any longer. To draw it out a little I said, 'Oops, left some lipstick,' even though I hadn't, much, and I allowed myself a lovely few seconds of rubbing my fingers on his face. He caught my eye and I looked away, quickly dropping my hand.

'You've met everybody?' I asked.

'Yes, just haven't said hi to Jim yet.'

Dan held out his hand to Jim. I held my breath.

They just shook hands. Looked each other in the eye. 'Hello,' said Jim, and that was it.

'And you must be Mr McKay,' I said, turning to Dan's father with relief. He looked a lot like Dan, though he had brown eyes and his hair was salt and pepper, and he was shorter. He looked English rather than American, not least in his smile. Dan's smile reached out and grabbed you and pulled you into his personality. His father's smile was cordial.

But I didn't mind shy people. 'I'm a huge fan of your father's, Mr McKay.'

'And your son's,' prompted Dan.

'And your son's,' I amended, and I felt again the brief touch of Dan's hand at my waist. No more than a clandestine acknowledgement that we were fans of each other. That we shared something together.

Who would've known that I could decipher the language of touch so easily?

'I'm not very *au fait* with comics, I'm afraid,' Mr McKay said. 'The gene must have skipped my generation.'

'They're surprisingly sophisticated in their narrative techniques,' my mother informed him. 'They require an almost unmatched participation from their readers to decode their semiotic lexicon. And of course there's the sense of an underground culture attached to them, which marks out their readers in a way that rather reminds me of the eighteenth-century female attraction for Gothic fiction.'

Mr McKay looked baffled.

His son nodded and said, 'You must be very proud of Philomena, Professor and Dr Brown.'

'Yes,' said my mother, 'we are.'

If I hadn't been surrounded by people I would have toppled over.

'Brown! McKay! Get over here and drink!'

Anthony's bellow swayed the balloons around us.

'He's known as The Chief,' Digger told Angelique as we twisted as a group through the tables to the UPC encampment near the front. 'I was thinking of changing my nickname, actually.'

'"The Stud" sounds too much like a Jackie Collins novel,' she said and I smiled all over in gladness that someone was calling Digger a stud.

Dan was walking beside me, a little ahead of everyone else. 'You look gorgeous,' he murmured to me and the words shivered pleasurably down my spine. He handed me a thick brown envelope that he'd had under his arm.

'What's this?'

'It's Episode Five.'

'Has Anthony seen it yet?'

'Not till next week.'

I tucked it under my arm, trying to make it inconspicuous. 'Only one more episode left. Have you figured out how it all ends?'

'I hope so. But it's a collaboration. I'd like to know how you feel about it.'

We reached the table, which was huge but didn't have place names. Within a few seconds Dan had us all organised into chairs, without being obvious about it. I slipped the envelope on to my seat and perched on top of it. I was between Dan and Jim, with my parents next to Anthony. 'Fucking good little artist, your daughter,' he said immediately to my father, who replied, 'Erm,' then cleared his throat and said firmly, 'Yes.'

Anthony began pouring out the bottles of champagne that were on the table. I didn't detect him saving any for his wife this time. I didn't detect his wife, either; he appeared to have come by himself, though Bradley the letterer was there, and several other people I recognised from marketing.

'How's your father, Digger?' Dan asked, and for the millionth time I marvelled at his social ease that let him navigate a conversation with these people he'd never met before, in a place brimming with the potential for *faux pas*. I was learning it wasn't a trick at all; it was part of being interested in other people.

'He'll be going home in the next week or so,' Digger told us. 'Angelique helped me sort out home help for him. I'll be doing PT with him two mornings a week.'

'I didn't help you with anything,' Angelique said. 'This man was on the phone bullying people night and day. Getting the best care for his father. He's going to get looked after better than he was before his stroke.'

'Two mornings a week?' I asked. 'You mean you're not moving in with him?'

Digger shook his head. He didn't say any more but I realised I should have known it from what he'd said the night before. He'd realised he deserved a life.

'Right, bottoms up, there's plenty more where that came from,' announced Anthony, finishing his pouring.

'I think I'm going to need it,' I muttered and at that exact moment Dan took my hand under the table and the house lights dimmed.

And this was it. My palms slicked with sweat and Dan tightened his grip.

I think this was where the adrenaline kicked in, as my body realised that this was really happening, because I don't remember who it was that came up to the podium, or what he said. I assume it was a man who spoke; the industry being as it is, odds were that it was a man, but for all I knew it could have been an octopus. My eyes were glued to the TV screen, which endlessly scrolled the nominees' names and categories. There was Dan. And me. And *Girl from Mars*. And Dan. And me. And *Girl from Mars*.

Then the screen stopped scrolling and only showed the nominees for the category that was being awarded. I kept staring anyway until I realised they'd got to Dan's category: Best Writer.

I looked at Dan. He seemed so calm. His hand holding mine was warm and dry, not clammy like mine.

'Don't you want to win?' I whispered to him.

'Fil, like you said, I don't know squat about writing comics. It's amazing I got nominated for my first ever script. I'd rather the award went to somebody who deserved it.'

'And the winner of the Peregrine award for Best Writer is . . .' there was a pause as the announcer attempted to do Chris Tarrant deadpan, 'Colin O'Leary, for *Apocalypse Cow*.'

Colin O'Leary was about sixty-five and had huge grey sideburns and hands which shook as they accepted his bird statuette.

'Now that's someone who looks like he's put in his time,' Dan said.

'It's like I told Stevo, the indie comics are going to get it all this year,' I moaned, and used my free hand to drink the rest of my champagne. Anthony filled it up again.

'Shut up,' called Stevo across the table. Digger threw a programme at me.

'You're going to win,' Jim told me.

I drank.

They did the pencillers first, and then the inkers. Since splitting up the job this way tended to be the way that major publishers did things, the penciller was for *Superman* and the inker was for *Spider-Man*. The three others in my category, which was for people who did everything, pencils, inks and colours, were all artists with indie imprints. Of course I'd checked out their stuff. Two of them, Chaz Herring and Gilbert Ortega, were amazing. The third, Big G, was just weird. Between them, I didn't have a chance.

'I'm going to lose,' I said. This time Jim hit me on the head with his programme. I didn't even feel it because they had got to Best Artist, and they said my name first in the list of nominees because I was Brown.

The breath halted in my chest. My stomach flipped over. My legs spaghettied. It was like that moment in a movie where the camera speeds through crowds of people all going in super-fast motion and then zooms in on one individual, fills the screen with her so that everything else disappears, there is only one moment, one person, everything focused on here and now, and the announcer did his Chris Tarrant thing and my ears filled with roaring and then, crystal-clearly, he said, 'Fil Brown, for *Girl from Mars* and *The TIME Temptation, Episode Two: Deeper*.'

I gasped a strangled gasp and felt Dan gently prising my fingers from his. 'Go up and get it,' he said to me and I have no idea how I got up to the podium, but then I was there. I took the Peregrine in my hands. It was lighter than it looked, cool and smooth.

'Thank you,' I said into the microphone. My voice was big in the silence. I knew I should say more, say who I was thanking and why. Daniel. Anthony. Jim, Digger and Stevo. My parents. Girl from Mars. Dennis McKay. But at that moment all I could think of was, 'This is going to look great in my house.'

I stumbled back down off the stage, laughter and approval and applause ringing through my head and body. When I got back to the table I was greeted by a sea of arms wanting to give me hugs. I was passed around, from Anthony's slap on the back to my mother's perfumed clasp, to my father's awkward hug to Digger's bear-arms and Angelique's warmth and Stevo and Brian's double-hug and then Jim, who held on for three full breaths. Then Dan, who lifted me up and spun me round and laughed and set me back on my seat.

I put the Peregrine on the table in front of me. I stared at it. I looked around at all of these people I cared about.

'This is exactly where and who I am supposed to be,' I said.

'Yes it is,' said Dan, and then Anthony poured some more champagne, and we had to be quiet because they were announcing the next award.

I stroked my Peregrine with one finger. My knee pressed against Dan's under the table. My mind floated on a cloud of champagne bubbles.

I closed my eyes for a moment and felt myself years ago, at school. My neck itched from the uniform. It was break time and all around me girls chattered, boys kicked footballs, and I curled up with my bare legs under my hated skirt and opened the latest issue of *Girl from Mars*. The one where she defeated the bad guys and she was bursting with power and she was strong enough to be alone.

Years into the future, I could still smell the ink from those pages.

'Right now, I wouldn't even trade places with Girl from Mars,' I said.

'About shitting time,' thundered Anthony, standing up so fast his chair fell over.

I lifted my head, blinking. 'What?'

Anthony was on his way up to the stage. 'Get up here, you pilchards,' he said over his shoulder.

'*Girl from Mars* won best comic,' Dan told me. His fingers threaded with mine and he brought me up to the podium with him.

I hadn't even heard the applause the last time I was up here, not until I'd stepped down, but this time it was a force, a miracle. Anthony held the statuette above his head as if he were Rocky and it was the belt for the heavyweight champion of the world. I looked down at all the people, the audience I hadn't been able to see when I'd been up here by myself. My parents were clapping, Jim was waving my Peregrine at the Peregrine that Anthony was waving, a matching pair.

If I jumped hard enough, I would be able to fly.

And then Dan grabbed me round the waist, held me tight against him, and kissed me. A proper, passionate, amazing kiss, a kiss that only Dan could deliver, with the memory of everything we'd done together.

Spinning, soaring, travelling not through space and time but through something deeper, more intimate and eternal. For an immeasurable moment I touched Dan's shoulder and his hair, his mouth with mine, and nothing else mattered.

In a comic book, it would be frozen. A permanent now. You wouldn't ever have to turn the page.

In real life there are no pages and nothing stays the same. I heard whoops and whistles, the applause grown to an almost unbearable level, the floor shaking with it, and Dan stopped kissing me and put me down so we were facing the audience.

The single still point in a heaving and thundering universe was Jim. In a clear line of sight, across the room, I saw his face and I understood everything I'd been trying not to see.

He put my Peregrine down on the table and turned away. I twisted out of Dan's arms and ran to my first friend, my brother, but he was already gone.

Me and Jim and the Elephant

I couldn't leave right away. There were hands thrust at me to shake and pictures to be taken. 'Go after Jim,' I told Digger as soon as I could but he shook his head.

'It has to be you,' he said.

But then I was taken away for more photos and I had to do an individual interview with *Comics International* magazine in which I have no clue what I said. I finished and, spotting Dan halfway across the room talking with someone who looked like a journalist, I threaded through the crowd and touched his arm.

'I've got to go,' I told him, and he immediately put down his glass as if he were going to go with me.

'No, you stay. It's Jim, there's something wrong. I'll – see you later.'

He bent his head to kiss me but I turned away quickly and went outside to hail a black cab.

The house was dark when I got there, but the way the front door opened and the scent of cut grass when I walked in told me that Jim was home and he'd gone outside to the back garden.

Now that I was here I moved slowly. I went upstairs and I changed into my jeans and a jumper, and then I came back down and I went to the fireplace. I knew the house so well that I didn't need a light, but some shone through from outside, enough to show me outlines. The candles stood on the mantel around my shrine, three of them lopped off at the top from when we'd taken our vow. Jim had dusted the empty plinth this morning in case I won.

I put the Peregrine in the space that had been waiting for it, and then used the waiting matches to light the candles, the straight ones and the crooked one. The yellow light flickered off the figurine's wings and beak and glazed its eyes.

Somehow, the award didn't fill the empty space. It displaced it, so that the entire room felt more empty, as if emptiness were a substance that could be moved but not destroyed.

I took a deep breath of my old life and went outside to where Jim was waiting for me.

It was chilly out here. Damp leaves squashed underfoot. Jim had dragged a lawn chair to the centre of the garden and was sitting in it looking up at the stars. You couldn't see many in greater London because of light pollution, but you could identify some constellations. We'd done that as teenagers, hanging around at night with not much else to do.

I pulled over a second chair. 'Why are you out here?' I asked.

'We need to talk.'

I didn't sit down, just in case. 'Are you sure?'

'Yes.'

He looked down, at the grass where Digger had

planted that first candle, the night we took our vow. Back when nothing had seemed so important as the three of us and being together and keeping everything the same.

'Don't say it,' I said in a rush of desperation. 'Please don't, Jim. Let's get everything back to how it used to be. We can just carry on and forget that anything ever happened.'

'And what about Daniel McKay?'

I bit my lip.

'I didn't set out to be with him. I tried not to. It just happened.'

'Things like that don't just happen, Fil. You can stop them happening if you want to. You can keep quiet. You can do it for years.'

I clenched my fists. 'Don't.'

'But you didn't want to keep quiet. You wanted Daniel McKay. How long has it been going on?'

'A little while,' I whispered.

'I thought so,' he said. 'Why didn't you tell me?'

'Because—' Because of how he was acting now. Angry and bitter, almost like a stranger. But he wasn't angry at Dan, even though he said his name so carefully. He was angry at me.

To truly explain why I'd kept it a secret, I'd have to admit what I didn't want him to say. 'I didn't want you and Digger to know that I'd broken the vow,' I said.

'We're your friends. You can't go around hiding things from us.'

'You have,' I said, and then instantly regretted it.

Jim gripped the arms of his chair as if they were the only things keeping him from falling off the earth.

'The vow was stupid,' he said. 'I knew why Digger started it. He wanted to keep us all together, and I thought it was a good idea. I thought it would be enough if you never had anyone else. We could carry on living together and seeing each other every day. I knew there could never be anyone else for me. But it wasn't enough. It can't be enough.'

'Don't say it, please.'

He shook his head. 'I love you, Fil. I'm in love with you.'

'Don't,' I said again, but it was too late. Everything I thought was for ever was swirling around me, dissipating like smoke into the night air.

'I can't help it. I've always loved you. Digger knew. He told me one time that the reason you and I argued so much was because if we agreed, I'd have to tell you how I felt. But you knew already, didn't you?'

'No,' I said. Then I said, 'Yes.'

I'd been standing up, but now I sat down. The world was too shaky for me to stay upright.

'Do you love me back?' he asked.

'You're – the most important person in the world to me, Jim.'

'Do you love me?'

'Of course I love you. But –' The words scraped my throat raw.

'Not like you love Daniel McKay.'

I swallowed. 'No,' I said.

Jim nodded, and looked down at the ground. The scorch marks had long since grown over. I thought of my weeks with Dan, all the wonderful, challenging, exciting moments, all the whirl of feelings that I wanted to cling to and never let go.

And then I thought of the years with Jim. The weight of everything we'd done, the people we'd become together. And how he was suffering in front of me now.

'I'll stop seeing Dan,' I said. The renunciation already tore a hole in my chest, but I ignored it, because it couldn't be as bad as this, not as bad as having my life ripped in half. 'You've been my best friend for so long. I can't lose you. I'll give him up.'

'And that will magically fix everything?'

'Sure it will.'

'How's it going to do that, Fil?'

'We'll go back to being friends. We'll do everything the same as we always have.'

'I don't think you understand what I'm saying, Fil,' he said, every word carefully enunciated. 'I am in love with you. I've been in love with you for years. It's been torture to sit beside you and not touch you, to talk to you and never mention how I've felt. To know you've been lying in bed down the hallway, or working upstairs.'

'I – I didn't know.'

'You just said you did.'

'I didn't want to know.'

Pain on his face, in the starlight, turned his eyes to dark holes and his cheeks to hollows, strangely beautiful.

'I'm sorry, Jim.'

'Yeah. So sorry you hooked up with a guy who you told me was your enemy. So sorry you had to lie to me and sneak around behind my back.'

The fury in his words made me jump out of my chair. 'What do you want me to do? I told you I'd stop seeing him.'

'That's not what I want.'

'No, you want me to love you back, and I can't do that.'

He actually, physically winced. It went through me like a knife.

'Why didn't you say something before?' I cried. 'Why not years ago, Jim, when I could have tried? Before I met Dan?'

'You mean so I could be second best even from the start?'

'That's not true, you're not second best, you've never been second best.'

'And that's why you lied to me, because I'm the best.'

'You never told me!' I yelled at him. 'If you'd told me I would have tried to love you but you were too scared!'

'Don't you dare call me a coward,' Jim said, standing up and towering over me, 'and don't you dare say you would've tried to love me. Not when you brought me to a party and kissed another man in front of everyone we know. I never told you how I felt because I didn't want to lose you. But I'd rather lose you than have your pity. Or have you *try*.'

'I don't—'

'And I'd rather lose you than have you humiliate me again.'

Jim turned on his heel and left me. He went into the house and banged the kitchen door shut behind him.

I stood in the garden, shivering as if the protection of my skin had disappeared and my body had turned into a mass of guts and raw nerves.

'Please,' I said to the stars, but I knew there was no use in it. There was no time machine, nothing I could do to go back and be honest from the start, to trust Jim, to value him enough not to ignore his feelings and not to hurt him.

And I could have loved Jim. If I'd never been afraid of

losing him, or seeing the truth. It only would've taken a bit more courage. But now it was too late. The gap was too wide, the habits too hard to break.

And now there was Dan.

I trudged across the lawn, the grass and leaves dampening my feet. As soon as I touched the kitchen door, I knew that as bad as things were, they were about to become horribly, tremendously worse.

Ash

The door was hot. I pushed it open and yelled, 'Jim!'

Smoke was beginning to fill the kitchen and through the doorway I could see the flicker of flames.

'Oh shit.' I grabbed the washing-up bowl from the sink, half-full with tepid soapy water, and ran into the living room.

Jim was by the fireplace. He had a blanket from the couch and he was using it to try to smother a fire which had burned from the carpet up the window curtains. His slim figure was a dark silhouette against the orange flames and smoke, and I could see that even though he'd extinguished some of the carpet, the fire had caught the other curtain and was moving rapidly across the room towards my girly chair.

And The Baz, who was in his cage against the far wall. I threw the contents of my washing-up bowl over the fire heading in his direction. It doused some of it with a hiss and a billow of smoke and steam, but as soon as I'd done it I knew it was nowhere near enough.

Grab The Baz? Or fill up the bowl and try to prevent the fire from spreading? It was difficult to see where it had started, and for a horrible instant I suspected that Jim had lit it himself because he was so angry with me.

'Don't just stand there, get more water.' Jim's voice was choked, and the smoke was beginning to grip at my own throat. I took in a deep breath while there was still some clear air and turned towards the kitchen.

But the flames had fanned behind me, around Jim, blocking the way into the kitchen. I dropped my bowl and pushed the lid off The Baz's tank. He was lukewarm and rough in my hands as I tucked him under my arm. He clung to my jumper with his claws.

'I don't think we can put this out,' I said to Jim. I could only see him as a shadow. The flames had reached my girly chair and were licking, curling around it, turning the flowers black. My eyes streamed and my mouth was full of the taste of burning upholstery.

Of course we couldn't put this out, this was a fire, a proper fire, not a little domestic accident. I had to call 999, but the phone was in the kitchen, and my mobile was upstairs. Could I get upstairs before— *No, silly, Fil, the house is on fire and you're not a superhero.*

The lizard in my arms thrashed his tail as if to remind me this was actually quite urgent, human, get a move on.

'Out,' Jim choked and he grabbed my arm and pulled me and The Baz out of the living room, into the hallway. As soon as he opened the front door the cool night air rushed past us, into our lungs and into the sudden great roar behind us in the house. We stumbled on to the path, turning round immediately to see our house with red and orange and yellow streaming through it, visible through the upstairs windows now.

'Shit, Fil, you didn't leave the back door open, did you?'

'I – think so.'

'That's fanned it.' He dropped my arm. I clutched the iguana. Our house, our place, our world on fire. I shook my head again and again. Was I trying to believe it? Or trying to deny it?

Behind us, below the roar of the fire, I could hear people spilling out on to the street. When I blinked I felt smoke and grit in my eyes and I saw Jim's *Star Trek* wall melting.

'Where did it come from?' I asked.

'It was burning when I went in. I think a candle fell off your shrine.'

Shit.

I sank to the pavement, The Baz's prickly head beneath my chin.

'You mean I set the house on fire?'

Jim didn't answer. He also didn't remind me again that I'd left the back door open to fuel the fire with oxygen, which was kind of him, I supposed.

'Are you all right? Anyone else in there?' One of our neighbours put his hand on Jim's shoulder. 'I've called 999.'

'There's nothing in there,' Jim said.

There was everything in there. In my mind's eye I saw the caricature of Jim, Digger and Stevo curling up and turning to ash, along with the couch. The books, the comics, the packets of cereal, the wooden chopsticks, the dog-eared decks of cards. I watched the fire climb the stairs and visit my room, eat my fuchsia dress, move on to melt Jim's computer and blacken the photograph of us at the Zoo.

All that time, all those memories. I looked up to the top window, the window of my studio, and I could see an orange glow there already. Behind me, getting closer, there was the sound of sirens, but it was too late.

'It's gone,' I said. 'We can't save it.'

I couldn't bear to watch everything being destroyed. I stood and turned to Jim and leaned my forehead on his chest, trying to hold him. He stood straight and tall, watching the fire, and did not touch me. He had a smudge on his cheek.

'It wasn't worth saving,' he said.

Finished

My parents' house was much noisier than mine in the morning. I'd forgotten how my father liked to sing *The Barber of Seville* all over the house, and how my mother believed that a good session of hoovering cleared the cobwebs out of her brain before a day's work.

They were up ridiculously early as well, considering how late I'd turned up at their house last night, stinking of smoke, covered with soot and needing several whisky-laced cups of tea before I could stop shaking enough to go to bed. When I did, in my old single childhood bed which still remained in a room that long ago had turned into overspill space for my parents' books, I couldn't sleep. Whenever I closed my eyes, I saw flames.

I gave it up and crawled out of bed. Though I'd taken a shower before I went to bed, the pillow was streaked with black. I considered my clothes, in a jumble on the floor, but even from a distance they stank, so I put on my mother's borrowed brown dressing gown instead.

The hoovering and the singing rose and fell in counterpoint. As a kid I'd found it pointlessly loud, especially when I wanted a good teenage lie-in. This morning, it sounded almost like a duet. My parents prepared for their day in effortless harmony with each other.

The singing stopped, and then the hoovering, and a moment later there was a soft tap at my door. 'Philomena, your friend is here for you,' said my mother.

My heart leapt and my stomach sank, joy and dread all at once. It couldn't be Jim. Jim had refused to talk to me once the fire engines appeared. I wasn't sure where he'd gone to spend the night; if he'd gone to his mother's he would be less than a quarter of a mile away.

Maybe it was Digger. Maybe Jim had gone to stay with Digger and Digger was here to try to sort things out. I tied the dressing-gown cord and flew down the stairs.

It was Dan, standing just inside the door. As soon as he saw me he grabbed me and hugged me tight to him. He smelled clean, but the scent of burning upholstery was lodged in my nostrils.

'Thank God,' he said into my hair. 'You didn't answer your phone so I went to see if you were all right and I saw your house.'

I wondered what it looked like this morning, with the fire cooled. I pictured an empty blackened shell with blank eyes.

'I burned it down,' I said to Dan's chest.

'You burned it?' He sounded disbelieving.

'One of my candles fell over. It was crooked but I lit it anyway. And then I left the back door open.'

'Oh.' He loosened me slightly and stroked my hair with a gentle hand. 'You mean it was an accident.'

'I did it,' I insisted. 'I ruined everything.'

And then I remembered properly how Dan was

part of my ruining everything and I stepped back from him.

'I can't see you any more,' I said.

'What?'

'I took a vow. I promised Jim.'

'But – I thought you and Jim weren't together.'

'We're not.' Not in any way. I remembered the stranger in Jim's body, a smudge of ash on his cheek, and I shivered.

'So why did he ask you to break up with me?'

'He didn't ask me. I said I would.'

'Why?'

'Because –' Because Jim couldn't have the person he loved and I shouldn't, either. The thought tore open the hole in my chest all over again, as if it had slightly scabbed over during the night and now I'd ripped it even wider.

What was wrong with me, that I'd only realised I loved Dan at the very moment I offered to give him up?

'Because my friends are more important than anything else to me and I don't need anything else.'

Dan frowned. 'Fil, you can see me and still see your friends. I like them. I thought we got along okay last night.'

'That's because you don't know me. You don't know them.' Every minute he was standing across from me was making it more and more difficult for me to make him go. 'Listen, Dan, you just have to leave, okay?'

Dan crossed his arms and shook his head. 'I can't let you break up with me without understanding what the hell you're talking about. What's really the matter, Fil?'

'Stop it!' I cried. My throat hurt from the smoke and I could smell it everywhere. I thought I would probably smell it for the rest of my life. 'Stop asking me how I feel! I don't want to talk about it and I don't want to think about it. I've ruined everything and all I want is for it to go back to how it was before I met you.'

'Philomena –' He reached out a hand for me and I stepped back, tightening the belt of my mother's dressing gown. It felt like very flimsy protection, from Dan and from my own temptations.

'Don't touch me, Dan. Please, just go away. I should never have started anything with you in the first place. It was all a mistake.'

His blue eyes were puzzled, the set of his mouth angry. I'd hurt him.

'I was a mistake?' he asked.

'Yes.' I turned my back and looked at the bookshelves in the hallway, seeing them as lines and bands of colour. There was a pause behind me.

'When you want to talk, you know where to find me,' Dan said at last. I felt him leave before I heard the door close softly.

'I'm finished with talking,' I said to the books.

Tell Me That Later, When My Hands Aren't Full of Evil Genius

I spent the next few days getting underfoot at my parents' house. I wandered outside once, to their little patio garden, and the autumn sun on my skin gave me more pleasure than I deserved. Mostly I wore brown, I mooched, and I ate the sandwiches my father made for me: tuna and pineapple, and (a favourite of my youth) butter, lettuce and poppy seed on white bread.

All of my own comics and books had been moved out of the house long ago; I read *The Mill on the Floss*. It was about a woman who fell in love with someone other than the friend who was in love with her. Then she drowned.

'Those Victorians really knew how to write a happy, upbeat story,' I said to my mother that night at dinner, and she explained to me at great length about the plight of the fallen woman in nineteenth-century fiction.

I let it wash over me. It was actually pretty comforting. Before bedtime, my father came to me with a biscuit and a copy of *Much Ado About Nothing*. 'This will make you feel better,' he said. It didn't, but it did lull the hours between bed and fitful sleep with iambic pentameter.

From my single bed one afternoon, cocooned in a duvet for protection, I rang Digger. As I'd suspected, Jim was staying at his flat and by the sounds of it, he was spending most of his time umbilically attached to the Wii. 'He needs time,' Digger told me. 'He's got to come to terms with it. He's blowing up aliens, but in his mind he's thinking it all through.'

'Does he want to see me?'

'No.'

'Does he know I'm on the phone now?'

'No, I'm on the balcony.'

I sighed and felt like crying. 'Digger, nothing's ever going to be the same again.'

'No. But that might not be so bad, Fil.'

There wasn't any answer to that.

'Are you still my friend?' I asked him.

'Don't be an idiot,' he said affectionately.

'Tell Jim that I—' My voice faltered. What good would it do, even to bring up Dan? 'Tell him I miss him.'

'Yeah. Bye, Fil.'

I pulled the duvet over my head. When I emerged, I found a cup of tea and a copy of *A Midsummer Night's Dream*. Quarrelling friends and mistaken love, all solved by the fairies.

'That Shakespeare was deluded,' I told my father at dinner.

The next day a box arrived. I opened it on the living-room floor. It contained my entire *Girl from Mars* collection, and on top of that, a brown envelope I recognised as the one that Dan had given me at the awards ceremony, and which I'd left behind on my chair.

I combed through the box for a note, but clearly the contents were Dan's message.

'What's that, Philomena?' my mother asked from behind me on the couch, putting a bookmark in her tome.

'It's my comics. I lent them to Dan to read.' I took them out and stacked them, arranged by year, on the floor. He'd looked after them well. 'They're my last surviving possessions.'

'And what's in the envelope?'

I opened it. 'The script for Episode Five.' I flipped through. 'No, for both Episodes Five and Six. The rest of Dan's story.' And no note here, either. I brought the scripts to a comfortable reading chair.

'Hmm.' My mother leaned over and picked up one of my comics.

GIRL FROM MARS AND THE TIME TEMPTA-TION, EPISODE FIVE: SACRIFICE, I read.

The front splash page was Girl from Mars and Jackson Silver in the chamber at the heart of the caves, surrounded by the shadowy forms of the beings whose deaths Girl from Mars had not been able to prevent. It would be a great set piece to draw, a classic for posters, and I suspected Dan had written it precisely for that purpose. Then I read on, and got sucked into the story too much to think about set pieces.

The ghosts were in pain. All of the mortal pain they had felt at the moment of their deaths, except without death as a release. Jackson, the inventor of the TIME device, had suspected that its time distortion might have side-effects such as this, creating unnatural pathways between life and death, which was one reason he'd never built the device. However, it quickly became clear that

this particular device had been tampered with specifically to produce ghosts – the doing of Glypto, Jackson's
evil former lab assistant.

What had been a brooding, intense story meditating
on the nature of responsibility and grief became a classic
adrenaline-thumping chase story, as Girl from Mars and
Jackson Silver raced through countryside and city and
eventually space, kicking some arse on the way, to track
down Glypto and discover how to reverse the effects of
the TIME device's modification. Meanwhile, new ghosts
were turning up all over – not just from Girl from Mars's
past, but from Jackson's past as well: his uncle, dead of a
lonely suicide; his brother, who had survived three weeks
after birth. I began to see why Jackson had been
interested enough in time to invent a machine to change
it. And why he was so determined now to find the person
who had perverted what had been a clear vision.

I read straight through to Episode Six, which Dan had
called *TIME*.

For an evil scientific geek, Glypto could move like the
wind. They finally cornered him in his own orbiting space
station, cobbled together from space scrap (this was going
to be great to draw). As Girl from Mars held him in a
Martian Torture Grip, Glypto revealed that using the
machine any more would only rip open the fabric of
mortality even further. The only way to reverse the
ghostly effects of the TIME device was to destroy it
completely, now.

GIRL: WHAT'S THE QUICKEST WAY TO DO
THAT, JACKSON?
JACKSON: BUT IF IT'S DESTROYED YOU'LL
NEVER GET HOME.

GIRL: MY FRIENDS ARE IN *PAIN*. THERE'S NO OTHER CHOICE. ARE YOU GOING TO TELL ME, OR DO I HAVE TO USE THE TORTURE GRIP ON *YOU* TOO?

PANEL SIX: Jackson presses the buttons to open the service hatchway to the radioactive core fuel supply of the station.
JACKSON: THIS IS PROBABLY NOT THE BEST MOMENT TO TELL YOU I'VE FALLEN COMPLETELY IN LOVE WITH YOU.
GIRL: TELL ME THAT LATER, WHEN I HAVEN'T GOT MY HANDS FULL OF EVIL GENIUS.

'I knew it,' I murmured, but my heart leapt and throbbed. I turned the page. There was only one panel.

With a show of unnatural and previously unsuspected strength, Glypto broke free of Girl from Mars's hold and rushed towards Jackson, his arms outstretched to push him into the reactive fuel core to his death.

Dan had hardly described what the panel should look like, only the action in it, but I could see it exactly.

She'd save him. She had to. I turned the page.

Glypto grabbed the TIME device from Jackson and flung it across the room, out of the path of danger. The two of them wrestled on the brink of sudden fiery death, until Girl from Mars dived in and pulled them both away from the fuel core. That was the moment that Glypto unsheathed a hidden and totally unfair dagger and stabbed Jackson through the chest.

Death came quickly, in a panel that Dan described as having 'just enough blood to be beautiful', but not before

Girl from Mars softly kissed Jackson's dying lips, and he smiled.

> JACKSON: I WISH WE HAD TIME FOR A LOT MORE OF THAT.
> CAPTION: AND THEN IT WAS *OVER*.

But of course she could still save him. She had the TIME machine.

> GLYPTO: *USE IT*. YOU CAN HAVE JACKSON. YOU CAN GO HOME. YOU CAN HAVE *EVERYTHING* YOU EVER WANTED.

Of course she'd use it. That was what Daniel McKay stories were all about: defeating death. She'd discover some amazing way to use it that meant it didn't call up any more ghosts. And she'd have everything she ever wanted.

I turned the page.

She threw the TIME device into the reactor. For good measure, she threw Glypto in there too.

All over Earth, the ghosts dissipated with a final sigh of relief and forgiveness. And Girl from Mars cried.

> CAPTION: WE THOUGHT WE HAD ALL THE TIME IN THE WORLD. WE WERE WRONG.

> PANEL THREE: She looks out to the stars.
> CAPTION: THE PAST HAS TO DIE. THE FUTURE CAN CHANGE. ALL WE HAVE IS *NOW*.
> CAPTION: AND JACKSON, I CAN'T REGRET A THING.

I wiped tears from my face. I must have sniffed quite loudly because my mother said, 'What's wrong?'

I looked up at her. She had *The Neptune Nightmare* open in her hands, and quite a considerable stack of read comics beside her on the couch.

'It's a good story,' I said.

'So are these. I'm hooked.' She laughed, somewhat shamefaced, and I couldn't help but laugh a little too, wiping my cheeks.

'I've got a deadline coming up,' I said. 'I need to find somewhere to draw.'

'Well, I suppose you can use my study. I quite often work in the same room as your father anyway. Do you need a lot of equipment?'

'I'll get Stevo to bring my stuff over from UPC.' I glanced back down at the script. One of my tears had landed on it and puckered the paper.

'Are you all right, Philomena?' my mother asked.

'What do you call it when reading a book sort of takes all your bad feelings and throws them up in your face?'

'Catharsis. Aristotle believed that it was an essential function of tragic art.'

'And what about when it gives you this feeling that maybe the tragedy wasn't pointless? Maybe that the person learned something from it and might be able to move on?'

'Darling, we call that hope.'

The Real World

The day I finished inking *The TIME Temptation*, I opened my parents' front door to a rainy day that smelled distinctly of coming winter. I shrugged on my new coat, which was neither denim nor black but instead bottle-green, pulled the hood up over my brown and pink hair and tucked my plastic portfolio under my arm for extra protection.

Fortified as I was, I still had to take a deep breath of damp air before I set off towards the tube station. There was nothing else for it: my scanner and computer had been destroyed in the fire along with everything else, and the insurance money hadn't come through yet, complicated as it was by the fact that the joint claimants, myself and James T. Lousder, weren't on speaking terms and were doing everything through the intermediary of Digger. Who had a life of his own to be getting on with.

Anyway, it meant that I was going to have to scan my art using UPC's mega-scanner, and to do the colours using one of their computers. Maybe even the one in the sweatshop, if the sweatshop still existed.

I took another deep breath, though this one had nothing to do with steeling my nerve and everything to do with the fact that the air just felt good. I had spent most of the past weeks immersed in my work, in the world of *Girl from Mars*. Drawing Dan's story, living it along with Girl from Mars and Jackson Silver. I'd only emerged this morning, whereupon I had drunk an entire litre of orange juice, mindful of Digger's advice about scurvy, and prepared to go out into the real world.

The grey sky and drizzle made the traffic lights seem brighter than normal. For a moment, the sun struggled through the clouds and I had to squint.

I decided to take a detour.

The bus route took me past The Manhattan Project nightclub. Since our night of ignominy, it had closed down and been re-opened as a gym named The Body Factory. I got off near the Swan and walked through my neighbourhood to my house.

The windows had been boarded up on the ground floor, and the cream-painted front was blackened with smoke. I stood on the path and gazed up at it.

When Digger and Stevo had gone through the house, they hadn't found very much spared from fire and smoke and water damage. They'd rescued my Peregrine, which was twisted and melted and I'd immediately thrown it away. In my head the house had been like that: a blackened lump, beyond all redemption or beauty or life.

Actually, looking at it now, it wasn't that bad. The four walls were there, and the door, and the roof looked fine. All the basics were sound, and the house next door was untouched.

The grass was long and dandelions had sprung up on

Jim's carefully tended front lawn. Weeds tendrilled over the front path and ivy had made a tentative restart on the brickwork.

I sniffed the air: rain and grass and the smallest hint of ash. I could go inside the house and look, rummage around for any more stuff that belonged to a past life, but I had other things to do. I turned and headed for the Underground station, splashing through all the puddles on the way.

Stepping into the carriage of the Underground train, I recognised a head of auburn hair. Rachel sat on a double seat on her own, frowning down at her sudoku.

'Hey,' I said, sitting next to her.

She started, as anybody would upon actually being spoken to on the Underground, but then she recognised me. 'Hey, Fil,' she said. Friendly as she'd always been. 'I haven't seen you for ages. How are you doing?'

'Not bad,' I said. 'How about you?'

She shrugged. 'I keep pretty busy. I should be working on my dissertation today but I'm skiving to go to the movies.'

'On your own?'

'Yeah, sometimes that's the best way. You don't have to share your popcorn. I'm meeting some friends for dinner afterwards. I don't mind being alone, it's being lonely I don't like, you know?'

I nodded. I thought about how Rachel had a group of friends, and by knowing her I was connected to them. And then each of those had their own friends, and they had their own friends, all of them connected by these invisible bands of friendship.

You could be connected to practically everyone in the world, that way.

'Digger told me about your house,' she said. 'I'm really sorry about that.'

'Me too.'

'Where are you living?'

'With my parents. But my friends Stevo and Brian are buying a house together so they're both selling their flats. I'm going to see Brian's tomorrow. I wouldn't wish Stevo's flat on a hamster, but apparently Brian's is quite nice.'

'Are you – are you going to buy it with Jim?'

'No. On my own.'

'Oh.' She blushed. She was so pretty, with her orange jumper and her hair and her blue eyes. She had on high-heeled brown boots and soft, faded jeans.

'I know you're busy,' I said, 'but do you think you'd like to go shopping with me one afternoon? I've bought a few new things but in general I need a whole new wardrobe and I'm sort of clueless about what's in fashion.'

'Yeah,' she said, 'I'd like that.'

She smiled at me again. Maybe I could invite Angelique too. 'Have you – uh, seen Jim at all?' I asked.

'He came in for the pub quiz with Digger last week. They did it just the two of them.'

'Did they win?'

'No, it was a bunch of secretaries from the office across the road. It used to be much more fun when you guys were the reigning champions.' She put away her half-finished sudoku; I noticed that she did it the same way Jim did, in ballpoint pen. 'Maybe one day you'll all have a triumphant comeback,' she said.

'Maybe,' I said.

*

By the time I emerged from Victoria station it had stopped raining. Becca greeted me at the door of UPC and we chatted for a few minutes about what it was like to have your house burn down (it hadn't happened to her, but as a kid in Slough, arsonists had attacked her garden shed). I went to the third floor and scanned my artwork using the massive scanner, a piece of equipment that was meant to be all high-tech and futuristic but which reminded me of a cross between a photocopier and a sun bed. Once the art was downloaded on to the system, I went upstairs to get started on the colour on the sweatshop's computer. On my way quite a few people said hello; Anthony, in the middle of some phone conversation, even waved through his glass door.

The sweatshop was empty, of course. Stevo had removed all of my stuff and even Dan's coffee-maker and mug were gone. I stood in the doorway.

I could turn on the computer, call up my picture files, and spend a few more hours on *Girl from Mars* planet. I wouldn't notice the emptiness of the room, not until I was done.

But it was as if during all the time I'd spent drawing, my mind had been working on its own. It had thought about what I wanted and what I didn't want, worked through what I felt. While my hands created pictures, maybe I'd even started to understand the meaning of the story I was drawing.

And now, standing here by myself, I couldn't help thinking of one of its final lines: ALL WE HAVE IS *NOW*.

I left the UPC building and walked down the wet pavements and the now-sunny street to Suffolk Mansions.

I stood on the intricate Art Nouveau tiles in the doorway and rang Dan's bell.

'Hi.' His voice through the intercom made me suddenly thirsty, hungry, every possible craving at once.

'It's me,' I said. 'Fil Brown.'

There was a pause, during which my trainers squeaked on the tiles and my heart flipped around.

'Come on up,' he said at last, and buzzed the door open.

He was waiting for me at the top of the stairs. He wore jeans and a grey jumper and no shoes and he looked indescribably good. I climbed the last step and stood there, gazing at him.

'It's been awhile,' he said.

His voice, his whole manner, was cool and reserved. Exactly the opposite of the Dan I knew. I hadn't been sure what I was going to say anyway, but now I was really clueless. I fiddled with the portfolio in my hands.

'I've been drawing,' I said. 'I thought you might want to see them.'

'Sure. Come in.'

His elegant front room seemed different, though it was spacious enough that I didn't see how right away. Then I saw that the wall of DVDs was gone. In its place was a stack of cardboard boxes. I glanced through to the kitchen; his refrigerator was bare.

'Are you moving?'

'I'm going back to Philly.'

'Why?'

'I've finished my work with UPC, I've spent some time with my dad, I've done what I came for and now there's nothing keeping me here. Apparently.'

'You –' I was trying to work through that 'apparently' in my brain, but it had stalled. 'Do you think you might do some more scripts for *Girl from Mars*? Maybe we could – maybe we could work together again.'

He ran his hands through his already-dishevelled hair. 'Fil, I know when it's time to give up. I'm not interested in a relationship that's not going anywhere. I've done that already.'

'You don't think *Girl from Mars* is going anywhere?'

'No, Fil, I don't think you and I are going anywhere. You kicked me out of your life. I thought my script made it pretty clear how I felt, but I haven't heard from you in weeks. So that's it. I've got the message.'

'I've – been working.'

'Far, far away from any telephone.'

'I've needed time.'

'Well, you've had it. And meanwhile, I've been hanging around waiting. So now the time's up.' He began to turn away, towards the boxes, his hand reaching for packing tape.

'I've been too scared,' I said.

He stopped.

'You make me feel all sorts of things I've never felt before,' I told him. 'You don't let me ignore them or run away. It's bloody terrifying.'

'Surely it's not as scary as all that.'

'The last time I was honest about my emotions I ended up fleeing from a burning building clutching a lizard. It's scary, Dan. It can hurt.'

'So how has this ignoring your feelings worked for you this time? Have they gone away and left you in peace?'

'No.'

'Well, I might.' He sat down on one of the couches. He

was still angry with me, but I'd heard that 'might'. I hung on to it, and dared to sit down beside him.

'So what are these feelings you're so scared of?' he asked me.

'I think I'll mess things up. I think you'll get tired of me. I think I don't know how to have a relationship and I think I'm not normal.'

'Fil, don't you know that's exactly what I like about you? That you're not normal?'

'Really?'

But I knew that already, even as I questioned it. I'd been able to see that in him for a long time now. He saw something in me that was truly me, not the weirdness of me but the uniqueness. It was the same way I saw him.

'Really,' he said, and there was a hint of his smile.

'I think the thing that freaks me out the most is that maybe you don't love me, that I've gone and fallen completely in love with you and maybe you haven't fallen in love with me back.'

There. I'd said it. It left me breathless.

His smile grew. 'Did you even read my script, or have you been drawing something you've made up yourself?'

'Yeah, but your script is about Girl from Mars and Jackson Silver. It's not real.'

'Now I know I'm hearing things.' Dan moved over on the couch so he was sitting right beside me.

'And he dies.'

'Well, he has to. Like you said, Girl from Mars has to be alone. It's part of her appeal.'

'I thought – I thought maybe you killed him because you were angry that I broke up with you.'

'Well, that too.' He touched my face with his palm. 'Tell me how you feel about me again,' he said.

'I've fallen in love with you.'

'And I've fallen in love with you right back, Fil Brown.'

He kissed me. Dear God, it was heaven.

'Please tell me you aren't going to get stabbed in the heart now by your evil former lab assistant,' I said when we were finished. I was a little bit dizzy because we'd very quickly ended up lying on the couch with Dan half on top of me, his hand resting on my bare waist underneath my top.

'I don't have any evil former lab assistants,' he said, 'unless you count Betsy Stevens who helped me cut up a foetal pig in ninth grade. She turned into a lawyer.'

'I'd watch your back.'

'I was afraid you'd chosen Jim,' Dan said.

How had I thought I could give up Dan? He was so wonderful, so real and frightening and happy, so everything I'd never known I'd needed or deserved.

'I wanted to be able to choose him,' I admitted slowly. 'He's a part of me, Dan. Not being friends with him is like losing an arm or an eye. But I can't choose not to love you.'

That sparked off a whole new round of kissing. I couldn't believe I'd lived without it for so long.

But I still had something to say, so I broke off before we got too distracted. 'I can't live two lives, though. I'm not going to dump my friends because I've got a boyfriend. My friends are brilliant, Dan. They're talented and caring and we have so much fun together.'

'That's fine with me. More than fine.'

'We play *Dungeons and Dragons*,' I warned him. 'And we have weird private jokes and games that nobody else understands. And we do the pub quiz every single Wednesday and, for God's sake, never ask Digger how he got his nickname unless you want to feel sick.'

I realised I was talking in the present tense.

'I'm looking forward to it,' Dan said. He kissed me on the nose and I smiled at him.

'Does this mean you're not going back to Philadelphia?'

'Not without you.'

'So are you going to write more for *Girl from Mars*?'

Dan rolled over, pulling me so I was on top of him, until I overbalanced and we both slid off the couch on to the thick carpet.

'Ouch,' I said, though I didn't mean it. Nothing hurt. Not right now.

'I think', he said, laughing and kissing me, again and again, 'we should concentrate on our own adventures for a while.'

I Don't Hate Lunch So Much Any More

I was fifteen minutes early and I fiddled with the heavy restaurant cutlery while I waited.

It was a formal place, with white linen tablecloths and wine glasses on the table. I'd chosen it for that reason. I wanted to show how serious I was and how much I valued him. I wanted someplace separate from the old habits and the old arguments, someplace that would symbolise a new start. But now, surrounded by gleaming cutlery and uniformed waiters, I wondered if this was too separate from how it had been, if it only served to show up how much we had grown apart.

Every time the door opened my head shot up and my heart skipped. After the fourth time, I muttered under my breath, 'This is worse than going on a date.'

And as important as any mating game. I touched, briefly, my lips where Dan had given me a good-luck kiss, and then Jim was there. He wore a blue shirt and held a rucksack. His clothes and hair and face were exactly the same, though he'd always been changing and feeling and growing up, all these years. We both had.

'Sorry I'm late,' he said.

'I saved you a chair,' I replied.

Jim sat down. He looked around. He looked at me.

'Bugger this,' he said, 'let's go for a pint.'

Still hungry for love?
Turn over for the chance to read
our fabulous short story, Rescue Me,
by Susannah Lee!

Susannah was the lucky (and talented) winner of the GALAXY Ripple®/*Company* magazine Young Writers' competition run in conjunction with Little Black Dress in 2008. We know you'll love her great writing as much as the judges did!

Rescue Me

Susannah Lee

'This guy is amazing,' said Jaz.

Katie lowered her paper and looked across the table to see her friend scrutinising a newspaper article. Next to the story was an action shot of a male figure clad in skin-tight black lycra expertly jumping from a burning building, baby under one arm, cat under the other.

'Not Mega Dude again,' she said in a weary tone. 'I thought that was the wine talking.'

'Look at him,' Jaz said, pushing the paper towards Katie and pointing at the man in the picture. 'He's been saving kittens, babies and old ladies for the past two years and nobody knows who he is. If I could just get the scoop I'd finally be able to stop writing stories about Stacy and her ponies for *My Horse and Me*.'

'And disappoint your legion of seven-year-old fans?' said Katie with a smirk.

'I'm serious,' exclaimed Jaz. 'If I find out Mega Dude's secret identity I'll be able to take my pick of any national paper I want,' she said triumphantly.

'Have you ever considered that maybe Mega Dude doesn't have a secret identity? He's a government test gone wrong, Jaz, not someone from Smallville.'

'Oh you don't really believe that, do you? Is the *Daily Express* your morning read this month?' she asked suspiciously, referring to the daily newspaper Katie had to read at work every morning to keep abreast of current issues for her PR job. The rotation system meant that if she was on *Daily Star* for the month her going-out tops suddenly got more revealing; reading the *Independent* led to an increase in her wearing glasses; and faced with the *Express* or *Mail* it wasn't uncommon to see her tutting at the kids in hoodies who hung around at the bottom of their road.

'Maybe,' replied Katie sheepishly, knowing Jaz had her pinned.

'There has to be a clue in here somewhere,' continued Jaz. 'I mean, he turns up two years ago and stops a family from getting squashed by an overturned lorry with his bare hands. One week later he's back and thwarting a bank robbery—'

Katie let out a snort of laughter. 'Did you just say "thwarting"? All you need now are some "POW" and "WHACK" signs and you can follow him round as his sidekick.'

At that point they were interrupted by an advert on the television for the latest Mega Dude toy accessory. A Harley Davidson motorbike like the one he'd used a few weeks ago to chase a drug lord through the streets of London.

'Aww, what happened to his spraying Coke bottle?' commented Jaz. 'I really liked that one.'

'There were complaints about kids buying normal

Coke bottles and spraying them at each other so they had to take it off the market.'

'Bet Coke were gutted, their sales went up twenty per cent, didn't they? Ah well, at least the little buggers can't hit me on the way to work any more. Although it was a pretty ingenious use of a fizzy drink; who'd have thought you could catch a diamond thief by spraying a bottle of Coca Cola in their face?'

'Yeah, not bad for a lycraed-up pretty boy,' said Katie.

'Like you wouldn't,' snorted Jaz.

'No, I wouldn't, actually,' said Katie snootily.

'Sure,' said Jaz sceptically. 'You'd turn down a dark-haired, blue-eyed, six-foot guy with rippling muscles and, if the pictures are to be believed, quite a, erm, package, shall we say.'

Katie smiled. 'Well, when you put it that way . . .'

Jaz let out a loud laugh. 'Come on, then, help me figure out who he is.'

The two girls arrived at the Apple iPhone launch and boarded the large boat on the Thames where it was taking place. Katie had managed to blag them both an invite through work. They were early so they grabbed themselves a cocktail and walked around the boat.

'Seen anywhere good yet?' asked Jaz.

'Long as you can cause a distraction, I reckon over there is as good a place as any to fling myself off a multi-million-pound boat.'

Concern crossed Jaz's face. 'Are you sure you want to do this? Just because he's always spotted in this area doesn't mean he'll turn up now. We can stay here, drink free cocktails and talk to Z-list celebs instead. I've just seen at least three of the latest *Big Brother* people arrive.'

'How tempting,' replied Katie dryly. 'I think that's more of an incentive to jump.'

'What if you get hurt?'

'I won't, that's the whole point. Mega Dude will save me. That's what he does, rescues damsels in distress.'

'Okay, well, I'll be right here ready with my camera. Soon as he rescues you, reach up like you're struggling and grab his mask. I'll get the picture.' She gave her friend a hug. 'If there's no sign of him after ten minutes I'll raise the alarm and get you out of there.'

Katie grabbed another cocktail for Dutch courage and waited for her signal. After about twenty minutes she heard a familiar voice yell 'Oh my God, Beckham's here!' and a stampede of stiletto feet rushed past her. Katie quickly took off her shoes and looked around the boat to check no one was watching. She hitched up her dress and clambered on to the side, keeping one arm around the pole next to her. She looked out at the shimmering water in front of her, and with one, deep breath, she leapt.

The water hit her body hard and the coldness of it took her breath away. She kicked her way to the surface and started swimming away from the boat to warm herself up. Once she felt her body get used to the water she turned back to see Jaz standing on the side of the boat waving. Katie lifted her arm in response to indicate she was okay. She swam out a little further to put a bit of distance between herself and the boat. She didn't want some have-a-go-hero trying to rescue her when she was waiting for the real thing. Okay, here goes, she thought, and she began to splash about. Did she need to shout? Lois Lane always called Superman for help and that worked.

'Help,' she shouted unconvincingly. 'Help,' she tried

again. 'Mega Dude, help me!' Thank God no one could see her, she wasn't very good at this fake rescue lark.

'Ow,' she cried, reaching down to grab her calf. 'Ow, cramp, oh that's cramp!' Katie kicked her left leg frantically to counteract the fact that she couldn't move the right and started to panic. The boat looked smaller than the last time she had looked and she couldn't see Jaz any more. Katie slipped a bit further down into the water and felt the liquid in her mouth. Spitting and struggling she pulled her head back above the water. Her arms flayed helplessly and her one good leg kicked as the other one got more painful.

'Help!' she yelled, this time with more feeling. 'Help me, someone, he—' She went under again and her words got lost. Her last thought before she slipped into the black water was that this had been a really stupid idea.

Katie woke coughing and spluttering.

'Hey,' said a deep voice above her. She blinked the water out of her eyes and a handsome face came into view. She reached out to touch the strong jaw line that was inches away from her face and looked into the bright blue eyes surrounded by a black mask. Her hand reached up further to the mask but he placed his hand on hers to stop her.

'No,' he said softly. 'I'll take anything else off but that,' he finished with a cheeky grin. Katie tried to sit up but he pushed her back down. 'Don't try and move; it's better if you stay still.'

'Did I hit my head?' she murmured, reaching up to feel for a bump.

'No, but we need to wait until the photographers get off the boat.'

'What?'

'Look,' he said, gently turning her head to her right so she could see they were lying in front of a Sony Ericsson billboard advertising its latest phone.

'So?'

'I've been looking for a phone sponsor.'

'You've been what?' she said, not quite believing her ears.

'Well, it's not like I get a regular paycheque,' he said slightly defensively. 'In fact, this job costs more than it pays. Ever seen *The Incredibles*?' He didn't wait for a reply. 'Not so far from the truth. After I saved the first family the lorry company hit me with a bill for the damage and the council tried to sue me for the pile-up on the motorway. If Coca Cola hadn't stepped in I wouldn't be much of a Mega Dude to anyone.'

'So this', she said, referring to the advert behind them, 'is going to get you a sponsor deal – and then what? You prove how good their phone reach is by placing a call to Earth from your home planet?'

'Of course not,' he said dismissively. 'That's way too obvious. They just place their products in my way.'

Katie's brain flicked into gear, she remembered the photos of Mega Dude picking up a Coke bottle at a museum – where no food and drink was allowed – and spraying a diamond thief in the face. Or, that ever-so-conveniently parked Harley Davidson with the key still in the ignition . . .

'It's all a set-up, everything,' she murmured disbelievingly. 'It's just a big PR stunt. Oh my God, I have to tell someone, you can't do this. Everyone believes in you, counts on you.' She struggled to get up but he held her down easily.

'You can't tell anyone,' he said firmly. 'Ninety-nine per cent of what I do is real; I saved you, didn't I?'

'Because you thought upstaging an Apple iPhone launch party would guarantee you a deal with a rival company.'

Mega Dude looked at her sheepishly. 'True, but I still did it. Just like I saved a baby from a burning house last week and pushed a car off the railway tracks two days ago. This isn't a comic book and I'm not Bruce Wayne. Someone has to pay my mortgage and someone has to cover the cost of damages to the city or your taxes would be sky high.' He paused for breath. 'I still save people,' he said sincerely. Katie looked deep into his eyes and sighed.

'Okay, I won't say anything . . .'

'Thanks.'

'. . . If you'll do a PR stunt for one of my clients.'

He grinned. 'Deal,' he said.

'Look, people are getting off the boat.' Mega Dude glanced quickly at the pier and without a word placed his mouth over hers as if to give her the kiss of life. Katie heard footsteps pounding towards them and through her closed eyes sensed hundreds of flashes. She was sincerely considering that maybe she had drowned after all and that this was actually heaven until she heard Jaz screaming her name.

'Katie, Katie,' she cried, pushing her way through the paparazzi. Mega Dude pulled away and Katie opened her eyes.

'I'm sorry, I'm so sorry. I got moved away from the side. I couldn't see . . . tried to tell someone . . . no one listened . . . you're okay. Thank God you're okay,' she rambled through uncontrollable tears as she hugged

Katie. She pulled away and flung her arms around Mega Dude. 'Thank you, thank you so much.'

'All in a day's work, ma'am,' he said in a Queen's English accent. Katie rolled her eyes at the change in his persona. 'Take care of yourself now,' he said, looking at both girls and touching Katie's hand. It was only after he took off that she realised he'd placed a business card in her palm.

One Month Later . . .

'Oh my God, have you seen this?' Jaz said, thrusting the front page of the paper at Katie. In big bold letters the headline read: 'Mega Dude's Soft Landing', and there was an image of the superhero nestled in a crate of Kleenex toilet rolls with a crook he had apprehended.

'You can't pay for this kind of advertising,' Jaz said. Katie smiled to herself. No, she thought, but it's worth the rescue.

little black dress

**brings you fantastic new books like these
every month - find out more at
www.littleblackdressbooks.com**

**Why not link up with other devoted Little Black
Dress fans on our Facebook group? Simply type
Little Black Dress Books into Facebook to join up.**

**And if you want to be the first
to hear the latest news on all things
Little Black Dress, just send the details below to
littleblackdressmarketing@headline.co.uk
and we'll sign you up to our lovely email
newsletter (and we promise that we won't share
your information with anybody else!).***

Name: ————————————————————————

Email Address: ————————————————————

Date of Birth: ————————————————————

Region/Country: ————————————————————

What's your favourite Little Black Dress book?

————————————————————————————————

How many Little Black Dress books have you read? ————

*You can be removed from the mailing list at any time

You can buy any of these other
Little Black Dress titles from your
bookshop or *direct from the publisher*.

FREE P&P AND UK DELIVERY
(Overseas and Ireland £3.50 per book)

TO ORDER SIMPLY CALL THIS NUMBER

01235 400 414

or visit our website: www.headline.co.uk

Prices and availability subject to change without notice.